A WORLD
BETWEEN

A WORLD BETWEEN

a novel **EMILY HASHIMOTO**

THE FEMINIST PRESS
AT THE CITY UNIVERSITY OF NEW YORK
NEW YORK CITY

Published in 2020 by the Feminist Press
at the City University of New York
The Graduate Center
365 Fifth Avenue, Suite 5406
New York, NY 10016

feministpress.org

First Feminist Press edition 2020

NEW YORK STATE OF OPPORTUNITY. | Council on the Arts

This book was made possible thanks
to a grant from New York State Council on the Arts
with the support of Governor Andrew M. Cuomo
and the New York State Legislature.

First printing September 2020

Cover design by Rose Todaro
Text design by Drew Stevens

Library of Congress Cataloging-in-Publication Data

Names: Hashimoto, Emily, author.
Title: A world between / Emily Hashimoto.
Description: First Feminist Press edition. | New York, NY : The Feminist
Press, 2020.
Identifiers: LCCN 2020016397 (print) | LCCN 2020016398 (ebook) | ISBN
9781936932955 (paperback) | ISBN 9781936932962 (ebook)
Classification: LCC PS3608.A78976 W65 2020 (print) | LCC PS3608.A78976
(ebook) | DDC 813/.6--dc23
LC record available at https://lccn.loc.gov/2020016397
LC ebook record available at https://lccn.loc.gov/2020016398

PRINTED IN THE UNITED STATES OF AMERICA

For my wife,
whom I like and love

The connections between and among women are the most feared, the most problematic, and the most potentially transforming force on the planet.

—ADRIENNE RICH

PART ONE

ELEANOR, 2004

SEPTEMBER

Her heart raced as she rushed, shoving a sweatshirt into her backpack to ward off chill in her classroom, stuffing in her notebook and pens and a magenta highlighter and her reading and her flip phone and her keys, and tumbling out of her dorm room and down the hall, racing for the elevator, because another late in Feminist Practices would bring down her final grade, and she was too Asian to let that happen, impatiently bouncing until the elevator arrived on her floor and the doors opened, finally, and she climbed on board.

And then everything changed.

At first glance the girl had brown skin and long, dark hair in a messy ponytail. A second stolen look revealed her built, curvy body. Maybe she was Indian. A third peek filled in the rest: short fingernails, a massive cuff of a wristwatch, and sandals that matched her own. In front of a beautiful girl, Eleanor was glad for unspoken elevator etiquette—where to stand, where to look, how to accommodate others—that freed her from thinking about how to be.

As the sluggish car descended, the fluorescent lights buzzed above them. The girl was hyperfocused on the notebook in her hands, like she could inhale what was written on the page. There was a luminescence in her skin that lit the elevator box, and suddenly the beige and chrome space was no longer as ordinary. The light

3

reflected onto Eleanor, warming her, changing her, brightening her whole self.

Eleanor couldn't let this moment go by. "Hey. You're, uh, studying for something?" She winced at her lackluster line. She could have done better. *You're very pretty. I would be interested in kissing you.* Maybe she couldn't do better.

The girl didn't even look up. "Epidemiology quiz." Her voice, smooth and low.

"Wow." Eleanor nervously scratched the back of her bare neck. "That's impressive. I can barely crack Intro to Bio."

"Ha. Yeah." The girl's eyes stayed steady on the page.

Eleanor took the hint. "Sorry. I'll let you—"

"It's just that I have this . . ." she interrupted, but didn't finish her thought, finally looking up.

Eleanor wondered what she saw. Her newly clear golden skin, thanks to the zap of chemical creams her mother had railed against; freckles that rained across her nose; eyes that marked her as distinctly Asian; and short, thick hair tamed with product. With any luck, this girl skipped over cheeks still thick with baby fat and a stature that never recovered from the freshman fifteen. She sucked in her gut, one arm hugging her stomach, across her Ani DiFranco T-shirt.

Whatever the girl saw, she smiled at Eleanor. "I have this quiz, and I've been so . . . distracted lately." Her dark eyes, warm and kind.

But there was also a certain heat that Eleanor felt between them that went beyond nice, that fizzed and fractured the air, that held the possibility of more than this.

Eleanor smiled back and opened her mouth to say more, to learn the girl's name, her sign, her first childhood crush, if she preferred to be the big spoon or little spoon, what she liked to do in bed—but the elevator dinged, signaling their arrival on the ground floor. She watched as the girl dashed away without turning around, taking with her the prospect of something tangible, something that Eleanor could hold with both arms. In a disappointed daze, she left the embrace of her dorm building and walked down Commonwealth Avenue.

With somewhere to be, Eleanor took off at a run: the freshness of the late morning all around her, the blue sky streaked with clouds above as she kept a determined pace, only pausing at the giant gap in the street where Comm Ave became a war zone of cars struggling against the tide. As soon as she got a walk signal, she was off again.

Eleanor bounced up the stairs to the entrance of the building, underneath low industrial lighting and past metal drinking fountains punched into the walls. She tripped up to the second floor and entered the small lecture hall that had become familiar to her in the past few weeks.

Maneuvering into her chair, she pulled out Audre Lorde's "The Transformation of Silence into Language and Action." She loved this reading, the simplicity and beauty of the words. *Your silence will not protect you*, Lorde lectured from the page, but more than admiring her blunt economy of writing, Eleanor was set aflame by the way Lorde called women to action. She had highlighted the words *it is necessary to teach by living and speaking those truths which we believe and know beyond understanding*, and scrawled four exclamation points in the margin beside them. She felt the text speaking directly to her, clearer than her own name.

There was so much that she believed and knew. Being in school, reading incredible writers, she began to comprehend a language and framework to explain the floods of rage that she felt on a daily basis for the injustices she saw around her and in the news. Wars waged a world away based on faulty intelligence. Unequal access to abortion and sex ed. Gay people who couldn't just get married.

So much felt wrong, and she felt called to fix what she could. Tikkun olam. Even if Hebrew school and her bat mitzvah and a relentless childhood faith felt far away, her Judaism compelled her to put hands in the dirt and repair what was broken in the world. But it was the what, and the how, that stumped her. These were the big questions floating nebulously around her brain—clouds of fluffy white or stormy gray depending on how she felt about the world that day. This class in particular, Feminist Practices, got the wheels turning. With graduation looming, figuring out what feminism looked like beyond theory was paramount, because her postschool life after the academic bubble burst had to have meaning. She wanted to go to work and make a difference, moving the heaviest boulders. She was a queer biracial Asian Jewish girl, but she had the power and privilege to help people.

She just didn't know how yet.

Class began, and with it, the same conversation patterns: the white girl with blond dreadlocks liked Lorde's piece, as she liked all the readings, but had a

But to offer. "It lacked connection to practice. It was so academic." Her face was sharp, angled, like her tone. "What pathways do women have to action?"

Eleanor took a deep breath, raising her hand and speaking without waiting to be called on by Professor Post. "Yeah, but, no. She offers, like, a ton of ideas. Learning how to conquer your silences." She flipped the crisp page to read more of her marginalia. "Defining yourself. Coming together in unity. Moving across predetermined borders and separations to really understand others." She held up the reading, glaring. "Also, it's in the title: 'The Transformation of Silence into Language and Action.'"

As the girl began her counterargument, Eleanor felt her blood flowing, her brain warming up, in her element. Some of her classmates were argumentative for the sake of argument, or didn't take it seriously, or just didn't get it, but the class was still a community of women, and here, Eleanor felt like her voice was all hers to use.

Some hours and another class later, she was still high on Feminist Practices as she darted into an old building on Bay State Road. Eleanor climbed up, up, up the stairs inside the mansion converted into administrative offices, dark polished wood alongside office furniture. At the top, she reached the campus Women's Center, a space with pitched ceilings that sat under the eaves of the old house, and which felt like home. The walls were a bright lime and complemented by a rainbow flag, a banner that yelled FEMINIST in pink spray paint from last year's Take Back the Night rally, and a poster of Sojourner Truth looking sternly down at all of them.

Cath and Sam were already in place for their volunteer shifts, while Eleanor was late, but it didn't matter. The only visitor was a girl with frosted-pink hair, probing the zine library. Eleanor sighed at the disappointing quiet, the lack of action in the empty safe space. So much for feminist practices. Still, there was work to be done. "Hey, dykes." Eleanor took a seat behind the desktop computer, booting up the ancient system to print more promotional flyers for the Women's Center, across the room from Cath and Sam. "Whatcha doin'?"

Cath lifted her book off the table and showed it to Eleanor. *The Vagina Monologues.* "I'm trying out," she replied brightly, pushing her tortoiseshell-framed glasses back up the bridge of her nose.

"Sam, are you trying out too?" Eleanor asked.

Sam shuddered. "Hell no." She brushed a hand through her newly short, orange hair, which had been longer and black until she'd cut and bleached it at the beginning of the semester, out of reach of her Filipino parents, who would disapprove of such butchery and butch-ery. "But I'm a good girlfriend. I play my part." She produced her own copy.

Sam *was* a good girlfriend, and she and Cath were good to each other. They had met during freshman orientation, drawn together by their shared love of *Buffy the Vampire Slayer*, and maneuvered themselves into a double room by the spring semester—and that was it, an old married couple. Eleanor was envious of their connection and contentment, but not their stodgy lifestyle, because her heart was set on romance and drama and excitement. Her mind drifted back to earlier in the day: the elevator, that girl, the promise of something moving yet solid all at once.

"What about you, Suzuki?" Sam asked with lesbian-softball-player huskiness in her voice. "Trying out?"

Eleanor shrugged, collecting the stack of flyers from the printer and shoving them into her backpack for later distribution, and pulled out her knitting, joining Cath and Sam at the folding table. The project was a half-finished scarf in hunter-green wool for her obachan. She could envision her wearing it as she worked in the family bookstore in San Jose, chatting with customers, minding the aisles of titles that slid down the spines of Japanese books and videos. The scarf gaped with holes from dropped stitches, but her grandmother wouldn't notice. She would be pleased to see Eleanor do something industrious, with a hard pat to her back and an appraising, "Yokatta desu ne, Chieko-chan!" If she closed her eyes, she could almost feel the affectionate whack and the gentle ease of being in her grandmother's company.

"Maybe I'll try out," Eleanor finally said. She had acted in high school, not since, but this wasn't acting anyway—it was performance art and activism.

"Oh great. You help." Sam tossed the book to Eleanor, who fumbled the catch.

Cath scrunched her face. "I think that's cool. But, um, you should know that Zoe is one of the codirectors."

Eleanor winced at the mention of her ex-girlfriend's name, even though she was over her. They lasted six months and Eleanor had fallen dangerously in love, but it was ages ago, last semester, that Zoe had broken her heart. She was basically over her. "Whatever. It doesn't matter. I actually met someone today."

Cath and Sam conferred silently in a language

between them, unknown to others. Cath turned to Eleanor. "So, we're finally over Zoe?"

"We?" She picked up her knitting again, completely forgetting how many stitches she'd done in that row.

"Dude, like you ever say this little about anything. Spill," Sam said firmly.

She stared at the green yarn, knotted in her hands, and thought of the girl in the elevator. *I actually met someone today* was a grand overstatement of bravado, overshooting their actual short and bare nonconversation. It might as well have not happened at all, and yet it had, and she'd been struck by this girl who was beautiful, yes, but also magnetic. She couldn't precisely remember what Elevator Girl looked like, but Eleanor knew how she had made her feel: Hopeful. Like she didn't have to spend the next weeks and months weighed down with the hulking pain of Zoe's rejection. Like there could be spring in her life, in her heart, romance blooming in her body. Kissing, sex, cuddling, long walks, movie dates, long and drifting hours with someone who made her feel so much. Even if it wasn't meant to be that girl, it would be *a* girl. She was ready.

"She was cute and kinda gay. She was Indian. She had long hair. I don't know," she finally replied, regretting mentioning it at all, not ready to give voice to the nascent feelings inside, picking up *The Vagina Monologues* script, hoping to wipe their brains clean. "Okay, so which monologue?"

She helped Cath practice for a while—"You cannot love a vagina unless you love hair. Many people do not love hair"—as Sam set up for a Latin American Womyn's Organization meeting. Then Tomás called her cell phone.

"Ladies, I'm downstairs waiting. Whenever you're ready to go to dinner."

Eleanor rolled her eyes. "Tomás, you can come up. You're not going to break feminism or anything."

"No," he said firmly, his voice coming in tinny. "It's your space, and I won't. Your space, your choice," he added. She knew without seeing his face that he was proud of that one, and she rolled her eyes again.

The vice president of the Latin American Womyn's Organization entered a few minutes later. "I ran into your boy downstairs, Eleanor. You should go claim him. Tell him he's bad at flirting."

Eleanor stuffed her knitting into her backpack. "We'll do that. That's a promise. Have a great meeting!" They wound down the staircase, rushing with momentum and gravity. Eleanor hit the sidewalk with a smile. "Tomás, I hear you're bad at flirting."

"*You're* bad at flirting," he countered. He was right.

They walked to the dining hall as a group, but divided along their usual lines of comfort: Cath and Sam, Eleanor and Tomás. He had been her best friend since their days at Mission San Jose High School, and their attending the same college had been her security blanket in the days when everything at school was overwhelming and unfamiliar, when all she wanted was to go for a hike with her family back in Fremont, or work with Obachan behind the bookstore's register, anything that felt like the life she remembered. Then, the homesickness faded as her life caught up to the present. Exploring Boston. The Women's Center, classes, friends. Girls. Girls, mostly, with Tomás as the only link to the past.

They sat down with their trays of food, piles of fries

and slices of congealed pizza and limp stir-fry and banana-cream pie. As Cath and Sam debated the new potato wedges, Eleanor felt her phone vibrate in her backpack down by her feet. It was MOM, or so said the screen on the outside of her phone. Eleanor groaned, returning it to her bag.

"My aunts are coming for parents' weekend," Tomás announced with his mouth half full. "I've put them off for years, but they finally strong-armed me."

The thought of Adelina and Inez visiting elated Eleanor, made her bounce in her chair. They were the first lesbian couple she had observed up close; through living their lives, they gave her a playbook of what a great relationship between two women could be. They squabbled, yes, but they delighted in small absurdities and cracked corny jokes at Tomás's expense. Their lives seemed fun, vivid, attainable. Exactly what a younger Eleanor needed to see as those budding, intoxicating feelings of queerness began to fill her teenage body. Adelina and Inez were bulwarks as she tried to fit words to the turmoil inside: "I think I'm bi?" and "Can you be a lesbian if you've had a boyfriend?" They never pushed her, they only listened, and it was because of them that she could see the possibilities of her own life unfold.

"I can't wait to meet them! Finally!" Cath enthused.

"Yeah. It'll be great to meet the dykes that raised you," Sam said, wiping her mouth clean with her forearm. "Maybe they'll take us out for dinner, like when El's parents came to town."

Eleanor knew what Tomás wasn't saying, could tell it from his glum, resigned face. As much as he loved his aunts, was grateful for them, they were still stand-ins for the parents that couldn't be there. But she knew he never let himself dwell for long.

"They're out of control," he said, his face screwing into a smile. "They're really looking forward to meeting you two, and seeing El." His grimace could almost be mistaken for a grin.

They parted after dinner, and she flipped her phone open and listened to her mother's message as she walked down Comm Ave back to her dorm.

"Hi, it's Mom." Her voice was as it always was—an impossible mixture of cheer, concern, and exhaustion. "I'm on a break and was just thinking about you. I saw on the Weather Channel that you had a nice day in Boston. Warm, sunny. Just like my little girl." Eleanor rolled her eyes. "We haven't talked in a couple days and I wanted to hear your voice, and your voicemail greeting didn't cut it, so call your mother, won't you, and tell her how you are? Love you, honey, so much." And then she did the most offensive thing: she made a kissy, smoochy sound before hanging up, punctuating the end of her message.

Ugh. Eleanor sighed and pocketed her phone, walking past the student union softened by street lamps, the walk made theoretically safe by blue-lit campus emergency phones. Her mother was too much, so overwhelming, so smothering, parenting like she was sucking all the air out of the room, leaving barely enough for Eleanor to survive. Her mother had no inner life of her own, all work and her kids; she had let go of meaning and activism and priorities to be somebody's mom. Eleanor yearned to live for herself, to pursue purpose, and to share her life with someone in a spirit of equity, not like she was giving herself away to the world.

Eleanor called back reluctantly, and when her mother didn't answer, she left a message, relieved. "Hi, Mom. I'm calling you back, as requested." Her voice sounded young and bratty as it met the large quiet of the evening, the wide-open Boston streets only sporadically dotted with cars in contrast with the earlier rush of traffic. She kept on her path home. "I'm walking back from the dining hall. And you always say I don't call you, but I do. I am, right now. Um. I had a good day."

Here was an opportunity, one of a million. *I met a pretty girl.* Saying it seemed so easy. Words coming out of her mouth; she did it all the time.

Her parents were liberal, or liberal enough, and her mother had gay male friends, and she knew intuitively that she could be honest with her family and not face the consequences that other people feared.

She crossed over the highway, back to the narrow sidewalk and old buildings.

And yet she wasn't ready to share this part of herself with them, needing it to be hers, to exist only at school, for a little while longer.

She slowed her pace, feeling the air descending into cooler temperatures against her skin, passing a building under construction that she remembered standing tall and weathered throughout her freshman year.

"Hope you had a good day too, Mom. Love you." Eleanor expressed a lungful of breath when she hung up, happy to sever the connection and leave the gray area between who she used to be and who she was now. Into her building she went, one of three matching dorm buildings on this side of campus. She swiped through with her card and boarded the elevator, the

14

car feeling more familiar and intimate than it had the day before, though there was still no sign of Elevator Girl anywhere.

Down the hall and into her room, she flicked the lights on, greeted by cinder-block walls covered in a beige-yellow-nothing paint pasted over with the markers of her life: family photos, protest posters, inspirational words. Clothes were strewn across her dresser and over her desk chair and on top of her unmade bed. It would be responsible to set the room right before settling in.

She flung T-shirts and shorts off the bed, settling into her nest of pillows with a highlighter and black pen and her Adrienne Rich reading—but was too comfortable, falling asleep with the lights on, and it was technically morning when she woke at three a.m. The dining hall wouldn't be open for hours, so she ate a pre-breakfast of pretzels and microwaved tea while finishing her reading and stretching out in bed, absolutely awake at this god-awful early hour. She considered tackling another assignment or using her vibrator, but instead queued up *When Harry Met Sally* on her DVD player, her comfort-food movie, and sank back into bed. It was a movie she'd watched on television with her mother, staring with bewilderment as a kid during Meg Ryan's fake orgasm scene in the deli. Now it felt like her movie, how she imagined love and friendship should work. Love was walking around New York in the fall, and banter, and taking time to get to know someone. Emotional shenanigans and dead ends until the right place, right person, right time.

She fell back asleep as Sally and Harry wandered the Egyptian exhibit at the Met, fall exploding gloriously in red, green, and gold outside the giant windows behind them.

A FEW WEEKS later, the season turned, blustery wind now coming off the Charles. Eleanor was on her way to a queer studies lecture, encased in her red plaid winter coat for the first time that semester, when she received a call from Cath.

"I know we said we'd be there, but our plans changed," her friend apologized.

"We're going to do queer studies in our room," Sam shouted in the background.

"Sam!" Cath chastised, but there was a coquettish laugh in her admonishment. "I have a quiz tomorrow in my Global Governance class, and I really need to focus," she said to Eleanor. "I'm sorry. Don't be mad at us."

Eleanor paused at a street light, starkly dark against the fading sunset. She debated not going to the talk, turning back around to her cozy dorm room, but she was already out and on her way. She was, in fact, mad, because although she believed there was an impending quiz, she was also sure Cath had already prepared; that was Cath's way. This was the luxury of being a couple, of having a playmate available at all times, and feeling no remorse in letting other people down. "Whatever, Cath. See you later."

She continued her walk down Comm Ave, hugging her coat tighter around her, until she reached the student union. She clambered in and through to the small multipurpose room at the back of the building. It was packed when she arrived, late, and she searched for a seat, slipping into a row toward the back, climbing past chatting women seated in black plastic chairs. Once settled, she scanned the room for familiar faces.

Her ex-girlfriend Franny was standing in the front row, talking with friends Eleanor couldn't identify. She waved when she spotted Eleanor. Aggressively nice Franny, who worked hard to do and say the right things, who hadn't ignited anything in Eleanor. Their months together had compelled Eleanor to rethink her queerness, that maybe it had just been an experiment.

Then she met Zoe at Spectrum, the LGBT group on campus, and she was sure again, just like that. Zoe was hot—short hair and an angular face and piercing blue eyes, with butch energy seeping from her lanky body. She was so enthralling and intoxicating, with whispered intermediate-level French and planned romantic outings, that Eleanor barely clocked the ways that Zoe held her at bay: never using the girl-friend label, freaking out when the word *commitment* was invoked, panic attacks when things got too serious between them. When Eleanor finally faced the reality, the damage amid the charm, she pledged to fix and take care of Zoe, because love meant understanding and devotion—but it wasn't meant to be. She felt too much, and Zoe too little, and her heart was broken after six months' time.

Seeing Zoe now, whispering to a willowy blond dyke that Eleanor recognized from Spectrum, lit her with smoldering disgust. She wanted to stand up and yell, *She's just going to use you! You're not special! She's trying to catch you just for the fun of it!*

But she was basically over her.

The professor, a soft white man with a receding hair-line, began his lecture on same-sex unions with a light and looping voice, highlighting recent successes in Vermont and Massachusetts while strongly advocating for the work that had been left to the side in order to shine a light on weddings and happily-ever-afters: work that tackled hate crimes, housing and employment discrimination, homeless queer youth. The professor had more to add: "If marriage was available nationwide tomorrow to same-sex couples," he said, "my beloved Jim and I would have to weigh the opportunity to skip down to city hall with real thought. To be recognized, to enjoy the benefits of tax relief and status, is no doubt persuasive, but it doesn't alter the fact that we'd be endorsing an inherently patriarchal institution that's not made more queer by our joining up." He paused for a sip of water amid abounding applause.

Eleanor itched to yell and use her voice, but she scratched out notes instead with the pen in her hand—the socially acceptable way to open the valve on what she was feeling. She hated what the professor had said, like there could only be one strategy or one issue at a time, like the LGBT community wasn't complex and vast, able to fight on all burners. Of course, it was depressing to see President-fucking-Bush and his cronies repeat "marriage is between a man and woman" like homophobic robots, but she believed in the potential of movement. People could change their minds, eventually. The winds and tides would shift, and then all of the bad for her community would fall like dominoes.

But what really got to her was the idea that marriage was so bad of its own accord, without caveat. When she was younger, before her queer renaissance, she never wanted to marry. The idea of being someone's wife, of being Mrs. Someone, sounded like a prison made of cockroaches, but marrying a woman was something else entirely. It was renegade, Bonnie and Bonnie instead of Bonnie and Clyde, rebellion against the status quo, changing systems from within. In her mind, idly, she envisioned what could be hers, someday: white and pale dresses, flowers in her hair, her parents walking her down the aisle, a chuppah, a thousand paper cranes for good luck. A wedding on her terms. A marriage and partnership of her own creation.

She wanted a special person who made it all worth it, all the struggle, all the human-shit-misery. She needed a life fueled by political purpose, but without someone to share that life with, none of her good works would matter. She required a partner, someone to complete what felt missing. An equal, a woman to love who would move mountains, climb with bloody hands to the summit, reach higher, and foolishly. Someone like her, but better.

Eleanor also thought of real gay couples who didn't prioritize the destruction of patriarchy but still deserved the protections that straight people had, like Adelina and Inez, people who worked and paid taxes and gave to charity when there was leftover money. Thinking in the abstract infuriated her, because it smoothed over actual stories, actual lives lived in days and weeks and years, and downplayed the massive civil rights violation that people seemed to accept. That she wouldn't accept.

After the lecture, she shrugged on her coat, arms into sleeves, facing the front of the room. That was when she saw Elevator Girl in the first row, standing, talking to Franny. Where Eleanor had remembered only the broad outlines of her long, dark hair and that she was beautiful, now she saw more: her wide and sparkling smile, her deep brown eyes, the slope and roundness of her breasts through her long-sleeved T-shirt. The way she looked when she laughed, eyes closed in pleasure and her head thrown back. Eleanor liked everything about her. With a racing heart, she advanced to the front row. Her stomach flipped like an eager, crisp pancake.

"Hi!" she greeted Franny, but her eyes darted to Elevator Girl. "How are you?" She sucked in her gut, smiling widely in what was hopefully an attractive way.

Franny nodded enthusiastically. "I'm good, Eleanor! We're gonna do dinner. Do you—"

"Yes." Her eyes flitted again to Elevator Girl. Eleanor gave a warm hello, and the girl said hello back without recognition. She wilted a little to not have been remembered, but she rallied, blood thrumming in her veins. It felt like fate to see her again, their paths crossing here and with someone in common. She floated to dinner, no longer cold and instead feeling only summer inside, down to her bones.

At the dining hall, she sat across from Elevator Girl, butterflies blooming in her stomach. "It's that weird thing," Eleanor volleyed across the table, "where I don't know your name? But now it feels, like, too late to ask, but—"

"Leena," Elevator Girl replied, with a mouthful of bright teeth and the slightest slip of a laugh.

Not Elevator Girl anymore. Leena. Leena, the most lovely name she had ever heard. Leena still didn't appear to recognize her, but she was smiling and friendly, talking about her premed studies. Eleanor was lost in thought, imagining Leena in scrubs with a stethoscope around her neck, when she heard Leena say to Franny, "Jennifer Beals is fucking hot." She looked excited, her cheeks lifting and her eyes sparkling. She was so cute.

"Fucking hot," Eleanor echoed, jumping back into the conversation, which had to be about *The L Word*.

Any concerns she had about crushing on a straight girl were put to rest as Leena went on about her favorite characters—"Dana, sometimes Shane"—and her least favorite couple—"Obviously Jenny and Marina." Eleanor listened intently, agreeing, hanging on to each of the words as soon as they left Leena's lips.

They parted at the end of the meal, Franny heading to one end of campus and Eleanor and Leena peeling off to the other, alone together. It was dark, the black sky dotted with glowing, burning street lights, guiding them up Comm Ave and back to their dorm. She felt the cold air rushing past her cheeks and smelled car exhaust, hyperaware of her footsteps on the sidewalk, of the person at her side, and it all made her feel like one huge exposed nerve. Without any idea of what to say next, she opened her mouth and let her rambling mind take over. "So what was Franny like in high school?" Like she even cared. It was just something to say that wasn't *Can I kiss you?* She rubbed her lip with her thumb.

"We were friends of friends. I didn't know her that well. She was like she is now? Nice. And kind of like an adult."

Eleanor snickered. "She's very serious. When we were dating—"

Leena stopped in her tracks, at the part of the

journey where Comm Ave felt more industrial, traffic rushing past and headlights blaring. "No way. Really?" Leena smiled, sounding skeptical.

Eleanor brushed a nervous hand down the back of her neck. She needed a haircut. "Yeah, but it didn't work out."

Leena shook her head and resumed walking, Eleanor following. "I can't imagine Franny dating anyone. Is that mean?"

Eleanor shook her head vigorously. "No. Well, maybe." Leena laughed then and it lit Eleanor up inside, fireworks spreading and rising inside her chest. She put a fine point on what she was trying to say. "She's a good person, but we didn't have chemistry." Franny never made her feel like this, raw and nervous and blooming all at once.

"So, where are you from? Not . . . that. I mean, where did you grow up?" Leena asked.

Eleanor cast a look toward the girl at her side. For the whole of her life, "Where are you from?" usually meant: *Why do you look like that? Why are you not more Asian or white? Where are your parents from, so I can easily judge who I think you are?* But Leena had clarified her question. Maybe she had heard a similar query her whole life too.

"Fremont, in the Bay Area? Like, near San Francisco?"

Leena brightened. "Really? That's so cool. I've always wanted to go to San Francisco."

Eleanor smiled at that, swiping into the building past the RA on duty.

They boarded the elevator, and the sense memory

of their first meeting washed over her as she pressed the 7 button and Leena pressed 9, their fingers almost brushing against each other. The feeling of destiny topped up her confidence, like maybe this was something to pursue if only she gave it a little boost. As they neared her floor, she turned to Leena. "Hey, we should get together sometime to watch *The L Word*. With Franny." She added that last part as padding, to save her heart if it came to it.

Leena nodded. "That sounds fun."

The elevator doors opened and the devastation of leaving washed in. She wasn't ready to go, not when they were only getting started.

"Give me your email? We can make a plan?" Eleanor produced a pen and blocked the elevator with her body, rolling up her coat sleeve and offering her arm as a notepad. She hadn't considered how it would feel for Leena to hold her limb, a touch that almost singed, that sent Eleanor into territories of desire. The elevator made a panicked sound, and Leena released her arm with a long string of a school email address now inked on her skin. She leaped out of the doors' path.

"See ya." Leena looked down at the floor then back at Eleanor, lips parted as if she had one more thing to say, as the elevator closed and she disappeared.

Eleanor couldn't sleep, abuzz from the night. She sat at her desk, in that cold and hard wooden chair, and looked Leena up online, but there were too many Leena Shahs on the planet. How could that be, when there was such a perfect one? All others should be sued for trademark infringement. She rubbed the skin on her inner forearm where Leena had left her mark.

> hey leena: it's eleanor, franny's friend. i had such a fun night! i'm going to have people over to watch L Word on sunday. you should join us.

She pressed send before thinking any more about it and closed her eyes. When she read the sent message, she gritted her teeth—forced cheer and casualness!—but it was out and gone. She ran through scenarios in her mind. Leena would read her email, think she was a weirdo, and pretend they'd never met when they inevitably ran into each other. Or: Leena would read her email, they'd fall in love, the end. Eventually she went to bed, drifting off to the sounds of *Four Weddings and a Funeral*.

In her inbox the next morning, alongside an assignment reminder from the professor of her Queer Jewish Culture class and a syllabus change from Professor Post, was a reply from Leena Shah. Her adrenaline spiked, nervous to know. With one eye open and fingers crossed, she clicked.

> Hey! I'd love to hang out but I'll be at a family wedding this weekend. What about Thursday? There's a documentary on street harassment playing at the Union.

Eleanor grinned at the screen and barely took a breath before formulating her reply.

> sounds great! not street harassment itself, but the documentary and hanging out thurs night. i'll see you soon!

And just like that, she had a fucking date with Leena Shah, the best of all Leena Shahs. At least, she hoped it was a date. She also had Feminist Practices that started in seven minutes, so off to class she raced.

ELEANOR WAS RUNNING late again on Thursday, cursing her fate on the T and tapping out a message on her phone, keying through each number until it produced the desired character, and kept on going:

running late so sorry :(

Eleanor charged off the train and across the street and into the student center and upstairs to the right room—and there was Leena in muted light, an empty chair next to her, listening intently to the speaker. Eleanor slid in and Leena plucked her placeholder scarf up with a smile. "Hi," she mouthed, looping the deep-ocean-blue wool around her neck.

Eleanor was glad to be there with Leena, glad to be anywhere with her. She couldn't help but nip glances at her during the film, eyes darting away to the gentle curve of her neck and the slope of her nose. At one point, Leena caught her, and Eleanor immediately redirected her line of sight. Being caught staring was not ideal during a documentary on street harassment.

The lights went up after the film, as the question-and-answer portion with the director began. Eleanor's stomach rumbled loudly and she clutched her belly, willing it silent. Leaning in, she whispered, "Are you hungry? Could we leave, like, now?"

Leena nodded vigorously, darting out of her chair with her coat in her arms, proposing the Lebanese place by Kenmore.

Eleanor readily agreed, although she would have followed her anywhere: McDonald's, a park bench to eat sticks of butter, the hotel dining room at the Four Seasons.

She discovered they were both vegetarians while contemplating what to order, the fact of their sameness a heady connection, one more reason they could be a perfect match. *Who knows what else we have in common?* she thought dazedly. She swam in their conversation, first about the documentary, then school.

"I'm glad my program lets me study abroad, not all do."

Study abroad. Eleanor's heart sank at those words, but she applied a smile to her face and asked where Leena was headed.

"South Africa. I'll be in Johannesburg in the spring. Well, technically, their summer."

They met approximately seventeen seconds before the start of this conversation, and so Eleanor knew she had no claims to Leena's semesters, or where they took place, and yet it was loathsome to think they would be separated by a spinning globe, a map, and a dotted line of adventure before they could really begin. But that wasn't a good reply.

"Wow. That's great," she said instead. "Why South Africa?"

"Some of my family lived there before moving to England, so it's almost a homecoming. I've heard the stories of what it was like there, under apartheid, and I'm looking forward to seeing the country for myself. I mean, it's not under apartheid anymore, but. To see the progress. To see where my family was . . . and I'm just babbling. I'm excited to volunteer in a hospice while I'm there. It'll be hard, I'm sure. But great."

Eleanor's mouth hung agape, pleasantly surprised

at this woman in front of her, gorgeous and caring and action-oriented, principled about being of service no matter the challenge. She cleared her throat, took a sip of water, and resumed their conversation when she recovered. "Wow. That sounds really meaningful and amazing, and also kind of heroic."

Leena looked startled, eyes wide and eyebrows high, but then she smiled, softly, into her lap. "It's just . . . I want to be a doctor. It's the least I can do."

Eleanor's dad, who worked in biomedical research, took pride in what he did, and often said something similar like, "It's important to use your talents to the fullest extent." Then again, he worked long hours for a pharmaceutical company, chasing dollars, and therefore forfeited the moral high ground.

"Why do you want to be a doctor?"

Leena bit her lip, nodding, a smile spreading across her face. "That's a hard question. I guess the short answer is that my dad is a doctor, and I got to watch him in action. It always seemed like a good idea." Leena's fingers traced the rim of her plate, and Eleanor watched the long, artful digits move, picturing them inside of her. A deep blush rose to the skin of her cheeks. "But I guess the reason as I get older is more about helping people. My dad does good work, but he never got to practice his specialty. That wasn't in the cards. I'm excited to do more. Make a difference."

Eleanor knew that feeling intimately, in her every-day, in so many moments where she yearned and grew toward her still-unknown purpose. "What do you want to do?"

Leena shrugged one shoulder. "Probably a pediatrics specialty, maybe infectious diseases. Childhood mortality stands out to me. Something often with an easy fix: more doctors and trained professionals in parts of the developing world. It's a way for me to have an impact. To give back when I've been so lucky." She took a bite of bread. "What do you want to do?"

Eleanor's mouth hung open like a cartoon character until she snapped it shut and took a gulp, unaccustomed to time spent with someone so obviously out of her league, gorgeous and cool and on her way to sainthood. "Well, it won't be anything like you, but I hope to have an impact too. Working on causes that I care about. Women's rights. LGBT rights."

"That's amazing," Leena remarked with an occupied mouth. Amazing was an overstatement. "What's your major?"

"Women's studies."

A look crossed Leena's face that Eleanor couldn't read, her stomach responding with pangs of anxiety. Maybe Leena didn't think she was a serious person, with her liberal arts pursuit. Maybe she thought she was too serious: a man-hating feminazi. There were plenty of lesbians who weren't really feminists. She waited with a breath clutched tightly in her chest.

"Oh, wow, that's really cool. I took the intro class, but because of my schedule I can't take more. What are you reading? Anything that stands out?"

Relief flooded her body and turned her bones to jelly. They were on the same page here too. She scanned her memory for a reading she could succinctly and fully discuss. "So, Adrienne Rich wrote this article about compulsory heterosexuality, enforced in, like, so many ways, including the erasure of lesbian existence in art and literature and film, and in the idealization of straight romance. But the thing that really got me was this concept, that all women live on a lesbian continuum of intimacy." There was a lot of stuff about the *erotic*, but she preferred not to use that word in front of Leena right now. "We're connected through intimacy, whether as friends or coworkers or . . . more. If it wasn't for compulsory heterosexuality, it would be more obvious that we exist on distinct parts of the spectrum during our lives, whether in love or in anger, or in a mix of the two."

She thought this was one of the more brilliant things she had learned in her coursework. Adrienne Rich's analysis glued together breaking taboos and rejecting compulsion, and the article was one of a few academic readings that felt more relevant to her life—practice rather than theory.

Leena looked like she was reviewing data on a spreadsheet, brows furrowed and eyes intensely focused. "So, we're all lesbians?"

Eleanor nodded back seriously, overdoing it.

"Knew it all along." Leena grinned.

"Do you identify with *lesbian*? Is that a word you use to describe yourself?" Eleanor saw a look of surprise cross Leena's face and immediately regretted her question. She thought it would be okay, because they had a shared code—queerness of some kind, whatever its label—and a certain element of affinity because of it. "Sorry I asked. Sorry if that's weird that I asked."

Leena waved her off, then stuffed a falafel ball into her mouth, holding up one finger against her lips as she chewed. She swallowed.

The suspense was killing her.

"I don't really have opportunities to identify. Or

describe myself. But if I did." Leena tilted her head side to side, almost like nodding. "Yeah. Lesbian, I guess."

It made Eleanor burst into laughter. "You said that so casually, like you'd just thought of it. I mean, I'm sure you didn't, but . . ." This had gone off the rails. There was more to say. "I've spent so much time agonizing over what I am, what to call myself, how to handle," she traced a wide circle around her head, "all of this. So it's just really cool to hear you have such clarity."

Leena waved at her again. "No, no. Don't misunderstand. I'm a mess." She laughed too. It would be okay. "I've agonized. In the past."

Eleanor leaned in slightly. "In the past?" Leena was confiding in her, her face more open, eager. Her smile timid, lips parted, cheekbones raised, eyes trusting. Eleanor could not look away.

"My best friend. Well, she was my best friend. Siobhan. We first bonded over substitute teachers mispronouncing our names. When we got older, in high school, I had these . . . dreams about her. Like. Sex dreams," she said, whispering the last words, then smiling into her lap.

Eleanor was hooked. "Did you tell her that you—"

"Never," she said in a rush. "And nothing ever happened. But for a while I felt guilty, like I had done something wrong just by dreaming. And I know now that it was a mix of my brain transmitting how I felt about her, but also how I felt about girls in general. At the time, it didn't feel that clear. It felt—" Leena stopped in her tracks, crossing her arms. She looked like she was biting back a smile. "You're easy to talk to, Eleanor. I usually don't have this much to say."

Eleanor grinned and blushed, pleased, tucking into the end of her hummus and rice, eyes purposefully on her plate. "I'm glad you have a lot to say. I like it." She wanted to learn every fact about Leena, every nuance, and wanted more of her, as much as she could give. When she finally looked up, she found herself without words, dazzled by Leena. The dark, magnetizing color of her eyes; her cheeks like apples when she smiled. The neon light from the Open sign in the window reflecting on her lovely brown skin.

Leena nodded her chin up in one jut. "So, what's your first-date secret-spill gonna be?"

Eleanor grinned, elated in her veins. "I'm really glad you said that. I wanted it to be a date, but I wasn't sure how you . . . anyway. Good. Yay!" she released in a whisper-shout. All of this was making her sweaty and she peeled off her cardigan, adjusting her bra straps and T-shirt as she settled. "It's hot in here. Are you hot? I'm warm."

Leena wagged her finger. "Don't try to derail me from your secret. I can't be deterred."

Eleanor searched her archives for something mildly embarrassing but not too scorching. "My mom found me and my friend kissing when we were seven. She's a nurse, so she's always over-the-top about bodies and sex stuff. She sat us down to ask if we had any questions, and to reassure us that exploration was human." She shook her head, exhaling, a laugh bursting through her lips.

With Leena's cheek propped in her hand, elbow on the table, she almost looked fond. "That sounds nice. But I'm kind of surprised. Asian parents aren't usually so open or cool."

Eleanor half shrugged, confused for a second until the realization hit. "Oh, well, my mom is white, and Jewish, so." Since Leena looked confused, she elaborated. "My dad is Japanese American."

Leena laughed in one short puff. "That took me too long to put together. I guess I don't know many biracial people."

That boggled Eleanor's mind. "Wow. Really?" Growing up in Fremont, she knew so many kids like her and her brother: hafu, hapa, and it wasn't until coming to Boston that she'd felt like an Other. At college, for the first time, she felt seen as Asian, period. "You know one now," she replied, touching her nose with the tip of her pointer finger. After she put her hand down, she recognized that gesture as the way that her Japanese family indicated to themselves. Her obachan, her dad, her uncles. Eleanor propped her head in her hand, elbow on the table between them. "What would your parents have done if they found you kissing a girl?" She realized she'd subconsciously mirrored Leena, and committed to the position, smiling at her dinner companion—who was not smiling back. Eleanor's stomach clenched.

"Oh, I don't . . ." Leena laughed nervously. "I don't know. Probably not have been as cool as your mom was." She pursed her lips and nodded. "We don't talk about that. I'm not really out to them." She checked her watch. "It's getting late. I have to get some homework done tonight. Sorry. Can we?" And she slid out of the booth, up to the counter to pay. Eleanor stared at Leena's back for a few seconds, feeling reckless and wrong, and followed suit, taking her wallet out.

Silence sat between them on the T back to their

dorm, in the space between their shoulders and legs. Eleanor regretted what she'd asked, her mind replaying Leena's response over and over. It had been careless to ask that question like it was no big deal. Like she knew anything about Leena's life.

The T lurched and knocked her shoulder into Leena's, and she glanced over.

At first Leena's face was serious, contemplative. It broke as she furrowed her brow, seriousness sliding into faux seriousness. "Quit bumping into me," she muttered, barely disguising her smile.

Eleanor kept their shoulders pressed together, relishing in the luxury of this for the rest of the ride.

Back in that elevator again, she offered a smile. "I had a good time tonight."

Leena beamed back. "Yeah, me too."

Eleanor felt hungry for the perfect moment. She wanted to push the emergency button to stop between floors—an action created by movies, and not of the real world—then press Leena gently into the wall of the elevator. Their faces would be close, Leena's breath on Eleanor's lips, until Leena leaned in closer, closing the gap between them with a kiss. A good kiss, one that burned, hot and maddening. *You should come back to my room*, Eleanor would have said breathlessly, reaching behind her to resume the elevator's journey.

She was knocked from her rampant imagination with a nudge.

"It's your floor."

She looked up and saw the doors open, exposing her hallway and the end of their date.

"I'm going to have a busy weekend with some family stuff, but maybe we could hang out next weekend?"

Leena asked, hope on her face, sprouting in her wide eyes.

As if there was any way Eleanor would say no. She bit her lip, trying to remain placid in the face of such unexpected goodness, and nodded, moving toward the elevator doors, putting herself in the way of their metal conclusion. "Yeah, definitely," her voice breathy and squeaky, like some kind of very uncool, unkissed virgin.

Leena tipped forward and gave her a hug: a good, brief squeeze that made Eleanor's pulse spike. Her hair smelled so good. She floated back to her room, high on possibility.

They made plans to watch *The L Word* next Sunday night, but then there were no more phone calls or emails or text messages. Eleanor invented reasons to be in touch, drafting emails every half hour that she didn't send.

How's your day going?

Should we study together tonight?

I keep thinking about your lips.

OVER THE NEXT few days, Eleanor flooded conversations with mentions of Leena, recaps of their world-spinning-off-its-axis date and reminders that she would be with Leena for next week's *L Word* viewing instead, until her friends groaned, exhausted by this invisible stranger. "She sounds too good to be true. I think I need to meet her," Tomás announced with crossed arms, his impression of a tough guy. Eleanor rolled her eyes at the idea of his vetting. As if his verdict would sway her. As if anyone could make her feel any differently about Leena.

On Thursday she opened her email to draft another message she probably wouldn't send, and was delighted to see an email reply from her brother instead.

ellie:

glad to hear about this leena girl. she sounds much smarter than you and way out of your league, so dont screw it up. how are you going to stay together if shes abroad, tho? wont she find someone better?

school is okay. i know you said i shouldnt go home on weekends, but id rather see my friends, and berkeley is so close to home. and i know youre right that its an adjustment from high school, but its not as great as everyone says.

but ill be fine.

and i can almost hear you saying "this is why men die sooner, because they dont say how they feel" but this is how i feel and im just being honest okay.

fuck you,

fitz

She snorted at his sign-off, but still worried about the things in him that she couldn't fix. He was his own person on his own journey, but he would always be, no matter what, that little kid who followed her around like a duck for almost his whole life. She never signed an oath in blood or anything, but she was his protector, and the idea that school wasn't going well—well, she would have to talk more with him during Thanksgiving break, if he wasn't in a better place by then.

Lost in Fitz's email, she almost forgot why she had originally logged in. **Dear Leena, it's almost time for our next date and the wait is murdering me from the inside,** she typed.

Delete, delete, delete.

PRIOR TO SHOWTIME on Sunday, she prepared for her visitor, burning incense and washing three weeks' worth of dishes in the communal bathroom sink. Leena arrived right on time; a second earlier and she would have seen Eleanor shoving dirty clothes under her bed.

Leena's eyes first locked on the wall above the bed, the story posts of her life. A taped-up photo of Obachan and Ojichan, and her uncles Atsutomo and Shigeto, and her aunt Keiko, frozen in time as young parents and children, dour and worn in black and white on the day they left the Poston internment camp in 1945. The photo did not, could not, show her obachan's cough that never receded, or Uncle Shigeto's imitation of the brutal whistling desert winds that ripped through their temporary housing.

Then to the right, another photo from a decade later, in front of the brand-new Suzuki Booksellers, her infant father in her grandmother's arms, her grandmother's face lined with time and struggle.

Below that was another family photo, this one of her mother's parents on their wedding day in 1951, her grandfather in a sharp, dark suit and her grandmother in a light-colored skirt suit nipped tight at the waist. They wore prim, somber faces, which matched what she knew of that time in their lives: being rescued from

Germany on the Kindertransport in 1939, growing up in England without family during the war, resettling in Philadelphia, then meeting at a Keneseth Israel temple dance.

And then there were more pictures of Eleanor, the product of all that horror and displacement. Protest signs, hand-copied poems, and quotes filled the wall. Audre Lorde. Ani DiFranco. A long excerpt from Martin Luther King Jr.'s "Letter from Birmingham Jail."

Eleanor watched Leena peruse, hands tucked behind her back as she leaned in over her bed, and felt dueling storm fronts inside of her: excitement and maybe a little fear at Leena examining everything so closely, like she absolutely wanted to know the things that Eleanor prized, and jolts of another category of excitement when Leena knelt with one knee on her bed to get a closer look. Her bed. Leena's body. Her bed. Her mind leaped to a swirling landscape, pulsing and rushing rivers of desire, of ecstasy, of bodies intertwined, and—

"You went!" Leena turned to Eleanor, underneath her large, yellow sign with MARCH FOR WOMEN'S LIVES blazoned in purple text.

Eleanor nodded enthusiastically, guiding her brain back from where it ambled. "Yeah! It was incredible. Being around all of those women, all kinds of women, and everyone so passionate. I felt powerful, you know? Like we could take on anything."

Leena didn't reply, looking lost in thought.

"You—how was it for you?" Eleanor asked.

"Um. Good. It sucks it was necessary, but the march was great," Leena said, then paused for a moment. "Sorry, I was thinking about my ex." Leena blanched. "Is that weird to say?"

Eleanor did find it weird to be on a second date and talking about an ex, but there was nothing she would do to obstruct Leena from talking, confiding, sharing every secret. She shook her head no.

"She was premed too. We marched with Physicians for Reproductive Choice and Health. She's in med school now, so she's on her way to literally being a full-fledged physician for reproductive choice." Leena scoffed at herself, landing a seat on the edge of the bed. "And again, I'm just like, blah, blah, blah. Sorry for going on about my ex. There's something about you, I feel so at ease. Like I can say anything."

"You could say anything," Eleanor offered, probably too quickly and with zero panache. She opened her mini fridge and grinned widely, leaving her expression there, grabbing iced tea borne of a powder mix—the solution for a hostess without a kitchen—then a bowl of pretzels she'd stolen from the dining hall. "Only the finest."

"This is so fancy," Leena teased.

Eleanor grabbed two hard plastic tumblers, worn souvenir cups from a Yosemite camping trip, and filled them with tea. "So, what happened with you and the Physician for Reproductive Choice?" Eleanor handed Leena a cup and the pretzel bowl, taking a seat on the opposite end of the bed, extraordinarily aware of her space and their proximity to each other. She sat very still, and waited.

Leena squinched her face together like a shar-pei, then let it go. "Well? It . . . ended. She's in med school in Ohio. Distance was too hard. And other stuff. But we're friends. Everything's good." Leena took a sip of tea, then coughed. "This packs a punch. What's in this?"

Eleanor took her own exploratory sip and wrinkled her nose. Too heavy with scoops of powder. "Just tea. And by tea, I mean chemicals." Eleanor turned the television on and flipped to the right channel as scenes from last week's episode played. She looked to the tie-dye pillow with arms at both of its sides. "Husband pillow?" she offered.

"I'm sorry, what?" Leena grinned, looking incredulous.

"A—uh, maybe that's not what it's called in Massachusetts?" Eleanor gestured to the pillow's back and its inviting, open arms. "That's what my mom called it when she sent it."

"Husband," Leena muttered under her breath, teasing, eyes flashing to Eleanor.

"Life-partner pillow?" Eleanor offered instead. Leena nodded, accepting it, placing it between herself and the concrete wall.

They watched in silence, even though Eleanor was ready to rip into it like she usually did with Cath and Sam. She didn't know if Leena thought it was actually a solid show, or whether lesbian media scarcity made her loyal and steadfast.

Jenny popped up on-screen, her long, dark hair frizzed and burnt-looking, whisper-talking to her ex-fiancé Tim's new girlfriend about toast.

"She is so weird," Leena said, eyes locked on the screen. Then, "Sorry."

Eleanor nodded, pleased. "Sometimes this show doesn't make sense. I'll still watch, but."

"Like when Snoop Dogg guest starred?"

Eleanor spread her arms. "Yes, exactly! Why did that happen?"

Toward the end of the episode, after lots of color commentary, Eleanor and Leena both fell quiet, fueled by a mutual appreciation for Dana—her newly improved haircut with bangs and layers, her always-toned tennis-player arms. After sitting alone in a dimly lit, old-school lesbian bar and nursing her broken heart and a beer, Dana went home with Jenny, who also happened by the bar that night.

"Jenny is always wearing tights. Have you noticed that?" Eleanor whispered. This pair was rust red.

They watched Jenny clear detritus from her bed. "There aren't too many places to sit," she apologized. The two women were sitting side by side on the bed in Jenny's garage-turned-studio as they drank juice.

The characters were awkward as they struggled to connect, talking about their careers and failed relationships, and they were so awkward that the act of watching them became awkward, made worse because she and Leena were also two women sitting on a bed. Eleanor felt thoroughly aware of herself and of Leena, and who they were in relation to what they saw on-screen. These characters had no chemistry; the absence of it was glaring. She wondered what someone would say should they be watching her and Leena, and how they would stack up.

Jenny tugged down her top to reveal her breasts without provocation, and she and Dana kissed as if by obligation, like leaving together had to mean one thing. Jenny laid down on the bed. Dana took her top off. Jenny reached up to squeeze Dana's breast as if it were a stress ball.

"Why is no one wearing a bra?" Leena sounded mystified.

Eleanor thought of Leena without a bra, but that perhaps had not been her point. "No one put their hair up," Eleanor added. "Sex is harder with long hair in your face."

Leena shifted her gaze to Eleanor then blinked, her face softening with the slightest smile. Her face looked kind, it always did, but this was something else. There was a wicked blaze in her eyes. Maybe she was thinking of sex, and of them, and considering it. It made Eleanor's limbs buzz with a nervous energy, tingling with possibility.

In what she hoped was not as awkward as anything Dana and Jenny had done, Eleanor applied one hand to the bed between them, her heart thundering in her chest, planning her move to lean in for a kiss—and realized they were still so egregiously far apart on the bed. With heavy, faltering breath, she scooped her legs up, knees to the mattress, and closed the distance between them, pressing a kiss to Leena's lips.

It was perfect. Perfect when they bumped noses, Leena giggling low, perfect when they were at the right angle, her ripe lips between Eleanor's, perfect as they clashed teeth, as Eleanor's arms shook from supporting herself, *Fuck, why don't I ever go to the gym*, perfectly perfect when Leena put a palm to the back of her neck, drawing her in, asking without words to stay.

Then there was a knock at the door. Eleanor briefly considered ignoring it before another one came. "Fuck," she groaned, slipping away from Leena. "Sorry." She walked backward toward the door, watching Leena, whose eyes were still glassy and her lips puffy with kiss.

It was Tomás, who pushed the door open wider than

Eleanor allowed, and slid his way in. "Hey! Sorry to interrupt, just had to drop something off." He held up a chemistry textbook, a prop in his charade, since Eleanor wasn't even taking chemistry. So here was the promised vetting after all.

She sighed as he pushed in toward Leena.

"Hey, I'm Tomás."

Leena stood up from her spot on the bed and shook his outstretched hand, throwing a bemused look at Eleanor. "I'm Leena. It's nice to meet you, Tomás."

"Same here!" He didn't say anything else, standing there with his hands on his hips, looking dopey, his gaze swinging back and forth between them.

Eleanor patted his back in two firm, abrasive pats. "Well, thanks for—"

"What are you two up to?" He said, settling on the bed, and Leena followed suit, shooting a quick glance, then a smile, to Eleanor.

We were kissing. We were on the way to a lot more. Eleanor crossed her arms, still standing. "Trying to watch *The L Word*. Alone."

Tomás reclined against one end of the wood bed frame, ignoring Eleanor. "It's nice to meet you," he said to Leena. "I've heard good things about you."

Eleanor's gut contracted in on itself, hoping that no follow-up questions would abound.

Leena snuck a look to Eleanor, face down but her eyes peering up. "That's nice to hear." Then, to Tomás, "I have to say, I haven't heard anything about you yet."

Tomás put a hand to his chest like a scandalized old Southern lady about to faint. "How dare you," he rasped, total overkill. She always thought he would fit in better with gay men, save for his unfortunate heterosexuality and omnipresent uniform of sweat-shirt, cargo shorts, and flip-flops. "But it's totally fine," he said, replying to Leena's original comment with his actual voice. "You've had other things to talk about."

"Tomás! It's been so nice seeing you," Eleanor said, her tone a dart, "but you probably have to get going, right?"

Tomás gestured to her with his thumb. "Me and this one, we went to high school together," he said, ignoring her. "We met in the straight-edge group."

"What's that?" Leena asked.

"Oh, it's people who don't drink or do drugs," Tomás told her proudly.

And there it was. The thing that Eleanor kept guarded, because to disclose it was often met with disapproval or confusion, from people who couldn't understand why a college student didn't desire nights of blurred forgetting, of personality displacement, of vomiting indiscriminately. She had seen it before and knew it well. Alcohol didn't interest her, no matter how alienating it was to stray from the norm. But this was hard to acknowledge when Leena's opinion of her mattered so much, when all Eleanor wanted was for Leena to think she was cool and worth her time.

Leena nodded slowly. "That's interesting." She said it in that way people do when they don't know what else to say. A pit formed in Eleanor's stomach.

Tomás, being a literal soul, seemed to take her at her word and began to elaborate. "Yeah, I joined because I was an athlete and took it seriously. El joined because Micah joined, and because her dad dri—I mean. Um." His always warm-beige skin was tinged pink in the cheeks. "Sorry," he mouthed to Eleanor, then grimaced.

43

She blanched at his indiscretion and felt deep embarrassment seep into her own cheeks, to be outed like that in two different directions, and she closed her eyes, shaking her head, to spare herself anyone's expression. "That's . . . not . . ."

"Who's Micah?" Leena asked quickly.

As Eleanor opened her eyes again, she smiled gratefully at Leena, but thought of Micah. Micah and his curly, brown hair, those dimples, the lean body honed by skateboarding. In high school, she thought she might literally die when he told her he liked her back. But that was barely anything in comparison to what Tomás had started to say.

It wasn't discussed. Japanese culture and adult behavior weren't up for conversation. But her dad's propensity toward a drink or two or more was as present in her life as anything else she knew to be true.

"Micah was Eleanor's boyfriend, but before he was that, she wanted him to be, so that was why she joined the group. Micah's mom was an alcoholic until she found Jesus, like George Bush."

Eleanor's eyes strayed to the television screen, where the show's credits were rolling, grateful for the way the conversation was diverting away from her family and toward a more comfortable mortification. "But then he wasn't my boyfriend and I'm a homo, and here we are," she said, still staring at the screen.

Leena asked about Tomás's major—as if she was kindly and carefully trying to change the subject, as if she was reading the words unspoken on Eleanor's face—and off he went as always on the importance of a diverse prelaw curriculum, about the law's relationship to everyday life. It was unbearable, and Eleanor ate two handfuls of pretzels out of boredom.

But Leena looked delighted. "Exactly. That's exactly how I feel about medicine. I need to prepare for med school, but it's more than that. I'm learning about health and the environment, and how diseases migrate. The intersection of things."

Tomás beamed at Leena. "Yeah. You get it. She gets it," Tomás said, moving his gaze to Eleanor.

When Tomás and Eleanor made eye contact, Eleanor slashed at her throat with one finger.

Tomás stood. "Well, I did my job, dropping off that book. So. Nice meeting you, Leena!"

Eleanor walked him out. From the hallway as she closed the door, he mouthed, "I like her."

She shook her head, shutting him out, and turned to Leena with her back against the door. They needed a reset. "Do you want to go for a walk?"

They bundled up and headed into the night, toward Brookline with its big houses and hushed streets. It had rained while they were inside, and the wet pavement shone with borrowed light from the street lamps above. Their hands brushed as they walked, until Eleanor grasped for Leena clumsily, then weaved their fingers together intentionally. She needed to know they could still be connected. Leena's digits were cold and dry, but she was touching her, they were touching. Eleanor's heart raced. "Is this okay?" she asked toward the pavement, unable to bring up her line of sight.

"I don't mind," Leena replied. They walked together, linked, like this was going somewhere. Like they were going somewhere.

"Sorry about Tomás," Eleanor said after her sense returned. "Sorry that he was awkward."

"I like him. He seems like a nice guy."

Eleanor signed. Nice, and nosy and indiscreet. "Yeah, he's okay. He's a dork. But it was great to come to school and already know someone, to have a little piece of home."

"I bet. Someone you have a past with, that you share things with. That must be nice. So. You don't drink. But does it bother you if I do?"

Eleanor veered them to the left on their walk, keeping words out of her mouth as she considered the question carefully. Yes, it bothered her, despite knowing it was unreasonable and unfair to expect them to be in sync about everything. Yes, it bothered her, because she watched people transform when they drank, become unrecognizable, when all she wanted from anyone was truth and authenticity.

At a party one night, Zoe accused Eleanor of being self-righteous about her prohibition. Eleanor felt burned. "I can't trust you when you drink," she'd lashed out. "I don't know who you are or what you're doing." It made her heart cramp to think of it, how much she'd been hurt then, how angry she'd felt. How much it was and wasn't about Zoe. Maybe it wasn't only alcohol that caused people to transform.

Eleanor gave Leena the answer she wished was true. "No, it doesn't bother me."

"Lots of surprises tonight," Leena murmured, squeezing her hand again.

Eleanor stumbled through her breath. "Yeah, I know." She took another gulp of fresh cold air, feeling like tiny icicles were forming down her throat as she inhaled. "I like you, Lee." *Lee*. It was an error coming out of her mouth, but with it delicately floating in the air—Lee—she liked it very much.

Leena paused them in front of a dark-green house with porch lights still on. It cast this little bit of light against Leena's beautiful face. Her white teeth, crooked a little in the front. Her gorgeous lips. Leena opened her mouth to speak, then shut it, then leaned forward and crushed their lips together.

Woozy with kiss, it felt like a promise, a true link between them.

They looped back to Comm Ave, to the rush of traffic on the four-lane street, leaving behind the quiet pocket of darkness that had been theirs for a little while, and headed home.

OCTOBER

Eleanor was rushing around, hiding stray papers and laundry before Leena arrived. They had both been caught up in homework and papers and tests, tabling to promote the Women's Center and Premed Society meetings, so there had not been time after that night when they'd kissed, when maybe-something-more had been interrupted. But that night, it would be just them, watching a movie together in Eleanor's dorm room—really an excuse to be in the dark, in proximity to a bed. To prepare, Eleanor shaved her legs, which felt unfeminist but like a practical investment in her evening, and lotioned her body with an apricot-and-rose scent.

The knock sounded as Eleanor dressed, hopping around on one foot to tug on her second sock, flushed as she answered the door. "Hiya," she said cheerfully. Leena held up a DVD, *Kabhi Khushi Kabhie Gham . . .*, depicting six attractive Indian people and a quote on the cover. "It's all about loving your parents," Eleanor read aloud from the case, then looked up at Leena. "Is it?"

"Oh yeah. That's totally what the movie's about. Hell, that's what being Indian is about." She leaned against the dorm frame. "Can I come in?" Her smile was teasing, her eyes bright and hooded. There wasn't any question she could pose to which Eleanor would say no.

The movie, promised by the DVD packaging to be 210 minutes long, was not a strong preamble to making out. It was family drama with sweeping musical numbers, featuring disapproving parents and sibling relationships and, inexplicably, pyramids. The movie was engrossing and Leena was laser-focused on it, despite it being her fourth viewing, and Eleanor could not find the right moment to kiss her, so she settled in for the long haul, with their heads together and shoulders knocking, bodies extending toward opposite ends of the bed. Eventually, two hours in, Eleanor yawned.

"Should we turn it off?" Leena murmured.

Eleanor yawned again but said no, repositioning their bodies so that she was spooning Leena. "Is this okay?" She asked into Leena's hair, holding her breath.

"Yeah," Leena said with a gentle sigh.

Eleanor had been lost to sleep minutes before, but now she was keyed up, her breath coming in and out in stuttered rhythm. She stroked one hand over Leena's hip. It was so hard and bony, unlike hers, and she couldn't help exploring the differences between them. Leena had hard juts to her body, but there were places where she was curvy. Leena let out a little sigh, content like a cat being pet or because she was rolling into sleep. Eleanor wasn't sure.

She knew soon enough when Leena spun in her arms, awake. It was dark in the room but she could see Leena's face well enough, some shades of her expression, the outline of her nose and cheekbones, so beautiful. So close, no space between them. Leena combed a hand through Eleanor's hair, then took a deep breath, sliding in to kiss her.

Leena kissed her gently, deeply, and held her close like she was something precious. "I could get used to this," Leena whispered against her lips.

Eleanor crushed their mouths back together. She reached out to graze her fingers against Leena's breast and Leena cracked up, wrenching away, putting a trench between them.

"Sorry, I'm ticklish."

Her laughter felt like a dismissal, but Eleanor wouldn't be deterred. "That's okay." She kissed Leena again, slipping her tongue between Leena's lips. It felt so good, intimate, like a preamble to the rest of the night. Eleanor slipped her hand down into the tight space between their bodies, rounding lower, between Leena's legs, Eleanor's fingers touching the hardy cotton of Leena's sweatpants. She imagined pulling them down, pulling off Leena's T-shirt, getting them both naked, under the covers, skin against skin, pressing into each other—

Leena moved Eleanor's hand, halting them again. She put as much space between them as she could on the narrow bed, and then lifted Eleanor's hand to her lips, kissing her knuckles one by one. "I like kissing you," she said quietly, her breath hot on Eleanor's skin, cooling once it disappeared.

"Me too," Eleanor whispered back.

"Can we just . . . kiss?"

Eleanor shrank back against the wall. Her mind flashed through various scenarios.

One: Leena liked Eleanor, she had said as much, but upon reflection, with their lips together, Leena just wasn't into her.

Two: Leena had never had sex, not even with the future Physician for Reproductive Choice. No one had ever touched her breast or clit or anywhere of note. Maybe an elbow or knee, but that was it. This was her first time and she wasn't ready.

Three: Eleanor was terrible at sex. She was awful. The worst ever. It was so bad that Leena laughed at her, and maybe there was even more laughter stored up. Nothing had even begun, and yet that's how bad.

"Why? Why just . . . kiss?"

Leena buried her face into Eleanor's shoulder and mumbled incoherently.

"Say that again?"

Leena lifted her face an inch off of Eleanor's shoulder. "I have my period? Which isn't all that alluring to say, but then again, neither is having your period. I'm sorry."

Eleanor had to catch up, which she did, slowly. Her body in the throes of desire, her brain in analytical mode, then this, a real barrier between them that was elemental, and no one's fault. She giggled, relieved, running a hand up and down Leena's back. "I went to some real weird places. I'm glad this is all—hey. Are you okay? Achy? Do you need anything?"

Leena leaned back and assessed Eleanor with a look of wonderment. "I've never dated a guy, but this is why I can't. Women! Women get it. I'm okay, but thank you for asking." She grabbed Eleanor's hand tightly. "I could, you know . . ." With their hands still locked she traced the top of Eleanor's pants.

Eleanor understood what she was being offered. Sex, and the smashing uplift of passion, and she went hazy considering it. As she played out the hands and moans and mouths, it wasn't what she wanted, not tonight. When they had sex for the first time, she wanted to undo all of Leena's snaps and buckles, to be bare to each other in the same way and at the same time. There would be no enjoying herself while Leena had cramps, so they kissed and kissed and kissed. She could barely contain her desire for Leena's touch, but she could wait. They had time.

LEENA KNOCKED ON Eleanor's door Friday at 9:15 p.m., a full fifteen minutes before the time they'd agreed on in advance. Eleanor yanked her inside with a kiss, flattening her against the door. "You're early," she mumbled against her lips.

"Of course. Because I knew you'd be late otherwise," Leena said when they broke apart.

Eleanor delighted at being known so well, a force field of intimacy around them that made her world feel soft, and cozy, and like she had nowhere else to be.

She was still in pajamas, not yet bundled for the cold trip to the restaurant. "I'm close to ready?"

"Yeah, you totally look it." Leena took a seat on the unmade bed, leafing through an issue of *BUST* magazine. "Let's leave right now."

With an upright presence in her room, Eleanor started running around. A quick rinse in the shower, product in her hair, jumping into jeans and a sweater and thick socks and clunky Moon Boots meant to conquer Massachusetts winters, darting over to Leena with kisses between tasks. This outing was their first with her friends, infinitely more pleasurable because it would be with her girlfriend, this person who had stolen her breath, and because she wouldn't feel like a third wheel or like Tomás was her de facto date. She had a someone to bring somewhere. They left at 9:30 on the dot, on time, Leena with a wordless smile on her face.

They hit the pavement, on the way to the center of campus, down the main road, walking quickly with the frozen wind whipping past their faces. She grabbed for Leena's hand once, then again, then once more, but Leena kept slipping loose of her hold. It made her feel like Leena was ashamed of her, like she didn't feel the same as Eleanor, who wanted everyone to know they were together.

"Hey, did I do something wrong? Is everything okay?" she asked.

Leena looked perplexed. "Yeah. Did I do something wrong?"

Leena's expression said nothing of being annoyed or ashamed or any of the things that Eleanor feared. She sighed, reassured. "No, no, of course not. Just, you wouldn't hold my hand." As soon as the words left her mouth, she felt so immature. *You didn't hold my hand and my feelings are hurt!* "Never mind, it's not anything, really. Sorry."

Leena nudged Eleanor's shoulder with her own. "It's okay. I'm just not always into PDA."

Public displays of affection. Maybe Comm Ave was too public for affection, or maybe Leena was ashamed, but whatever the why, it stung like a bee. She slid her hands into her coat pockets, privately tightening them into fists. "You were into it other times." She thought of roads shimmering after a rainstorm, feeling connected and tethered, like she belonged. Not like now.

"Well," Leena started, but paused, for a long time, for an eternity. The wind whistled. "I'm not a robot. You can't expect the same thing from me all the time." Her voice was stern, bluntly honest, without the usual softness and sweetness that encased their conversations.

Eleanor was freezing, didn't think it was possible to grow colder, and yet she felt ice crystals forming between her vital organs once she heard the chill in Leena's rebuttal. Usually she'd open her mouth and let the hurt pour out, but Leena's dourness prevented her admission. She didn't feel like anything she lobbed out between them would be caught.

Instead of talking, they kept up their hustling, speed walking through the cold, and reached the vegan Chinese restaurant in a stony silence.

Eleanor still felt weird in her limbs and stomach, prickly and numb, and she had leagues more to say to Leena, but there were Cath and Sam, already tucked in a red banquette, sharing a menu. She pasted a smile on her face and raised her arms. "Happy birthday!" she called to Cath, leaning over the table when she reached it to give her a hug and a kiss on the cheek. Casting a look at Leena behind her, she made introductions to her friends, wearily, with more restraint than she usually displayed. A storm cloud brewed above her head.

"Hi!" Leena offered cheerily, shaking their hands in turn, so formal and adult. "It's nice to meet you two."

They slid into the booth as Leena asked Cath about school, *of course*. Across from her, Sam gave Eleanor a knowing nod of approval.

Normally that cosign from a friend would be affirming, but in this moment, Eleanor only felt left holding a bag full of fish heads. Public displays of affection. PDA. It wasn't a big deal for two girls to hold hands on a college campus, in the middle of a city, in a state where gay people could get married. She wasn't so Bambi to think that marriage suddenly evaporated homophobia, but it meant something about who they were and who shared their sidewalk. They could fucking hold hands, and Leena knew that, and so it had to be her original suspicion: that Leena was embarrassed to be seen with her. Eleanor smiled blithely as the other women chatted, getting to know each other, becoming enmeshed, while she sat on the sidelines, blinking, unable to let this go.

There was something wrong with her, something uncool or loud or chubby or broken. If she was what Leena wanted, more of something, or less of something, then maybe she could be seen as whole and worthy of being present at her girlfriend's side. Working herself into a lather she could not undo, she felt hot tears pricking her eyes.

"So, we'll share?" Sam asked.

Eleanor dropped back into the moment. "Sorry, what?" She listened to Sam tell the server the list of dishes they'd share—scallion pancakes, dumplings, edamame, tofu with three kinds of mushrooms, sweet-and-sour faux chicken, and vegetable fried rice—and nodded her assent, though she couldn't care less what they ate because she no longer had an appetite.

She felt a small tap on her side thigh.

"Are you okay? Hungry? I am too," Leena whispered.

"Cath, how are rehearsals going?" Eleanor asked, bypassing Leena's question, focusing on her friends.

Cath delicately sipped from the straw in her water glass. "You know, it's actually going pretty well. We haven't rehearsed together as a cast, it's just one on one, so it's me talking to one other person about vaginas."

She grimaced, arms folding tight across her chest as her shoulders hunched protectively toward her ears. "Maybe that's better than a whole bunch of people. I'm finding it's kind of embarrassing, more than I thought it would be. To say it in public will be weird."

"Babe, it's gonna be really public when you're on a stage performing that monologue."

"What are you guys talking about?" Leena asked, bewildered.

Eleanor repressed the smile threatening her lips.

"Cath is going to be in *The Vagina Monologues*. They're doing it in December," Sam answered.

"Having a whole public-slash-private mindset is kind of limiting, don't you think?" Eleanor said, her heart and brain racing, running against each other, petty and self-righteous. "What's private should be okay in public too. That's . . . just my two cents." She didn't dare look at Leena, didn't want to, couldn't, but she felt her tense all the same.

"Well, I think there's a difference between saying *vagina* in public—"

"And, like, fucking in the street."

The double punch of Cath and Sam, united even in extemporaneous speech. Eleanor waited for Leena to weigh in, but she studied the menu as if there was something new to be gleaned from it, and felt a low mix of atomic fury build up her spine.

"And everyone has different boundaries," Cath added. "I guess mine stop at talking about oral sex with a man in front of Zoe."

At the mention of that name, Eleanor felt her own vagina tighten with phantom agony. *I'm over her*, that was her refrain, and it was always true, but tonight made her play the comparison game. Zoe was many terrible things, including emotionally unavailable, but she had not been ashamed of Eleanor. She even ventured to think that Zoe had been proud to be seen with her. "How is Zoe doing? We haven't talked in a while."

Eleanor ignored the knowing looks exchanged between Cath and Sam.

"Who's Zoe?" Leena asked. "Sorry, I feel like I'm playing a lot of catch-up." Her hostess smile thinned, her easygoing mask starting to slip.

Eleanor felt guilt, but also a pang of righteousness. *Good, lose your cool, lose your patience, react, feel something!* "My ex. We were pretty serious." *Express yourself!*

The food arrived en masse, and the conversation devolved into the passing of plates and silence of happy eating. Eleanor stealthily watched Leena from the corner of her eye. She wanted to know how she felt, but Leena was a clam, everything trapped inside, hard shell on the outside, and she wanted to bust through with a hammer.

After paying the bill, they walked in pairs—Cath and Leena; Sam and Eleanor—to Machine, and their 18+ night. The last thing she wanted to do was dance, but she groped for the silver lining: the frenetic energy of movement and a thumping bass would take the edge off a shitty night. While Sam filibustered about Halberstam's *Female Masculinity* and the problem with gendered bathrooms—which Eleanor followed but didn't totally empathize with—she tried to unsuccessfully eavesdrop on Cath and Leena.

Inside the dark club, with a dance floor drenched in rainbow-colored lights, Eleanor didn't try to manage her face at all, pouting instead, and scanned other faces, other people, other groups. They were mostly surrounded by clumps of young men, reeking of Curve and wearing slutty, elaborate Halloween costumes, everyone preening, wanting to be seen and recognized.

Cath pulled Sam onto the dance floor in the middle of a dancehall song—a tune with questionable lyrics, like most music played at clubs—and Eleanor felt her hips move of their own accord, at the edge of the dance floor at the back of the room, silent next to someone who was supposed to be her girlfriend.

Leena asked something, but her voice was too soft over the din.

"What?"

"Is Tomás joining us?" Leena asked loudly, right into her ear.

The close contact thawed her heart slightly, but the almost-touch reminded her of what was lacking all night, what Leena withheld. "No, why would he?" Eleanor retorted, irritated all over again.

A Shakira remix gushed out of the speakers.

"You're mad, okay, I get it, but I don't know what I did." Leena took her hand and stared, wide-eyed and plaintive.

Eleanor looked down, admiring their grasp, loving it more than she wanted to, because she wanted to be furious with Leena. That was more comfortable than whatever this was, a gray area of hurt and confusion and upset. "So you can touch me now? So now it's okay?" Eleanor looked up, finally taking her gaze off of where they were joined. It was dark, but she saw Leena flinch.

Her girlfriend opened her mouth, then closed it, then shook her head, eyes away. "I'm not out. Not out-out, at least. Here, a place like this, it's okay. Can you understand that?"

Eleanor let out a deep sigh, and that release let relief flood in. It wasn't her, it was about Leena. But then the sadness of that fact hit her in a rolling wave, washing over her. *Not out-out.* Eleanor wasn't out-out either, but there were no walls or barricades she had to observe. It seemed exhausting to look over a shoulder. She nodded, acknowledging her, because this she could understand. "Do you . . . dance?" Eleanor asked. "Do you want to dance?"

Leena squinted. "I'm Indian. It's, like, not even a question. But if I'm not at a family party, I'm usually drunk while I'm doing it."

Eleanor felt her face fall. This night wasn't going well. They weren't a match, and there wasn't anything she could do to change that. She sighed. Maybe she could sneak out to drown her sorrows in a pint of cookie-dough ice cream.

"If I was at a family party," Leena continued, "I couldn't do *this*." And she pulled Eleanor onto the dance floor, close, and started to dance, which surprised her and made her sweat even more than she already was.

Leena wants me, she realized in the haze of her blooming arousal.

Leena, as it turned out, was a phenomenal dancer, shaking her hips with a rhythmic bounce, bending her knees, rolling her shoulders. She seemed so unusually confident with the way her body moved through the air, in the room, how it fit with her dance partner.

Eleanor was, at best, a dorky dancer with flailing

limbs, but she focused on Leena, who still wanted her, who couldn't desire her in public but could give her this. She bopped and ached at being this close as one song slid into another.

"*I'm so caught up,*" Leena mouthed along with the music, smirking and staring. "*This girl's got a hold on me.*" Eleanor was overwhelmed by the attention, by the blatant flirting. It was so unlike her, so broad and boastful of who they were to each other. It was too good to be true, and she didn't ever want to leave.

Leena put her hands on Eleanor's hips, pulling her close, and their hips synced and rolled in tandem. Then she slotted one thigh between Eleanor's legs, her hands tight and insistent on her body.

Eleanor felt her brain decelerate, the motion in the room crawling in front of her, as all of the blood in her body rushed to her clit. Up until this second, her interest in Leena was physical, no doubt, but she had been fascinated by the whole of her. How smart she was, interested in subjects that Eleanor could not understand. Her dry sense of humor, her open heart, her curious and inquiring mind. With their bodies intertwined, all of that faded into the background. Her interest became simple, broken down to its elements, to the root of her body. She wanted to fuck her.

The music transformed into a twitchy, bubbly pop tune, and bodies around them flailed.

"I'm having fun!" Eleanor shouted into Leena's ear, pulling on her arm to stop her bouncing. "But we should leave."

"What?" Leena yelled. Her body stilled and she stared, appraising, eyes scanning, and then her expression turned warm, her eyes visibly lit even in the dim.

A wide, slick smile spread across her face. "Let's leave," Leena said, before Eleanor could repeat herself.

She spied Cath and Sam on the dance floor, wrapped up in each other in the way they always were, and slipped in behind Leena on the way out, briefly touching her waist before they hit the sidewalk. They walked down Boylston, then on Jersey Street past Fenway, which was alive with floodlights as workers in orange vests prepared for the World Series victory parade the next morning. As they left the cacophony behind them, Eleanor stayed silent, wanting to preserve the heat between them, suspending the moment they'd shared in amber. They crossed over the Mass Pike on Brookline Ave, the Citgo sign glowing in the dark, lighting the way ahead. From there, they were on familiar territory, on Comm Ave, dark and chaotic with late-night partiers dragging themselves to their next destination.

In the elevator of their dorm, she pressed the button to her floor only, and turned to Leena, realizing they had nonverbally agreed to something that required coordination. Would Leena come to her room? Did they need to get ready? Did they still even feel ready?

Three women barreled in loudly behind them, forcing them apart to opposite sides of the elevator.

"Um, hey," Eleanor called over the bursts of shouts and laughing. "Do you want to . . . come over?"

Leena seemed to be weighing the decision, blank-faced with a sway of her neck, but then she grinned like a sun-shower, and nodded.

At her floor, Eleanor pushed past the noisy girls crowding the hallway, then looked back at Leena, who was still in the elevator, gesturing up then down with her finger, which maybe meant that she would go to her room first, but the elevator closed before Eleanor could confirm.

She rushed to her room so she could make it impeccable before her guest arrived: clothes shoved under the bed and into the hamper, books stacked on her desk, unwashed dishes thrown into the microwave, a lit candle thrusting out the scent of cucumbers and cantaloupe. She debated a quick shower, but before she could make a strategic decision, Leena arrived bearing her toothbrush. Her pajamas were similar to her hanging-out clothes: black sweatpants and a black Lowell Soccer T-shirt.

"Soccer, that's right! You're a soccer superstar."

Leena rolled her eyes. "You heard that story wrong."

"I think I'm remembering your accomplishments right."

In the harsh overhead light, Eleanor kissed Leena and stroked her back, her fingers on the worn cotton of her shirt. She felt the back of Leena's bra and ran her hand back and forth over the strip of material, then flicked off the light.

"You can take it off," Leena murmured into her ear. "If you want to." Then she went back to kissing with intention, strong and burning kisses with her tongue.

Eleanor's mind spun. With a faltering hand, she traced her way underneath Leena's shirt, stroking her soft skin, then made her way up to Leena's bra and strived to unhook it with one hand. A failure, but she kept kissing her, Leena's tongue in her mouth. She wedged her hand underneath Leena's side, sliding it up to meet her other hand. It took several tries as Leena chuckled into her mouth, but she got it unhooked and felt powerful. Unmatched. And yet. She shimmied back on the bed, a little. Leena's ponytail was askew and her eyes glassy, her lips plump and shiny from kissing.

This was it. Her mind raced. "Okay?" That was all she could muster, especially when Leena plucked off her shirt and bra, and buried herself underneath the blankets. She tugged on Eleanor's hand to follow.

Eleanor marveled at the swell of Leena's bare breasts, at her stomach, at so much gorgeous brown-tan skin that contrasted against her golden-beige coloring. She pulled Leena's sweatpants off, kissing her way down her body, the birthmark on her inner thigh, then her kneecap, then the knob of her ankle bone. She draped herself half on top of Leena and got lost in kissing her, kissing so hard that their teeth clashed. Skimming her fingers down Leena's rib cage to the lowlands between her legs, rubbing against the cotton panel of her underwear. Leena's breath going out of her like static.

"Okay?" Eleanor asked.

Leena's stout laugh, then, "Yeah. Yeah, I'm okay. It's okay."

There was too much sensation for her to register in its entirety. Touching Leena, learning what worked, what produced what sounds, what position of Eleanor's fingers caused Leena to sigh then moan. Feeling Leena's body go slack, or become rigid. Her wild, frantic kisses. It was too much goodness, too many of her desires realized.

Leena pressed Eleanor back onto the mattress. She kissed her neck, trailing those kisses with her tongue. "There's a problem. You're still entirely clothed. Can we change that?"

Eleanor's breath came out in one staccato bleat,

her heart pounding with anticipation. As much as she liked sex, and liked thinking about it, it came with the unveiling of her form. A body that served her well, to do the things that she thought were important, but one that was not toned or slim or even curvy. She wasn't sure Leena would like what she found, but it was too late and they were in too deep. Eleanor nodded.

Leena worked quickly, shucking her out of her clothes, and then she moved like molasses. Kissing up and down her arms, her legs, her sides, like Eleanor's body was a world to be circumnavigated. Being cherished like that was almost painful, and she leaned into her discomfort until the awful feeling turned to gold.

They had sex for hours, until they were too sore for more. Rounds and rounds of Leena's strong, dexterous fingers and Eleanor's persistent tongue, and switching. And vice versa. Eleanor had been starved for Leena, and apparently the reverse was true too. Everything was perfect.

NOVEMBER

It stopped feeling perfect on Wednesday morning. Whatever optimism she had as she went to vote on Tuesday after class was demolished by John Kerry's concession speech. She stayed in bed, blankets to her chin, dwelling in sorrow and anger. It wasn't so much that she loved Kerry; it was that she would support anyone who could unseat the disastrous religious oligarch running her country. Carol Moseley Braun would have been her pick, but the country was too racist to elect a Black person and too sexist to elect a woman. She couldn't find hope in Kerry's defeat, in the mandate of Bush's reelection. She chided herself for not doing more. She could have knocked on doors or made calls—she should have tried, at least. She could have done more than just vote. She wouldn't fuck up next time.

Eleanor called her mom, who was getting ready for work. "It's too terrible. I'll call you back after I have my coffee" was all her mother could manage.

She called her girlfriend next, limp like a noodle as Leena ran between classes. "Why are you in bed? Why aren't you in class? Are you okay?"

Eleanor scoffed. "Did you see the news?"

There was a pause on Leena's end. "Oh. Yeah, but. Life goes on. You have to go to class and graduate and get a good job that undoes whatever he's going to do in the next four years." Though Leena had never spoken to her in that way, she recognized the steadfast tone. Her father, uncles, and grandmother all had it, that tinge of Asian Immigrant, or Asian Immigrant–Adjacent. She could remember being little, with the last sniffles of a cold, and her dad saying, "Ganbare. Go to school." In Leena this severity felt reassuring, like a compass and a map, a way forward.

She eventually got out of bed and showered, and waited for Leena outside of her last class. They walked back to the dorm and had sex until it was dark out, until they were drained, until she had nothing left in her head. The dining hall was closed when it finally occurred to them to eat something, so they ordered a pizza and ate on Eleanor's bed, watching television. Something with a laugh track was playing, but she was too tired to pay attention, and fell asleep with one slice still on her paper plate.

FULL, GLORIOUS WEEKS with Leena passed, spending stolen moments together between classes, and every night tightly tangled in an extra-long twin bed. The Tuesday before Thanksgiving, as she looked at Leena, who was leaning against her life-partner pillow and "getting a jump on end-of-semester reading," Eleanor could not stomach the idea of boarding a plane the next day home to Fremont, to a Thanksgiving at her parents' home filled with family that she did not want to see. Or rather, she did not want them to see her: the Eleanor she was at school, the Eleanor she was still becoming, who she was with Leena and to Leena—pure and raw and alive. She couldn't leave her girlfriend, not with her dark, wavy hair spread on the pillow, her eyebrows arching, shockingly engaged by the reading for her Organization and Delivery of Health Care class.

Eleanor sat up at the other end of the bed. "I can't go home. I'm going to cancel."

"You can't cancel. Your parents bought a plane ticket," Leena replied with eyes still on the page.

Eleanor wormed her way in next to Leena, pressing her front into Leena's side, curling around her body, taking in a lungful of the scent of her shampoo, clean and floral. She held it inside for the longest time, not wanting to let go of any part of her. "You're not doing much of anything for Thanksgiving, right? A family thing on Thursday night, but otherwise no plans? We could hang out." She kissed her ear, then tugged on her earlobe with gentle, persistent teeth. Without school in their way, their days could be their own. Like their days might look, later on, after graduation.

Leena spun, her reading forgotten, her smile languid. "You're right, we could hang out."

Her warm breath was soft and inviting against Eleanor's lips, and she closed their gap and kissed Leena, gently at first, then insistent. When they pulled apart, Eleanor took a moment to catch her breath.

Leena tapped her nose. "You should call your parents."

Eleanor buried her head in Leena's shoulder, groaning. "It would be easier if I just didn't show up at the airport. 'Whoops, I missed my flight!'" She paused, then groaned again, because Leena was right, and why was her girlfriend always so responsible? She left her on the bed and rooted around on her desk for her phone, flipping it open, paging through her address book. She perched on her desk facing out, feet on her chair, and waited for someone to pick up the home phone.

"Hi, Eleanor. What's up?"

Her heart sank. Her more permissive mother would have been the better parent target in this moment. "Hi, Dad. Um, so I'm not going to be able to make it home." Her head raced, visionless, because in her haste to get this business over with and back to Leena, she had not thought through an excuse that wasn't the truth.

I'm sick.

I have a lot of homework.

I've been suddenly stricken with an intense case of aerophobia.

I don't believe in celebrating this bullshit holiday.

That last one was true enough, but he wouldn't care. She'd already heard twenty-three verses on "this country imprisoned my family, and I don't want to celebrate its founding, but I'm not going to turn down an opportunity to eat a turkey." She thought of what might best hold his attention and empathy.

"I have a lot of homework. Just, like, papers and reading, so much of it, and I would hate to get behind."

"You can bring your reading here. And papers— that's why we bought you and Fitz that very expensive iMac to share. What's going on? Are you not doing well in school? It's not like you to be this studious."

She felt caught. It wasn't like her father to question her, to go beyond what she offered. He was a stats and science guy. If he was detecting feelings, or something amiss, was it her place to jump in with the truth, with a part of her he didn't yet know? *I don't want to come home because I have a girlfriend, and she's leaving soon for another continent, and I'm going to miss her more than anything I've ever known in my whole life.*

Before she could search for words, her father sighed, a rattling sound that whistled through the phone. "It doesn't matter. The ticket is nonrefundable. We'll see you at the airport. Your mom will pick you up."

Then the line disconnected, and that was that.

She could pull a fast one and pretend that she slept through her flight, but there would be a cloud of wrath headed her way, conjured by both parents, and though she was stupid, she wasn't that stupid. She launched herself at Leena, committed to making the most of their evening.

SOLEMNLY, SADLY, ELEANOR packed her worn Camp Tawonga duffel bag the next day. They bid each other farewell, Eleanor kissing Leena like it was the end of the world, mouths wet, tongues roving. She clutched her girlfriend, sure she'd otherwise disappear.

"I'm going to miss you so much," she mumbled into Leena's shoulder.

"Okay, weirdo, I'll see you in a few days." Leena beamed through her teasing.

That only made Eleanor miss her more, on the spot, and she embraced her again, until it was really time to go—to the T, to Logan, to her afternoon flight to San Jose, which she made by mere minutes. She finally hit her narrow, stiff airplane seat and conked out, ready to let go, to be still and prostrate for as long as the trip would take.

She awoke over farmland, yawning, stretching. A pang of missing Leena sounded in her chest, her heartbeat unsteady at the thought of being without her skin and smile and laugh, and then she yawned again, fidgeting in her seat, ready to get this long weekend the hell over with and return back to the life she was creating for herself, which had nothing to do with her aunt Margaret's ostentatious mochi ice cream fortune, or her cousins Yumiko and Saya's vapidity, or the negative space occupied by her aunt Keiko's untimely death. It was all too much—baggage she didn't want to claim. The only person she was really excited to see was her obachan, with her surprisingly strong hugs and skin like a wrinkled paper bag.

Fitz was a pleasant surprise at the airport in their mom's new Prius, and they bickered about radio stations for the duration of the car ride until they arrived home. Long and ranch-style and looking like everyone else's tan suburban fantasy with a two-car garage and a terra-cotta roof. Boston homes were stately—red-brick and multilevel with turrets and bay windows and peaks and slanted roofs in different shades, without the tyranny of a homeowner's association. They stood out, unique. Not like the house where she had grown up.

But it had been her home, the only one she knew. The driveway she walked now, sneakers on pavement, where she tripped and skinned her knee so badly she still had the faint white whisper of a scar. The front door she jammed her key inside of after school, on the way to microwaving Hot Pockets before her mom got home from work.

She dropped her duffel bag in the vestibule and peeled off her jacket, throwing it on top of her bag, then slipped out of her shoes, lining them neatly alongside other pairs, and gazed around the house, eyes tripping on living room furniture that had been rearranged, a new armchair, a Japanese tablecloth patterned like a roiling sea. Strains of the KQED pledge drive floated in from the kitchen, along with the warm, yeasty smell of baking bread and tempura frying in an oily bath.

Her mom poked her head out from the open kitchen doorway. "There's my baby." Her short hair was highlighted in an effort to cover the gray, her only allowance for vanity. Otherwise, her glamour was what she was presented now: turquoise scrubs, little to no makeup, and an embarrassing grin as she advanced on Eleanor with a crushing hug.

"Hi, Mom," Eleanor said, wiggling away and darting to the kitchen, opening cabinets and the fridge to raid what was there, Fitz at her heels, in her shadow, doing the same. College was so much better than being at home, because here the concept of junk food was dark chocolate or a kale salad with dried cranberries. Here there were eyes in the walls to watch, and judge, and there would not be two helpings of Lucky Charms cereal. Instead she toasted two thick slices of healthy, almost-gray bread and slathered them with butter as her mother peppered her with nagging questions about school and friends, and buzzed around the kitchen making Thanksgiving preparations.

When her dad called, her mom picked up the yellow corded phone in the kitchen and gave orders into the receiver while Eleanor peeled away into the living room, slumping on the couch next to Fitz, zoning out to a *Friends* rerun. Rachel had a baby, Chandler and Monica were trying to have a baby, and the episode ended then spilled into the next without so much as a commercial interruption. This was nice. Easy. Boring.

She missed Leena.

She missed her in a way that felt akin to homesickness, for her long arms that hugged so well, the gorgeous waves of her thick, black hair, the span of her hips, those soft lips. Her clever mind and the nervous, dizzy feelings that she engendered inside Eleanor. This brief separation felt unendurable, with nothing substantive to occupy her mind.

Dinner was pizza—albeit pizza laden with so many vegetables it might as well have been a salad—delivered by her dad, home at his routine hour of seven p.m. He dropped a kiss in Eleanor's hair. He still looked so young at forty-nine, save for the slight brush of gray streaks in his black hair and the crinkle of lines around his eyes. It was good genes that kept him that way, and for now kept her looking like a fourteen-year-old.

"Chieko-chan."

Chieko. Her middle name—in honor of some great-aunt she had never met. It felt like second nature to hear it from her dad, in this house, in this state, but at school it would have been so foreign.

Her dad watched *Friends* for a second, standing in front of the television with hands on hips, blocking their way until he turned, hands in the pockets of his khaki pants. "Genki desu ka?"

She shook her head at him, rating his corniness with an eye roll. "You're still on this?"

He shrugged. "As long as my failures as a Japanese son are on display with your dismal grasp of the language, then, yes. Hannah," he called, walking toward the kitchen.

Eleanor turned to her brother. "I'm not trying to say

I don't want to learn Japanese, but he's really intense about this, right?"

He burped a reply and grinned, and she groaned.

THE NEXT MORNING she awoke completely disoriented, forgetting for a second that she wasn't with Leena. Long moments passed before she remembered that, instead, she was in her childhood bedroom filled with the detritus of her life, with light filtering in bright and harsh alongside dust particles. She stretched, yawning, her skin rubbing against starchy sheets, and stumbled out of bed, down the hall toward the fragrance of coffee.

"Did you ever leave the kitchen last night?" she asked her mother, already dressed for the day in a flowing top marked with dizzying paisley, like something under a microscope.

Eleanor fixed herself a cup of coffee in her treasured Garfield mug.

"No, I slept with my head on a loaf of challah," her mother replied smoothly, snapping a dish towel at Eleanor's back. "You got a lot of sleep. I forget what it's like to have you here. It's been, what, ten hours?"

Eleanor slumped against the counter, mug in her hands. "I need it. I'm a growing girl." Her mother had boundless energy, an indefatigable spirit that made her tired just to watch. It was disgusting to witness, in this moment, her mother's whole hand inside of a turkey. She picked up the *San Jose Mercury News* and scanned frivolous pieces befitting a national holiday: visa loopholes for tech workers, a Nasdaq board resignation, parking in downtown shopping areas in preparation for Black Friday. An article on a proposed housing project on the site of the old Del Monte plant caught her eye, but she was depressed to see the lack of coverage on other issues. Were there not wars being fought in multiple countries, a regressive Congress, civil liberties on the line? What was the point of journalism if it wasn't going to get into the meaty heart of the matter?

After another cup of coffee, Eleanor banged on Fitz's bedroom door, entering his dark room without permission. It smelled like boy, sweaty and musty, and she wrinkled her nose. "Wake uuuuup," she sang. "Waaaaake up." She opened the blinds to his groan, then jumped on the bed. "I'm bored."

Fitz squinted, then yanked the sheet over his face.

She lay back on his bed and looked around, his room a museum: baby-blue paint from when his room was newly his, a framed photo of his T-ball team, a trophy cup from a high school science competition. A giant poster of a red sports car.

"I'll get up if you pour a gallon of coffee down my throat," Fitz said, his voice muffled.

She took off to make good on that offer, bumping into her dad in the hallway, rumpled in his pajamas.

"Ohayo gozaimasu," he called.

"Ohayo," she offered back, speeding toward the coffee pot.

When Eleanor got to the kitchen, her mother was putting the turkey back in the oven to cook. She wiped her hands on a dish towel and, upon seeing Eleanor, let out a sigh. "I could have used a hand here."

Eleanor let out a sigh of her own, filling her brother's Snoopy mug. "You always do this, Mom. You could have asked for help earlier, but instead you always complain when you're almost done."

"Steve." Her mother's voice like gravel.

Her dad mugged at Eleanor, eyes wide and smiling. "Chieko-chan, listen to your mother." He shrugged, wandering out of the kitchen. "I need to get some more work done." He wouldn't be getting involved.

"Ooookay." She put her hands on her hips, turning to her mother. "How can I help?"

Her mother turned her back, tending to the bubbling pots on the stove. "Set the table. The nice plates and the nice silverware, please. And then report back for your next assignment."

Eleanor saw future Thanksgivings and a future her, also leaning over the stove, black hair turning gray with age. It filled her with terror to think of herself as so conventional, walking such a well-trodden path. Her life, the one she was making for herself, gave her the space to decide how she would be, and what she would become.

"I think Fitz should help too. And Dad. What is this, 1952?"

Her mother looked exasperated, wiping sweat from her brow. "Does it matter who does it? We're feeding a crowd of people today. Your hands are as good as anyone else's."

Eleanor kept her arms crossed and her mother threw her head back. "Fine. Fitz!" Her mother yelled down the hall. "Get in here! You're being drafted because of feminism."

It was a minor victory, but Eleanor felt triumphant all the same.

After all the preparations, flatware and dishes for the occasion in place, food ready ahead of schedule, a weird lull fell, as it always did before everyone arrived.

They assembled around the television and watched football, waiting, although Eleanor barely paid attention because she didn't care about football or the accompanying beer commercials and sexism.

"Where is Tomás? Usually he's here by now." Her mother checked her watch, pouring a glass of white wine. "Steve? Wine?"

"Yes, please."

Her parents clinked glasses and Eleanor's mouth set into a line. She could practically set a watch to the day and what would happen next, once her dad drank more, outpacing her mom, once her uncles were here. This first part was relaxation.

"Yeah, Tomás isn't around this year. He went with his aunts to Mexico to visit his parents."

Her mother clucked her tongue. "Oh, well, that's wonderful. Although it's still awful."

"Yeah. Awful." Eleanor's eyes fixed to the screen, arms tightly crossed over her chest.

"Eleanor, are you sure you don't want some wine? A small glass won't hurt."

She sighed. "Mom, we've talked about this."

"I know, and I worry that someday you'll fall off your horse and really have a bender." She chuckled.

"I don't see that happening," Eleanor replied tersely. She was so sure of herself, in herself. Her mother couldn't see into her, not anymore.

"I miss getting to see Tomás more often. What a good kid. How lucky you are to have him at school."

Eleanor's default was to disagree with her mother, but it was impossible to argue that point. She was lucky to have him.

"You've always had great friends, huh? Tomás. That friend of yours from high school, Talia."

That friend of mine that I kissed during sleepovers.

"And Micah." Her mother's face brightened, softening, sappy. "What a gentleman. What a great boy. A great first boyfriend."

Eleanor adjusted in her seat, curling into a ball, arms around her legs. "Yep."

"If you start with a good one, like him, then the others that come will be as good, or better. At least that's my hope."

Her mother was prying. She wanted to hear about what boys she was dating. She wanted an in-depth peek into her life, a life she assumed was straight. It wasn't, and there would be no peeks allowed.

When her mom stood, she brushed Eleanor's head with her hand, then a palm on her cheek, so much tenderness and smothering love.

It made Eleanor squirm like the first time she had a bra fitting.

Soon the whole family arrived: Uncle Atsutomo and Aunt Margaret, her cousin Saya, and Uncle Shigeto, trailed by Obachan. She gave out cursory, perfunctory hugs until she reached Obachan. Stiff as always in her embrace, she thumped Eleanor on the back. "Chieko-chan, genki desu ka?" She was short, and beautiful, tan with brown speckles and spots.

Eleanor gulped down another look at her grandmother, nodding when ready. "I'm doing great," she replied, and let her grandmother's survey continue to Fitz, who teased her with a bow, before she grabbed at him with spidery arms.

"Daigaku wa do desu ka?" she asked, swiveling her head between her two youngest grandchildren.

"It's good. I like my classes," Eleanor answered first, before Fitz.

77

"Atama ii desu ne," Obachan said in wonderment. This from a woman who didn't understand women's studies but who thought Eleanor was amazing just for being in college. She happily accepted her grandmother's pride.

There was mingling in the living room, football still blaring on in the background, shrimp and vegetable tempura, plates of crudités and ranch dip. Aunt Margaret in the kitchen with her mom and Obachan, her uncles making whisky cocktails, Fitz wolfing down appetizers.

Out of boredom, with no other escape from this mandatory family time, she turned to her cousin, who was pouring herself a flute of sparkling wine. "Saya, how are you? How's . . . the business?"

Her cousin smiled primly, running a hand down her long, dark hair from scalp to ends, her ostentatious engagement ring glaring in the light. "It's great. Getting into new markets, launching a new print campaign. Putting that ol' MBA to work."

Oh, you have an MBA? she wanted to ask sarcastically. *You've never mentioned it.*

"But working with Mom and Dad is, like, always challenging," Saya continued. "I'm always in the middle."

Eleanor shuddered at the idea of working on anything with her parents—an impossible thought, because they were such polar-opposite communicators. Her mother never stopped talking, her father never had anything to say. Not exactly a dream team for teaching their children how to interact in the world. "I can imagine. Where's Yumiko?"

"She's on a shoot. She got a job as a photographer's

assistant. I think they're in . . . Cape Town? I can't remember. My sister is always all over the place."

"Oh, that's really cool. My girlfriend is going to study abroad in South Africa," Eleanor said, the words slipping out of her mouth before she knew what she was saying, eyes bulging, heart racing—*fuck, did I just come out to my cousin?*

"Yumiko can totally give your friend tips, I'm sure," Saya replied with a cloying smile.

Eleanor forgot that straight women did that, referring to women friends as their girlfriends. But as relieved as she was not to be detected, she was disappointed too. Just to say it, to be honest, to claim Leena as hers, because it was all she wanted. Here she was, talking with her cousin like it was any year, any Thanksgiving, when she was unlike she had ever been. "I . . . forgot something I had to do. I'll be back."

She ran down the hall to her bedroom, shutting the door and rummaging for her phone, then pulling up Leena's number and dialing. No answer. "Hi, it's me. Eleanor. You probably know my voice by now, but voices sound funny on the phone sometimes. Um. I was just thinking about you. My cousin was talking about South Africa, and I thought about you." Her eyes pinched shut, thinking of Leena's face, how warm and supported and enveloped she felt in Leena's arms. She could almost feel her now; her girlfriend, so real to her even in this emotional hologram state. This distance, temporary and countrywide, felt unbearable. How would she fare when they were time zones, continents, eons apart? Her stomach turned. "I miss you." *I miss you now. I'll miss you later.* "That's what I was calling to say. Hope you have a good time tonight with your family." She hung up, bereft, and sat at the edge of her bed, looking up at an *X-Files* poster for the longest time.

At the dinner table, they passed platters and filled others' plates—sweet potatoes and tofu and turkey and stuffing and sashimi and onigiri. Eleanor filled her plate twice, ignoring her obachan's indictments of "takusan," as if this were the unhealthiest food she ate, as if she would let someone control how much she consumed.

At her mother's urging, as it was every year, they took turns sharing their annual expressions of thanks. Her uncles and father, having put away half a bottle of Japanese whisky, were at the giddy stage of their inebriation, laughing and joking, a state that only made her frown. It was a farce—men who couldn't relax enough to be themselves otherwise.

"I'm thankful for tax cuts," Uncle Atsutomo said in between giggles.

Uncle Shigeto grabbed the sashimi platter and it skidded out of his hands, clattering on the table with a jarring thud. "Lost my grip there," he said with a whooping laugh.

All the women around the table—wives, soon-to-be wives, mothers, and grandmothers—accepted the personality changes and mood shifts that came from drinking. It made her feel so uncomfortable, and so out of control, to experience this instability, to not know what would happen next.

"Okay, Eleanor. You're up," her mother said, smiling.

She sighed. "Well, I'm not thankful for this racist holiday." Her brother groaned. "What? It is!" She looked around the table at her family, people who knew her as a daughter or granddaughter or niece or sister or cousin, people who thought they understood her. Some people were drunk, which felt like lying about who they were. She couldn't do that. She couldn't sacrifice the truth, ever, because she thought of Audre Lorde and what she might say. *It is necessary to teach by living and speaking those truths which we believe and know beyond understanding.* "And I'm not grateful for the way this family pollutes their bodies with alcohol. But I am thankful for my girlfriend," she said, with a clear voice like a bell, and released a breath she didn't know she had been holding.

Uncle Shigeto nodded sagely, thoughtfully, and gave her a thumbs-up.

"Okay," her dad said, as if she asked him to pass the potatoes.

Aunt Margaret and Uncle Atsutomo exchanged looks, and said nothing.

Saya shrugged.

Fitz looked at her blankly, squarely, and shook his head slowly.

"I have to—excuse me," her mom said, rising from the table and heading at warp speed down the hall, away.

"Nani?" her grandmother asked the table, confused, her forehead wrinkling in slats.

Eleanor gulped. She had not considered her grandmother, short and feisty and loving, who had lived through the hell of racism, of internment, of losing her husband then her daughter. She was tough. This news would not compare to anything she had been through. And yet.

Her grandmother was old, eighty-five, intolerant, and there were lots of things in the world that she did not care to understand. Even if Eleanor found the words, she would struggle with what to say. Her grandmother was less conversant in English—but Eleanor didn't know the Japanese word for *gay*. And it couldn't be overstated how worried she was about how her obachan would react, because any shade of rejection would have felt awful. There was a subtle border between them, strong and wide enough to keep Eleanor from what she had to say.

"Chieko-chan ni wa tomodachi ga imasu," her father translated, but slant.

And yet the reality of sanitation was worse. She didn't just have a friend, as her father had said. "Īe," she said, shaking her head, her eyes aimed at the table, too scared to look up. "I have a girlfriend. Not a friend who's a girl," she said, directing her words at Saya, "but a *girlfriend*. Wakarimasu ka?"

It was quiet for a long time, dust settling on the ellipses of the moment. When Eleanor dared to look up, her grandmother was nodding slowly, her eyes dark and serious.

"Hai, wakarimasu."

She didn't say, *Oh, Chieko-chan, thank you for telling me, it's so important that young people tell their truths.* Or, *Thank you for coming out to me. What an important moment in your life.* She also didn't say, *You're dead to me.* "Yes, I understand" felt like something she could work with.

With her eyes up, she looked around, saw the empty chair, and was reminded of the one who had fled. "Excuse me," she mumbled, cheeks hot with embarrassment as the moment continued to sizzle silently. She left the table, creeping down the hall.

She was always almost coming out to her mom, knowing she would be safe. She dropped hints—talking about why same-sex marriage was such a riveting current event, or discussing her choice in music and books and movies—because she understood instinctively what her mother's response would be to such news, from a woman who had treated HIV-positive patients at the height of the crisis, who wrote a letter to ABC in anger when they canceled *Ellen*.

Eleanor traversed the hallway, white walls covered in family photographs, with track lighting above her head. She saw herself and Fitz as small kids, then as awkward, hunched teens, then back again to toddlers, running through grass or at the zoo or swimming in a pool. Her bat mitzvah. A family camping trip to Yosemite. The last time they went to Japan. She had already been so many people.

She poked her head into her mother's room, but the light was off. The door to her own room was pitched open a crack, light seeping out, and she pressed on the wood, hand to the knob. "Mom?"

She thought her mother would greet such happy news more graciously. Staying at the table at least. She wasn't sure what awaited her now.

Her mom sat on her bed, forearms resting on her upper thighs, hands clasped together, eyes on the salt-and-pepper wall-to-wall carpet. From this angle, Eleanor could see the roots of her real hair, that which was not highlighted to mask her age. From this angle, she looked small.

"Eleanor, I don't know what to say to you. Except, that was rude." Her mother looked up slowly, meeting Eleanor's eyes first before her gaze fell to the bridge of her own nose, narrow where Eleanor's was wide like her father's. Her lips were pursed, almost in a pucker, and her pale skin was tinged pink from drinking wine. Usually she was ebullient in this state, but she was somber now.

Eleanor stood in place in the doorway, hanging her head as the frustration built in her chest. Her breath heaved until words came. "That wasn't rude. Being honest about yourself is never rude."

"No, not that," her mother said impatiently. "Talking about body pollution? That was incredibly disrespectful. I know you don't drink, and that's okay with me, because you're underage and basically still a child without a fully formed brain, but you have no right to tell other adults what they can and can't do." Her mother's chest heaved, her eyes wide and ablaze, unusually wired and amped. "I'm disappointed."

Eleanor lifted her eyes, forehead pointing toward the popcorn ceiling. *Disappointed* was certainly the word of the hour. "Okay, fine. I get that." She kept her eyes up, away from her mother. "But—"

"No, sorry, no. Look, I don't care about the drinking. I don't know why I said that. I guess . . . Eleanor."

At the utterance of her name, because of years of training, she looked at her mother.

Her eyes were dark, serious, holding Eleanor tightly. She sat up ramrod straight, though there was an energy coming off her body, as if she was holding herself back, her hands clutching her thighs. "I guess . . . I'm disappointed that you didn't tell me. About . . . you. Why wouldn't you tell me? You know who I am, and where I've been, and what I've seen. You know my mind. At least, I thought you did. I'm so upset—with you, maybe, but maybe more myself—if you thought that you had to hide this. If you thought that I wouldn't understand."

Eleanor shook her head, crossing her arms tightly. "I didn't think I had to hide. I knew I could tell you. But maybe I wasn't ready? Because maybe I want something that's just mine and isn't, like, yours to know and own and be in charge of? I'm my own fucking person, but you always treat me like a baby, like I need to be taken care of, like I need your protection. And maybe I don't want that all the time. I know I'm a kid, but I'm growing up too, like, I'm an adult. I can vote."

Her mother laughed, her shoulders hunching, her head thrown back. "It's not funny, it's not funny, but it's so funny," she gasped, one hand over her heart, one out to Eleanor. "*I can vote.*" She only laughed more. "I'm sorry, I'm sorry." She wiped at her eyes with the pads of her fingers. "I've been up since I don't even know when, and it's been an eventful day. Come here? Please?"

Eleanor stayed glued in place. She wasn't about to be summoned after being laughed at. Like the day hadn't been hard enough on her. "Mom, I told you this really big thing, and it was really hard to tell you, but then I did, and you just walked away. You ran away." She tried not to cry, but she felt the tears prick her eyes anyway in hot, wet bursts. "And then you fucking laughed at me!"

Almost immediately she felt her mother's arms around her, warm and comforting, and it wasn't what she wanted—or rather, it wasn't what she wanted to want. She sagged into her mother's embrace, feeling exhausted.

"It's okay, I've got you," her mother soothed. "I'm really sorry. For the leaving, the overreacting, laughing. Although it was really funny." She stroked Eleanor's hair, then down her back in sure, smooth strokes. "What's her name?"

Eleanor wiped her nose with her sleeve. "Huh?"

"Your girlfriend. What's her name?"

"Leena." She brightened just to say it.

"You go to school together?"

"Uh-huh."

"She's nice to you?"

Eleanor grinned, her cheeks pulling upward, so happy her face hurt. "Definitely." She pulled back and saw a deep calm on her mother's face.

"I want you to be happy."

Eleanor nodded. She knew that.

"I—I think we should not tell my parents. For a little while, at least."

Her back straightened. If she were a cat, her back would have arched, all the hair on her body standing up. "Why?"

"Well . . . I think that news was a little shocking for your obachan, and Grandmom and Grandpop aren't going to take it any easier. I worry, you know. They're older." The expression on her mother's face was somewhere between a pitying smile and a grimace. "They're not as healthy as I wish they were. I worry news like this could be . . ."

Eleanor was left to fill in the blanks. "Are you saying I'd kill them if I came out?" They escaped Germany, separated permanently from their families, schlepped to England, only to resettle again. They were made of metal.

Her mother shook her head. "No, no, I'm not saying that. Except—well, look. Just, let's hold on to this. For now. Okay?" She leaned away, hands braced on Eleanor's arms, eyes sweeping her face like she was searching for something, anything, to fix. "It can be difficult to tell your parents things they aren't expecting. Like me bringing home a Japanese guy. They did not start out thrilled."

Eleanor was struck by having something in common with her mother. They were both women who'd made choices, women who pushed, barreling toward what they wanted. Similarity was comforting but binding, because if they shared this, there might be other aspects of her mother that lived inside her, dormant for now, and that thought left her achingly uneasy.

"I'm glad we talked, sweetie," her mom said, pressing a kiss to Eleanor's cheek. "Let's join everyone. You know Margaret brought enough mochi ice cream to fill two freezers."

The thought of seeing anyone was unbearable, drained as she was. "Yeah, maybe not. I think I'm just gonna stay in my room."

A blip of hesitation passed over her mother's face, lips parted, eyebrows raised, as if she were about to unleash guilt or a lecture, or both. But she closed her mouth and her forehead went slack, neutral, and she nodded, patting Eleanor's shoulder. Letting it go. Letting her be.

She listened to her mom's footfalls until they were no longer audible. She pulled out her phone and opened it, dialing Leena's number and hoping desperately to hear her voice, but it went to voicemail again. She dropped to her bed with the lights off, door closed.

Hearing Leena's voice—"Hello, you've reached Leena Shah's cell. Please leave a message!"—then that menacing beep made her teary all over again. "Hi. Sorry to leave another message. I just wanted to . . . I hope your Thanksgiving is going well." She had no idea how Indian people celebrated. Like everyone else? She knew the Shahs were vegetarian, but she doubted Tofurky played a role. Maybe Indian foods only? There was so much she longed to know. "I hope you're having a good day. I know you had a lot of studying to do, so . . . Hey, I just came out to my family." A shaky burst of laughter left her throat. "I didn't mean to do it, it just kind of . . . came out. And I told them I have a girlfriend." She squeezed her eyes shut, imagining a future where her family could actually meet the girl she had mentioned. "I guess it went okay. Nobody disowned me. No one is throwing me a party." She was reminded of Sam and Cath's fears, of what their families would say and do if they were to come out, and no matter how upsetting tonight was, she would not face what hung over her friends' heads. "I just wanted you to know. And sorry for telling you in a voicemail. But I just wanted you to know." She was repeating herself. It was time to hang up. "Well, I better . . . go. I'll talk to you later, I hope. Bye, Leena," she said, her voice wistful and bright.

She couldn't fall asleep, though her eyes ached and her body longed for restoration, and she picked up her worn copy of *Cunt*, hoping to be lulled to sleep. Her mind was too wired, all of her desires and the demands made of her jumbled together in an unhappy knot. *Moving from phonetics to etymology, "vagina" originates from a word meaning sheath for a sword. Ain't got no vagina.*

She kept reading familiar words in the waning early evening light, until her eyelids weighed heavy, until sleep came.

ELEANOR SPENT THE rest of the long weekend days sleeping late, drinking coffee, and waiting for Leena to return her voicemails. No such luck. She didn't know what to make of it when she knew her girlfriend was unscheduled, with aimless hours to fill. With nothing but her own time, she drove nowhere, driving around simply because she missed it, that feeling of being a ship captain. She blasted the Smiths and the *Hedwig and the Angry Inch* soundtrack on a loop as she cruised Thornton to Fremont, doubling back to Paseo Padre Parkway, rounding past Central Park, Quarry Lakes, and Coyote Hills, and trying not to end up at the mall.

On Sunday, she packed her duffel bag again, hastily throwing in clothes laundered by her mother, ready to get back to her life, her friends, her girlfriend. She ate a quick standing breakfast of coffee and toast, urging her mother along until her dad appeared, dressed in jeans and a sweatshirt and a worn baseball cap.

"Come on. I'll take you."

She eyed him warily, uneager to spend any time alone with him in a car. It just wasn't something they did. Her eyes danced between him and her mother.

"That would be great. I can get ready for the week." Her mother rose with arms outstretched and a soft grin on her lips. She hugged her so hard that all the air fled Eleanor's lungs, but then it came back as the squeeze lessened, became more reasonable and measured. "I love you, sweet girl."

Eleanor sighed. "Love you," she muttered fast, and ducked away.

"Ready?" her dad asked.

Without answering, she turned on her heel, heading toward Fitz's bedroom with the door still closed. She paused before knocking, but decided waking him up was worth the wrath and gave it two pounds, calling his name. He was up, on his laptop, slumped over it and furiously typing.

"Hey," he said without looking up.

"What are you doing?"

"Homework. You leaving?"

Homework. That was his problem, taking school so seriously. Or maybe it was the solution. She strode to his bed and gave him the best hug she could given their awkward, disconnected positions. He was so lanky and stooped now, but he was still small to her, the little baby bird of a brother she wanted to protect.

"Bye, Ellie," he said, no longer with the voice of someone barely paying attention.

She pulled back and saw the angles of his jaw, the thickness of his eyebrows, someone she could see with eyelids closed that was also growing into his own person. "Bye, Fitzwilliam."

Steeling herself, she took a breath and traveled back down the hall to pick up her bag and follow her dad out to his black Honda Civic hatchback, chucking her bag in the back and slinging the seatbelt across her body.

He started the car, reversing them out of the driveway and down the street, curving out of their subdivision and toward the highway. They drove, and it was silent. No radio. No talking. Eleanor didn't know what to say or what was happening. She played a game with herself as her eyes followed the power lines: It was seven now. She'd be in the air by nine. She would get into Boston around five, home to her dorm around six.

She sighed, sliding tired eyes across her dad, and sighed again. "I feel like I'm in trouble. I'm a dead woman walking."

"We just didn't have a lot of time together this weekend. You seemed to want . . . space."

"Mom usually does stuff like this. Taking us to the airport. Taking us places."

He made a muffled sound, his hand over his mouth, one elbow up on the door.

"What?"

"I said, I do 'stuff like this' too. You just forget," he said, checking his rearview mirror, "because you've been away for so long. I'm still your dad. Always." He cleared his throat. "And it's fine, what you said. It's fine," he said, without looking at her. "You know that."

She didn't know that at all. Her eyes attached to his side profile, a nose that looked like hers, skin that matched her own. He was not an expressive man, and to hear his sparse support felt like everything.

"We are who we are," he continued. "Wired before we leave the womb."

Eleanor imagined herself but a seed in the wild, vast expanse of her mother's uterus, growing that part of her that would make her gay. Maybe it was the wiring in her elbow or behind her knee or in her earlobe. Wherever, however, if that's how it even worked, she was grateful for her father's words and understanding—a gift of compassion she had not expected.

She wanted to confront him about how their family's drinking made her feel: unsafe, untethered, like the world could fall off its axis at any moment. As free-spirited and go-with-the-flow as she wanted to be, maybe that wasn't her at all; and yet as much as she wanted to tell him off, she knew this was not a barrier she would be welcome to cross. She could only stand here on this shore looking over, and wanting more.

They arrived at the departures curb and she had no more time to consider it. She dropped a kiss on his cheek and thanked him for the ride.

"Of course, Chieko-chan. Ki o tsukete, ne?"

With sun raining down on his shoulders, she could answer her mother's question from the day before: she was thankful for him. "Hai. I'll be careful." She grabbed her backpack, rushed into the terminal, and paused inside, to the right of the revolving door, the emotional toll of the weekend hitting her with a dull thud. But she regrouped, enough to head through security and toward her gate, ready to be home.

AS SHE DRAGGED herself toward her dorm, she saw Leena. Leena, who could deliver her from the foibles and missteps of the past couple of days, and she breathed easy. Just seeing her lifted Eleanor's spirits, eager to connect after so many days out of touch. She called to Leena, then noted the two adults behind her girlfriend that looked like her—lithe and Brown—and the pieces locked together. Eleanor's back straightened as she smoothed her hair down. Fresh—or not so fresh—from a plane and wearing old sweatpants was not the way she expected to meet the Shahs. She applied a bright smile to her face.

"Oh hey!" Leena said, as if she were greeting someone she once had a class with, and not someone who knew about the birthmark on her inner thigh. "Mom, Dad, this is my friend Eleanor."

Eleanor kept smiling despite her demotion, no matter how much it pained her to be painted as a friend. *I just came out! I'm so gay! We're more than friends!* She pushed down on these thoughts that clamored to break free.

"Nice to meet you, Eleanor," said Leena's dad, adjusting his wire-framed glasses. Her mom nodded politely and stared. "So, what are you studying?" He had a lovely Indian accent and a soothing voice. She bet he gave grave news to his patients and they took it so, so well.

"Uh, women's studies?"

"What is that?" He sounded genuinely curious, not incredulous like most people.

"It's about, like, women in society and culture and history. And outside of America too. Around the world. In India, for example." She immediately felt like an idiot. Why did she have to mention India? As if they were so Indian that they would only be interested in India?

"Is there men's studies?" He was teasing her now, she could tell. He had this little glint in his eyes that she had seen before in Leena.

"No, because everything is men's studies?" she said, her mouth in a rush while her brain winced. She pressed on quickly. "But it's nothing like what your daughter is doing. She's incredible."

He nodded in this way that she'd seen Leena do once or twice, a quick seesawing of the head in an arc, from

93

side to side. "Sometimes I wish she'd study less. She can't seem to find a nice boy—"

"Eleanor has to go," Leena interrupted. "And we're late for dinner." Her eyes pleaded with Eleanor. *Please let me go. I'm sorry.* "See you later?" She grabbed her parents by the arms, tugging them along, forward, away.

Eleanor nodded to herself. She stood for a second, watching them go. "It was nice to meet you!" she called, an afterthought. She walked toward the building alone, feeling the full weight of her body and the weekend and this thing with Leena that felt like an open wound.

Leena can't seem to find a nice boy. Those words resounded through her body, echoing and ricocheting off her organs. A hundred retorts flooded in.

Leena's not looking for a boy, nice or otherwise.

Leena found a nice girl—me!

Why does it matter? She's going to be a doctor who heals everyone in the whole entire universe.

Leena's too busy going down on me to find time for a nice boy.

She took a long shower and changed into new sweatpants, heading to the dining hall to sneak out food. In her dorm and the dining hall and everywhere, people were pouring back into the campus fabric after arguing and coming out and being sad over the election and throwing footballs and eating and talking and laughing.

On her way out of the dining hall, she felt a vibration in the kangaroo pocket of her sweatshirt. She set her bag of food down on the ground and slumped against an empty bike rack, sighing as she read the preview screen. She flipped her phone open. "Hi, Mom."

"Hi, honey. Listen, there was something we didn't get to talk about. Safe sex. Well, safer sex, you know, because there's no such thing as completely safe sex. Disease transmission between women is lower than in other populations, but still, protection is important."

Eleanor could throw her phone away. She could refuse to reply to another one of her mother's emails, she could never go home again, she could move to another continent, perhaps Antarctica. Anything to prevent this conversation from continuing. "I know what safer sex is and I know how to have it," she said through gritted teeth.

"Yes, but—do you use dental dams? I know it probably doesn't seem cool, but it's your only way to protect yourself. Other sex acts aren't as much of a transmission worry, but you know, I would be careful with vaginal fluids. Flora and fauna. Your system is unlike your girlfriend's. If you swap fluids by touching each other then touching yourselves, you can definitely get bacterial vaginosis."

"I'm going to die if you keep talking!" Eleanor yelled. "I have to go." She hung up, Nurse Suzuki's words ringing in her ears as she walked back to her dorm. Nurse Suzuki, the woman who showed up on occasion, who was so clinical and exacting, well informed on public health statistics and practices. So dissimilar from the mother who made smooch sounds into the phone.

Eleanor sat down at her laptop to work on her Comparative Feminisms paper, but the words and paragraphs eluded her. Her topic: the clash between Western white-savior feminists and Muslim feminists, specifically as it related to the veil. She was supposed to critique the conversation itself, the obsession with head coverings over more substantive policy issues.

Her eyes fell to the short stack of books on her desk. Her related readings were already printed out, read, and highlighted. She was prepared. And yet she couldn't concentrate. She stared at the blinking cursor. Blink, blink, blink.

Fuck.

Leena had been so dismissive of their real relationship in front of her family, in front of people who mattered a great deal to her. Eleanor understood the reality of being closeted in front of family, but at least now she knew that it could be so much better. Open and honest. She didn't have to feel like this, underappreciated and punted to the side.

She tried once again to focus on her paper.

In 1998 Mavis Leno started a campaign to save the women of Afghanistan from the Taliban. In the years between 1998 and going to war with that country in 2002, a picture emerged of the plight of Afghan women as being defenseless, forced into burqas and other constrictions. Feminists like Leno focused on the garment as the symbol of their oppression because they saw themselves in contrast to these women, and as people who could rescue them.

Leena can't find a nice boy . . .

She banged her head against the desk, then ate cake until she heard a knock at the door. She shuffled over, still holding her Styrofoam plate and fork, and found a gleeful Leena waiting.

"They finally left. I thought they'd never go." Leena pushed inside and took the cake, closing the door behind her, then turned off the glaring overhead light so that only the desk lamp remained on, the room transformed with a soft glow. She moved toward Eleanor, stealing a bite of cake before setting it aside.

It was Leena kissing her, so there was a lot to soak in and enjoy: the sweet pressure of Leena's lips, her tongue, the taste of chocolate icing. Then, Leena's mouth at her throat, trailing kisses and her tongue along her neck. Eleanor's body sagged, letting Leena make her mark.

"Missed you," she heard Leena whisper into her skin.

As relieved as she felt to have Leena close again, there was something eerily wrong. Shrugging off recent events—Eleanor's coming out, meeting Leena's parents—struck her as callous, and didn't make her feel the intimacy in this moment, even as her body craved her girlfriend. She lightly pushed on Leena's shoulders, watched as Leena's eyes opened and refocused, her lips parting. Confused. Eleanor took a deep breath and sat at her desk chair, closing her laptop and crossing her arms. "I kind of want to talk to you."

Leena was still trying to catch up, blinking dumbly. "Oh." She came and perched on the desk, at Eleanor's side, careful to mind her books and papers. "Okay?"

Eleanor felt a ball of anxiety starting to snowball in her stomach, getting larger and larger. Leena's lack of empathy and understanding was out of character. Or was it? Maybe she didn't know this about her yet. "I guess. Like. I came out? And I thought you'd ask me about it? And I met your parents but didn't meet them as your girlfriend?" That was the best she could do, the closest she could come to bold eloquence. She

97

pursed her lips, watching Leena's body language shift. She had become so open to Eleanor, but now she closed up, crossing her arms, crossing her legs.

"Sorry. From your voicemails, I thought you were feeling okay about coming out," Leena said, her tone like a jagged piece of glass, topped with whipped cream and a cherry.

Eleanor shook her head in a twitch. "Yeah, I am, but still, I thought you'd ask me about it. That's, like, something people do." What was wrong with Leena that she didn't know that? "And also, it was . . . unexpected to meet your parents."

Leena shook her head. "Yeah, sorry about that. I didn't think we'd run into you. But don't worry, you probably won't see them again."

Of that she was sure. Leena barely talked about her family, but they were the reason why they couldn't hang out most weekends. A wedding, a party, a thing. It was so obvious now that Leena's worlds were kept absolutely separate. This was how she had designed it. On the precipice of another question, Eleanor was afraid of the answer, but she asked anyway. "Do you think you'll come out to your family? Anytime soon? Even . . . for the right person?"

Leena smiled sadly, then looked toward the floor with its ugly beige-speckled tile. She shook her head no without hesitation.

"Why?" Eleanor asked. "I've been out to my family for all of, like, five minutes, but already I feel like this is the start of something better. I feel better. More open. And yeah, they'll probably ask me annoying questions, they already kind of have, but that's the worst of it." She took a breath, but it barely filled her body. This was a moment, a spark of time when she could push Leena to open up, to consider her options. "You could, you know. It's 2004, and this is Massachusetts. There's no better place to be out."

Leena pushed off from her perch on the desk and backed up. She kept her arms crossed as she traversed the space of the room, as if looking for something on the walls that she had misplaced. Finally she stood still, close but not touching Eleanor. "I think that all sounds great, for you. But our families are just . . . different. It's not that my family is bad or hateful, but it's not what they have planned for me. And to go against that is not something that I'm going to do. Not now, at least." Leena's words flowed quickly, as if she had already prepared for this conversation. That was her Leena. Always prepared.

"But what about in the future? What happens when you fall in love? When you can no longer deny to your family who you are, and have the physical proof of what you feel inside?" Eleanor stopped herself short of asking if Leena was in love right now. That, she wasn't ready to hear.

Leena knelt next to her. With Eleanor in the chair and Leena on her knees, their heads were almost at the same height. She shook her head. "I don't know. Can we skip it for now? Can I kiss you?"

Eleanor's shoulders sagged. Her body and brain were so simple. That question was sexy, and she felt depleted, defenses down. There were so many things she couldn't have. She nodded and Leena kissed her, her hands on Eleanor's knees. Then Leena led her to bed, where they lay together and continued to kiss. She brushed Leena's thigh with her open palm. Even through sweatpants she felt the soft heft of muscle and bone.

Ambiguity shut off for the evening as Leena undressed her, drowning her with kisses, filling her with this moment, this exact moment, looking straight ahead.

DECEMBER

That Friday night, Sam came to pick Eleanor up from her dorm room, wearing a blazer annotated with a pocket square, with a bouquet of pink carnations in her hands ("They're not for you, dummy," she said).

Of course Eleanor was late, rushing to leave to watch Cath in *The Vagina Monologues*. Shaking off snow and the chill in the night air, they entered the lobby to a queer undergraduate women's Who's Who. No night would be complete without Zoe looking gooey toward some new woman. This one was femme, the obvious push-up bra and high heels contrasting with Zoe's obvious sports bra and ill-fitting jeans. Zoe grabbed Eleanor's elbow as she passed and asked, "How are you?" in a completely patronizing manner. Like they'd divorced after a decade and stuck Eleanor with the twins, while Zoe had gotten a sports car and a pageant queen out of it.

"I'm awesome." Eleanor gave her a huge, phony smile. "You remember Sam?"

Sam cut in. "Oh, I remember Zoe."

Zoe gestured toward her blond. "This is Kiki. We met at a kiss-in on the Common."

"Of course you did," Sam said swiftly, putting an arm around Eleanor, which Eleanor promptly shrugged off. "Listen, we . . . have to get out of here. Bye!" Sam steered them far away. "Before you say anything, I know you can handle yourself, but it's always better to have reinforcements when in the presence of an ex."

"Aw shucks," Eleanor said, punching Sam's bicep. "I'm glad to have you. Hey, how do you know what to do with exes? You've only had one girlfriend."

They sat in the back row of the black box theater, borrowed for the night from the theater kids, and took up room across three seats.

"Dude, I had a girlfriend in high school. We only talked through AIM, but still."

Eleanor watched the blank stage, listening to the feminist music mix playing in the background, some folky voice with a guitar that she couldn't place. "That counts. I guess," she teased.

"Where is your girl tonight?" Sam asked.

"Studying. She has an exam next week." Smugly, she kept to herself the words Leena had whispered—"I need to focus, you distract me"—before kissing a stripe down Eleanor's torso. She thought idly of Leena as she looked around the space, taking in the black-painted walls and floor, and the audience that filtered in, shuffling through narrow rows and negotiating with saved seats, her thoughts so vivid she was sure she saw Leena entering the theater. Actually. That was her. *Why wasn't she studying?* Confused, Eleanor watched her walk down the aisle, laughing, her body loose. She seemed happy. Leena was with some soft-butch Latina girl who stumbled, missing a step, making Leena explode with peals of laughter. She seemed so uncharacteristically jolly and untethered, as though all of the times they were together Leena had been weighed down.

"Did we tell you what we're doing during break?" Sam asked, delight in her voice. "We're going to rebuild houses in Appalachia. Isn't that awesome? We'll get all that time together. Time alone. Under the stars, in nature. I can't fucking wait."

Eleanor was happy on a base level for her friends—one of whom was trying to spin a service trip into a Tahitian honeymoon—but she couldn't devote any attention to Sam because Leena had lied to her, and worse, was quiet-talking in the second row to some woman, their heads bent together. She said that she had to study, but had this been her plan all along, to spend time with this girl, whoever she was?

Or maybe she was just a friend.

But on the lesbian continuum, a friend can also be more, given time. It left Eleanor spinning, the briny taste of distrust oozing into her mouth.

Sam sighed audibly, poking her. "You've stopped listening to me. You're a terrible friend."

Eleanor wasn't listening, and she was a terrible friend, but she didn't have time for that, not now. She gestured forward and Sam squinted. "Huh. You're having a variety of girl problems this evening."

When Leena smiled soft and gauzy at the woman she was with, a powerful cyclone of agony smacked Eleanor. She was sure this girl was not a friend, was clearly someone more than that to arouse that look in Leena. It could have been them tonight, Eleanor and Leena, but instead they were rows apart, separated by whoever this girl was who made Leena laugh, who seemed to make her so happy. *Why aren't I the one doing that? Am I not enough?* Enough was enough. Eleanor got out of her seat, legs propelling her forward before her brain could catch up. She scooted into the aisle behind Leena and tapped her on the shoulder.

She turned, slow to recognize Eleanor in the faint light of the theater and whatever haze she was in. But then she got it. "Hi," Leena said loudly, surprised. "It's you." She indicated with her head toward the other woman. "This is my friend Noa. Noa, Eleanor."

Noa was butch in demeanor and handshake. "Hey there. Nice to meet you." And voice. Eleanor pasted on a smile and took in her short, dark, curly hair, her curvy frame, her khakis, her jean jacket rolled up at the sleeves. *Was this the future Physician for Reproductive Choice?*

They were both drunk. Eleanor was sure of it—from both the smell and the loopy less-than-Leena she was getting. And here was her test, the one she didn't want: When the idea of drinking was in the abstract, she told Leena she could be cool with it. Here in this room, with this company, she wasn't going to be cool. Being drunk wasn't something she could trust. "I thought you were studying tonight," she directed at Leena. "At least, that's what you told me."

"Oh, well, yeah. I was studying, but Noa called, and this sounded more fun."

Eleanor nodded. "Definitely more fun. It would've been *more fun* if you had come with your girlfriend instead of saying you were studying when you weren't." She could hear herself, the jagged-edged tone in her voice, and couldn't back down. She felt too hurt and bruised for generosity or understanding.

Leena pursed her lips and looked toward Noa, then back to Eleanor. She shrugged. That, apparently, was the end of this conversation.

"Cool. Well, I better get back to my seat and my friend. Sam. Leena, you know Sam because we went on a double date together? So. Nice meeting you, Moa," she petulantly threw over her shoulder. With each step, she replayed her reckless reaction and compared it with the dull aching in her heart.

"Who is that bitch?" Sam asked when Eleanor got back to her seat.

She appreciated the show of solidarity, taking secret pleasure in the word she'd wiped from her vocabulary. "Her ex." Eleanor sank low in her chair. "I don't want to talk about it."

Sam scoffed. "Hilarious. Of course you do."

"She lied to me. She told me she had to study, then she went out with that . . . girl."

Sam scrunched her face in contemplation. "Well, I don't think that's being a liar. I think her plans changed, and her ex called, and they came here. I'm sure it's not something worse."

Eleanor crossed her arms and sighed. "You don't get it. You've had a girlfriend since freshman orientation."

"I know. I'm really lucky."

Tomás appeared in their row, plunking down next to Eleanor and dusting snow off his peacoat. "Hey! Here before it started, awesome. Did you guys see Leena a few rows up?"

Eleanor rolled her eyes and sighed. "Yes, Tomás." The lights went down in the theater and up on the stage. "Also, hi," she whispered to him. The cast entered wearing black, getting into their places. Cath looked out with a nervous smile, adjusting her shapeless black dress. Sam let out a whoop, and Eleanor covered her face.

"I bet you're worried," one actor said.

"We were worried," Cath added.

And another: "We were worried about vaginas."

The show went on. She had never heard the word *vagina* said more frequently, which was saying a lot given her mother. The play was heartfelt in some places, sad in others, and definitely mortifying. Cath's piece was called "Because He Liked to Look at It." Cath was nervous at first, her voice wavering as she tried to emulate a sarcastic, fast-talking woman. Eventually she got into the rhythm, telling the story of Bob and his desire to look at vaginas. Sam mouthed along with Cath, entranced, word by word, beat by beat.

When Cath delivered the line "Bob continued. He would not stop. I wanted to throw up and die," Eleanor saw Leena throw her head back and laugh. She wished they were sitting next to each other, holding hands in the dark, cocooned in their own impenetrable bubble.

The show ended, the audience and actors crowded together in the lobby. Sam bounded off to find Cath, and Eleanor and Tomás waited, getting jostled around, an impediment to other people's goals. She watched Zoe leave with her new girl, and as her eyes sought Leena without success, she felt alone, even with a friend at her side.

Cath appeared, now with her flowers in hand, with almost all of her stage makeup removed save for smudges along her hair and jawline. Still on a post-performance adrenaline spike, she glowed beatifically, and despite everything Eleanor hugged her friend, happy for her. "You were wonderful." They fought their way out, leaving to go find a restaurant, Tomás in the lead. It continued to snow as Sam put her arm around Cath. Some people had it easier.

LEENA DIDN'T CALL or email that weekend. Eleanor knew the end of the semester would be a busy time, but radio silence seemed foreboding. She was sure it was how she had behaved, ferociously jealous, without constraint. She still felt entitled to such behavior, but was rational enough to know that not everyone enjoyed such displays. She didn't call or email either. She gave Leena space, so they could reconnect with cooler heads.

A crowded elevator wasn't a great place to give someone space. It was already almost full when the car arrived on her floor Monday morning before class. She saw Leena right away: her hair in a ponytail, her form made puffy by her black down jacket and giant clunky boots to face the snow. She didn't look up from the notes in her hands and Eleanor made no attempt to grab her attention, to interrupt the intimacy of whatever important symbiosis was at play.

A tall boy elbowed Leena at her side, causing her to look up. She saw Eleanor across the car and grimaced, putting up a hand like a wave, then went back to her notes.

Being cast off, like she was nobody, broke Eleanor's heart.

As the elevator landed, Eleanor swore to peel right out, get out of there, show Leena she could brush her off too. But once the car unloaded, Eleanor broke the promise to herself and tugged Leena to the side. "I know you have to go to class. I just. Can I walk with you?"

"Fine." Leena tore out of their building and toward the street. "I'm running late. This is the last session before the final."

"Where are you going?" Eleanor asked.

"Dalton Hall. I have Global Environmental Health." Once they hit Comm Ave, Leena took off at a run-walk.

Eleanor worked hard to keep pace. "I was harsh the other day."

"Yeah, that was a side of you that I hadn't seen before. You were . . . intense."

"I know, I know. I just—you said you had to study, but then you were out with her. And I know she's your ex, and that's a gay thing to do, like, to be friends with your ex, but it sounded like you and Noa had a complicated past, and so to see you two together, when you'd bailed, and you'd been drinking . . . I didn't know what to think."

They paused at the stoplight as traffic zoomed past. Leena looked like she'd prefer to run right into it. She marched in place, quiet for a long time before shaking her head. "You overreacted."

"I know, I'm sorry. I should trust you—"

"You should. Nothing happened with me and Noa. We're friends. I don't have a lot of lesbian friends that I can talk to." The traffic light changed and Leena took off like a shot across the street.

Eleanor dashed too, as fast as her reaction time would allow, and caught up with Leena, wheezing with exertion, cold air in her lungs like sharp stabs. "I'm sorry, I was feeling . . . exposed. I came out to my family for you, and then I saw you with Noa. It felt like we weren't in sync."

"Whoa, whoa, whoa." Leena stopped then, a sudden standstill so fast that Eleanor almost kept moving past her. "Coming out *for* me? I didn't ask you to do that."

"No, I just meant—"

"I'm leaving in a couple of months to go abroad. We can't be serious, not like this."

For Eleanor, time halted. Cars stood still. People paused midstep. She froze inside as her blood stopped pumping and muscles ceased operation. She had accepted this as a possible option, but she'd thrown her weight into optimism. Weren't they a perfect match? How could a perfect match not overcome the odds? A knot took shape in her throat. "This is serious. Serious to me. I know you feel the same way. I know we have something. We can outlast study abroad and not being out, and we can be together. We can make this work."

Leena looked at her for the longest time. It added an extra chill to Eleanor's body. "I wish we could have everything. But there's too much in the way." She took Eleanor's hand, glove in mitten. "Let's say, this was fun. That's easier. I'm sorry, but I have to go."

"So that's it?" Eleanor asked.

Leena dropped her hand, nodding, averting her eyes.

Eleanor turned so Leena wouldn't see her cry, so she couldn't see Leena take off. Hot tears ran cold on her skin. She kept her eyes on the street, retreating to the dorm. There was no way she could make it to her Queer Jewish Culture class.

She got back, shed all of her clothes, and got into bed naked. The flannel sheets her mother had insisted she buy came in handy and warmed her body immediately. They did not, however, make her feel better—nothing could do that—and she spent the morning in bed feeling sorry for herself. She struggled to track where she had gone wrong. Her heart was too open. She was too susceptible and trusting. Zoe had hurt her, and now Leena. They were both alluring in their mystery, and she had confused the black box of attraction and chemistry for what was really at play: they were unknowable, aloof, emotionally unavailable. Or it wasn't them—it was her, and she was a fool. Or she was rotten to her core. There had to be something wrong for her to be so unlovable. She let herself cry, depressed herself with more sad thoughts, and cried more.

She washed her face in the late afternoon. "Life goes on," she said aloud to herself in her room. Leena's words to her, when she was upset about the election. *Life goes on.* She made it to her shift at the Women's Center with two minutes to spare.

For the remaining weeks of the semester, she felt brittle and vulnerable. Usually she loved that, being honest and truthful and letting it all be, right out there for anyone to see, but it had lost its sheen. She locked herself up and away from her friends. She finished knitting a scarf for her grandmother. She put her head down and got through, ready to get out of this room that had been tinged with so many memories.

She had not imagined the semester ending like this. She had envisaged a week fueled by caffeine, pushing through finals, spending every spare minute with Leena. Sex on every surface. Being tucked together in bed. Dreaming of how things could be, reunited after time apart. She knew now it was a pipe dream, a fantasy, because she refused to recognize what was in front of her, obvious: they weren't meant to be. Realizing that their love wasn't destined called into question her deepest-held beliefs. She had been bat mitzvahed, but her real religion was love. She wasn't sure what to believe anymore.

She ached for a last-minute reunion, like in the movies: She would return Leena's sweatshirt. Leena's roommate would be there, so Leena would come into the hallway and close the door behind her. Eleanor would hand over the sweatshirt. "I miss you," she'd say.

Leena would say the same and add, "We can't work it out."

Eleanor would say, "But we could try. Because I love you."

They'd kiss in the hallway as the camera crane drew back, the music swelling.

But none of that happened.

"PROFESSOR POST?"

Her shaggy blond head bobbed up, dark eyes warm behind her gold, wire-framed glasses. Her long face softened as she looked away from the glaring glow of her desktop computer. "Hi, Eleanor."

"You wanted to talk about my paper?" She sagged in the doorway, the left side of her body against the door-frame. The fluorescent lights felt like melting snow against her eyes.

"Yes, I did. Sit down, make yourself comfortable." Professor Post stood, rounded her desk, and scooped a pile of books off of her visitor's chair, a wood-frame chair with nubby orange material on its seat and back.

Eleanor sat as her professor did the same, and set her backpack between her legs, coat draped behind her. "I didn't mean to take down the Madres de Plaza de Mayo. I'm, like, totally in awe of their activism, but their identity framed as mothers, and that being the reason why people should have listened to them flies in the face of—"

"Eleanor, relax. You're not here to defend your paper." Her professor flipped through a stack of papers in a folder, then pulled out one stapled packet. Eleanor's paper. On the first page a giant, gleaming A+.

Her heart, which had been so bashed in and exhausted, gave a fluttered beat. "Wow. I . . . wow." Eleanor worked hard, could work harder, but generally she tried to be proud of her academic performance without prioritizing it above friends, sleep, or carbs. Perfect marks were not common in her life.

"I do have a few suggestions," Professor Post said, handing over the paper. "You love a run-on sentence. And sometimes you use seven words when you could use two. But generally, it's good. Far and away the best in the class."

Eleanor beamed. The heart that let out a gasp now drew blood, in and out. Something about the compliment, the small, fond smile on her professor's face, and how low Eleanor had been feeling all congealed together, and she burst into tears.

She heard a sigh. "Take a tissue. And don't be embarrassed. You'd be surprised how often this happens, though at this point I am not."

She took from the box when it was offered, drying her cheeks, blowing her nose, looking up at Professor Post through watery eyes. "It's just that my girlfriend broke up with me and I came out to my family and this semester feels never-ending and I kind of thought she was *the one*, but she's going abroad and her ex-girlfriend is a med student and she's going to South Africa—"

"Eleanor, I'm going to stop you there." Professor Post reached up, her fingers running over the book spines in her above-desk shelving unit. She pulled down a white-and-red book. *Communion* by bell hooks, paperback and slightly fuzzy at its edges. "It's not one of her academic titles, but it's a worthy read. It's as if that *Men Are from Mars, Women Are from Venus* book were written by a feminist. Borrow it, enjoy it."

Eleanor took the book from her professor's hand and nodded, grateful for whatever it was that was being offered.

Professor Post found her over the top of her glasses. "You've had a hard time. You're not the first women's studies student to have their heart broken by their girlfriend, and you won't be the last. Focus on school, your friends, your activism. There will be another. Take it from someone who knows."

Take it from someone who knows. Was Professor Post coming out to her? *Focus, Eleanor.* "Thank you so much," she said. As she gathered her backpack and coat, she noticed a brochure on the desk: *Explore Feminist and Queer Theory across Europe!* She picked it up, intrigued. "What's this?"

"I don't really know. One of my students asked for a recommendation letter. A women's studies program abroad. Czech Republic, Sweden, Germany, I forget where else," Professor Post replied, distracted, already turning back to her computer. "You can take that if you want."

Germany, where her grandparents were from, where half of her was from. The chance to escape the confines of this campus and country, to go elsewhere, to where history comes from, instead of staying in a muddy half-cocked nation that was still becoming. She left the office with the brochure in her hand, a thank-you over her shoulder, and her mind gratefully clouded with thoughts other than Leena.

IN THE END, Eleanor packed up after her last final. She saw her friends for one last celebration, splitting pizzas and a raucous game of Scattergories. She'd see Tomás at home, but it wouldn't be the same without the whole gang. She hugged Cath and Sam so tight, too tight, grateful that everything in her life hadn't collapsed.

On her night flight to San Jose, she was glad for a window seat. She leaned her head against the curved wall, trying to sleep, but she couldn't quiet her mind as it flipped through the months. One moment at a time, backward, forward. Feelings only. Images. The plane roared and lifted up. In the dark, Boston was lit like any other city. She said goodbye to her adopted home, shutting her shade.

At ten thousand feet, she watched a Nicholas Sparks movie. Two people destined to be together despite the odds, looking gorgeous while they did it, with a lush Southern backdrop. But it was too painful, and she shut it off.

While she tried to sleep, she kept returning to the night they'd shared after first having sex. Eleanor felt drugged, so high on Leena. After, they'd lain together, half-asleep. She'd twirled a lock of Leena's hair with her finger, a slow loop that she kept dropping and picking up again. She'd kissed Leena's bare shoulder. "Who knew this would happen after meeting in an elevator?" It was so dark, save for the slick line of light under the door.

"What elevator?"

"We met—you don't remember? In the dorm? We met before we officially met?"

Leena squinched her face. Then, "Are you sure it was me?"

Eleanor had been sure, as sure as she was about the destiny that had brought them together again, and to this moment. "Definitely you," she had said, as Leena let out a delicate snore.

PART TWO
LEENA, 2010

JANUARY

The definition of chaos was getting to the airport. There were so many discrete, random possibilities that could delay Leena's commute before her flight: congestion on the A/C/E lines, a delayed train, a sick passenger, an AirTrain stalled on its elevated track, a seemingly never-ending TSA line. To combat the unknown, she allotted double the time predicted, departing at five a.m., and no matter how slow the handoff was at Hoyt-Schermerhorn from the C to the A, her investment paid off. She slid into the security line with plenty of time to spare, allowing herself a moment of self-congratulation.

The TSA agent beckoned her forward after she made it through the full-body scanner, arms above her head. "Ma'am? Step to the side."

Leena sighed. This, too, was a reason for leaving extra early. Her belongings loitered at the end of the conveyer belt as the agent patted her down. It was invasive, like a bored doctor—clinical intimacy—with gloved hands skimming over her body in precise strokes down her limbs and tapping at her sides. Her skin a threat. She kept her head up, eyes straight ahead, not diverting her gaze. She held her breath, waiting for the call for a supervisor, which sometimes came next.

"Okay. You can go."

"Thank you," Leena said to the agent, like her parents had coached long ago.

Once settled near her gate, with her carry-on suitcase and backpack wedged between her legs, she called her mother.

"Your plane is delayed. I see it on the computer screen," her mother said before Leena could get a word in.

Leena de-escalated her mother's anxiety, answering each question exactly, no more or less: "Everything is fine. It's only a ten-minute delay . . . Yes, I'm staying with Neha . . . Of course I'll see Dhaval while I'm in San Francisco . . . No, Dhaval isn't proposing this weekend."

With her mother assuaged and off the phone, she relaxed backward into her seat, sagging against the leather, and indulged in one of her favorite pastimes: watching those magnificent machines leave the tether of the ground, running so fast before becoming airborne, a smooth sail into the sky and away. She loved the science, though she knew less about aerodynamics than she would have liked. It was a privilege to board a plane, and she did it today with pleasure before slumping into her seat, succumbing to exhaustion from waking so early.

Leena woke to turbulence and tuned into the in-flight movie, some Nicholas Sparks tale about two sad white people in love. Normally she couldn't care less, but she found herself crying at its climax, unsettlingly and against her will. To put an end to that, she pushed the shade up and saw the West unfold below her: straw-dry arid patches of rock formations, then illuminated green farmland and rhombuses of water.

The West Coast. She was getting closer to California, to San Francisco. A place she had always wanted to visit. With airfare loaned from her sister Binita, she was on her way to a weeklong visit with Dhaval. To share a space and be in his life in a way that remote, electronic pathways could only attempt to mimic.

Leena was grateful for a vacation from her tiny studio apartment, so hot she was always in underwear—contrasted with the wind and snow outside, and blistering frozen treks around New York City. Plus, it would be nice to spend time with someone who knew her beyond a classmate or internship supervisor. New York was lonely. She felt lonely when she was alone, but also in the scorching crush of a packed subway, or in the dull blur of a movie theater. She didn't know many people well in the city, or in life. She had her family, whom she saw when she could get home to Massachusetts, and Dhaval; he and her mother were the ones she could count on to always take her calls on the first ring.

It was unexpectedly sunny when she arrived, more like California as an idea than San Francisco as a reality. The hazy mountains greeted her as soon as she was past baggage claim and outside on the pavement, bag in tow. She saw Dhaval right away, though he didn't see her, and it afforded the opportunity to examine his tall, lanky body with accidental biceps; his brand-new, full beard that was starting to fill in past the patchy phase; and his warm complexion of honey and almonds. He was undeniably handsome. Her guy, her man, the one who took a half day off work to pick her up, in a T-shirt and jeans and high-top sneakers.

Dhaval looked around, a coffee in his hand, scanning. When he saw her, his eyes lit up, and he advanced quickly, almost stumbling over a small child with a large backpack. She let him hold her tight when he reached her, inhaling his familiar scent: detergent, and cologne that his mother bought him in sets. Being with him was soothing. The feeling of home, the smell of her grandmother's chai on the stovetop. She ran a hand over his bearded cheek.

"San Francisco. What a hipster."

He grinned and kissed her, and she felt his smile press into her lips.

They hopped into a cab, both of his hands gripping one of hers. He asked about the flight, her classes next semester, her parents, Binita's wedding—as if they hadn't been talking about these subjects on an endless loop already. When he would get out of work, they talked after her night classes. They texted and emailed and called and Skyped, and sometimes he sent a corny postcard, like one with a cable car and Coit Tower in the same shot. They were never not in contact, and yet there was something about seeing him in the flesh. She could touch him and watch him breathe. Here and now, he was three-dimensional and tactile, putting her at ease to have him near, with the sun on his skin.

His skin was a beautiful shade darker than hers. Her mother had worried to Binita, who immediately told Leena, about future grandchildren and a darkening of the gene pool. Her mother's colorism was not a surprise, but she was surprised that pigmentation concerns were not superseded by her desire for Leena to conform. Become a wife. A mother herself. When it was clear that no other suitors would be in the picture, her mother begrudgingly took to Dhaval, taken with his smarts, his trajectory, and his love for her daughter. Leena tried to be worthy of that devotion every day, but was currently failing, zoning in and out as he talked about his software-engineer job and his manager Mark, who was in a death-metal band on the side.

The cab arrived in front of a statuesque white building. Dhaval drew out his wallet.

"Are we here? Is this it?" Her eyes took in another look, of smooth planes and bulbous windows that resembled a cruise ship. They climbed out of the car and went through the glass doors, Dhaval wheeling her bag through the courtyard and past the fountain to the elevators. It was a stark comparison with her three-story walk-up in Clinton Hill next door to a storefront church. She shook her head at the opulence, at the thought of the salary that afforded all of this. "Somehow you left out the fountain when you described your new place."

In his apartment, she noticed the view first. She saw a sliver of a bridge and the bay, the bridge cutting into the gray sky and choppy water as the day grew overcast. It was a formidable scene, one that must have had quite the price tag attached. Leena and Dhaval always talked of money only in the abstract, in the ways that it was mutually understood that she had none and he had lots.

She spun and looked around at the apartment itself, which she'd seen over video chat. A low-backed couch, a flat-screen television affixed to the wall. White untouched walls and shiny parquet floors. Her eyes glossed over new furniture, a square table and two chairs, all in boxy black wood. "Did you go shopping recently?"

He nodded, his smile embarrassed. "Before that, I ate on the couch. But you were coming, so . . ."

Her eyes caught on to the only personal item in the room, the only thing that wasn't from an IKEA showroom: a framed photo from Binita's engagement party—Leena in a sparkly black lehenga and Dhaval in his plum kurta, the same one that he wore to her friend's wedding, where they'd first met. That Leena from six months ago beamed at her, with rosy cheeks from dancing and whiskey. She looked so happy.

"I'm glad you're here," he said, and she offered him a kiss.

He was handsome in the photo, and he was handsome now. He kissed her with urgency, with hands tight around her waist, then her hips, then a hand at her breast, and she sagged into him. They got into bed first, naked second as she yanked the blankets up around them. He rolled on top of her, skin to skin.

"Wish we could do more. Want you so bad," he groaned against her neck. He gently rocked his hips to touch hers, and she felt him, hard.

Her desire had been a surprise. Falling for him made her crave his hands. And insistent, teeth-clashing, feverish kisses. And the feeling that she would explode, then melt, from the spice of him in her orbit. And yet, she had heard her mother reverberating through her keyed-up body: *Girls must be careful. Boys pressure. It's up to us to think about the future. About families.* Suddenly those words applied to her, alive in a way they had not been before. And so Leena and Dhaval stuck to limits that were first hers then theirs, shared.

It felt absurd at times to be twenty-six years old and saving herself for marriage, especially given how much sex she had had with women, and yet this was what felt right for her now.

Leena moaned as his lips encircled her nipple. "I know, I know." She, in fact, didn't know, had no clue what she was missing, because this seemed to cover all of their bases. Sex wasn't a one-way destination; pleasure came in all forms. His mouth on her body, hers on his. There wasn't anything that left her unsatisfied. But she needed to please him, even if it was with lies. "Remind me again why we're waiting?" she asked breathlessly.

Where he had been ravenous for her, he now turned reverent. A hand in her hair, an adoring smile on his face. "Because I'm going to love you forever. You're going to be my wife. A few more months don't matter."

"You're such a sap," she teased, but she loved that they were synced in this way. They would one day join their families—lines of history and fate—after being married in front of their community, walking around the fire tied together in a blaze of symbolism that she didn't really understand, but felt was important. Sex—the kind that could produce children—would be the territory of her new life, singed clean. Emerging like a phoenix.

"I'll show you sap," he said, which made no sense, but it didn't matter when his mouth was slipping down her body and between her legs.

After her orgasm, and his, he curled around her, a shade of affection that wasn't in her repertoire. After sex she had no desire to spoon, to avoid the wet spot as a team, to bask in a sparkling afterglow. She wanted to be alone. At her side she grabbed her phone and saw the notice: a missed call from her mother. It reminded her of her subterfuge to-do list. She texted Neha: **Thanks for putting up a Facebook post about me staying with you! I'll be sure to do the same for you while you're in Hawaii with Ben :)**

She stroked Dhaval's forearm down to his hand, over knuckles sparse with hair. His breathing was slow and thick.

When he woke from his nap and she was done reading her *Scientific American* article about curing tropical diseases, they went out for an early dinner: small plates, low lighting, narrow reclaimed-wood tables. Leena swigged cava from her glass and looked around at their fellow patrons, a few older couples and parents with a small baby. He lightly kicked her under the table, grinning. He was so stupid after sex it was almost adorable.

"What should we order, honey?" Although she had her own menu, he pivoted his so they could peruse it together.

She rolled her eyes but humored him, strategizing on vegetarian selections: croquettes, patatas bravas, tortilla española, manchego cheese, and vegetable paella. "But that's too many things. It's too expensive."

Dhaval shook his head, reaching a hand across the table, silently asking for her to hold it. She did, begrudgingly. "I can afford a nice dinner with my girlfriend. I can afford more than one nice dinner." He squeezed her hand. "When you graduate and move out here, we can order whatever we want for dinner, all the time," he teased, a mischievous gleam in his eyes.

Leena drained her flute and reached into the silver

ice bucket at their side, refilling her glass with more wine. "Mm. I hope you like restaurants and takeout. I'm not going to be the kind of wife who cooks every night."

"I know," he said, because he did, because these days he knew her better than anyone else. "Maybe you'll learn. Or I will. Or we'll get our kids to cook for us."

"Toddlers are great chefs," she deadpanned. As much as she couldn't fathom a child right now, the thought of being a mother made her pulse speed. Watching a tiny human develop, helping them along the way, learning with them. She found it fascinating. Whenever it happened—down the road, after marriage and a house purchase and more life lived—she would be ready.

They ordered, then indulged in each dish as it arrived. When the paella finally came, Dhaval mentioned that he'd started thinking about towns they might like in the South Bay. Redwood City, Fremont, Mountain View, Sunnyvale. "Commuting is okay right now, but I bet I'll want to be closer when we . . . have a family." His voice started out confident and matter-of-fact, but by the end it was soft and bright. So were his eyes.

She polished off their bottle of cava. She liked planning. No. She loved planning. But this was all premature; it was months before the end of her master's program. Discussing the map stretched out in front of her, already charted down to the details, served no purpose. Not now. But she didn't know how to tell him, so she said nothing and let him go on, let him be flushed as he tallied the tip on his phone and settled their bill.

"Ready?" he asked, smiling. "Ready to head out?"

She wasn't, but nodded. They walked back to his place and she found the darkness of night comforting. Less to process and take in. "I like your place. Did I say that?"

"You didn't." He draped an arm over her shoulders.

She flinched. She couldn't help but flinch. It wasn't his touch; it was anyone's touch delivered with a surprise, out where anyone could see. But she tried to relax into it. The heaviness of his arm could be calming if she reframed it. She put her hand up to her shoulder and wove their fingers together. He pulled her in tighter.

"Well, I do. The view is incredible in person."

"My mom says it's too extravagant."

She smiled to herself, knowing exactly the tone of voice his mother must have used. "I'm sure she's also really proud of you at the same time."

Dhaval squeezed her hand. She let him.

She thought of his apartment as they walked on dark streets heavy with construction sites. Buildings in the midst of being razed. Deep holes in the ground. Skeletons of metal frames and scaffolding. Newness being built. Beginnings for some, tragic endings for others.

"What do you think of the city so far?" he asked.

"I've seen your apartment, one restaurant, and this street. My review is not yet ready."

He snorted at her side. "Please let me know when it is."

Leena had woken up that morning in New York City and was ending her day here. San Francisco shared a profile with most cities in the United States: tall buildings, traffic lights, street lamps. Somebody in pajamas walking their dog. A Brown person waiting for a bus. It was familiar. And yet, this city was different from where she had begun the day. Air that was warmer but sharper. Wider sidewalks. Clothes that lacked the finishing polish of fashion-conscious Manhattan, and instead were more relaxed, rumpled. Beyond what little she had seen and felt, the jury was out on San Francisco. And in some ways, it didn't matter what she thought. Dhaval's work was here. She would move to be with him, a tacit fact of their shared life.

Once they were back in the apartment, she could tell he wanted to have sex again, his hands pawing her. Desiring her. She begged off sex, and opted for cuddling and television instead. "Tomorrow. I'm so tired."

His eyes dimmed, but he did what she asked, on that she could rely. He flipped the television on and brought up the guide, the glare from the screen reflecting on his neutral face. "That cake show you like is on."

"*You* like it," she pressed, teasing, wanting his favor and willing to win it. She pressed into his side, wrapping her arms around him, looking up and giving him a look he deserved. Filled with a somber love that only he engendered in her.

They drank more wine and watched the cake show. It was the same each week: struggles to get cakes out the door on time, well-photographed reveals of the final product, and ebullience from satisfied customers. It was silly, but that mattered not at all when they were intertwined on the couch. As if this was every night. As if this was her lived-in norm, watching the fast-food equivalent of television and falling asleep on the couch with her boyfriend.

SHE AWOKE TO gray morning light streaking through the plastic blinds in his bedroom that needed dusting, to Dhaval's mouth kissing up her thighs, higher and higher, his sweeping kisses and tickling breath. A puff of exhalation left her lips and her eyes closed. She fumbled for his head with one hand, then stuffed a pillow over her face to stifle the volume of her moans, until he made her come after a long while. Without coffee she was basically still asleep, but she took him in hand and returned the favor.

They were a mess. There was brunch to be had, things to see, photos to take so her parents didn't assume the worst. They showered together, which only delayed them more. She dressed in jeans and a T-shirt, with a sweatshirt over the top of that, and a rain jacket tucked in her bag to combat erratic weather, as her mother suggested before she left—and then she was still waiting five minutes later.

Leena popped back into Dhaval's bedroom, where he stood in front of his walk-in closet that housed not clothes or towels or household items but sneakers. Sneakers lovingly displayed, arranged by color and style. Enough pairs to outfit more than one man. He appeared genuinely confounded at the decision ahead of him, one arm crossed over his chest while the other was diagonal, with one hand on his chin. His eyes swept and swept. And she grew decades older as she perched and sank on the bed.

"Just fucking pick!" she finally exploded.

Dhaval turned to look at her, his face vacant. As if he'd forgotten she was there. "I am. It's a serious process."

Leena shook her head. "No sir, it isn't. We are going to go eat brunch. Your shoes don't matter."

He held up an arm, gesturing to his abundance. "But I have so many options. It's hard to choose."

She was tempted to storm out of the room, to deliver the tough love he needed, but she didn't know how long the selection process might stretch on in her absence. "Dhav," she said calmly, with a reserve of patience stored for moments like this. "Please." But the *please* was filled with the tension of an aimed bow and arrow.

He took one more exhausting minute, then gingerly removed a pair of blue sneakers with a Nike swoosh that looked ordinary. "Classic Cortez. Can't go wrong."

Leena kissed him with fever and flourish, then shoved him out the door.

After huevos rancheros and blood-orange mimosas, they walked down Market Street and crossed Castro on their way to Mission Dolores Park. Leena stiffened at the giant vertical CASTRO sign at the Castro Theatre and the giant rainbow flag, with baby rainbow-flag offspring everywhere against the now-cloudless blue sky. This had once been a place for her, in books at the library and in documentaries she saw in college.

She looked to Dhaval, smiling as he observed a pack of old white tourists, two gay bears walking their dog, two beautiful Black women walking hand in hand. "See anyone you like?" he whispered, then laughed softly.

Her back went up until she looked at his face. He was teasing her. Of course. Because there was nothing he knew that would make his intonation any different. She breathed a little easier, gripped his hand a little more, no matter how sweaty it was.

"Do you?" she asked.

He laughed and held her tight around the waist as they walked down to the park and found an unoccupied plot of grass. Leena produced a blanket from her bag, a bright patchwork bedspread that looked like it once resided in his mother's closet. They settled down on their backs, eyes up to the sky, but eventually she turned her head to peer around at the park filled with people, even on this winter day. Homeless people carting their possessions, groups of friends smoking weed, people sharing from a flask, dogs, and brassy Mexican music performed by a circle of men. All of these people together under a blue sky now tinged with gray, low-hanging clouds.

"Is your review ready yet?" Dhaval asked. "Now that you've seen more than my apartment, a restaurant, and . . . a street, is what I think you said?"

"It depends how much of a contact high I get."

Leena's eyes fixed on a straight couple embracing, huddled together on a blanket. It was such an ostentatious display. *We get it, you're in love.* She was in love too, but that was private. Intimate. Her heart was carefully guarded, shared only with Dhaval, and she couldn't understand another way. He, on the other hand, was an affectionate guy. Touchy-feely, arm around her shoulders, preferring to be hand in hand. He probably saw a couple like that and thought they looked sweet.

She felt the bedspread underneath them, the fabric between her fingers. Her future mother-in-law was uncertain about Leena at best. Dhaval's mother never said anything outright, but it was in the way that she conspicuously doted on Dhaval's brother's wife, who wore makeup and carried nice purses. She was all surface and flash, unlike Leena, and Mrs. Patel seemed as if she couldn't get enough of her.

She knew so many Patels. Her mother was a Patel.

She herself was on the way to becoming one too—the devoted Mrs. Dhaval Patel everyone expected her to be. Or she could chart her own way, on her own terms. That was the allure of a young, American-born man like Dhaval, who wasn't conventional, who didn't ask her to conform. His family might be from Uttar Pradesh, but he was from New Jersey. He was not someone who would fight her on staying Leena Shah. That's what made her his.

Leena turned to him now, and watched his serene face and closed eyes. He trusted her implicitly not to hurt him, and that aching responsibility made her want to poke him in the eye just to see what would happen. She tweaked his nose instead and he turned too, brown eyes blown open and a smile on his face.

"I think I lost you for a while. You looked so deep in thought."

She shrugged. "Yeah, just thinking."

"Anything specific?"

Leena brushed at the bangs on his forehead. "I can't remember this cloud type and I've been trying to recall it. Stratocumulus, maybe."

"When I hear the word *cloud*, I only think of it in a computer context."

She tweaked his nose again. "Nerd."

They sat until the air grew cool and clouds overtook the sky. She shivered.

"Are you cold? Do you want my coat?"

She was cold, warmed by his thoughtfulness. She dropped an impetuous kiss on his cheek.

"I know a great bar nearby, with spicy Bloody Marys. Is that a good next stop?" He was worried. It was so saccharine and endearing. So Dhaval.

They packed up and climbed the steep hill of Church Street to get there, on the way to the rest of their day. Leena was out of breath at the top, heaving and panting. She spun for a 360-degree view, fog hanging ominously over the city. Breathtaking, literally and figuratively. She took his hand as they descended.

"I can't get my mind off these sneakers I saw online the other day. Jeremy Scott, he's this designer. He took the normal high-top Adidas design and added wings to it and, like, wow. They come in so many colors and I'm trying to decide between metallic silver or gold, or white with gold stitching? It's figuring out what will be of better value and what I'm more likely to wear. They're awesome but they're, like, a look."

Bored into a lull, she felt like she was asleep with eyes open. She squeezed his hand as they crossed onto Twenty-Fourth Street and Dhaval's phone rang.

"It's Mark. It's my boss." He sighed dramatically. "I gotta pick up, I'm so sorry." He pulled over, his back to a construction site's plank-board wall. "Hey. Yeah, it's no problem. Was there something wrong with the patch they rolled to production?" He mouthed again that he was sorry.

Leena couldn't care less. It was Saturday, she was on vacation, without homework or chores, and she was about to drink Bloody Marys for the rest of the afternoon. She left Dhaval under the scaffolding and gazed into the shop window next door. It was a paperie store—with an *ie* at the end—with Valentine's Day cards on display. Hearts and lace and rolling script. She couldn't understand what any of this had to do with real love.

She turned her head away, and her eyes caught on

someone walking down the street. Someone who looked like someone she once knew.

"Leena?"

Eleanor's voice. Eleanor herself. Leena's stomach flipped over, then over again with unease. The moment slowed to a crawl in front of her, sun jagged through the clouds, Eleanor gliding forward with long hair, in a dress and a cardigan. Looking straight. The Eleanor she remembered—whom she'd actively avoided all senior year—had short and spiky hair, and dressed like a sloppy boy. Leena could feel the other woman's frenetic energy pulsing out of her. That hadn't changed. Once it had been something pleasantly attractive, but in this instant, Eleanor's energy was a wave crashing over Leena's head. Pulling her under. Limbs twisting and fighting against the tide.

"What are the absolute fucking odds?" Eleanor pressed forward and gave Leena a tight hug.

A flood of unwelcome emotions washed right into Leena's body, stiffening her muscles and bones with archived feelings of heat and comfort. She looked quickly at her boyfriend. He wasn't paying attention. Leena pulled away.

"What are you doing in San Francisco?" Eleanor asked.

She considered Eleanor's earlier rhetorical question, concluding the odds were high, but not astronomically so. It was statistically probable that they would eventually run into each other, being two young women of similar socioeconomic groups; it wasn't fate at work. But there she was. Eleanor. In the flesh in front of her. Her sweet face, her genuine smile. Invading her today.

"I'm here visiting a friend." These words came out of Leena's mouth with ease. Delivering convenient untruths was the path of least resistance. She cast a quick look over her shoulder to Dhaval, who was still wrapped up in his phone call. "I have to go. It was so nice to—"

"Wait." Eleanor put a hand on her forearm, firm and anchoring. "We should catch up while you're here. Give me your number?"

Leena hesitated, a nanosecond, a fear impulse striking her amygdala. She had already turned that page. Reintroducing Eleanor to her ecosystem would be retracing dangerous steps, but then she looked at her again. Long hair, kind face, trusting eyes. It was nothing. There was nothing to worry about. Leena recited her digits for input.

Leena's phone rang and Eleanor's name came up on her screen—still in her contacts after all these years. She pushed it back into her pocket before Eleanor could see. "Cool. So now I've got it, because I didn't have it." She moved to leave. "It was nice to see you."

Eleanor nodded, a bright smile still on her face. "Same here." Eleanor leaned in, kissed both of Leena's cheeks, and leaned out. She walked away, beaming over her shoulder as she went.

Leena kept walking for a building or two. She paused in front of a bar, the large window displaying a raucous crowd inside watching a game. She hid in plain sight outside, her heart pounding in her chest, feeling dazed, like she walked away from a car crash. Nostalgia broke loose inside her, for who she used to be: a college kid open to endless possibilities. Eleanor was from that time, and seeing her again recalled when Leena hadn't yet known her path. She could have become anyone.

A hand clapped her shoulder and she spun around with trepidation, unready to confront Eleanor again. "Hey, you found the bar," Dhaval said with a grin. "Did I see you talking to someone?"

"A friend from college," she replied numbly as he led her inside. In a total haze, she ordered a gin and tonic, skipping his earlier drink recommendation. She tried to transition from this unbelievable moment back to regular life. A bar, her guy, her drink. This was her now: public health school, not med school. On track toward a husband and a family of her own. This was her path.

"I'm so glad to have you here," he said more than once. He watched the game as they split fries and veggie burgers, leaning in to kiss her during commercials.

Leena couldn't concentrate on him, the food, or the game. She felt trapped in remembering. Noa and Eleanor and the other girls from her past. She thought she had gotten away clean.

She drank.

They took a car home after the game and Dhaval was handsy like he always was when he was drunk. A hand between her thighs, a hand slipping around her waist, and down. A few drinks in, it stoked the fire inside of her, longing to be touched. But they were in a car with a driver, and she had rules about strangers and PDA. Her mother could find out. Desi networks were powerful and far-reaching. She regretfully removed his hands.

He paid it no mind, smiling goofily at her. "I can't wait to have you here, all to myself."

She cracked open the window, clamoring for fresh air no matter how cold it was. She breathed in deeply but received no solace.

"Hey, let's do something fun tonight," he said. "There's this little park with adult-sized slides. Or we could do a bonfire on the beach. Or skinny dip?"

She snorted. "That's silly." She ruffled his hair, then affectionately tugged at his earlobe. She still couldn't catch her breath.

At Dhaval's, they ordered Uyghur food, which Leena had not heard of before. "Halal Chinese food? Is this some kind of San Francisco fusion thing?" She perused the menu and found options she'd seen on other Chinese menus, deciding on mapo tofu and vegetable sides. He insisted on paying again and she hadn't the energy to argue. She still felt breathless.

Dhaval lit dusty votive candles and placed them on the table, in between their takeout containers. "I bought these a while ago with the vague idea that it might be for your visit," he said shyly. "Glad to be using them." He turned down the dial on his overhead lighting so that the texture of the room grew rich and buttery. All the ingredients of a perfect night in with her boyfriend.

And yet she felt queasy, her stomach churning. It must have been the food she ate earlier. What she was eating for dinner. All that drinking. With her gut in turmoil, her breath couldn't make it past her chest.

They settled on the couch. "Can we open a window?" She tugged at the collar of her T-shirt.

"I can put on the air?" He went to the bulging unit jutting out from the white wall.

"No, no, that's okay." She didn't want hermetic air.

That's not what would help. She drank a glass of ice water instead and sunk into *I Love You, Man* on TBS.

She made it to sleep, her body and mind fighting until they gave in to rest. She woke up in the middle of the night to pee. Too much to drink. She turned in bed. Dhaval was sleeping and snoring at her side. She picked her phone off the floor to check the time, 2:29 a.m. Maybe it was jet lag. She crept out of bed, taking her phone.

Her feet scuttled against the parquet floors that creaked with newness. When she was done in the bathroom, she wandered out to the living room. She sat backward on the couch, away from the television and facing the windows, with her chin hooked over the top, the fabric coarse against her skin. It was a dark night, moonless, and yet the bridge glowed, glinting in outline. Leading somewhere. She hadn't done any preparation for this trip and had left it all up to Dhaval.

She got up to putter, living room to kitchen and back, her bare feet on the cool floor. She felt so restless. Wide awake, alert, ready to start the day. She wondered how early she could get up and go out for coffee. A muffin. She could bring it back. Five a.m.? Was that a time people did that?

She wondered if Eleanor was awake. What she was doing. If she was happy or hungry. Or thinking about Leena. She woke her phone, ignoring the missed call from her mother, and opened her messaging app, searching for Eleanor's name, just to look. There it was. Eleanor Suzuki. She selected her as the recipient and watched the cursor blink. A dividing line. She could delete Eleanor's name, put her phone away, and go back to bed. Or she could satisfy her latent curiosity.

See who Eleanor had become. Not think so hard about what could be so simple. Be ever-so-slightly reckless.

Hi, it's Leena. I'm here for a few more days. Do you want to meet up?

Sent.

Then she started freaking out. It was out there in the world, and what would Eleanor think of her texting at such a late hour? It was a terrible decision. She hadn't adequately thought this through. She buried her phone under a cushion, pressing her face down into the couch's arm. It was fine. It was fine, because she could block Eleanor and never speak to her again, forgetting this ever happened. She was on this train of thought when she felt a vibration from underneath her.

Yes!!!!!!! Lets get a drink? At the Lexington? 3ish?

She had texted back so fast, and she had said yes. Without any caveats. Leena stared at her phone, a device that couldn't help her absorb the rush of satisfaction and the pulse of concern running through her body. A drink with Eleanor.

A drink. Eleanor. In college, Eleanor blew up in anger over two vodka cranberrys.

Leena felt like she should say more. They were both up. She should acknowledge that.

Great! Then, **You're up late.**

Eleanor quickly sent back a text. **(: I'm out at a thing. Is it late? See you tmw!**

It was late. There was a certain stillness, even in the city, and that's how lateness was decided. Everyone knew that. She imagined Eleanor out at some party,

with loud music and pretty women and everyone dancing and women kissing.

Leena brought her phone and person back into the
bedroom, creeping in along the shadows. Dhaval didn't
stir when she lifted the covers and slid right in.

She stared at the ceiling. White. Smooth. It should
have been boring enough to put her to sleep, but she
was revved up. She rolled toward Dhaval, stroking a
hand up and down his bare chest. Desire cropped up
within her. He was so lean, with some muscle at his
pecs. She sidled up to him, close, lining up their bodies,
her face in the crook of his neck. His body had become
so familiar to her even in their distance. The feel of it,
the heft. She took a deep breath and exhaled, and he
laughed drowsily.

"Are you tickling me?" He turned toward her. "What
are you doing awake?" he asked, his mouth still slow
with sleep.

"I don't know." She stroked his hair, raking lightly
against his scalp with her short fingernails. She kissed
the side of his neck, his clavicle, his chest. The flat-
ness of his stomach at the brim of his boxer briefs. She
tugged his underwear down, and off, and took him into
her mouth.

Dhaval sighed, then said her name, sounding
wrecked. She was already craving sex, but knowing
she had this power over someone was even more of a
high. She had her own sigh as she balanced her body
on the bed, a hand snaking into her underwear.

LEENA SLEPT LATE and rushed out the door the next
day, but still made it to the bar before Eleanor, who
had already issued an apology text about her tardiness.

She recalled their brief romance: Leena always waiting for Eleanor to show up, or waiting for Eleanor to be ready to go.

When she walked into the bar, she was startled at the abundance of women. Perhaps she shouldn't have been surprised. Eleanor was gay, and they had been gay together. It was a natural meeting place.

Light from outside filtered in, hitting the walls painted red with wide, black baseboards. Photography and paintings hung over the red, her eyes scanning images she couldn't quite decipher. She ordered a gin and tonic, and gazed around at all of the women. Women everywhere. In knit caps over shorn hair, in ill-fitting button-downs, with long hair like a beauty queen, with red lipstick. So many black, plastic-framed glasses. White women and Brown women and Black women. Lanky, tall women and women with natural hair and older butch women and trans men. No one who looked like her—curvy and Indian and dressed to underwhelm, because she couldn't be bothered past jeans and a shirt that fit.

She could have once belonged here, but there was no room for her now, and it wasn't her personal dress code or the person with whom she shared a bed. Everyone seemed cool, too cool, and not even gay or lesbian—but queer. Political. Radical. Fluid. Her life was none of those things, because it wasn't set up to function that way. Her life was grown-up and responsible, structured and ordered. She had a path. Straight ahead, moving forward.

Leena was midsip when she saw Eleanor zip in, hair wet on her shoulders, wearing a delicate scarf wound around her neck, another dress, and boots. A turquoise coat over top, in a loud announcement of her arrival. Eleanor held her hands up in the air as she approached.

"I'm so sorry. And I don't have a good excuse. Hi!" She leaned in to hug Leena, arms tightly wound around her, smelling clean, of honey and jasmine. She shucked herself from her coat. "I'm so glad you could meet up!" She shook her hair out and took a seat at Leena's side. "How crazy is it, running into each other? Hey!" She called to the bartender. "Can I get a whiskey ginger? Like, with whatever whiskey is cheapest?"

The tornado of Eleanor left Leena struck silent. All of this Eleanor in front of her, long hair and possibly eyeliner, skin that Leena had kissed, rushing toward her in a ball of seizing energy, the past crashing into the present.

Eleanor looked at Leena expectantly.

"What?" Leena asked.

"What are you drinking?" Eleanor repeated.

"Hi." Leena laughed.

"What?" Eleanor asked.

Leena shrugged. "Just . . . all of this. It's surreal."

She nodded eagerly, leaning forward and putting one hand on Leena's knee. "How are you?"

The heat from her hand seeped through Leena's jeans. She could practically feel it on her skin. She crossed her legs the other way, displacing Eleanor.

"Good! Yeah," she replied on autopilot. Then she really thought about the question. She was fine. Life was complicated, but not more than anyone else's. "So much time has passed since I last saw you." She refrained from specifying when that last time was: crossing the street near the student union, then running the other way.

Eleanor's face fell a degree or two, a subtle shift. "It's true. And Leena . . . I just have to say." Her drink arrived and she gulped at it. "I didn't like the way we ended. I was so . . . immature. I made such a big deal of everything. When we were just—" She shrugged, her eyes glancing away. "We weren't serious. So I'm just, so sorry that I was so dramatic. It's embarrassing, the few times it's crossed my mind."

Their end was not something Leena liked to revisit. How she had backed off, too scared of their potential, their chemistry, and the impending separation of her study-abroad semester. How she had let bad advice cloud her judgment. She was the one who had said they had not been serious, implanting the false idea in Eleanor's brain. Unless that's how they had actually been. Not serious. Only fun.

Leena could accept this narrative. In fact, it fit better. She recast the memories, reimagining their relationship as a flight of fancy. Everything was instantly easier, and she sipped her drink. "You don't have to apologize. We were young. You're right, we weren't . . . serious. No need for apologies." The truth of her younger feelings tugged at her, but she felt overwhelming relief at Eleanor's remembering it this way. And it was true. Eleanor had been dramatic. About Leena drinking, and about something else she could no longer recall.

Eleanor exhaled and worked on her drink. "That's really cool of you, Leena." She held her glass up, and Leena clinked it with hers. "So, what have you been doing? Catch me up."

Leena's mind scanned. She thought of her second round with Noa when she transferred from Ohio State to Tufts for med school. The intensity of their reunion kept Leena grounded in Massachusetts, canceling her South Africa trip, unwilling to disturb their restored love. They dissolved disastrously right before Leena's graduation. That cannonball-sized scar inside of her. She felt a phantom ache to think of how she had let her plans unravel. How she had let Noa invade her life again. If she hadn't, Leena would be finishing med school this year. Leena couldn't be trusted around women. She got too close, lost herself. Women were a threat to her path.

Leena thought again about what Eleanor had said. *We weren't serious.* That made Eleanor safe now, in this moment. Eleanor was just a friend. She could disclose the texture of the previous years—Noa, living with her sister in Boston, getting a job at Mass General doing outreach, trying on different women and finding that no one fit. The loud, dark bars smelling of spilled beer, and her desire to sink her teeth into anyone who made her feel like she wasn't standing still. Meeting Dhaval at a wedding. Starting grad school. The first time she and Dhaval went to bed together, pretending it was her first time, erasing all of the women who came before, because she was with him. For good.

Looking at Eleanor, Leena felt a rare sensation of comfort and trust. Something about Eleanor's face, sweet and smiling. Her round cheeks, her kind eyes.

"I live in New York. I didn't go to med school. I have a boyfriend."

Eleanor craned her neck back, her eyes popping wide. "No fucking way," she sputtered.

Leena nodded slowly. She wasn't sure how Eleanor

was taking this news; she hadn't had practice telling anyone else. She furrowed her brow, watching.

"Hey, can I get another round? Can we both, actually?" Eleanor called to the bartender, flagging her down. They both still had liquor lingering in their glasses. "What did you have? Vodka? I was drinking a whiskey ginger but let's switch that to whiskey with, like, ice."

"Gin and tonic?" Leena added, putting her order in with the beleaguered bartender.

"What happened to med school? You were so passionate about becoming a doctor."

She shrugged. "I went to public health school instead."

Eleanor shook her head. "But that's not the same."

"It's not," Leena acknowledged, "but it's where I am. And I know that I can make a difference with this work too."

"I really want to know what happened," Eleanor said, eyes dancing, "but I think I'm prying. I am. I think. When I knew you, before, sometimes you were so quiet. Like you had a secret held between your cheeks." She leaned in and narrowed her eyes, smiling, like she could suss out the full truth that way.

Leena squinted. "I could tell you anything. That's what I remember." She squirmed in her chair. "It was just . . . something about you."

Eleanor looked skeptical. "Says the woman who omitted a fucking boyfriend until now!" She punched Leena in the arm with zero power behind her fist, then rested her arm on the bar, hand cupping her cheek. "When I last saw you, you were a confirmed dyke." She straightened up. "Oh my god, and then I invited you to a dyke bar. I invited a woman with a boyfriend to the fucking Lex."

"Where is that drink?" Leena muttered under her breath, loud enough to be heard, and it made Eleanor laugh. "He . . . Dhaval, he's—Indian. There are just things that we share, that I don't have to explain." She shook her head, self-deprecating. It wasn't just culture that made them a pair. "He's a nice guy. A good guy."

"I'm sure he is." Eleanor shifted, leaning back, hand over her mouth, rubbing her bottom lip. "He'd have to be." Her lip was turning pink from the friction.

Their drinks delivered, Leena clinked hers against Eleanor's. "And talk about changes. You didn't use to drink."

Eleanor's cheeks reddened as she took a sip. "Yeah, I used to be a real pain in the ass about it. People change, I guess." She sought out Leena's eyes, like a challenge.

"So, what about you?" Leena adjusted herself on the hard wooden barstool. She had had enough of being in the spotlight. "What's your six-years-in-five-minutes update?"

Eleanor laughed with her head down, then looked up, eyes shining. "That's all you're gonna give me?" Her voice was low, smoky, smooth. It sounded like flirting.

At first Leena was flattered, in some core part of herself deep down. She was hit on randomly by guys when she wasn't with Dhaval, a gesture of masculinity and heterosexuality akin to dogs lifting a leg and pissing on a tree then moving on. It wasn't sincere or genuine, not like Eleanor's face. But the more she reveled in and weighed Eleanor's attention, the more she thought better of it. Eleanor knew she had a boyfriend, knew she wasn't interested. Leena no longer knew how to read lesbians.

Her thought spiral had no impact on Eleanor, who began speaking again. "Well, I went on a study-abroad trip, this women's studies trip in Europe—god, it feels like so long ago—and it was so, like, life changing to be among women, feminists, and out of my element. Walking along ancient streets in Prague, or staying out all night at girls-only parties in Berlin." Her eyes were crinkly, dreamlike. "It was wonderful. And then, I graduated. So, check. I moved home, which was a disaster, and I had to get out of there. I started working for a congresswoman, in her district office, which was really meaningful to me. A Japanese American woman in politics, you know? I wanted to be active and make a difference, blah, blah, blah."

Leena smiled.

"But the job was in Sacramento, which was not, like, my favorite place to be, and it ended up being mostly spreadsheets and data entry. Not exactly glamorous, action-packed work. I moved back home to the East Bay and got a job on a mayoral race in San Francisco. Living with my parents was still a disaster, but I couldn't afford to live on my own. That was fucking exhausting, and really strenuous. Long hours and random cranks calling to complain and events on the weekend. When he won reelection, I guess I could've tried to get a job at city hall or with city government, but I was way the fuck burnt out on politics, so I started working for this nonprofit that supports gay-straight alliances in schools."

Leena couldn't believe Eleanor was still monologuing;

she herself never had that much to say. Yet what she had to share was so impressive. In school Eleanor had been a sociology major, or a women's studies major, one of those nonscientific, fuzzy concentrations. And here she was. Accomplished. Driven.

"I was delirious for a new job," Eleanor continued, "and didn't pay attention to the fact that I'd be fund-raising, which is really fucking hard! And awful. Like, asking people for money. It's mostly gay white male couples who dress alike. They're nice, or they're nice and mean at the same time."

Leena didn't understand what that actually meant, but bobbed her head like it computed.

"When I worked in politics, everything was more . . . scrappy. On a campaign, everyone worked hard. A good idea would get implemented. It didn't matter how old I was. But at work now no one trusts me. I just feel like I can't get a break. I can do more, I can handle more responsibility, and it's frustrating when my bosses and the senior team don't see that."

Eleanor ran her hands through her hair and Leena noticed a few strands of gray, just a few.

"How long have you been there?"

"Eh, a little over a year. I'm thinking about leaving. I'd miss the kids, though, the few times when I get to work with them. The world is changing so much, even from when we were in school. You'd never believe how many straight kids are so moved by this issue, or how many queer kids are out."

Leena felt a sway in front of her eyes. Everything was hazy, not sharp, not confined. Drunk. She was delightfully drunk.

"That's so cool," Leena said. It was all she could

manage. She smiled then grasped at Eleanor's drink and, uninvited, took a pull from the glass. It was so different from her gin and tonic, cool and almost savory. This was spicy, wooden, a bonfire.

Eleanor had talked about work with intensity, but had not divulged anything personal about her nonwork life, leaving Leena curious. What were her weekends like? What did she think about in the shower?

"That's a good drink. I like it. Are you dating anyone?" she asked, the question falling from her mouth. "I think I'm drunk," she announced.

Eleanor raised an eyebrow. She nodded, reclaiming her whiskey, glass sliding against the wood of the bar. "Yeah, you are. And yeah, I am." Her face shifted with an enthusiastic glow. "We've been together for about a year."

That settled that. Nothing to worry about.

"So, then, you've been living together for about a year? U-Haul style?"

Eleanor visibly winced.

Leena had attempted a joke, but her aim had fallen short of her goal. "That's great," she tried again. Because it was. "You deserve to be happy." Somebody did. Everybody did. "What's she like?"

"Nasrin?"

Leena mouthed her name. *Nasrin.* A name that seemed Indian at first sound, but upon second thought was probably Middle Eastern. Her name began with a certain softness and ended with an edge.

"She's great. She's passionate and driven and tough." Eleanor roughly clapped a hand to Leena's shoulder. "You should meet her. You will. It'll be great. Man. Look at us. Having a drink and talking about our girlfriends—significant others, sorry. It's amazing. Seriously. Like, the odds of seeing each other again. Being in the same city, on the same street, at the same time. Crossing paths. Recognizing each other, even, because that wasn't a given. Although you look the same, still pretty, and, um, like you."

Apparently Leena wasn't the only one who was drunk. She tried to forget that Eleanor called her pretty while still letting the word reverberate through her head.

They poured themselves out of the bar an hour later, Leena laughing at Eleanor's truly atrocious British accent.

"All right, love? Bangers and mash. Havin' a pint. Dingo . . . Nope, that's the wrong one. So now what, guv'nah?"

She thought of Dhaval's inquiring texts and her noncommittal smiley-face replies. "I could eat the fuck out of a pizza."

Eleanor guided them down Valencia to a hole-in-the-wall with bright-orange laminate booths and glaring overhead lighting. A television blared a soccer game in the background like white noise. She ordered a pie and a giant bottle of soda, and they waited.

Leena leaned against the glass case. "This is like a pizza party, like fourth grade. Like a roller-skating birthday party."

Eleanor nodded way more than was necessary. "I was fucking great at roller skating." She started skating a little in place, forcing her shoes to slip. She looked like an incredible fool, someone who didn't care if people noticed or had something to say. She did whatever she liked, straight from her gut. It went beyond admirable. Leena skated a little too. She needed more shenanigans in her life.

They brought the pizza to Eleanor's place. Leena remembered visiting her dorm room for the first time, soaking it up like an archaeologist. She felt the same now. Eleanor and Nasrin shared a studio, with end-of-day sunlight seeping in and covering their couch, their bed and the patchwork quilt draped over top, their large square table low to the ground. The apartment felt lived in. A home for two. It was so different from Dhaval's, which was new and lonely in comparison. Guilt set in behind her teeth that they were spread across two cities, instead of comfortable like this. They could blend too.

Eleanor threw the pizza box on the table. "Should we drink beer? Definitely or definitely? I'm getting it." She disappeared into the kitchen.

Leena perused the walls. A sketch of a naked woman's torso on tracing paper, pinned with a tack. A photo of Eleanor and a pretty, aloof dyke with short, curly hair and light brown skin, in a lush rainforest, each with an arm around the other's shoulders. Possibly Nasrin? Then possibly Nasrin, with her head covered in a scarf in front of a dramatic backdrop of ancient, squared-off ruins. A black-and-white photo of a Japanese family that must have belonged to Eleanor, that looked somehow familiar to her. A photo-booth strip of Eleanor and Nasrin: giving each other bunny ears, then hugging, then making out, then looking at each other with what looked like abundant affection and love. A photo of Eleanor surrounded by a gaggle of women, in what appeared to be a European city square. It warmed Leena's heart to see Eleanor's life splayed out like this. A life lived well. She could barely stop looking, even when Eleanor reappeared with four beers and the two-liter soda bottle in her arms.

"I'm like a drinks-carrying champ. I won't drop it. I won't. I won't."

Leena heard a concerning crack on the ground behind her.

"Fuck." Then: "It's okay! Drinks-carrying champ!"

She tore herself away from Eleanor's past and looked at her now, tearing into pizza and opening two brown bottles of beer.

The light steadily dimmed outside as they sat and ate and talked and drank. Leena felt good and heavy with booze in her bloodstream and pizza in her gut, and was similarly satisfied in her mind. Being with Eleanor was as if no time had passed at all. She could be comfortable. Literally. They sprawled out on the couch at opposite ends, backs against the armrests, facing each other. What was different was the flame of her attraction, which had been extinguished with time. Eleanor was cute, and had a certain frenetic, seductive energy that made Leena's pulse spike, but now she could appreciate that from a distance. The connection she felt, that she had needed without knowing it, was friendship. A friend.

Perhaps this melt of attraction was indicative of something larger, a straightforward answer to all of her romantic inconsistencies: she was not an overly sexual person. Dhaval didn't particularly light her up; here she was with someone who had once made her feel like she could combust during sex, and now there was barely a spark. As she aged, her sexuality was receding. It was a natural evolution. Maybe.

Leena nursed the end of her second beer, knowing she had overdone it with booze, but it was too late. She let herself be slow and semiconscious, nodding along to a story about Eleanor's postgraduation trip to Japan to see family. She was half listening, half processing, when the front door opened.

Eleanor grinned, looking toward the door. "Hiii!" She put her arms up in the shape of a V.

Leena swiveled her head, surprised to see a lithe, curveless woman walking toward them. Someone she'd never met, but had just seen in a rainforest, in a photo. Here in person she just looked gay, in tight jeans that hugged her frame and a fitted plaid shirt and a down vest. Aggressively gay. Leena couldn't stop staring. So this was the kind of woman Eleanor wanted. If she had ever been her type, she was no longer.

Nasrin sauntered up to the couch. "Hey, you must be Leena. I'm Nasrin." She held out her hand and shook Leena's with a firm, tight pump. Then she leaned down to Eleanor and kissed her with abandon. Like she was ravenous. Like they'd been apart for years.

Leena averted her eyes. It wasn't her business who Eleanor kissed, or how, or when, but she was happy when she saw Nasrin straighten up.

"Did you two have a good afternoon?" Nasrin pinned her question to Leena with a look.

Leena nodded, intimidated. There was something in the other woman's tone that made her feel unwelcome, and with which she agreed completely. This wasn't her space. It wasn't for her. It belonged to her ex-girlfriend and her new girlfriend.

"I should get going. It was nice to meet you, Nasrin." She searched for her sneakers, dizzy as she stood.

"You don't have to go. Stay!" Eleanor commanded, getting to her feet.

Nasrin sat on the floor and munched on a slice of cold pizza. "Babe, she said she has to go. But hey, Meow Mix is on Tuesday night. You should join us."

Leena's head was spinning. She needed to get out. "Yeah, sounds good. Um. Thanks, Eleanor. It was great." She caught her brown eyes and smiled, nodding, then left quickly, closing the apartment door behind her. She paused in the hallway, eyes shut as her pulse raced. She looked around the deserted, dim hallway then headed down the stairs, overly careful with her drunk body as she descended a flight, rounding the landing toward another. *Steady, steady.* Finally she was downstairs and out through the glass front door. Once she was on the sidewalk, she took a breath of the air that must have chilled as afternoon turned to night. She stood at the corner of Valencia and Sixteenth, not sure what to do.

He picked up on the second ring. "Leena. Are you okay? I haven't heard from you since you sent that winky face." He sounded so serious when he said *winky face.*

She laughed, hard. "I'm sorry. I'm so sorry."

"Where are you?"

She looked up again, confirming. "Valencia and Sixteenth."

"I'm going to call you a car. Stay put."

She sighed, hearing him gone. While she made it to the Lexington on her own, now in the dark she felt helpless. Stranded. Drunk. She watched people walk down the street. Alone, in couples, in groups. She wondered where they were going. Dinner plans? Drinks?

Home to their boyfriends? Her phone rang in her hand.

"It's on its way. Listen, I'm not mad, but it was all day, and I didn't hear from you. I was worried."

She sighed into the phone. She wished she was magically back at the apartment. "I lost track of time. I'm sorry."

"It's not like you."

An ordinary car pulled up and the driver rolled down his window. "Are you Dhaval?"

"No? But that's my boyfriend? He called?"

"Technically he used the app, but yep. Hop on in."

She was so confused about what was going on, but wrote it off. *Tech. Whatever.* She got in, and her stomach lurched as the car took off. Most of the drinking had been poorly executed, but that last beer had been a particularly bad idea. It was too late now. "Can I go?" she mumbled into the phone, remembering Dhaval was still there. "You can continue to lecture me in person."

"No, honey, that's not—I didn't mean—just come home."

She nodded. "Working on it." She hung up, looking out as the buildings passed, ignoring a call from her mom. As the city passed in a blur, she thought of her day, and of Eleanor. So fun and carefree, a jaunt through an earlier time. She sobered incrementally in front of Dhaval's building and walked gradually toward his apartment. Eleanor was the past. So was the person Leena had been. That's where they both belonged.

WAKING UP THE next morning was violent, her throat dry and her stomach in turmoil and the light blasting in, hitting her eyes. Her first thought was: *Vomiting would be preferable right now.* But everything in her body stayed, to fester and rot. She dragged the blankets up over her head.

Dhaval yanked them down, pressing a kiss to her temple. "Gotta go, but I'll leave work early."

"Good. I'll try not to die." She grabbed his pillow to block out the brightness.

She heard him laugh mirthlessly. "You did this to yourself!"

From under the covers in her spinning stupor, she was grateful for one thing: Dhaval's grace. The night before when she'd dropped on his couch, he'd only been understanding, more concerned with her safety and well-being than anything else. He was great. He was better than waves of nausea.

She woke later to a text from Eleanor: **Yesterday was suuuuuuch a blast. Lunch? I know a great place. Meet me by work?**

Leena left her phone in the bedroom, stumbling to the kitchen for a glass of water and then to the bathroom, rifling through cabinets to find any kind of pain reliever with ibuprofen in it. She sat on the cool tile with her back against the wall, three pills chased by a gulp of water, then another. *Lunch with Eleanor. More time with Eleanor.* Last night she had sworn to herself that the past was the past, but spending the day with an old friend had been time travel to a lighter, freer time.

There wasn't anything wrong with lunch. She had to eat. Dhaval was at work. She had no schedule. What could it hurt? After she struggled to her feet and went back to the bedroom, she replied: **I think I can make it. Let me know where and when to meet you!**

She trudged through the dreariness of her hangover, wincing, showering, caffeinating, and eating a piece of white toast. She pulled on clothes, threw on sunglasses, and was out the door.

Outside the restaurant, a hazy sky hung over her head as she waited, hands jammed in her pockets as it grew chilly. She could have sworn it was sunny a few minutes ago. Everything seemed so much brighter with her hangover. Her eyes drifted from squat building to squat building, so different from New York. Here in this neighborhood, there was so much sky. While she waited, she finally called home.

"Hi, Beta. I saw it was you on the caller ID. Such wonderful technology. How is your trip?"

Her grandmother's voice was almost a cure for the headache beating in her temples, her measured tone that sounded like a thousand bedtime stories. "Ba! Hi! It's going great. How are you?"

"The one time I traveled to San Francisco, I went to the Alcatraz. It seemed very secure. Have you been to the Alcatraz?"

"I have not been to the Alcatraz," she replied, trying her best to stifle the smile in her voice.

"Oh, you should go. You must," her grandmother said in a rush. "You take a boat to an island. It is magnificent."

"Thanks, Ba." She closed her eyes for a second, thinking of afternoons after school with her grandmother, eating chaat and drinking soda and doing homework. Ba had read everything already and always had something to say about her English class: *Great Expectations* is sad and grimy. I don't know why you're not reading *Pride and Prejudice*. It has everything.

A clever girl, romance, scandal, family expectations. Like my growing up in India! What is wrong with your school?"

Leena felt a bop on her nose and opened her eyes, panicked. Eleanor stood in front of her, grinning, bright in her jacket against the dreary day.

"Ba, I have to go. Can you tell my mom that I called?"

"Of course. Have a wonderful time, Beta."

"Bye." She pocketed her phone. "Hi. Sorry."

Eleanor shrugged, leading them toward the door and inside the bustling café with exposed wood beams. "Sorry I'm late," Eleanor said as they joined the line. "I really like the kale pesto chicken wrap, but the tuna and avocado sandwich is fucking awesome."

"Weren't you a vegetarian?" Leena asked, the mix of flavors a revolting nightmare in the wake of her hangover. She pursed her lips.

Eleanor's eyes went wide and she smiled sheepishly. "Yeah, I was. But I wasn't healthy at all. French fries over . . . French green beans. So. I eat meat, but you know, only good ones. Organic, ethically raised. Are you still a vegetarian?"

Leena nodded. "It's religious." Religious to her mother. "Cultural, I guess. It's more than what I eat."

Eleanor nodded back seriously, thoughtfully, getting a look that Leena had seen on many non-Indian faces. "Yeah, I get that. You have a different connection, because of Hinduism, and reincarnation, and animals. Yeah, I get it." She radiated patient pluralism.

Leena bit her lip, smiling. "Yeah, you get it? All those years of classes at the local temple? Praying with your grandma at home?" It was exhilarating to tease her like this. She had been careful when they were dating. She could be more herself now, unguarded.

They moved up in line.

Eleanor shook her head. "I just mean, I guess, that I—" She looked at Leena with trepidation in her eyes, a timid whisper of a smile on her lips. "I made it weird. I really shat the bed on that one. I'm sorry."

Leena's face cracked into a grin. She grabbed for Eleanor's elbow, briefly squeezing it. A gesture to say: *It's okay.*

They ate at the reclaimed-wood counter, on stools tucked in close together. Leena ate a veggie burger that tasted flat. They talked: Nasrin, Dhaval, the health-care debate. The best gin and tonic in New York City. Eleanor's crush on Rachel Maddow. They talked so much that Leena was exhausted, unaccustomed to this level of interchange. There didn't seem to be a ceiling. When they finished their meal and returned their trays, Leena ambled outside with Eleanor, ready to say goodbye.

"I sort of 'went home sick' today," Eleanor admitted with air quotes. "Do you . . . want to hang out?" She looked hopeful, nervous.

Leena was at once incredulous at such slackerism and flattered to be the one for whom Eleanor was taking the time. The push and pull of those things formed her answer. "Yeah. Let's do it. But, coffee?"

They wandered like it was six years ago in Boston. Only Leena wasn't trying to be cool, or battling a complex tangle of feelings. So much time had passed. So much geography traversed and transformed. They were both so different now. Leena and Eleanor walked up and down slopes crowded with scaling houses and emerged from pockets of shadow, climbing to meet bright, clean sun.

"I'm not, like, always playing hooky," Eleanor said. "This was a special occasion. You're visiting. But, I guess, sometimes I don't want to be there. I just feel like they don't trust me. I can't get a break. I can do more, I can handle more. It's frustrating when my bosses and the senior team don't see that."

It was almost verbatim what Eleanor said to her at the Lex. Leena found it irksome when people repeated themselves, with brains too messy to recall whom they'd talked to about what. But being a friend, if that's what they even were to each other, was about support. "I get what you're saying. That's so frustrating," Leena replied. "But it sounds like a good job and a great organization. You just need to be there a little longer." She tightened her ponytail, tugging at her hair in two handfuls and forcing the band toward her scalp.

Eleanor shook her head. "I wish it was that easy." She crossed the street, heading up the incline, sloping up and up toward the sky.

Leena followed behind, speeding to catch up. "You can do it. I'm sure you can. You've done impressive work already. You're . . . taking on the world, taking responsibility for what's broken."

They were again in stride, at each other's side. Eleanor brightened, nodding. "I am. There's this thing in Judaism—I'm Jewish, did you know that? Did we ever talk about that? Anyway, I'm Jewish, and there's this thing, tikkun olam, which means, to repair the world through good acts and deeds. There's lots of reasons that I do what I do, like my family's histories and what they've been through, that whole World War Two thing." She scoffed to herself. "That's an understatement. *That thing.* That terrible, horrible thing of fleeing on one side and internment on the other. But. I'm also inspired by repairing what's broken."

Leena didn't know what to say. Despite her lackluster adherence to every tenet and principle, religion had taught her that actions mattered to who you were going to be, and doing good was imperative for a prosperous life. She watched family and friends interpret this in their own ways, but for her it was about a life of purpose. Serving communities, as she had hoped to do after graduation, by helping them become and stay healthy. Doing what she could with what she had. She agreed with Eleanor about how to use their breathing hours on Earth, to use their energy toward a better future. She caught her breath and scanned the row houses crammed together, the stunning views of the city below, and looked to the grand sweep of the bay, of rolling hills beyond it. She felt simultaneously small and like the world couldn't contain her. She turned to Eleanor. "This is stunning. This is how you grew up?"

Eleanor took in the view too. "I grew up in the suburbs, with houses that all look the same, malls. This is something else." She started walking down the hill and Leena followed, careful on the decline. "This is where I choose to be."

"When I think about California, this is what I think of," Leena said with a sweep of her arm. "Wide-open spaces and possibility. Arnold Schwarzenegger is your governor, which is weird, but anything is possible here. That's a kind of magic. You can be anything." Which was alluring even as it was frightening. To be free and limitless. No boundaries. She could not fathom it.

They paused to cross a street. A biker struggled up the hill and quit, walking the rest of the way.

"Because I'm from here it holds none of that romance." Eleanor shook her head. "California is my parents, my grandmother, my stuck-up aunt, traffic, subdivisions. My awkward-as-fuck teenage years. Where you're from is always fraught. It can be mythical, or whatever you said, but it's also a place where people live and fall out of love and buy groceries. Like, I used to feel that way about New England. Foliage and sweaters and old money, and smart, liberal people who love the Kennedys. It just had the air for me of a place where you could triumph. Be better. I thought it was those things, but I lived there for four years, and certainly that was just a place too."

"Massachusetts, to me—except for my family—is white kids in classes talking loudly about immigrants taking their parents' jobs. And using racist accents gleaned from *The Simpsons*, as if that was clever." Her memory stretched and burned. She winced.

Eleanor rolled her eyes and shook her head. "Kids are the worst. And adults. Everyone."

She still rolls her eyes, she noted. *Like a bored teenager.*

"Last year I was by myself, it was late, and I was on the Muni platform waiting for my train. These two drunk bro motherfuckers kept screaming 'CHINK' at me." Her face scrunched, incredulous. "Like, first of all, be creative. And I'm not even Chinese, so, inaccurate."

"So, what did you do?"

Eleanor snorted. "Well, I, too, was a bit wasted." She grimaced. "So I yelled back that they should fuck off, or fuck each other, or their mothers."

163

Leena's eyes went wide. "And then what?"

Eleanor grimaced. "They yelled more, and then they chased me, and they only stopped because one of them fell. I got onto a train; my heart was beating so fucking fast."

Leena's mouth opened. She would have never done that. She would have kept to herself, made herself smaller, and tried to stay safe. Drunk racist men were not worth provoking. And yet, she felt proud of Eleanor for being so reckless. "You're really brave."

"I'm really stupid too, but thanks. I better stop hanging out with you. I'm going to get a very inflated sense of self, worse than I have now."

Leena knew Eleanor was joking, but a current of dejection raced through her body. Her eyes caught gratefully on a café down the hill next to a construction site, and she made a beeline toward caffeine. "There's also the run-of-the-mill stuff," Leena offered. "I'm sure you get that too."

Eleanor looked intrigued as she held the door open for them.

"People always tell me about their favorite Indian restaurant, or about their cousin who went to Goa for two weeks."

"I know exactly what you mean. Everyone has an awesome Asian girlfriend they can't wait for me to meet," Eleanor said, eyes flashing with annoyance, but perhaps something else too. A shared camaraderie. "And people think it's hilarious that I'm not good at math."

They put in their orders.

"I mean, you are pretty bad at math," Leena said under her breath, and it made Eleanor explode with peals of laughter, so bouncing and inviting that Leena couldn't help but join her.

While waiting on their drinks at the counter, Leena felt her pocket buzz. It was a text from Dhaval, leaving work early as promised. She wasn't ready to say good-bye, and she weighed her options as they waited on their coffees: inviting Eleanor to Dhaval's or blowing Dhaval off entirely to spend more time with Eleanor. As they went outside, Leena blew on her drip coffee and made an impetuous decision. "You should meet Dhaval. You should come over."

Eleanor sipped her soy cappuccino, her eyes hooded. "You sure?"

"No," she said, laughing. She shrugged. "It just came to mind. It's only if you're okay with it." She shocked herself when she realized the other side of what she had proposed. "But he doesn't know. About us. He doesn't know . . . you know."

"That you were a raging homosexual?" Eleanor's tone was joking, but Leena could see concern in her eyes.

Leena started to feel like this was a bad idea. "First of all, I don't know that I was raging anything? But he doesn't know that I dated women. I said you were a friend from school."

Eleanor didn't reply. Leena watched the parade of random people file by, men with thick beards, pasty male nerds in impractical shorts and flip-flops, families with distantly but distinctly Asian faces. The last vestiges of sun appeared as the clouds parted, the sun on its way to setting.

Eleanor finished weighing whatever was heavy in her brain, and she nodded. "No."

The nod threw her off. "No?"

Eleanor played with the fringe of her scarf, shoulders frozen in a shrug. "Yeah, I don't know, I don't think I could, like, pretend. That's just not me."

Leena felt her own face fall from that heavy indictment. She nodded numbly. "I need to get home to Dhav. Where should I . . . ?"

Eleanor wrinkled her nose. "You're mad. I can tell."

She shook her head. "No, not at all. It's fine, but I have to go."

Eleanor's eyes went round, planets in orbit, and she clapped a warm hand to Leena's wrist. Her gaze pierced and Leena wished to be anywhere else, somewhere without searing pressure. "I'm sure he's as great as you say, he'd have to be, but I don't think I should meet him. Not like this."

Leena didn't care if they ever met. It didn't matter. Eleanor had it wrong, simplifying the situation into a digestible tablet. The truth was much more fractal. "Okay." And she smiled, hoping to kill this conversation where it stood.

Eleanor seemed satisfied, looping an arm through hers. She put Leena on a bus headed to Dhaval's with a hug, then waved from the sidewalk.

Leena was not as satisfied, uneasy in the last strands of what had otherwise been a good day. The bus darted then inched through a tunnel, a Chinatown that looked like every other, past construction downtown and tall buildings. Closer to his neighborhood, she began to see the arc of three cranes in the sky. More construction. This was a city in formation, crafting who it would be.

Dhaval greeted her at the door with a kiss. Arms like an octopus, drawing her in. Safety in his embrace.

"Do you want a beer?" He led her inside.

"Yeah. No. I don't know." She sat on the couch, feeling the way she did that one time she smoked pot with Neha. Like her head was detached, floating above her shoulders. "How was your day?"

He joined her on the couch with a beer in one hand and a glass in the other. "Just in case you want to split. Uh, it was good!" He scrubbed his face with two bare hands. "I always feel a little glazed over at the end of the day. All that staring at a screen. How are you? You met up with a friend?"

"She used to be a friend," she replied stiffly and quickly. Defensive. "We knew each other in college."

"How'd you meet?"

Her mind wove a lie: *We met in a class. We hung out a few times.* The truth wasn't that much more interesting. What she could remember, at least. A dining hall, a shared meal, something about street harassment. A lecture? She couldn't remember if they met through someone or bumped into each other and struck up conversation. If it had been more important, she would have remembered. "We met in a psych class. We hung out for a semester."

"And she lives here now?"

Leena took him up on that beer, chugging the hoppy brew from the bottle. "Yeah. She's from here." She suppressed a burp.

"Where does she live?"

"In the Mission." She wished she felt drunk already, loose and relaxed. No such luck.

"Oh, nearby. That's cool. We should all hang out." He rubbed a hand over her knee. "Double date? Assuming she has a boyfriend."

Leena shifted in her seat. "Nope, no boyfriend. You ask a lot of questions."

He let out a stout laugh. "Is this a lot of questions? It's just a normal conversation."

More beer down her throat. It wasn't a normal conversation for her, doing backflips around her past and present. "Feels like you're interrogating me."

He shook his head in even swings. "I want to know about your day, about your life, about your friends, because I'm your boyfriend and I'm curious about everything Leena."

She stood, arms over her chest. "Yeah, but you don't get to, like, own me." An unfamiliar wave crested above her head. She felt bereft, and mad at Dhaval. She turned away from him, making her way to the kitchen. For—something, she would figure out what. She rummaged through the cabinets and, unsurprisingly, found them bare. Save for packets of ramen, like some joke.

"Leena."

She turned around and saw his plaintive face.

"What's the matter?"

"Nothing." She slammed the cabinets.

"Clearly something is wrong."

"She doesn't have a boyfriend," she snapped, spinning back around, venom spiking hot in her veins. "She's gay. She has a girlfriend. I can't believe you'd be that homophobic." Anger churned inexplicably inside of her with bright, cold licks.

Dhaval held up his hands in surrender. "Whoa. What the hell did I do?" He rose, moving closer. "I don't know where this is coming from. I don't know why you'd automatically assume that about me. I just, like, asked my girlfriend a question and then got accused of a hate crime." His normally sunny face twisted. He looked like a petulant baby.

Leena shook her head, crossing her arms tightly. "I need to be alone."

Dhaval didn't reply as she entered his bedroom and closed the door.

She snapped out of it almost immediately, feeling deep remorse for the person she had just been. She sank into a seat at the edge of the bed, foolish and alone. Marooned on an island by her own hand.

Eleanor had told the truth. About how she felt, about the moment, about Leena. *I don't think I could pretend. That's not me.* Leena valued accuracy and empirical evidence, but only in the physical realm. As it related to feelings and the inner workings of brains and hearts, she reasoned that not everything she thought or did needed an audience.

So much for being impetuous. So much for letting a spark of an idea come to fruition. She wished she had never asked Eleanor to meet Dhaval.

With a cooler head, breath came in and out like a calm tide. But she still wasn't ready to call a truce. With her hand on her phone, she dialed her parents.

This time it was her dad. "I heard you haven't gone to Alcatraz yet!"

She laughed hard, surprised. "What is it with you guys and Alcatraz?"

"It was just so memorable. Anyway. How is Neha? How is Dhaval? How is your trip? Are you getting ready for the semester?"

She sunk back on the bed, her body molding into the memory foam. "My trip is great! I caught up with an old friend from college. We've been hanging out. That's been fun." She cleared her throat, having forgotten his other questions. "I am reading for the semester, but just some recommended reading. I finished the requirements for the first day."

"Of course you did." She heard a burst of pride in his voice. "And how is Dhaval? How is my man?"

Her father's love for Dhaval could not be contained. He was fascinated with Dhaval's technical skill in both hardware and software, and thought he was a genius when he hooked up their printer to function wirelessly. Her dad was known to print unnecessarily and marvel at the results.

She sighed. "Your man is good. He's probably playing video games."

"He has to keep his mind sharp, Beta. How else will he do it? Okay, I have to go, thanks for—"

"Wait! I need to talk to Mom too. She's been calling, and I know how this works." Her mother's panic when she didn't receive the required quantity of communication from her children was notorious.

"You're right about that. Okay, hold on."

She heard him call for her mother and walk the cordless device to her. He had probably been in the living room, her mother in the kitchen cleaning up from dinner. She could almost smell the house, fragrant from cooking, and see the lights on overhead, and for a second she felt the pinch of missing her childhood home.

"Leena. Are you okay? What's happened?"

The missing only lasted a second. "Yes, Mom, I'm okay. The time difference makes it really difficult to call you back." She stood, putting her back to the wall.

This was supposed to be relaxing, grounding. She found it lacking.

"What am I doing that you couldn't interrupt, eh? You're traveling by yourself, you're young."

Leena stifled a laugh in her twenty-six-year-old mouth. "I'm not alone. I'm with Dhaval. And, uh, Neha," Leena added, quickly recovering.

She heard her mother exhale. "Beta, I know you're a good girl. You just need to keep it that way."

It was an intricate threat that indicted her, Dhaval, premarital sex, pregnancy, and marriage, and hinted at a potential shame that could engulf her family. Her mother's ability to communicate volumes in just a few words had been painstakingly honed over the years.

Leena had also been honing skills. "I've been spending most of my time with an old college friend, Eleanor. She's half-Asian."

She could hear her mother sniff her approval. There was nothing else for her to say. "That's good. Are you eating enough?"

"Always."

Once her mother was reassured, Leena proceeded to coax her off the phone. She sighed. She had to leave the bedroom at some point. Before she went, she sent a text: **See you two tomorrow night! Looking forward to Meow Mix!**

"WHERE IS IT again? What's going on? I could come for a little bit."

She was concentrating on applying eyeliner, her only concession to makeup. Dhaval leaned against the doorframe in the bathroom. There was a hairline fracture still between them, only awful if she thought about it. So she avoided it like the bubonic plague.

"Um. Yeah, I don't know. It's kind of a girls' night thing."

He shifted, crossing his arms. He didn't say anything, which said enough.

Her eyes were done but she wasn't ready to turn and look at him quite yet. She pretended like there were touch-ups to do.

"Leena, you came to visit me. I just want to spend time with you. I wanna, like, go to bars, come home, and have sex, be a normal couple. For once. Why can't we do that?"

She capped her eyeliner pencil and gazed down into the bowl of the sink. This messy energy between them was so unusual. Normally they were in sync. A match. There was nothing to explain.

"And you won't even talk to me. Leena, what is going on?"

Being apart was easier. Being in the same space meant she was accountable to another person. She hadn't realized how suffocating that squeeze would feel.

"I hate when you do this," he muttered under his breath, sounding wounded and small. "Go quiet. And you're not here. Even when you are here, you're somewhere else."

Her heart cinched. The things circling her head like a nimbus cloud were not things he wanted to know. She was almost sure of that.

"You know what? Go," he said, his voice rough. "Have your girls' night. I will . . . see you later. I guess."

Her frustration bubbled and brewed on the bus ride and as she arrived at the bar. She tried to tell herself that it didn't matter. She mattered. What mattered was that now she could focus on drinking, dancing, and slipping away from the quotidian confines that held her in check.

She took in the space: a large, square room with dark, red-tinted lighting. And: women. They were leaning on the bar's edge toward the bartender, clustered around the room, or bravely and terribly dancing in groups of three. She joined the bar-leaners and checked her phone. No new texts, emails, calls. She ordered a gin and tonic, and as she waited for it and Eleanor, her gaze traveled over her fellow bar patrons: Black women with natural hair wearing heels and tight skirts, dykey Latina women looking dapper, and sturdy white women in plaid. She'd put these women into boxes at the Lex, feeling self-conscious and set apart. But now she took these women in with fresh, open eyes, and saw that she was one of them. Straight or gay or bi or queer, they were women in a women's space. Maybe there was even a woman like her here: someone with a past, who was solid in their present, and trying to make peace with who they'd been. Leena felt her body relax, to think she could breathe easy here and simply exist.

"Hey!" It was Eleanor, and Nasrin, who each kissed both of Leena's cheeks with breezy, impersonal affection. Eleanor looked dykier than she had previously. Gone were the dresses and tights, and in their place were jeans and a button-down shirt, as if she had dressed for the occasion and location.

Eleanor introduced a third woman, Joan Liu. She

pointed at Leena, "My ex," and then at Joan, "Nasrin's ex."

Joan laughed. "This is so gay."

Leena observed her uneven teeth first, their braceless legacy, her cute smile. Her gaze pulled back and swept quickly, with one brush of her eyes, along Joan's short, black hair and blazer and tight-fitting jeans and bare ankles. Then she cut herself off from further perusal of Joan's person, beautiful though it was. She took a deep, controlled breath and smiled at her new acquaintance.

Leena drank her gin and tonic, then got another. By then the music had kicked up and women were dancing in couples and groups. Their quartet went to the dance floor, and she danced and danced. It was like breathing. Innate. Hopping around her bedroom with her sister, then formal dance lessons with other Indian kids. Performing at family and friends' weddings, dancing in bars. Dancing was when she trusted her body entirely to do as it would. She never questioned herself.

A hydration break with Joan turned into shots at the bar, a something Nipple, a name that was meant to be gross and provocative, and it burned going down, sweet when it was over. She felt loose and impervious to gravity, her back to the wooden bar. She watched Eleanor and Nasrin dance, their bodies tight together, Nasrin plastered to Eleanor's back.

"Why aren't you and Nasrin still together?" Leena asked, the words slipping out of her mouth as she turned her head toward Joan.

Joan tilted her face away, in lovely profile, and Leena thought she was considering her question, but then she ducked back, close, with her mouth at Leena's ear.

"What?" she asked over the din.

Leena repeated her question louder.

Joan's cheeks tinged pink—from blushing or from Asian glow, Leena wasn't sure. "It wasn't meant to be. But she's a friend now, and I think Eleanor is great. Plus, it was forever ago. Like, two years ago. How about you and Eleanor? Why didn't you work out?"

Leena considered those questions with as much clarity as she could muster. "Shit. I didn't realize you'd ask that."

Joan laughed, tossing her head back with abandon. It was cute. When Joan's gaze settled back on Leena, she licked her lips, then her eyes strayed to Leena's mouth. It was so overt. In a split second, Leena decided she didn't mind.

"We were young. We only dated for a few months. We didn't have time to work out." It was a brutally uncomplicated answer, but it felt honest. She couldn't remember everything, but she remembered great kisses, good sex, laughter, connection. Their time together had held promise. But it didn't matter anymore.

"I'm just getting over my own thing that didn't work," Joan said. "I'm so done with drama. And I'm happy to be single." She smiled, her face briefly bathed in the shifting colored lights that roamed the space. "It's a great time to meet new people. See who's out there. I just feel really open to whatever happens next. To whoever I meet."

Leena felt the gentle drill of Joan's focus. Her gaze tightening. It was thrilling to be under someone's watchful eye, someone who was doing advanced trigonometric analysis to predict what would happen next, but it also felt dangerous.

Dancing. Dancing was always the answer, never talking, and she dragged Joan to the dance floor. The liquor in her body was an elixir, her limbs even looser than usual. Joan was in front of her, full of fervor, bopping with confidence. Then she slowed her pace. She was within kissing distance and Leena's body thrummed with lust. What would be so bad about it, in the dark of this club, where no one could see? Where this moment could be hers alone? This recklessness felt too good. Leena leaned in, so little her body barely moved, and kissed her.

It was a good kiss. Soft, a gentle press of lips, but insistent, like the next would be even better. She barely had time to feel the second kiss before hearing Eleanor's voice over the thumping bass.

"Whoa whoa, Joan."

She felt out of her body as Eleanor yanked them apart, her hand cuffed at Leena's bicep.

"What the actual fuck. She has a boyfriend. She's basically engaged."

But Leena was no docile drunk. She shrugged Eleanor off with a roll of her shoulders. To Joan she argued, "Not engaged. And sexuality is fluid."

"Ugh, gross," Eleanor interjected.

Joan was appraising Leena, scrutinizing her. "When I said I was open, it wasn't for kissing a straight girl."

Hearing those words, she felt a clarity that she lacked only seconds ago. *I shouldn't have kissed her.* She had sharper words for Eleanor. "You don't know me anymore. You don't know my life. Go spend time with your wife. I don't need a babysitter." What she needed was air. She charged toward the exit, shaking her head. Once outside, she tipped her head back against the brick wall behind her. She was starting to feel woozy.

"Hey!"

Leena didn't turn when she heard Eleanor's voice.

"You're right, Leena. I . . . I don't know you anymore. But I can't imagine your boyfriend would be cool with you, like, scissoring with a woman on the dance floor."

Leena snorted. "Scissoring." Her amusement transformed into a bitter taste in her mouth. "Why do you care? We haven't seen each other in years. You live in San Francisco. You have a hot girlfriend. You work at a magical gay baby organization. You have your queerness on lock. Why does mine matter? I feel like I'm going to be sick."

With all of the alcohol catching up to her, she stepped down to the curb, taking a seat with her head between her legs as the world spun around her. She didn't want to throw up like some drunk college sophomore at a party, and yet purging some of this awfulness that she felt, emotionally and physically, would be a gift. When she looked up, Eleanor was nowhere to be found, and that only made her feel worse. She rested her elbows on her knees, her chin in her hands. Somehow she managed to turn a nice girls' night out into a monstrosity of guilt and nausea. Dhaval didn't deserve this, and now Eleanor had walked away too.

While she fumbled for her phone to try and call a cab, Eleanor dropped down at her side, handing off a bottle of water.

"It's you!" Leena exclaimed. She was so relieved to see her, and reached out to hug her, holding on tight.

"Drink some water," Eleanor urged, untangling from Leena's embrace.

"Water! Oh my god, you're the best." Here was another person that she didn't deserve, someone to come and interfere, and care. To have her back.

Leena chugged half the bottle in one long gulp, then offered it to Eleanor, who declined. She looked out onto the dark street as cars occasionally whisked past. The night was turning cold. She zipped her jacket all the way up, then crossed her arms.

"I really fucking liked you," Eleanor said in a small voice, her head lowered. "I thought we could work. I liked you so much."

From Eleanor's face in profile, Leena could see enough. She looked terrified. Leena thought of the apology from days ago, when Eleanor said they weren't serious, and now here she was going back on her word. Being vulnerable. Letting Leena in. She grasped for Eleanor's hand, which was soft and damp. "I really fucking liked you too." They sat so close, but there was difference and time and distance between them. There had been so much she had wanted and didn't know how to get. She could have burst at the seams with longing for the lives she could have led. Now all she craved was the feeling of solid ground. Safety. An adult life. To keep her focus away from the stray, loose ends of her life. A car blared past, noisy with music and engine trouble, and she watched it pass by. "I want us to be friends again."

Eleanor slipped her hand free, hugging herself. A flurry of air made her loose hair swing. "In that case, as your friend . . ." Eleanor paused, looking like she was revving up for what would come next. "Leena, what are you doing with a man?"

Leena leaned back, averting her gaze. She wished she could puke, right now, to detour this conversation. "I don't want to do this."

"Well, we are. Tough shit. What do you really want?" Eleanor asked, undeterred.

What a wide-open question, broad, scary in its scope. A question that assumed that what she wanted mattered. "A mountain of chocolate soft-serve frozen yogurt."

Eleanor groaned, and Leena reconsidered the question itself. What she wanted in her heart, in the deepest parts of her, was still unknown, because she wasn't accustomed to asking herself such questions. Even as she pondered it now, she couldn't hover near an answer. She told Eleanor what she told herself: "Women never worked out, not really. Dhaval is a good guy. And my family likes him." She thought of her dad's admiration, and Ba's elation when Dhaval visited. She was proud of her honest selection, of her ability to find someone she could bring home who wasn't anything like window dressing.

Another sigh sounded from beside Leena, this one aggravated and sharp. "Okay, but, like, you're really gay."

She thought about Noa. How her fingers had carded through Noa's short, dark, curly hair. Their shared passion. Their fights during their sex droughts. How Noa would get aggressive and pushy, picking every battle, and how Leena was powerless against her. She lost herself. It wasn't going to happen again.

"I don't know what I am. But this is my life as it's unfolded. I want to have a family and live a life where I make my mark. The rest doesn't matter as much."

Eleanor scoffed. "You know two dykes can have

179

babies? Like, it's possible? There's more than one way to get to any end point."

Leena felt a dull spike of annoyance start to form in her chest. "I don't know what to say." She looked at Eleanor, face to face, right into her dark eyes. This was going to be it for them. If Eleanor couldn't accept this about her, then they would be done before they'd begun again.

Eleanor stared right back, but there was no sharpness in her face. She looked kind, caring. She nodded, putting an arm around Leena. "So let's be friends, Lee."

Her heart glowed warm over that, even when Joan and Nasrin came stumbling out and it was awkward, even when she was back at Dhaval's throwing up at four a.m.

Despite whatever emotional property Leena had destroyed, or any semipermanent marks she'd left, he stroked her hair when she got back into bed and whispered his offer of help.

He was a sunburst in a dark room. She gripped the side of his face with one hand. "I'm sorry," she croaked, wrung out. "I love you." She was recommitted to him. More than ever. "My head wasn't on straight." She laughed at her unintentional phrasing.

He kissed her hair and told her it wasn't funny. She completely agreed.

LEENA GAVE HER liver a break. She set off early in the morning and watched the sea lions at Fisherman's Wharf for a good half hour, their massive bodies in shades of brown, like floating fields of mushy rocks.

She took off for Alcatraz on the ferry after that, because apparently she would not be welcomed home without having gone. Since it was a beautiful day with blue skies and a green-glass sea, the boat ride was lovely—but then the island was just a museum. Old and weathered buildings from another era. On the audio tour, filing through narrow hallways and cells stacked toward the roof, she felt claustrophobic in the dim atmosphere.

That night, while she and Dhaval ate Goan takeout for dinner, she regaled him with educational highlights from the day. The Native Americans who occupied the island. The prisoners who possibly, but not probably, escaped via the cold waters of the San Francisco Bay.

He nudged her foot with his. "The way you sounded just now. Like you're planning your escape."

She shook her head, grinning. "Are you kidding? I'm too smart to risk freezing water."

He took hold of her chin and kissed her, chicken xacuti on his breath, and she let him, content with him. Happy, even. She kissed back.

The next day she checked more things off her list: the intersection of Powell and Market to watch a cable car turn and trundle back from whence it came. Alamo Square, famous for the Painted Ladies Victorian houses that bordered the park and were featured prominently in the *Full House* opening credits, burned into her mind over years of watching endless reruns as a child. She settled on a bench, people-watching as clouds crossed a sky heading toward sunset.

An Indian couple taking their engagement photos swung into view with their photographer snapping behind. The woman was in heels and a red dress, belted at the waist and full in the skirt. Her fiancé was in a matching red shirt and blue jeans. This seemed to always be the case: women dressed up, dressed well, and men barely looking a match. They posed awkwardly, plastic smiles on their faces, as the photographer walked them through a battery of standard poses: him holding her, arms around her waist. Kissing, holding hands. Kissing, dipping her backward. Walking away holding hands, looking back at the photographer over their shoulders.

In her ideal, there would be no photo shoots, no spectacle, no attention. Her wedding would be about her and Dhaval, and no one else—until her mother inevitably interceded and made demands requiring pleading and compromise. They would likely settle with no mehndi party, a low-key sangeet, and a guest list under two hundred. The baraat would have dancing, but no theatrics. No horse-drawn carriages or helicopters.

Her wedding would be a public affair, one for her parents to brag about, to show off at, to announce that they had succeeded as good parents. Her marriage, which was far more interesting, would have substance. In Dhaval she had a partner, a friend with whom she could grow old and have a full life with, way past the bang-pop-fizz of a wedding.

A text came in from Eleanor: **We're doing dinner with Tomás tonight. I kno it's last minute but would be great to see you agan. Join us!!** Then: **Both of you!!**

She considered Eleanor's pledge to be her friend. Perhaps this was a way to demonstrate that commitment. A group dinner, typical of friends. With girlfriends and boyfriends invited. She hoped that meant no, or limited, weirdness. That Eleanor would be on her best behavior. Since she wanted it to be true, she decided it could be, and texted back that they'd be there.

Rereading Eleanor's text, she saw Tomás's name. She had almost forgotten about him. He was one of the first gay men she'd ever spent dedicated time with, and had always enjoyed seeing him. His endless, cacophonous cheer. She was still smiling at the message when another text came in, this one from Dhaval.

Hey leaving now. See you at Montgomery st bart.

Ok, she replied. **What do you think of dinner with some of my college friends?**

Yes definitely! Sounds great! came back almost instantaneously. **See? The Bay Area is great for you. You already have friends here.**

He wasn't wrong. She did have a friend here now, and that made San Francisco a better prospect. Her mind drifted toward weekly dinners and grabbing lunch and hanging out on the weekends. A friend who knew her well.

Outside of the Montgomery BART station, people bustled past her. It reminded her of Midtown Manhattan, only with wider streets and more drifting wafts of weed. She felt two arms grab her from behind, jolting her nervous system, and she twisted quickly to see, reassured, that it was Dhaval. Annoyance ran through her veins. "That's not a good way to approach a woman."

He put his hands over his heart. "I'll do better next time." Earnestness on his face was replaced with what looked like a scheming smile. "I wanna show you something." He tugged on her hand and led her through the streets, buildings dense together with little sunlight shining through. Outside a pair of gilded doors, he stopped and kissed her cheek, and led her in. An upscale jewelry store. She gulped as he rounded them toward a display case full of diamond rings that caught light and glittered.

He turned to her, leaning on one side against the case. "I've been talking to your sister, to get her advice, but I wanted you to look at some options before I, well . . ." He dropped her hand and spread his arms wide. "Whatever you want. I want you to have what you want. I can afford it." He smiled meekly but expectantly.

She looked in. So many rings, most in platinum, or at least not yellow gold. Round-cut diamonds. Princess cut. Cushion. Oval. Radiant. Pear. She had learned these words when her sister was ring obsessed and was disappointed that they'd remained in her memory bank.

She yearned to tell him she didn't care, that whatever he bought would be fine, but that wasn't supposed to be her answer.

"I'm overwhelmed. There are so many options."

"Binita gave me some ideas. She said you might like a cushion cut with small side diamonds in platinum."

Leena groaned. "That's literally her ring." She hated knowing these details, but more to the point: "My sister doesn't understand my taste. She doesn't get me."

He leaned on the glass case, his lanky body draped over it, impervious to the blatant glare of a white-haired saleswoman. "Tell me, wife-to-be, what *is* your taste?"

"I don't know. But definitely not a lot of flash. That's not me." He knew her well, but sometimes his brain switched over and she became just A Woman, not her singular self, like he didn't know her at all. If he really recognized her, saw her and not through her, he'd know an engagement ring wasn't something she wanted at all.

She took a deep breath, pushing down her feelings. "Tell you what. Try again." She smiled, as big as she could muster.

He looked back, confused.

"Knowing what you know, pick something that I'll like."

He grinned. "So, this is like a challenge. Like a test."

It wasn't either of those things, she simply didn't want this burden, but she nodded slowly.

Dhaval rubbed his hands together, eyes raking the display cases with a laser focus. He shook his head after a few minutes, heading to a case of wedding bands. And then he stood up straight, face triumphant. He tapped on the glass. "This one, right here."

She was skeptical, but peered in where he pointed. It was a platinum band, with simple details and small diamonds spread across the circumference. For another woman, this would be a complement to a giant rock of an engagement ring. To her, the ring seemed like a plain proclamation. The right one. Or, close. She could imagine it on her hand every day.

"Did I pass?"

Leena nodded once, pursing her lips with a smile. "Yes."

He pulled his wallet from his pants pocket, but she stopped his hands.

"Let's not rush it. We have time to look." She wasn't ready to make such a final and expensive decision. "Let's go to dinner."

RING SHOPPING HOVERED over her head like a demented halo as they rode the train, climbed off the escalator, and walked down Mission Street. She shook it off when she saw Eleanor and Nasrin waiting in a line that extended outside a whitewashed building trimmed in turquoise, with rounded arches and La Taqueria blazing in red neon script. Nasrin had an arm tucked around Eleanor's waist and they were low-talking, looking intently at each other, on the precipice of kissing or fucking or who knew what.

"Hey!" Leena called, to make their presence known. "Eleanor, I can't believe you beat us here."

Eleanor laughed and shook her head. "Without Nas, that wouldn't be true." Her eyes darted between Leena and Dhaval, a performative smile on her face. "Dhaval, right? It's so nice to meet you! I'm Eleanor. This is Nasrin."

Dhaval stuck out his hand so formally, like he was someone's dad. "It's nice to meet you."

Nasrin nodded to Leena. "Hey, nice to see you again. Hope you're doing okay; you were pretty fucked up last time I saw you."

Shut up shut up shut up.

Dhaval laughed. "She came home and puked. Quite a night you all had."

"Tomás is visiting family around the corner, but he'll be here in a minute," Eleanor said quickly, changing the subject.

Leena was grateful. "I thought he grew up in the suburbs with you?"

"He did, in high school. But he lived here before that with his parents."

Something about that last part of the sentence bothered Leena. "Oh. Does that mean he didn't live with them in high school?"

As they moved up in line, inside, Eleanor dropped

her voice. "Yeah, it's a really fucked-up thing. His parents were deported."

A mixture of surprise and shock rose up in Leena. It was the kind of thing she read about, not something that happened to people she knew. She could joke in her cynical mind that it sounded like paradise, but she could barely imagine it. To be without. "I . . . I had no idea."

"He doesn't like to talk about it. And there he is." Eleanor waved. "Hi!"

Tomás in college was the kind of guy who always had stubble, whose hair stuck up at the back and was out of sorts, who wore cargo shorts in the snow. Now he was in jeans and a T-shirt, clothes that skimmed his body. She remembered him doughier in shape, but the man in front of her now was lithe. Handsome.

Leena was third in line after Eleanor and Nasrin for a hug. "It's so nice to see you!"

"Just so you know," he said into Leena's ear, "I've been briefed." He kissed her cheek as he pulled back, then shook Dhaval's hand, pausing to talk with him.

She wanted to ask him questions, sympathize, anything to acknowledge this challenge in his life. She wanted to apologize for not knowing. But her sorry would not undo the damage or bring them back. To stop herself from saying the wrong thing, she stared at the overhead menus. "Should I go veggie tacos or burrito?" she asked Tomás.

"What, are you asking because I'm Mexican?" he said, then grinned, seeing the horror on her face. "Well, the carnitas is where it's at, but I think you're a vegetarian? Maybe go veggie burrito."

"Thank you," she said. "And I, um, wasn't asking

because . . . Eleanor said you grew up around here. I thought you might have been here once or twice."

"Oh, definitely, despite being packed with tourists." He nudged her shoulder with his, like they were thick as thieves.

Relieved, she looked over to the rest of their party: Dhaval on his phone. Eleanor and Nasrin strategizing over dinner, an unexpected intensity in their interaction. It seemed exhausting.

Tomás must have noticed her noticing. "They're pretty much always like that," he said, answering a question she hadn't posed aloud. "They like to share, but getting there is a blood sport."

"So, how are you?" she asked. "What have you been up to?"

He shrugged. "Not much. Working. Living at home with my aunts, saving for law school. Waiting to hear back and stressing about that. But hey, a couple of schools are in New York. Maybe we can live across the hall from each other, like on *Friends*. I'm definitely a Joey."

She shook her head. That show provided an impossibly inaccurate view of New York City real estate. But she liked the idea of friends close by, like college. There was an appeal to that, even as her own residence would soon be unknown. Somewhere in the Bay Area, close to Dhaval's job. After the wedding. They moved up in line, where she could watch the cooks and their flat-top grills churn out food.

"It's nice to have Eleanor nearby. I stay with her and Nas sometimes. Just to not feel so crazy in the suburbs."

She nodded. "I imagine it's easier to meet men here too."

Tomás opened his mouth, eyebrows knitted together. Then he burst out laughing. "I know I only hang out with queer women, but I'm not gay. I mean, I wish. But no such luck."

They joined their group at a tight table in the middle of the room. Leena was mortified as Tomás repeated the story to the rest of the group. She hid her face in her hands and heard Eleanor's voice first.

"It's not a big deal. He's culturally gay. Look at those jeans. Look at how many times he's watched *9 to 5*."

"And those vivid sex dreams about Bradley Cooper," Nasrin added absently, eyes on her phone.

Tomás shrugged. "Who hasn't?"

Leena looked to Dhaval, his face blank. This wasn't his scene, conversations like this. He looked uncomfortable. Or thrown. Like it said something revealing about her, that this was the company she used to keep. She fretted.

"I haven't," he finally said. "But do you know who Hrithik Roshan is?"

Lots of headshakes. No.

Dhaval pulled up a photo on his phone and passed it around. "If I had one guy crush, this would be the dude."

Not only was this new information, she was riveted by him saying it. That he felt comfortable enough with himself. She beamed up at him and held his hand, her intimacy a reward for his emotional largesse.

Nasrin collected their food, doling out tacos and burritos. Leena bit into her giant burrito wrapped in foil, recalling Taco Bell—a family favorite—but knowing it wasn't in the same league. This had more flavor and depth. It would fit in a similar paradigm of frozen Indian food versus her mother's cooking.

"Do you come back to the neighborhood a lot?" she asked Tomás.

He nodded, taking a giant bite from his burrito. He chewed. "I do, but it can be weird to be here. All this hipster gentrification."

She nodded back. From a public health perspective, gentrification was very much present in her mind and studies. The physical- and mental-health impact of displacement, from higher cancer rates to the loss of social ties, could not be understated. Knowing the harm was one thing, but she was still a gentrifier in her Brooklyn neighborhood. It didn't matter that her skin was darker than most of the other people new to the neighborhood. She still didn't fit in with the Black families who had lived there for decades. Who would remain, if they could, when her lease was up. And yet, as a student without a paycheck, her access to other neighborhoods was limited. She was stuck. And she tried to tell herself the trade-off for her encroachment was her public health studies, which could help her Clinton Hill neighborhood and others in Brooklyn. That's what she told herself.

She imagined Tomás as a younger man, living in the Mission with his family. Once again, Leena wanted to acknowledge what she had learned about him. She wanted to say she was sorry, and that she hoped his parents were okay. When she looked at him, she also saw the man he was now. A guy in jeans applying to law school, a straight dude with occasional Bradley Cooper sex dreams. He seemed . . . okay. How was that possible? Her imagination could not contain that kind of loss.

"So, not gay," she clarified.

He nodded. "Not gay. Not that I know of. And you?"

She smiled tightly, because she was being teased. She checked in on Dhaval with a sidelong look: he was in conversation with Nasrin, distracted. "Not that I know of." She was struck with the possibility of being outed at this dinner, and a hot burst of panic seared her gut. She had not considered it, not seriously, and it felt like a grave error. Upon reflection, her dinner companions became a fun-house mirror: her ex-girlfriend, her ex-girlfriend's new girlfriend, and her ex-girlfriend's best friend. People she barely knew, all of whom held a damning secret.

She turned to Dhaval. But what would be so awful about his knowing? She weighed the facts: he was born and raised in New Jersey, and not the rural part. Although he didn't have openly gay people in his life, he wasn't hateful or judgmental. He had a theoretical crush on Hrithik Roshan. She imagined his kind face twisted with anger or understanding, a coin toss for her to lose or win.

If he took the news badly, it would spell their end. She would lose him, which she was not prepared to do, not in front of her parents and Ba, and an extended network of family and friends who knew them as a couple. Who expected a wedding and marriage. To do anything to threaten that was unthinkable.

"Babe," he said, interrupting her spiral. It was unlike him to use that word. Strange coming from his mouth. He put a hand on her knee and she let him. "Next time you're here, Nasrin and Eleanor have a restaurant recommendation. It has this courtyard and shows old movies. That sounds kind of cool, right?

That's where they went on their first date. Where did you guys meet?"

Eleanor and Nasrin shared a knowing, layered look. They spoke with their eyes, then Eleanor spoke aloud. "It's not really that interesting."

Nasrin shook her head. "It's not. We met at our friend Karimah's party."

"You told me right off the bat that you had dyke drama," Eleanor interjected.

Nasrin nodded. "I did say that, yeah. Because I wasn't looking for a girlfriend. That's my way of keeping girls at bay."

Leena wrinkled her nose. She had never liked this kind of lesbian talk, the kind that made women into objects. Into things. Masculinity and machismo in a lesbian wasn't any better than it was in a man.

"Is your way?" Eleanor sought clarification, eyebrow raised.

Nasrin kissed Eleanor's cheek. "Was, baby. *Was* my way."

Gross.

"Then, if I remember correctly, Nas said something about not wanting to be tied down, unless it was consensual."

So gross.

"We left together and that was that." Eleanor smiled at Nasrin.

"Well, we went to my place, and on the way there you pressed me against a fence to kiss me," Nasrin corrected. "And then, that wasn't quite that."

Leena could nearly see the fence, the kiss, the night falling on their shoulders. The whole tableau. She, too, had been pressed by Eleanor, followed by a dizzying joining of lips.

Dhaval checked his phone. Tomás became interested in the remaining chips on his plate. Leena stole a glance at Eleanor, who looked uncomfortable. The moment required refreshing. She cleared her throat. "Dhav and I met at a sangeet, which is a party before the actual wedding. I was dancing with my friend Neha, but I was, like, dance-punching." She gave a sample, showing off the boxing-turned-dancing from her seat. "Because I was so sick of seeing girls dance slow and looking over their shoulders, like it's alluring. So Dhav came up to me and asked if what I was doing was a new dance."

He slung his arm across the back of her chair, with fondness in his eyes. "And she said, and I quote, 'No, I just think girls are dumb.' End quote."

That quote, while factual, was not good for her image. She winced, but her mission would not be deterred. "Well, it's the parading and the posturing. Everyone trying to be noticed."

He put a hand over his chest. "For the record, though, I defended women."

"And then you tried to hit on me. But you didn't do it well."

His hand then clutched at his chest in faux outrage until he mellowed. "It's true. But somehow I still tricked you into dating me." His expression was loving, looking at her with so much affection. Enough to make her squirm while still warming her heart.

"Yeah," she replied, giving him a smile. "Somehow."

"I met myself as a baby. It's been love ever since" was Tomás's contribution.

Eleanor and Nasrin groaned.

Finished and full, they ambled out at Nasrin's direction, walking up Mission Street to a bar. Elbo Room was dark with red highlights and pinball machines, and it smelled like last month's spilled beer. She ordered matching drafts for her and Dhaval, not minding his hand on her hip. Not minding much.

"This place used to be a dyke club," Nasrin yelled over the din to their cluster at the wood bar. "It used to be one thing, and now it's something else." She winked at Leena, then nudged her. Like some cartoon character. Literally wink-wink, nudge-nudge.

But she was her friend's girlfriend. And as much brimstone and rage as Leena felt, her best rebuttal was a prim smile. Inside, fire ants marched over her guts, and she took a pull from Dhaval's half-finished beer. She prayed Nasrin would not be amused by this bit for much longer.

"Leena, what's your deal?" Tomás asked, voice raised to be heard. "What are you up to these days?"

Trying not to fight someone. "I'm in grad school. Getting my MPH."

He knocked his beer bottle against her glass. "Good for you. Why public health?"

That was a big question. She considered it thoughtfully, avoiding any explanations that led to why she wasn't finishing med school this year. Why she made this choice. Why an MPH wasn't an alternative. A second runner-up. "Epidemiology? I know it sounds pretentious."

"I think it sounds like you use seven-syllable words with ease. I'm impressed! Tell me more." He propped his elbow on the bar, like someone settling in for a good story.

She shrugged, revved up but trying not to betray her cool exterior. "It tells the story of who we are today.

Global pandemics rely on movement. People traveling, people interacting. A flight pattern from an infected country will tell you which countries will get a disease and when, and at what rate. I geek out about the science, but it's really about people. How we move, grow, change."

Dhaval, who she did not realize had been listening, grinned with hearts in his eyes. "You are so amazing. Isn't she amazing?"

Her cheeks went pink as she looked down to the sticky floor. She felt exposed, talking about what made her feel passionate. Talking like this was not in her nature.

On her second beer, she felt the slow drag of fatigue set in. It had been a long week.

"Do you like living in New York?" Eleanor asked into her ear, out of nowhere.

She scanned their group, to Dhaval, Tomás, and Nasrin locked in conversation. Then she looked back to Eleanor and considered her reply. Yes, she liked it. How bustling it was, how it contained multitudes. And no, she hated it, feeling alone there and how exhausting it could be. "Yes?"

Eleanor nodded. "I've seen some great jobs there. I'm thinking about applying."

Something burst inside of Leena and spread across her chest, a firework or flare, she could not be sure, and she felt impossible, wild hope. She imagined what it could look like if Eleanor moved to New York—museum trips, movie outings, lunches and dinners after class, long walks around the city. But even in her excitement, there was an alarm bell inside of her sounding its fear of the unknown. Leena and Eleanor had shared a wonderful, complicated, intense week, but that was no guarantee of a restored friendship. So she tamped it down, played it cool. She nodded steadily. "That sounds great. What about Nasrin?"

"Not sure. She's thinking about grad school in New York. We're still talking."

Leena slowly nodded, taking that in too. "Keep me posted?"

As they parted outside in the cold, damp air—Tomás with a big hug, Nasrin with cool cheek kisses—she and Eleanor stared at each other for a brief, bright moment, then hugged tightly. "Keep me posted," Leena said again. When she walked away with Dhaval, she told herself not to look back.

HER FLIGHT TO New York left early the next day. Dhaval kept asking to take her to the airport, but she wouldn't be a bother like that. "My shuttle's here," she whispered at four a.m. She bent over to kiss him, her ponytail falling forward. "Love you."

He took sleepy hold of her hair. "I love you. Did you have a good visit?"

"The best," she said without hesitation, and kissed him again before descending in the elevator, down to a shuttle shared by other drowsy travelers.

Once through security, which, per usual, included an extra pat down, she called her mother. As the phone rang, she dragged her small suitcase behind her, her tote bag over her shoulder, and slowly traced the stores and restaurants. *Airports all look the same.*

"You're at the airport?" her mother asked by way of greeting.

"I'm here too! Hi, Beta," her father said next. She

could picture him hopping on the extension in their bedroom.

Leena waited for Ba to speak as well, but there was silence until her mother asked, "Leena. Are you there?"

"Yep. Yes. I'm at the airport."

"Nita needs help with the wedding. You should call her."

"My classes start next week," she replied, even though her desired answer was an anguished scream. Her sister was a nightmare bride, pretending to be cool while micromanaging and obsessing over every detail. It made the mind-numbing project of wedding planning even worse. It was a plague. She changed the subject. "Hey, I went to Alcatraz. It was . . . historical."

"Did Dhaval go with you?" her father asked.

"No, he had to work a lot. I walked around by myself."

"Were you careful?"

She knew the right answer to her mother's question. *Yes, I was always conscious of my wallet, and my person in relation to all possible criminals or unsavory types.* In thinking about her trip, she thought of ways in which she wasn't careful. Drinking until her liver ached, kissing a woman that wasn't her boyfriend. Nothing that her parents would want to hear, or that she was eager to disclose. "Yes, of course. I was careful."

Her father, ever interested in logistics, asked, "Do you have a window or aisle seat?"

"Window."

"Okay, I'm going to go, Beta. Have a good flight."

"Bye, Dad." She was pretty sure he had already hung up. "Mom?"

"Did Dhaval propose?" her mother asked in a whispered voice. "I know you said he wouldn't, but—"

"No. Can you stop asking me?"

Her mother sighed, a gust of wind coming through Leena's phone. "No. Because sometimes, you don't tell me things unless I ask and ask and ask. And ask."

"Fine." She wheeled to her gate, where a smattering of sleepy-looking people sat. "I have to go, I have to talk to the airline." There was no one behind the booth at the gate.

"Have a safe flight. And call—"

"I'll call you when I land. You know I will."

Leena took a seat and pulled out a book for her fun class, Social Epidemiology. Social inequality existed, and there were ways in which public health could be a great equalizer in policies and programs. She wasn't ever going to be the one at a rally or lobbying Congress, but she could use her chosen tools—health, science—to make sure that communities improved. She read with bated breath about a study that examined stress and cardiovascular health in Puerto Rican youth, both in the South Bronx and San Juan, taking cultural and social context into account.

She couldn't wait for the semester to begin, to return to school, where she knew entirely what to do.

MARCH

Once her Qualitative Methods class ended, Leena checked the updated flight time with twitchy fingers, then made a split-second decision. She rushed out of the building and along Washington Square as the snow around her swirled and gusted in clumps. She thought of Ba. Her grandmother was interested in precipitation from afar, but it was the going out in it that she always protested. "Why does snow have to be cold?" she was known to grouse. She should call her grandmother.

She swiped in at the turnstile, heading down the long sloping hallway toward the train. It was a long ride out to the airport, but she was excited for this visit to begin sooner rather than later.

The night before, Leena had taken the long walk down to Ginger's. It hadn't started snowing yet, but it was in the air. Sharp wind and a pregnant pause. The bar was quiet, a smattering of regulars on stools, a handful of women in the back at the pool table. Like most bars, like most gay bars, it was dark. Dark lighting, dark wood. She sat, nursing a gin and tonic, thinking of nothing and feeling very meditative. Watching women. A task she understood, but from long ago and far away. She walked home with a shot in her throat, keeping her warm for the whole walk home.

Now, she waited outside the security line, scanning

faces, and almost missed her until she saw her. She looked more like she did in college, with sweatpants and a chunky sweatshirt, and her hair in a messy bun.

"Hi! Eleanor!"

The woman turned, and upon recognition, blinded Leena with a grin. "I can't believe it!" she called out, and as soon as she was close she collapsed onto Leena with a hug. "You're so old school," she said into her ear and pulled back, tilting her head to the side. "Hey, Leena."

She had missed her sweet and happy face. "Hey, Eleanor."

Leena wheeled Eleanor's suitcase for her, back to the tram, then to the A, then to the C. They sat side by side on a two-seat perch, Eleanor's suitcase wedged between her thighs.

"I haven't been in New York in, like, I don't even know how long. My grandparents are in Philadelphia. We came here to see a show when I was in high school. This is really great. Really terrific."

Leena scanned the tan interior with bright-orange plastic seats. Its questionable smells and dim, flickering lighting. A young, loud cluster of teens boarded the train, one of them playing music out of their phone at top volume. Someone else started singing, but not in tandem with the phone music.

Leena was concerned for Eleanor. "This is terrific to you?"

"I can't believe you came to get me!" Eleanor's eyes sparkled, animated, like stars were about to come shooting out of them.

Leena shrugged. "My class ended early." That felt more appropriate than what happened: she ran without thinking. "What's your schedule like while you're here?"

"Interview tomorrow afternoon, then one the next day, in the morning. And then I head back."

"You lined everything up so well." She was pleasantly surprised at Eleanor's level of efficiency.

"I did. I'm excited. An LGBT organization and a girls' leadership organization. Honestly, I'm sick of the gays. I'd love to support young women. But what's new with you?"

Leena smiled. "What's wrong with the gays?"

Eleanor rolled her eyes. "I'm over it. I'd rather be a private gay citizen, rather than Gay for Pay. But." She wagged her finger. "You? School? New York? Apartment? Dhav?"

Leena shrugged. "Everything's good." She was suddenly shy, unfamiliar to questioning from friends. It was usually her family or Dhaval, and with them she answered selectively.

Eleanor furrowed her brow. "That doesn't seem good."

She tried again, not censoring and not thinking. This was Eleanor. There was no need to hide. "Everything is good. My classes are good. My internship at Vital Strategies is really interesting. It's mostly lit review and analyzing field research someone else has done, but it's so fascinating to see what's happening in South Africa around HIV and AIDS, and tuberculosis, and how they intersect."

Eleanor nodded, then shook her head like she was trying to get water out of her ear. "South Africa. Your study-abroad trip! That was forever ago, but how was it?"

Leena felt her cheeks flush with an old shame. It had been forever ago, but the wounds still stung. "Oh. I didn't go."

Eleanor's face softened, but her eyes stayed sharp. "But it was all set. You were going to go."

Leena rubbed her eyes with the heels of her hands, buying time. "I was, but . . ." She looked around the train car, hoping for a distraction, but everyone was keeping to themselves. "Did I ever mention Noa?"

Eleanor nodded slowly. "Yes, you did." She grimaced. "I met her once. Do you not remember me being a total jealous asshole?"

Leena scraped the archive of her mind for such an event and came up empty. She shrugged, shaking her head. "Anyway. She and I were together, then not—"

"Oh, I totally get that," Eleanor interrupted sagely, nodding her head. "I've been there."

Leena continued, "And when we started talking again, she was transferring back to Massachusetts, to Tufts, and somehow I talked myself out of going to South Africa." Hearing herself now, she couldn't believe that she had once been that woman. So untrue to herself and easily swayed, like girls she deplored.

Eleanor's face creased with confusion. "But you were so excited about your trip."

Leena nodded. "I know." Eleanor was arguing with facts, as well as with the past, as if either of those things could be altered. Leena shook her head. She had made a bad call. Her time with Noa was always amazing or terrible, nothing in the middle. They crashed, because that was the only way they could land as resentment built. It was behind her, far away, walled up in the vault of poor decisions no longer worth her time. "Anyway. I didn't go to South Africa. But my internship is pretty great." She sealed it with one sharp nod. She was done talking about this.

Eleanor raised her eyebrow and opened her mouth, but then closed it. She nodded once in reply. "I'm glad your internship is great." She fixed her with a stare that seemed to say, *We will pick this up later.* "What's on your calendar while I'm here?"

Leena thought of the literal piles of reading that needed to be done. Piles seemingly without end. "A little bit of homework. And I have a class, but that's all." Also her internship, for which she had already rescheduled her hours. "We can mostly hang out."

When they finally reached her tiny studio, after taking off their shoes inside the doorway, Leena inspected her own apartment with a stranger's eye. Books on shelves, photos from her December trip to India to buy stuff for Binita's wedding. A photo of her and Dhaval at Niagara Falls in translucent blue ponchos, the gray background of the sky hanging behind them. How cramped the apartment was, with a small couch, a multipurpose coffee table, a bookshelf, a bed covered in a spare comforter from her parents' home. A laptop that had seen better days. A spare pair of sheets for her guest, folded over one arm of the couch. Orange-and-pink striped like a popsicle, from her childhood bedroom.

But Eleanor examined nothing, flinging herself onto one side of the bed, hands behind her head. Like she'd been here a hundred times. So comfortable. So admirably sure of herself. "I like your apartment," she announced.

They drank cheap wine from Trader Joe's out of

juice glasses as they waited for their delivery order to arrive. A lull in the conversation hit, and stuck. She worried for the health of their visit. Would it be made up of stitched-together pauses and uncomfortable silences? Would their time together in San Francisco be an anomaly? Were they not as connected as she had hoped?

"What do you think happens when we die?" Eleanor asked.

Leena almost spit out her wine. She looked to Eleanor on the couch, who was lying on her side, head propped up.

"My dad is turning fifty-five this year. Same age that his sister and dad died. And my grandmother isn't doing great. But he's Asian? So he's not dealing with any of it well." Eleanor shrugged. "Shikata ga nai."

Leena didn't understand. She shrugged back.

Eleanor threw her a lifeline. "'It can't be helped'— that's what it means. It's such a Japanese thing, to toss up your hands and say, 'Eh, what are you going to do?' That collides entirely with my mom's side of the family, who say, 'It can be helped, go fucking do it already.'"

Leena considered Eleanor's original question and sipped from her glass. She didn't know that many people who had died. Her grandfather, but when she was young. She remembered trying to feel grief at the funeral, to drum up an emotion she knew was appropriate to produce. Only later did she feel his profound absence in her life.

"I think I believe in reincarnation?"

Eleanor put out a hand, as if to halt her in her tracks. "What makes you waver?"

She lifted her shoulders into a shrug. "Because I'm a scientist."

Eleanor nodded slowly and cocked her head. "I guess . . . I want to believe there's something. I just don't know. So I'm collecting points of view, Lee."

Leena nodded, feeling so fond of Eleanor and the way she shortened her name. *Lee.* "I'd like to believe that what you think happens is what actually happens. You think you're going to heaven, and you think that means clouds or angels or whatever, then it's that. Yes to reincarnation. Yes to whatever."

"But that doesn't sound like science." Eleanor was befuddled. It was adorable. "Is the afterlife so flexible?"

Falafel wraps and chicken kebabs were eaten, more wine imbibed. They slumped together on the bed afterward and watched some overwrought British television show on her laptop that she couldn't follow. All the white people looked the same.

With booze in her system, Leena leaned her head against Eleanor's shoulder and closed her eyes. "You smell good," she said. And then, "Remember when we used to watch stuff together, like at first? So far apart."

Almost into her ear, and so quietly, Eleanor replied, "I was scared of how much I liked you."

That made Leena laugh. "What's scary about me?"

Eleanor leaned her head heavier into Leena's, a sign she was getting sleepy. "You were perfect. That was scary," she finally said.

They both fell asleep with the lights and television on, still fully dressed, though Leena took a while to succumb. *You were perfect* rang in her ears, with cymbal clangs of disbelief. No one was perfect, least of all her. For Eleanor to believe such a thing, for so long.

It didn't compute. Her head swam while she reached, with challenge, for sleep. The couch stayed empty, the deliberate sleeping plan unexecuted.

LEENA WOKE THE next morning to melodic snoring next to her, then turned her head to see Eleanor, drooling. They had spent a handful of nights together that turned into mornings, but she didn't remember Eleanor looking this much a mess in dawning light. It helped. She no longer yearned to stroke her cheek.

Leena started her day: got out of bed, made coffee, checked her phone. She sat on the couch, drinking from her mug and tucking into her reading, but found it hard to concentrate. The couch faced the bed, with a front-row seat to Eleanor, and there was something about her presence, even when she was sleeping. It was hefty. Not literally, though she was heavier than she had remembered, but looming. Large. Eleanor took up room in this space, as she did in any space she was in. It made it hard to focus on work, and Leena reread the same paragraph, grasping for meaning and connection in what she was absorbing.

"Shit, what time is it?"

Leena's head snapped up. "Hi, good morning." She peered at the digital clock on her nightstand. "It's 8:57." She looked over to Eleanor, who was sitting up, her hair a mess, squinting. At some point in the evening, she had removed her bra, and now her nipples were hard through her tank top. Leena averted her eyes. "I made coffee?"

"I have to get moving. But all of the wine is in my legs."

It was day. Sobering light poured into the studio,

casting a slanted shadow of sunshine onto the scratched wooden floors. She winced to think of the words they'd spoken to each other the night before. Too soft, too kind. Embarrassing. "I have to get ready for class," Leena said, even though class wasn't for hours. She went into the bathroom to hide, sitting down in the small space at the edge of the tub—and to make matters worse, she had forgotten her coffee. Leaning with elbows against her thighs and cheeks in her hands, she devised her next moves: getting dressed, getting out the door, sitting in the library. Anything to escape the awkwardness she felt. She washed her face to make it seem like she'd done something in there, then emerged.

Eleanor sat in bed in a different state. Glasses on, for one, that Leena didn't remember from their college days. She was no longer squinting while she read through a sheaf of papers and drank coffee as if this was a normal morning for them. Seeing her relaxed in her space put Leena at ease.

"Your coffee is actually kind of good."

"Why would you think I have bad coffee?" Leena poured more into her own cup, then took her seat back on the couch.

Eleanor laughed, a short burst. "Thanks, by the way. For the coffee and . . ." She looked around. "Everything. Thank you."

Leena's throat felt dry. She fixed that quickly with coffee, to have something to do. "Thank you. For . . . staying with me."

"So, you have to get to class?" Eleanor asked.

Leena nodded, now regretting her choice. "In a little bit."

"I'm starving. Breakfast?"

Leena nodded fast.

They walked up to Choice Market for breakfast, selecting their meals—an egg and veggies on a crusty baguette for Leena, a giant horn of a chocolate croissant for Eleanor—and sat at one end of the long farmhouse table right by the window. She watched Eleanor take down her breakfast quickly, with relish, flakes of pastry on her upper lip. She seemed to do everything like this, like she was in a hurry to enjoy what was in front of her. Before Leena could ruminate on it further, she was called up to the counter, where she dumped hot sauce between the slices of her bread.

Then a strange thing happened: they didn't talk. Leena read for class, Eleanor prepared for her interviews, and they ate in silence, one that bonded them together at their end of the table, separate from everyone else. Leena couldn't believe how naturally they'd shifted into this mode. As if they'd been friends for years, with no gap in time or romantic stickiness.

Eleanor walked Leena to the C and handed off her apartment keys. "This one is for the front door. You've gotta jiggle it in the lock before opening the door."

"And what's the secret password? Just in case."

Leena couldn't think of a retort fast enough. She shook her head, smiling. "Early dinner? After your thing?"

Eleanor nodded. "Text me a place."

Leena was in a certain haze all throughout her subway ride to school, reading in the library, and class time. Being around someone who invigorated her was a charge to her nervous system. She felt alight. That feeling carried her after class as she navigated slushy and icy sidewalks from Union Square toward the Village, getting lost on streets that twisted like roots.

She arrived at the restaurant before Eleanor, early as usual, at five p.m. The third patron there. Her eyes scanned the fireplace, walls inlaid with stone, and votive candles on the tables in mismatching jars. Like a quaint cottage. She was satisfied; she had selected well, despite the price tag. She put in her order for a gin and tonic.

Her eyes dazzled on Eleanor when she arrived. Hair blown straight, mussed slightly by the winter wind. That green-blue overcoat with tall boots, a skirt, and tights. Like Bette from *The L Word*—looking nothing like her, but still projecting that same aura of professionalism and confidence. Swagger. There were times, years ago, when she'd be tripped up over a woman, unsure if she wished to be like her or be with her. Looking at Eleanor now, Leena was sure it was the former.

"Hey!" Eleanor shrugged off her jacket, revealing a blazer underneath and the hint of a pink silk blouse. A whisper of a silver necklace with a small, dangling heart.

"How was the interview?"

Eleanor didn't reply, eyes casting around the restaurant, and ordered a Manhattan from the server. Her gaze then settled on Leena, eyes narrow and lips tugged into a smile. "I'm flattered."

Leena whipped her head around, seeing the space with new eyes. The fireplace, the walls, the candles. It was romantic. Cozy. Its selection telegraphed something she had not meant to say. But Eleanor was smiling, teasing her. As mortified as she was, she was also pleased that they were in this place, where joking like this was safe. Leena shook her head, looking toward the fireplace, a smile on her lips.

Eleanor's amber-colored drink arrived, and they put their orders in with the server: vegetable phyllo pie for Leena, Alaskan salmon with couscous for Eleanor.

"So, how was the interview?" Leena asked again.

Eleanor nodded vigorously. "Good, good. Yeah. Really good. They work with young women through, like, programs, training, and support." She made a face into her drink, but kept gulping. "I'm so bored at my job."

"How long have you been there?"

Eleanor shook her head. "Over a year. Long enough."

Leena didn't think so. A year wasn't enough time to accurately calculate feelings. But she kept that to herself as the server dropped off bread. "Did you like the office? The people you met?"

Eleanor nodded, mouth full of bread, lifting her pointer finger. *Just a second*, she seemed to signal. "Yeah. Everyone seemed cool."

She suspected her friend was an interviewing pro. Excitable, engaging, a performer. They probably loved her.

"What does Nasrin think?"

Eleanor deeply frowned, almost as if forcing it. "I don't know. She had been thinking about grad school, but she's not sure anymore. All that exorbitant debt."

Mentions of debt, especially the exorbitant kind, made Leena shiver. She received scholarships, and there was that new loan-forgiveness program for working in the public and nonprofit sectors, but there would be a hulking bill at the conclusion of this semester nevertheless. She would need the best-paying job she could find, one with health-care benefits. From the other side of graduate school, Nasrin's hesitance made sense to Leena, while she also felt a certain judgment. Graduate school wasn't always necessary, but it was for her. These extra years of training had been fascinating, deeply invigorating, and the bridge to her professional life. *We can't all fight the Man without a degree.*

"We may just do distance for a while," Eleanor continued. "I mean, if you and Dhav can do it . . ."

At the mention of his name, Leena realized they had been out of touch all day. "I'm sorry to do this, but I just . . ." She plucked her phone from her bag and answered his messages: **I'm fine. Sorry! Busy day. Eleanor and I are at dinner. Love you and miss you too.** She sent the words without thinking. A standard communiqué.

"Is everything okay?" Eleanor asked, concerned.

The server returned with their plates and cracked fresh pepper over Eleanor's dish with a giant grinder.

"Yep." Leena cut into the flaky layers of her phyllo. Their relationship remained glued together through text messages, calls, and Skype dates. And the occasional visit. She would never tell him, but she preferred it this way. She was lonely in New York and yet felt immense delight at a schedule entirely of her own making. No one to consider, only her. It was decadent. It was the upside to feeling disconnected. "Distance isn't so bad. We're independent. It makes our time together even better."

Eleanor shook her head, her face spiraling with what looked like nerves. "Nas and I are totally co-dependent. We do everything together."

That much time with another person seemed like a recipe for friction. Utterly exhausting and such an

Eleanor thing. And probably not the best foundation for a long-distance relationship. But she did not have the heart or honesty for such words. "I'm sure you'll be fine. You'll figure it out."

Whatever Eleanor was feeling, she didn't say. The nerves dissipated and a smile filled her face, organic or not. She nodded.

Bellies full from dinner, they walked through cold and winding streets to the train, commuting back to Clinton Hill. Once aboveground again in the frigid air, they sped past the familiars of abandoned buildings and streets with refurbished brownstones, back to Leena's boiling-hot studio.

Leena discarded her jacket, then began peeling off her sweater. "This switch from cold to hot is going to give me pneumonia one of these days, I'm sure of i—"

"I think we should move in together if I get a job here," Eleanor interrupted.

Leena, still with her sweater on over her head, finally got it all the way off then held it at her side. She watched Eleanor take off her jacket, boots, winter accessories, shedding down to underwear and sliding into a sweatshirt and sweatpants before slumping on the couch. Leena blinked, her brain whirring wildly at the possibility of sharing a space with Eleanor. Splitting the rent, a kitchen, a bathroom. Utility bills. Fighting over what to watch on television. The dinners, brunches, and walks of her idle thoughts.

"I'm kind of wondering if you didn't hear me?" Eleanor whispered, laughing, her eyes crinkling.

Leena barked out her own laugh. "Sorry. It's a big idea."

"It's practical," Eleanor countered quickly. "If I move

212

here, I'll need a roommate. Tomás might be coming for law school, but it's still up in the air. And I'd guess that having a studio in New York isn't cheap."

It wasn't, but at this point she would owe so much to her creditors that rent was inconsequential. Leena had other concerns. Namely, a tall and cranky lesbian who would be a country apart from their two-bedroom apartment. "What would Nasrin say?"

"What does that have to do with anything?" Eleanor spread her arms wide.

Leena bent to unlace her snow boots, her hair hanging loose in front of her. All the blood rushed to her head. "That doesn't seem very partnerly of you." She stepped out of her boots and set them by the door, taking a seat on the bed. Smoothing out a wrinkle in the worn comforter.

"This is just hypothetical, Lee, but you don't seem into it." Eleanor shrugged. "It's okay. I'll figure out something else."

Leena took a deep, steadying breath and scooted to the bed's edge, to sit closer to Eleanor. "I just didn't expect you to suggest it." It was fine to cohabitate for a couple of days, but longer and more permanent accommodations seemed dangerous. Their past. Nasrin.

Sitting in close proximity, she could smell Eleanor's perfume, something musky and feminine.

Having a roommate would be practical—it would cut her expenses and fill this gap of isolation, but more than that, the idea was fascinatingly unpremeditated. She had not already planned for every inevitability. Sometimes she was so sick of herself, of her necessity to tame everything in her world. She needed Eleanor, to help loosen the ties and have fun.

This was simply a circumstance of being asked a question. All she had to do was answer. "I think we should," she said, taking a leap without looking back.

Eleanor beamed, then leaned forward to hug her. The scent was probably jasmine.

APRIL

Sweat bore through Leena's favorite T-shirt, soft and worn through with holes from countless washes. "Lowell High School" on the front and "Red Raiders" on the back, complete with an unfortunate outline of a Native American head and feather headdress. Despite being racist, the shirt reminded her of playing soccer, of running down the field and of corner kicks. The feeling of her left side skidding against the grass as she tried to score a goal. That time she sprained her ankle. She thought of that as the emergency-room doctor popped back in, flinging the curtain open and closed around their partition.

"Okay, Ms. Suzuki," Dr. El Khoury said, eyes accentuated with eyeliner and lips red, her face framed with a black hijab. Normally makeup didn't hold her attention, but the doctor was so expertly put together. Flawless. Stunning. "Based on your history, the lack of numbness, the X-rays, I think we're dealing with a grade-1 wrist sprain." She took Eleanor's hand in hers. "But the swelling still looks significant, and the bruising is substantial, so I want you to really take care of yourself. You should keep the splint on for about a month."

"But there was no tear? Just stretched ligaments?" Leena asked. She ached to look at the chart to get the full picture.

Dr. El Khoury appraised Leena, leaving her with a smile like punctuation. "You know your stuff. Yes, thankfully no tear."

Leena felt her cheeks flush.

"Ms. Suzuki, you'll want to wear the splint, ice your wrist for twenty minutes two to three times a day, and take ibuprofen as needed. And probably not move apartments again anytime soon. Feel better!" She flashed a bright-red-lipped smile at them before drawing the curtain closed behind her.

"Thank you!" Eleanor called. Then, despite the bruising and pain and eternity-long wait in the emergency room, she whipped her head around to grin at Leena. "You were totally flirting with her."

Leena shook her head, slinging Eleanor's backpack over her shoulder. "Were you slipped drugs while I wasn't looking?" She navigated them down hallways that all looked the same, down the escalator to the hospital lobby encased with glass.

"I wish!" Eleanor shouted in an inappropriate outdoor voice. She was so loud, in all ways, including her "We Can Do It!" T-shirt featuring Rosie the Riveter.

Dr. El Khoury was pretty, but that was beside the point. If there was anything to flirt with, it was possibilities. Being a doctor. Providing needed care. Eleanor, as usual, was wrong.

"There they are." Leena guided them to the rental car paused in the round loop of the driveway.

Mrs. Suzuki jumped out immediately. "Oh, thank god. Everything okay?" She examined her daughter's wrist with precise, clinical fingers. "Your dad is such a terrible city driver. All those formative years in Ann Arbor. Can't handle the stress of honking and one-way streets. If I didn't have to drive, I would've been in

216

the exam room to make sure they didn't pull any hack moves."

Mrs. Suzuki was a heroine. Driving moving vans, armed with helpful medical knowledge, all without mussing her tunic top or jeans. So different from her own mother, who shrank in the face of unknowns.

"Did you return the truck?" Eleanor asked, sliding into the back seat, her voice amusingly petulant and irritable. Amusing to Leena at least, who had heard the tone stapled to Eleanor's voice for the duration of her parents' weekend visit.

"Yes, we returned the truck. Leena, how was the patient? Sounds fussy." She patted Leena's shoulder.

"She was . . . fine. And the doctor was very capable. No hackery, Mrs. Suzuki." Leena jumped into the back seat of the sedan next to Eleanor, buckling in as they took off, merging into early evening Brooklyn traffic.

Eleanor's mom rolled her eyes in the rearview mirror. "Please. Hannah. Mrs. Suzuki is somebody else."

Mr. Suzuki, who did not offer a similar clarification, turned around to look at them. "Chieko-chan, daijobu desu ka?"

"Hai, hai," Eleanor muttered. "Can we go eat?" She turned to Leena. "Are you hungry, Dr. Shah?" Her face transformed with her wolfish grin.

"Doctor?" Hannah asked, turning her head slightly.

"Oh, no. Your daughter . . ." *Is a liar. Is mercilessly teasing me.* "I'm actually in public health school," she said to an interested nod from Eleanor's parents. "I'm getting my master's."

"Why public health?" Mr. Suzuki asked, more engaged than Leena had seen all weekend. "I ask because I'm in the health field too."

"Eleanor mentioned that. Um, I was premed,"

she said, words that always pinched as her throat and mouth worked in tandem to admit that difficult phrase. "I read *And the Band Played On* in a class, and was completely struck by it. How obvious it was. The action that was required. I, uh, didn't end up going to med school, but when I thought about what else made sense, it was public health all the way. I wanted to help."

Hannah's eyes glistened, a hand over her heart. "I don't know if Eleanor ever told you, but I was a nurse in San Francisco in the eighties. I worked at San Francisco General, mostly with AIDS patients. That book was only half of it. But I'm so glad it moved you to service, I really am. Steve was working for pharma then too, and he'd meet with my patients, and with activists that I met, to explain what the hell was going on." She patted his arm and shared a glance, something akin to fondness.

If she had been in awe of Hannah before, it was nothing compared to now. Being on the front line of an epidemic, dealing with literal and figurative shit. Her goodness felt infinite.

Leena also noted the way Hannah looked at Mr. Suzuki. A gaze that belied their years and where they'd been. She wondered, not for the first time, if she could have that kind of staying power. With anyone.

She snuck a look at Eleanor, who rolled her eyes.

Hannah must have caught it. "I can see you, kid. Eyes in the back of my head." Her face folded with a smile. "It was an important time in my life. This was all before I had kids. Before they destroyed my body and mocked me for having a heart."

Eleanor groaned. "It's not that! It's that you tell

this story all the time. 'Blah, blah, I was an angel of mercy—'"

"What a brat," Hannah replied, her tone good-natured where her words weren't.

Leena couldn't fathom speaking to her parents that way, her mother especially. She noticed this in white families, like when she would spend time at Siobhan's house. Parents and children who were playful, genial, like friends. Leena loved her parents, but they were not friends.

The drive was short, but finding street parking took ten minutes.

"We should eat something," Eleanor said, pulling out her phone as Hannah locked them in place. "I'll find a restaurant."

Leena took it from her grasp and got out of the car alongside Eleanor. "You need to rest your wrist."

"Ooh, I would love a cheeseburger. Cooked just medium. Fries." Hannah shrugged. "I'm on vacation!" she exclaimed breezily. She looked over to Mr. Suzuki, who was out of the car, glued to his phone. "Unless, of course . . . Leena, do you have any dietary restrictions?"

Hannah had offered her food wish with such fervor that Leena didn't want to say anything to get in the way.

"She's a vegetarian," Eleanor said almost immediately. "Can I have my phone back? I'll barely use my wrist."

"Steve? What do you think?" Hannah asked. "About dinner?"

He looked up, pausing. "Nothing is wrong with a good piece of fish."

"Or maybe we should just order in a pizza. We're tired. That's easy," Hannah offered.

This process was labor intensive in the Suzuki household. Leena could tell.

They walked down the street to their new home. Leena felt so full at the sight of it, a squat building with gray siding sitting between one freshened brownstone and one under construction. She pulled her new house keys out of her pocket, fumbling with the lock. It was a special science she had not yet learned. Fumbling and fidgeting led to the door opening, without a clear way of replicating it again.

The Suzukis continued to debate behind her, up the stairs and to their unlocked door.

"Hey!" Binita called brightly.

The tart smell of fresh paint hit her nose first, then the sight of an apartment in order. It had been hellish chaos earlier, when Eleanor tripped over a box of books and fell on her hand, halting the whole moving expedition in its paces. Now the coffee table and couch were in place, along with a bookshelf, book spines out, and a lit floor lamp. The two bedrooms, side by side, each had their beds and dressers. The kitchen, one long strip of appliances and limited counter space at the back of the apartment, housed a modest amount of remaining boxes, but Binita's fiancé Sagar was unpacking dishes from them.

Leena was exhausted. Drained within an inch of her life from the energy of the moving day's quick transition to hospital waiting-room purgatory, she felt near tears at Binita and Sagar's hard work. She would give them her firstborn. Naming rights, at least.

Looking at her older sister was like catching a

quick glance of herself in a distorted mirror. One that reflected someone a few inches shorter, curvier, with lighter skin. But otherwise the same. A look at herself if she did what she was supposed to do: Wear makeup, pay attention to clothes. Do something, anything, with her hair.

"So, we basically did everything," her sister reported. "Don't expect any more favors for the rest of your life." She tossed her side ponytail over her shoulder, her ostentatious engagement ring glinting in the light.

Good feelings gone. No naming rights, then. Leena rolled her eyes. "Whatever, like I'm not working just as hard on your wedding. You owe me forever." She was actually not working that hard, but it was on her to-do list to begin all of the mind-numbing tasks that were required of her. "But thank you, Sagar. I really appreciate you coming down from Boston. This is really incredible, and I bet you did most of this, since Binita is lazy." Where Dhaval was lean and lanky, Sagar was the opposite. As tall as Binita, but bulky from his fanatical gym regimen.

He shrugged, then closed the kitchen cabinet he was unloading Leena's things into. He put his hands on his hips, atop the waistband of his mesh workout shorts. "Well, I don't know about that. But you're going to be my sister. I'm more than happy to help."

She smiled and nodded, hating that. She wasn't going to be his sister. That wasn't how marriage worked. Sisters were people reared together, who fought over the family bathroom and the sole desktop computer.

"Wow, this is amazing, Binita and Sagar!" Eleanor enthused. "We're so grateful for your help."

Binita pressed a thin smile between her lips that

Leena knew she saved for judgment of others. It punctuated the opinions she had already made known on this move.

"Can you undo it?" Binita had asked when Leena called with the news. "Is there a lease signed? Urvashi massi's son is a lawyer, he can totally help."

Leena had had to shift from calling-to-convey-good-news mode to defense mode. "What's the matter with you?" She got up from her bed, standing, so as to meet her sister all the better prepared for this conversation. Bigger, stronger.

"What's the matter with *you*?" Binita countered. "I thought you were done messing with gay women."

"I am not messing with anyone," Leena replied sharply. "She's my friend. We're going to be roommates. You're making a big deal out of this."

"Leena!" Binita screeched. "I thought you had outgrown all of this. It was a phase."

She shook her head. Her sister had it wrong, had crafted an entire narrative of her own choosing. "I never said any of that."

"You said it with your choices. You let lesbians in, you made mistakes, like with that Noa person. And then you met Dhaval, and now you're so happy. You're on your way to getting engaged. Why would you try to ruin that?"

She hadn't been surprised to hear her sister's reaction. This from the woman who, when Leena tearfully came out in her senior year of college, said, "Thank you for telling me. That must have been hard. I'm sorry you're hurting. But you know you can never tell Mom and Dad, because they wouldn't understand." Those bitter words played on a strange loop in her head for years. She didn't question her sister's pronouncement because it felt inherently true, but it was without proof. Would they worry what their friends would think? Would they say it was anathema to their religion? Were they too traditional to embrace something foreign in their American-born daughter?

There was so much Leena wanted to explain to Binita—about the choices and decisions she had made, about how attraction was rich and complex—but she knew that her sister wouldn't be able to comprehend it. They shared so much as sisters, including secrets locked up and away from their parents. But they couldn't have been more different as women.

"I'm not going to ruin anything. Eleanor has a girlfriend; I have Dhaval. There are two bedrooms. I have no interest in Eleanor in any other way but as my friend and roommate." That last statement she tacked on for good measure, to put a fine point to her position. She nodded, even though her sister couldn't see her, as if confirming it to herself too.

Binita sighed a gust of judgmental wind. "This sounds entirely dangerous, but whatever, it's your life. I guess it's yours to screw up."

Now, her sister scanned Eleanor, analyzing her. There was no *whatever* in her stare. "We're gonna go. Leave you two roommates alone."

"Roommates!" Eleanor shrieked happily, throwing an arm around Leena's shoulders.

Leena turned to look at her. Her roommate. Her friend. Maybe her best friend.

"It's settled, we're going to a little Italian place down the street for dinner," Hannah announced. "It used to be a pharmacy. New York! Anyway, we're treating. Let's go."

"That is so generous, truly, but we were just leaving.

223

I think the girls are all set," Binita said with gravitas, like she and Hannah were the adults and decision-makers. As if Binita wasn't just two years older than Leena with the emotional maturity of a preteen. "We have our appointment with Tiffany's first thing tomorrow."

Leena shook her head. "Why can't you be like everyone else and ask for money? What are you going to do with china and fancy flatware that no one in our family can afford?"

"And glassware, you forgot the glassware," Binita added. "And serving pieces." She offered a syrupy smile piped with condescension. "You'll understand it when you're making your registry."

Her registry would only have a trip on it: the Galápagos or the Arctic. She had no desire for fine, breakable things. "No one is going to buy you a three-hundred-dollar pitcher," Leena argued.

"Okay. Bye, Leena," her sister said loudly.

Binita had annoyed, crowded, and patronized her, but Leena still hugged her tightly. "Thanks for coming," she said quietly, lest anyone else hear.

"Obviously. Like, what else would I do?"

She hugged her future brother-in-law too, thanked him, and watched over his shoulder as Binita daintily said goodbye to the Suzukis. Like a pageant queen. Like a poised diplomat at the United Nations. Leena was quick to shove her and Sagar out the door.

"Dinner?" Eleanor's mom looked eager to eat, and to feed her child. It was an expression with which Leena was all too familiar.

Eleanor sagged into the couch, chin to chest. Putting her feet up on the coffee table. There would be a conversation about how that wasn't okay, though not that evening. "I'm not up for going out. Can we just get, like, Thai takeout or something?"

So it was noodle dishes with protein variations, delivered within thirty minutes. Appetizers. Sticky sauces. They sat at the small kitchen table, pulled out to accommodate visitors.

"So, Leena," Hannah said casually. "Do you have someone special in your life?" She asked it like she was asking for the peanut sauce.

"She's engaged," said Eleanor, mouth full of spring roll. Her eyes were on her plate, cloudy and indecipherable.

Hannah seemed to deflate when she heard that. "That's wonderful. How did you meet? What's she like?"

Leena had been asked this question by family, by her parents' friends, by random aunties and uncles she had met exactly once before. *Is there someone special in your life? Are you dating? Leena, are you married yet? Why aren't you married yet?* Never was a female pronoun thrown into the interrogation. Eleanor's mother and father knew more about Leena's past romantic life than her own parents. That made her feel linked to them in this small and cozy way, like she could trust them.

"We're not actually engaged. But, uh, we met at a party. He's—actually, he's a man."

Hannah's mouth hung open slightly, her eyes drawn together, in deep concentration. "Is your fiancé—how do I put this delicately, and obviously I'm such an ally—a transgendered person?"

Again Eleanor swooped in. "For fuck's sake, Mom, it's *transgender*, it's not past tense. It's active, it's right now—"

225

"He's just a—man. A guy. Um. Biologically," Leena broke in.

"Cisgender," Eleanor whispered helpfully.

Leena nodded, parroting the word she had not heard before, but Eleanor seemed sure it was right.

Hannah nodded. "Oh, okay. I—huh. Okay. I thought you . . . aren't you the Leena that Eleanor wouldn't stop raving about that one Thanksgiving?" She leaned in, shaking her head. "She came out, right at the table. Right after dessert."

Mr. Suzuki shook his head, grimacing. "I think it was right after the turkey."

"That was a really long time ago," Eleanor objected, lacking the fire of her other retorts.

When Leena took in the blistered redness of Eleanor's expression, she had to look away. She didn't want to think of that time. "That was so long ago. We're much better together now," she told the table, reaching over to steal a roll from Eleanor's plate, slipping her friend a smile as she did it.

"There's one thing I know, having lived as long as I have, and being a nurse, and it's that sexuality is so personal. Everyone is on their own journey." Hannah brushed her short hair behind her ear.

They kept on talking, about 401(k) plans and her brother Fitz's new job, but Leena stayed stuck. Comfortable and uncomfortable at the same time. In a few short words, Hannah soothed and accepted her like no one else ever had. *She was on a journey.* She wasn't gay or straight or even bisexual. And it didn't matter. How she felt was personal, hers. How she felt belonged to her.

After dinner they said their goodbyes, with Hannah

and Mr. Suzuki off to the hotel before their flight the next day. On the street, Mr. Suzuki put up his hand to Leena in a frozen wave. Hannah hugged her tight, taking Leena by surprise. Her own parents weren't affectionate and would never think to hug her friends. It was nice. Hannah smelled like a burst of flowers.

Leena and Eleanor watched them go, their street buzzing with laughter, shouting, and the ambient hum of traffic.

"I live in New York City," Eleanor said, dazed.

They stood side by side, arms brushing, skin on skin. There was a current of cool breeze in the air, giving her over to goosebumps. "You do." She did. Eleanor made the enormous leap, and they were together. It was what Leena wanted, and she so rarely got what she wanted. She wished she could put them and this moment under glass, so nothing could spoil it.

"I'm going to eat pizza and bagels at every meal," Eleanor continued. "I'm going to go for long walks along the East River and just, like, ponder things."

Leena was charmed. "You didn't have to move across the country to do that."

Eleanor shook her head. "There's more energy here. Such cool stuff. Nas told me about an art thing she read about, an artist that sits across from people, totally silent, at the MoMA. We should check it out."

Leena wrinkled her nose. Paintings were lost on her. Performance art wasn't any more enticing.

"Tomorrow? Before I start work on Monday? If it's terrible, we can get drunk afterward. Actually, let's get drunk either way."

Sundays were for preparing for the workweek. Chores, errands, rest. Not art. But Eleanor was piercing her with expectant hope in her eyes, so there was only one answer: to roll with her friend's whims, to let go of her handmade constraints. "Okay."

Eleanor knocked her shoulder into Leena's. "Great! Amazing. I can't wait."

She sighed, her brain overtaxed as they went inside. Her thoughts drifted to Eleanor's parents, whose support seemed unconditional, whereas Leena's parents were all about conditions. As long as she kept in tight formation, she knew she would have their metaphorical embrace.

"Your parents are great," she said as they ascended two floors up steep steps. "It was nice to spend time with them. They're so . . . easy to talk to." *Like you.*

Eleanor was panting at the top, but it could have also been a scoff. It was hard to tell.

"They're overbearing. My mom is, like, out of control, a one-woman firing squad. She didn't give you a minute to breathe. And asking you about who you're dating. God."

A fleeting fiction blossomed in her mind: What her life would be like with Hannah in it. They'd talk about books and health care, and tease Eleanor. Maybe Mr. Suzuki would eventually encourage her to call him Steve. Leena had seen framed photos from a family camping trip. She added her own smiling face to the photo in her mind, also in a windbreaker and hiking boots.

Eleanor's phone rang and she immediately picked up. "Hi, baby! I just got in." She rushed to her room without looking back at Leena.

As quickly as her imagination had bloomed, it burst like a bubble, and she went back to her own space, taking a seat at the lip of the bed, unsure of what to do next. She stayed that way for a long time.

WITH MAINTENANCE WORK obstructing their subway stop, they hauled it to DeKalb Avenue early the next morning. Leena pushed her sunglasses up her nose, yawning into her bodega coffee.

This was not the morning she would have chosen, lining up alongside office buildings in Midtown at nine a.m., eating an egg and cheese stuffed into a croissant. April weather in New York was strange and unpredictable. Her lined rain jacket, which had been very necessary when she left the apartment, was no longer helpful as the heat crept up. So she shed it, breakfast held between her jaws. As they waited for the museum to open, she and Eleanor made lists of things to buy for the apartment: A standing lamp for the living room. A laundry cart. Another frying pan.

Once the doors opened, they stood in line to buy their tickets. Leena was thankful for her student ID, cutting the exorbitant admission by eight bucks. They climbed up the stairs to the exhibit, where many people were already ahead of them in line. She could see to the center of the room. A white woman sat slightly hunched over in a long, red gown across from a silver-haired Asian woman, who was silently weeping.

Leena cast a glance to Eleanor. "You didn't tell me there would be crying," she said in a hushed museum whisper, raising an eyebrow.

"What's so scary about crying?"

Leena sighed and watched as the crier got up, and was replaced by a thin white man with suspenders and a mustache that twirled at the ends. This was all so uninteresting to Leena. Not only was the artist watching the patron in front of her, but other people were watching the pair. Watching on watching. Literally in the spotlight, as there were huge photography canvases and lights set up to take photos of the proceedings. She had no desire to be observed, having who-knows-what feelings in front of all these strangers. When they got to the front of the line, she would step aside. This was Eleanor's thing. She answered a text from Binita, then another.

As they inched forward, Leena's interest piqued. This art was more science. The brightly lit square in front of them was the laboratory, the microscope. The constant stream of sitters was the experiment. The conditions were the same for everyone, yet produced different results. Fascinating, even as her legs began to fatigue from standing.

The woman in front of them in line took a deep breath and stepped into the middle of the square. It was her turn with the artist, who Leena had finally learned was named Marina Abramović. That name sent her back to watching *The L Word* with Eleanor in a dorm room as Marina the character weathered lesbian drama. A very different Marina was in front of them. Sturdy, plain, with a long, dark braid. Leena watched as this next participant's face bloomed into something approaching wonder and radiance. Like she was receiving something from this interaction that she hadn't ever experienced. The woman stood quickly, hands over her heart, and before Leena realized what was happening, Eleanor was shoving her forward, up next.

The artist was sitting there, still as ever, head bent

down. Leena turned back to Eleanor, shaking her head. She could change her mind right now, but something about crossing into the square of energy made her feel like she couldn't leave. If she was anything, she tried to be a rule follower. She kept walking toward the empty chair, with dread in her legs. She didn't want to feel in public. It was foreign. This whole thing was. She didn't grow up going to museums or experiencing art. And now, here she was, in the middle of a performance piece.

She sat. The artist's head stayed bowed, then her face rose, wide and waxy. She didn't say or do anything. She was still. Looking at Leena. Not with concern, impatience, devotion, kindness, disgust, heartbreak, or lust. Not with hate. Not love. She looked at her only with neutral concentration. Leena existed.

She could have run from the hall screaming. It was too much. Too much intimacy in the connection of their eyes. She felt so unnervingly, enduringly on display. *Can she tell that I'm going to lose it, right here in front of everyone?* She breathed small, shallow breaths. In, out. In, out. She focused on the artist. Marina. Marina, who didn't know her or demand anything from her except to share this moment. When she stopped struggling against the awkwardness she felt in her lungs, she relaxed. Her body sagged.

Marina. Marina, with dark eyes that seemed to reflect her own. As she kept sitting and breathing, Marina faded away, and Leena felt like she was looking at herself. Leena on Leena. She saw herself not through the distorted eyes she had when in front of a mirror, but how she really was out in the world. Aesthetically she was pretty. Warm, honey skin and black hair. Still fresh-faced at twenty-six. A figure that kept athletic without sports, neither slim nor overweight. A body polluted by cocktails, but nothing her liver and kidneys couldn't handle. Inside, she had a good heart. She was a good daughter and sister and friend and girlfriend. She worked hard to be worthy of the people around her. Of their love. Of their trust.

But she also saw the darkness within. Her doubts and insecurities. Her fears of being with Dhaval. How scared she was about this tenuous relationship with Eleanor. How awful the drop would feel after graduation, when the future would come knocking. Her outright lies. The way she could manipulate and sculpt the truth. She wasn't being the full Leena that lived inside of her. A change would have to be made.

She gradually came out of her trance, the other Leena morphing back into Marina. She smiled at her, truly grateful. She eased out of the chair and made it to the other side of the square, seeing Eleanor take her place—where she stayed for approximately thirty seconds before getting up abruptly, running for the other side.

"Are you okay?" Leena asked, following beside Eleanor as she booked it away from the crowd.

"Huh? Yeah," Eleanor threw over her shoulder.

Once they were down in the lobby, Leena grabbed Eleanor's elbow. "Hey. Slow down. Are you okay?"

Eleanor shook her head, eyes filling with tears. "I'm okay," she said, in opposition to her countenance.

"You don't seem okay." Leena searched her friend's eyes, looking for any evidence of what was transpiring inside her. "Are you—what happened?"

Eleanor bit her lip. She wiped her tears away. "I

don't know. It was overwhelming. It's not a big deal. Boozy brunch?"

Leena nodded wordlessly. It was peculiar for Eleanor to hold back instead of bursting forth with confession. An unsettling rarity. Had she also seen her true self?

Eleanor fiddled with her phone once outside, next to those waiting for admission into the museum. It felt quaint—to think about who she was hours ago, a clear line marking before and after.

"Got it. Let's go this way." Eleanor guided them up Fifth Avenue, past giant stores and tourist groups, and against the flow of cabs and traffic. Leena saw a peek of Central Park on the left as they went right, the landscape turning green again after winter. She was never in this neighborhood; it was like she was visiting for the first time. But then they turned, and it was buildings again, tall and pressed up into the sky. "Where are we going?"

"Oh, just some tavern-bar thing that also has brunch and bottomless mimosas," Eleanor replied, seeming elsewhere.

Instead of prying, Leena decided on a different approach. To say the thing that had taken small root in her brain. "I need to tell Dhaval. I need to tell him. About my past."

That stopped Eleanor in her tracks. "Why? Why now?" Her face was befuddled. Her tone hurt, perhaps.

"I don't know, but I have to tell him," Leena replied. "And it's not even about him knowing. It's about me saying it. I need to tell him." She had a brief flash, imagining how the conversation would go. Lots of questions. Spurts of anger, jealousy, hate. She didn't have a good feeling about it. "And then I'll deal with the repercussions."

On the corner of Fifty-Eighth Street and Lexington, right outside a Victoria's Secret store, Eleanor hugged her with crushing strength.

"If there are any," Eleanor replied, still holding on tight. She pulled back, hands tight around Leena's biceps. "If he's as good a guy as you say he is, maybe he'll just be cool with it. Because what is there not to be cool about, right? You're together. You have a plan. You love him."

"I do love him. But I don't want a plan," Leena said, from some deep pocket where the truth was hidden. Where the words had gathered, inchoate. "He's thinking ahead, he's drafting a life. I want to be here, where I am, right now. Not thinking about finals, or graduation, or anything that happens next. I just want to live now, and enjoy this lovely day with you." And with that, all of the tension fled her body as she said exactly what she was thinking.

Eleanor put an arm around Leena, nudging them back to walking toward brunch. "So, don't think about it now. Listen, Nas is going to come visit for Memorial Day weekend. Dhav should come, and you can tell him then, in person."

She slumped against Eleanor. "Maybe. What's the best way to deliver this kind of information?"

"Don't do it at Thanksgiving. Otherwise, you're good."

MAY

It poured on graduation day. Situated between two classmates she had never met, Leena sported a clear poncho over her purple gown and salmon-pink hood, an infinity sash that draped over her clavicle then down both sides of her back, signaling her master's in public health. This mass costuming exercise was absurd, but her mother had issued a plain, efficient, and to-the-point threat: "This is important. You will do it." From where she was in Yankee Stadium, she couldn't see her parents or Binita. Far too many faces to scan, difficult to make out anyone's individual features.

Her graduate school experience had drawn to a close. The expansion of her mind, the real-world problems she'd wrestled with, the irksome classmates, educational internships, tedious internships. A chapter closed. She grieved the loss of office hours with professors. Researching in the library. The fresh Word document before she started an assignment.

Once the ceremony was over and she was officially commenced, she received her sister's call. "Where are you? Let's meet."

Leena sighed. "Yeah, no shit. Let's meet."

She cursed the slowly moving hordes of purple robes in front of her, like cells in a sluggish bloodstream. She checked her email while she waited, to see if any more organizations had replied to her applications. With the weight of her student-loan payments approaching, she was in a submitting frenzy: coordinator jobs, analyst roles, data-evaluation gigs. Some organizations required a master's in public health alongside years of experience that she didn't have. Other roles were part-time without benefits, or temporary for six months. Nothing was all that appealing. It was not a job seeker's market, not with the recession still in the rearview mirror.

Once she passed through the gate, she rushed through the clusters of family and friends hugging, finally catching sight of her own family, chatting while looking for her. "Hi!" she called. She wished Ba was there, but at the last minute she wasn't well enough to make the trip.

Binita grinned and waved, holding her digital camera up to Leena's face.

Leena put her arms out over her face in a definitive X, but lowered them as she approached, hugging everyone loosely in turn. "So, now what?"

"Now we eat," her dad said. "Of course."

"We need to take pictures," her mother insisted. "Binita, ask a trustworthy person to take it with your computer camera. Try to find someone Indian."

There was so much future ammunition in her mother's demand, words to be mocked in front of her and behind her back. She looked at her sister, snickering in tandem. At a New York University graduation, it was not difficult to trip over an Indian family. Their graduate gladly took their photo, following their mom's required-shots list with a very patient "Yes, auntie" at every turn, umbrellas over their heads holding the rain at bay.

They found their way in the sea of families to her parents' Toyota, the maroon car in which she had learned to drive. She climbed into the back seat with her sister, her parents up front. Her dad steered them out of the parking lot and onto the highway.

Binita pinched her through the gown. "Sagar says congrats, by the way."

"It's a shame Dhaval isn't here," her mother said, not turning around.

"Yeah. He couldn't take off from work." He could have, in fact, taken time off, and had asked about it more than once, and so had Eleanor, but Leena had insisted that they not come.

"That guy. He works so hard," her dad said, his voice laced with admiration.

Next to her, Binita was viewing image after image of mandap ideas, and Leena grabbed her phone away to scan too. "Don't make it look like a dollhouse. I saw one last year at a wedding that was pink material, pink flowers, ugh."

Binita shook her head. "What is wrong with pink?" She took back her phone.

"Speaking of weddings," her mother piped up.

Leena groaned, realizing she had made a tactical error. If only she could go back in time one minute.

"Speaking of weddings," her mother began again, louder this time, "you've graduated. You had wanted to graduate first, before getting engaged. And now everything can fall into place." Her mother turned around, her face an unusual shade of serene. But there was something else there too: a challenge.

She was right. Today was a dividing line. Her anchor to New York was slowly dredging up from silt and clay, rising into sea and air. The path in front of her: California, marriage, children. School, for better or worse, was no longer in her way. Their way. But she had just moved into a new apartment. A summer in New York spread out in front of her. New residences and cities could wait. What was a little longer?

If she said this to her mother, Leena instinctively knew the reply. *You don't take your responsibilities seriously. You are playing a game instead of living your life.* Then, maybe to lay it on thick: *I am disappointed in you.*

She didn't want to hear that, not today or ever, and she let the quiet in the car fester.

"We should plan on a December trip to India," her mother continued.

She shook her head. "But I'm not even engaged yet."

Her mother made an indecipherable sound, like a scoff and a sigh had a baby. Whatever it was, it was dismissive at best.

Leena loved India for the ways it felt like home and family. India was rooftop sleeping with Binita on sweltering nights, waking to a pinch that she thought was her sister but was actually a monkey. Rooftops so low she felt like she could jump across theirs to another.

The country of her parents' birth was also a call to an ancient part of her that couldn't answer back. She was born in Massachusetts, a place that didn't always feel accommodating of who she was. But in India she felt truly and thoroughly like an American-Born Confused

Desi, set apart from the remaining family who had not moved to the States. It always left her wondering what her life would have been if her parents had never left India. What if her dad hadn't gone to medical school in Chicago and fallen in love with American culture, with *Saturday Night Live* in particular? What if he hadn't gone back to fetch a bride, only to return, eventually finding work as a doctor in Massachusetts?

During her last visit, India had changed when it became about shopping for Binita's wedding. Her next visit would likely be the same, clothing and jewelry and attending other people's nuptials, which she liked well enough—a time to dance and drink and eat—but it would all be in service of that march toward the mandap. It was calling her name whether she liked it or not.

"Let's not focus on what I'm sure will be a disaster," her sister finally said, barging in on the silence. "Can we talk about my day? I'm still waiting on RSVPs from too many people, including Asha massi, which I can't believe. Her kids RSVP'd, but I guess my cousins have more sense about these things. And Karan mama— well, I'm not surprised."

"Karan mama told me on the phone that he's not coming," her mother relayed.

"Why didn't you tell me he wasn't coming?" Binita whined.

The talk went on, but Leena tuned it out, staring at the river as they slung past Roosevelt Island. Lunch at a nice Indian restaurant blurred past her too. She was tired from the day and from considering what was next.

While they were saying their goodbyes, her mother

took her aside, handing off a plastic shopping bag. Peeking inside, Leena saw familiar recycled sour-cream and salsa-jar containers.

"That one's dal. The other one is chori nu shaak."

She could identify it on sight, from the black eyes of the beans that stared up at her through the curry.

"That's a package of pakoras, and that's a stack of chapati. Made fresh this morning," her mother continued, a note of pride in her voice.

Leena shook her head with eyes wide. "How early did you get up?"

The older woman sighed. "I never go to sleep. I'm always worrying about you and Binita. I didn't make rice, but you should. You need to learn how. The next time you're home, we're making all of these dishes together. I won't hand you off to Dhaval with him thinking I raised you like a boy."

Leena slow blinked, casting an eye to Binita, who only offered a shrug.

With a firm hand on her elbow, her mother yet again changed subjects. "You should move back home. You're done with school. Before you get married and move to California, you should be with family."

She mapped out that scenario: commuting to Boston for work, eating dinner with her parents and Ba. Her mother's old-school idea held appeal on a one-week basis, but not indefinitely. She couldn't go back to being a kid in their house, not when there was New York City. Her autonomy. Eleanor.

"I'm gonna stay in New York," she tried to say with conviction. "There are more job opportunities here." At least, she hoped that was true.

Her dad crowded in. "That is great to hear. Plus,

New York. It's so exciting. Maybe *we* should move here," he said, teasing her mother.

Her mother didn't even reply, climbing into the passenger side of the car. Leena hugged her dad and Binita before they, too, slid into the car, and away.

She trudged home on the train in her shapeless black dress, stuffing her drooping regalia into the food bag. More than one person sniffed and sneered in her direction. She wanted to toss the food up in the air and let it land, make it so the smells were even more potent and bothersome. But her hand stayed steady on her mother's delicious and nourishing cooking that always made her homesick.

In the small, poorly lit vestibule of their apartment, she found a huge box labeled with her name. She brought it up to their apartment, leaving it in the living room as she went to put everything away and disrobe in her bedroom. She changed into cotton salwar pants and her Lowell Soccer T-shirt, and went back into the living room.

"Hey, you're back!" Eleanor came out of her room in a bra, no shirt, purple sweatpants that ended midcalf, and her wrist splint that was on its final days. "Hey, graduate! Ooh, great pants," she said to Leena. She approached, grabbing a handful of the loose fabric at her thigh. "They're so baggy and flowy. Are they Indian?"

Leena nodded, looking away. This seemed to be a marker of Eleanor-as-roommate: very comfortable in various states of undress. It was something Leena couldn't broach, and so her only course of action was to get used to it.

It was a process.

"There's a celebratory bottle of wine in the fridge with your name on it, literally. Rosé. Leena."

"The brand is called Leena?" She flopped on the couch, legs parallel.

"No, I wrote your name on it." Eleanor perched on the couch's other arm.

Leena giggled, her fatigue from the day sliding into giddiness. "Why? It's not like we have a bunch of roommates. It's just us."

"I know-oh," Eleanor singsonged. "But, you know, it's an occasion. We need to mark it."

"Like, with a permanent marker. And my name."

"Okay," Eleanor grumbled. "I'm never doing anything nice for you again, ever. Except taking you out for dinner tonight. Don't forget about that box."

Leena giggled again, sweeping her legs down. She opened her box with the teeth of her house key, surprised to find a giant bouquet of flowers. Peach roses, sunflowers, and other blooms in blue and pink that she couldn't identify. Eleanor clapped from behind her, peering in.

"He did so well. I knew he could."

Leena turned, arms full of flowers. "What do you mean?"

Eleanor arched her fingertips together, tapping them rhythmically. "Scheming with your boyfriend."

That did not sit well with her, but before giving it more thought, she read the card.

Leena: I'm sorry I'm not there with you in person. Hoping that you had an amazing day. Sending you love, but also flowers (if that wasn't obvious). See you soon! —Dhaval

She smiled at the card, her thumb swiping against the type. She looked up. "So, this was you?"

Eleanor shook her head, heading back toward her bedroom. "He asked me what you'd like. I told him a wine-and-cheese basket," she called over her shoulder, "but he didn't think that was festive enough. Anyway, I consulted."

Leena put the flowers on the coffee table, covering the big gash on the table's right corner. She sat on the couch and leaned her head back, closing her eyes.

"Do you two . . . talk?"

"Yeah, all the time. We are in constant communication." She could hear Eleanor and her sarcasm moving closer, and cracked open an eye to see her on the couch, now wearing a giant T-shirt that proclaimed "I Rocked at Fitz's Bar Mitzvah."

"I was just asking."

"What you were asking was: Did you out me ahead of time?"

Leena shook her head, even if there were parts of her that worried.

"Should we practice what you'll say to him?"

Leena shook her head again. At least, she was sure she didn't want to rehearse with Eleanor. She'd had some wandering thoughts, when her mind went idle, when she was falling asleep. She would scribble down a list while on her way to an interview, then throw it away afterward. Without a doubt, her only plans were to be honest, direct, and brief. Workshopping her words with her ex-girlfriend would not be helpful. She was sure Eleanor would be a part of this, one way or another.

IT WAS ALMOST a relief when the weekend finally began. She headed into the city and met Eleanor for drinks at a small place on Orchard Street with French doors that opened out to the street.

"To Memorial Day weekend, and my splint being gone, and our significant others visiting, and to big announcements," Eleanor said, clinking her margarita with Leena's beer bottle.

Leena gulped. "And to hoping that I get that data-evaluation job with the city and not that one being an assistant for a chief medical officer." They clinked drinks again.

Eleanor unpacked her day of meetings and spread-sheets, already seeming worn by her role. Leena had nothing to report about her day. Still job hunting, reading blogs for interview tips, and trying not to think about Dhaval's visit. She was in such a liminal state and would have given anything for some stability.

Without anything to say, they fell into silence and people-watched as lazy breezes dragged across them. They ordered another round because it was still happy hour. Soon Dhaval and Nasrin would arrive, soon they'd need to clean the apartment and go shopping, but for now: shots, because the bartender knew Eleanor and her coworkers. Leena's neck became loose, free, like her head was untethered. She rocked it side to side, sloshing her beer, her ponytail swaying. As the alcohol melted into her bloodstream, she felt her thorny worries subside. She didn't have to focus on anything but being here, drinking and having a good time.

A synth-pop song bopped through the speakers, and Eleanor's body lit with recognition, dancing in her chair. Something about California girls being unforgettable. Something about bikinis and popsicles. Eleanor knew all of the dumb words.

Leena checked her email while Eleanor went to the bathroom. From Dhaval: **I'm emailing you from the air! Holy shit! We're flying over Utah right now. Can't wait to see you.** She put her phone away and ordered them another round, but it was a mistake. She was already drunk as she took another sip of her beer, now overpoweringly sour on her palate.

Eleanor stumbled back, struggling to methodically mount the barstool again. She smiled placidly. "I feel like an astronaut," she said proudly as she drank more.

"I don't know what that means."

"You know. Like, my head is in space, but I'm here?" Eleanor laughed, leaning in, one hand on Leena's forearm.

The light caught Eleanor's hair in a certain way, and it dazzled Leena. Eleanor with sunlight in her hair, with that small mole near her eyebrow that she had seen many times before but always forgot about, with the low draw of her neckline. This whole moment felt so magical—the late afternoon sun dissolving around them, the air feeling like spring before summer unfurled across the city.

"Do you miss having sex with women?"

Leena's eyes drew up, fast, locking with her drinking companion. Perhaps her admiration had been noted, or perhaps Eleanor was always thinking about sex. Either way, Leena took a sip of her beer, trying to stall. "That's not an easy question," she said, finally.

"I think it's a yes or no. Pretty . . . straightforward." Eleanor cackled at her wordplay.

The straightforward answer was: yes. She liked it,

she missed it, and she had on occasion fantasized about women when an attractive one crossed her path. But everyone fantasized. Everyone lusted. She had Dhaval—who cared for her body and mind, who wanted only what was best for her. Women. Women were not to be trusted. She shrugged her answer in reply.

Eleanor mimicked her shrug back at her. "You were really good at it. Sex with women. Too bad you're retired." Eleanor sipped, her lips around two narrow, black straws. Her eyes unflinchingly flirty.

Leena stared at the floor, where it was safe. She smiled to herself and tried to gain composure at such a compliment. And yet the flames licked up her spine, in ways she did not want but did desire. The only way out of this was with a burn. "Are you sure you're remembering right? I know there have been more than a few of us." She peeked up, looking at Eleanor's face slyly.

"Yeah," Eleanor said, laughing. "I think I remember your tongue correctly."

She grappled to get ahold of firmer ground. "I don't miss it. Not really. Dhaval is . . ." *Attentive, generous. Good.* She had no complaints. But this information wasn't Eleanor's to have. Not like this.

Eleanor rolled her eyes. "I'm sure he's fine, but women know women. Sex lasts for two hours, and everybody gets off." She shook her head. "None of this ten-minutes-or-less bullshit."

Leena pursed her lips. Eleanor was right but also off-center. That, she needed to correct. "Dhaval and I haven't had sex."

Eleanor's eyes widened.

"Well, like, sex-sex. We do other things."

Eleanor leaned in.

"Everything but," Leena clarified.

Eleanor burst out laughing. "I got what you meant, but for a second I thought you meant everything butt, B-U-T-T. That would've been surprising."

Leena laughed. "That would've been. No, it's—we do other stuff."

The bartender passed by and Leena asked for the check, swiveling her body away. They split the bill, signing their receipts. Eleanor always hesitated over tip math, so it took her longer.

There was straightening up to be done around the apartment before their guests arrived. Leena lit a candle, hoping to mask the weird, inherited smell of a previous tenant's cat. She plumped a faded throw pillow and tried to tuck the vacuum next to the bookshelf because there was no other place for it.

Eleanor emerged from the bathroom with a scrub brush and leftover paper towels. She shrugged. "Good enough."

Leena wished she was the kind of person who didn't inspect someone else's work, but there she went anyway. It was indeed good enough.

Eleanor's phone rang and she raced to pick it up. "Hi! You two landed?" There was nodding, then, "Bye, baby." She turned to Leena after hanging up. "I think they're friends now."

That was sobering. Leena headed to her bedroom to straighten up. There wasn't much to do, since she straightened up every day.

They flew together. Of course they talked; there were no rules against that. This had been the desired plan: they'd travel together, and everyone would have a nice couple's weekend with their respective bicoastal partner. She marched out of the bedroom toward their patch of liquor bottles on the windowsill and measured out a shot of whiskey. Down it went, quick and searing enough to make her cough.

Eleanor's eyes were incredulous on her. "Jesus Christ. It's not that bad, is it?"

Leena shrugged and wiped her mouth. She wiped down the kitchen counters one more time, fluffed the cushions again, until the buzzer sounded and Eleanor squealed. She opened their door and waited for the footsteps in the hall, hearing their chatting and laughing before she saw them. Once her eyes were on Dhaval, as he cleared the landing, she felt a flutter of excitement and belongingness. His long, sweet face covered with a beard. His thick, dark eyebrows. She pulled him into the apartment and he lifted her off the ground. That and the whiskey made her laugh. She tightened her arms around his neck. She kissed him and he kissed back.

When they untangled from each other, she saw Eleanor and Nasrin still locked together in a tender embrace. It was achingly saccharine, and she had to turn away, steering Dhaval toward her bedroom. "This is it."

"This is where the magic happens?" he quipped.

She scoffed. "Yeah."

She leaned in again to kiss him, feeling the brush of his beard, both familiar and irritating on her face. His lips were soft, though, and she ran her thumb over his full bottom lip. She put her hands into his curly hair that was growing out, and breathed his scent. "You smell like sweat and cologne. Why does that combination smell so good?"

He shrugged, looking down at her, tugging at her earlobe. "Science. You tell me."

"Hey!" Eleanor shouted. "Lovebirds. Dinner? I'm thinking Pequeña." She moved into the doorway.

Leena edged away from Dhaval. "It'll be so crowded."

"But it's the best," Eleanor said emphatically, with an immovable tone.

Leena turned to Dhaval. "It really is the best. Tapas? Sangria?"

He nodded, smiling warmly, eyes all over her. "Sure. That sounds great."

OUTSIDE, THERE WAS no air-conditioned reprieve from the early onset of summer.

"It's so humid," Eleanor moaned as they walked, holding hands with Nasrin and walking in front of Leena and Dhaval. "Maybe I won't last here."

Nasrin started fanning her and blowing a stream of cool air onto her neck.

Leena turned to Dhaval, pointer finger outstretched. "Don't do that to me." Her face cracked into a grin as he laughed.

The restaurant was cramped at eight p.m., with a long wait as expected. She was drained from day drinking, but her energy was upped with Dhaval at her side.

"On the plane," he said, "Nasrin was doing some social work with a tween."

Nasrin and Dhaval laughed at their shared joke.

"He saw my phone screen and had a lot of questions." She showed it to Leena, an image of Eleanor and Nasrin posing together, wearing only bras and shorts underneath a cage suspended in the air containing one barely clad dancer. On the street. In broad daylight.

Leena handed the phone back. "I'd have questions too. I *do* have questions."

"It's the Folsom Street Fair," Nasrin said, like Leena was supposed to understand what that meant.

"It's this annual event on Folsom Street that celebrates BDSM and kinks and fetishes. People wear leather, and some people are whipping other people, and there are leashes. And other things." Eleanor grinned, her cheeks lifting.

Leena smiled uneasily, not daring to look at Dhaval. Sobered. She didn't want to talk about whips or leashes ever, but especially not now, not this weekend. Not with everything else that needed to be said.

"So," Nasrin continued, "after a light primer about BDSM, and also my girlfriend, and I'm not sure how we got into it but also explaining how Farsi, Persian, and Iran are related words, he asked for help writing a letter to a boy who doesn't like him back. I gave him some tips."

"Like what?" Eleanor asked, her face lit with admiration.

Nasrin shrugged. "Like, don't fall for straight people. Always a mistake."

Nasrin's narrow and judgmental words put a foul taste in Leena's mouth. She sounded so dismissive. Like it was a premeditated arrow aimed directly at her. By the time their table was ready, she was pissed and exhausted, and ate silently as everyone else continued to chat.

BACK AT HOME, they split off to their bedrooms, Nasrin giving everyone kisses on both cheeks. Leena rolled her eyes when it was safe, and retreated to her bedroom with Dhaval. The sugar and tequila pulsing through her body had her amped, but not in the right way. She was irritated, her brain inflamed. Nasrin was just one of those people she was never going to like—a mismatch at their cores. She was too over the top, and honest as an ax to the head. The way she conducted herself was so anathema to Leena's understanding of the ordered world.

Standing in the middle of the bedroom, she kept these thoughts to herself as Dhaval kissed her neck and stroked her back, bringing his hand lower to the curve of her ass. She tried to give herself over to him, lose herself in sensory distraction, but her mind would not let her go. She pushed away from him. "I'm sorry. I'm tired. Later?"

Dhaval's face clouded with disappointment, starting in his eyes then falling into the frown of his mouth. But he rallied, nodding, his eyes brightening. "Yeah, me too. I'm tired. You're just . . . hard to resist."

She felt her face relax from its pinched mask. "That's a pretty good line." The irritation slipped ever so slightly, and she kissed him.

They took showers—separately, for propriety's sake. She turned to *The Immortal Life of Henrietta Lacks* while he faded at her side. She was stalled on a paragraph when she heard a low and clear voice moan, "Baby." At first she checked her computer to see if it was playing music, or if it was coming from the street, but then she heard it again and recognized the voice. She'd heard that low and clear voice too, years ago. Then there was more, the sound of escalating ecstasy. She got up and approached their shared wall, ear to plaster, her palm flat. And she listened to two voices losing their grip, rich in tone. "I'm coming, oh, Nas," she heard Eleanor say. Then a laugh. Silence.

She returned to bed feeling disturbed. Violated. That was not something she should have had to hear. They could have played music or tried to *shut the fuck up.*

As that first crest of feelings hit her and washed away, a new set emerged. Guilt, at feeling aroused. Her conversation with Eleanor about sex with women rang in her ears, and her hand settled on her lower abdomen, then stroked lower past her pubic hair, feeling so much pulsing heat.

Then she changed course. She pulled the sheet down Dhaval's body and took his dick into her mouth. He moaned faintly, not really awake but not asleep. He hardened in her mouth.

"Shit. What did I do to deserve this?" he asked rhetorically, still with sleep in his voice.

She put his hand to her head and let him guide her. Answering one kind of desire with another itched a certain scratch, but it wasn't enough. With one hand on his hip, she slipped the other between her legs, and imagined it was Eleanor's hand. And that was terrible, but it made her come before she could think more about it.

Once he came, and she spit into a tissue, she flopped back down, sweaty and ready for sleep. Drowsily Dhaval drew her close.

In his embrace, she sighed, her body loose and relaxed. She felt delinquent, to have used an imaginary Eleanor like that, but attraction and sexuality were complicated. That's all. Complicated.

MORNING BROKE WITHOUT relief from the heat. Weighed down by the weather, she couldn't shake off the lethargy she felt. As she woke up, she flushed, thinking of Eleanor and Nasrin, then of her and Dhaval. The arousal, then the sex. Now in the morning light, it disturbed her to think about being with Dhaval while clouded by the vestiges of old feelings that had come out of nowhere. She yawned and got out of bed, pulling on Dhaval's T-shirt and boxers.

Actually, it hadn't been out of nowhere. It had been provoked by her roommate and her roommate's girlfriend, who had been loud, rude, and inconsiderate; it was on them for how her night unfolded. If they had kept private what was private, she wouldn't have crossed a line. What she felt, she realized, was anger. In the kitchen she ground fresh coffee beans, despite the early hour. Despite the fact that it sounded like a mini mechanized tornado.

Eleanor was on her immediately, pressing Leena's palms together in a prayer. Her hair was wild, her eyes tired, and her voice rough when she garbled out, "What in the fucking fuck."

Leena looked down to see her in those boxer briefs she wore sometimes and a T-shirt with no bra, her breasts pressing against the thin material. She thought of last night—how she had imagined her hands as Eleanor's—and backed up, guilty. She set up the coffee machine.

"I need coffee. I had a late night. It was really loud," she finally said, pointedly. She was mad and couldn't keep that penned inside, not when she had other things to hide away.

Eleanor kept eyes on her and smirked. "What, no high five?"

Leena crossed her arms over her chest. "I just think we should be respectful."

Eleanor shook her head. "Look, this doesn't happen often. We're never together." Her face twisted from braggadocio to something more neutral. "It's like you and Dhav."

The coffee maker gave its last gasp and Eleanor's bedroom door swung wide. Nasrin sauntered out in underwear and Leena's Lowell Soccer T-shirt, rubbing her eyes. She stood behind Eleanor, her chin on her shoulder, arms wrapped around her. She yawned. "Hi, gays."

Leena's treasured shirt had somehow migrated from Eleanor to Nasrin. Her favorite shirt. Leena pulled her jaw up and forced her cheeks into an approximation of a smile. "Good morning, Nasrin." She turned away from them and grabbed mugs out of the cabinet, milk from the fridge.

"We kept Lee up last night," Eleanor said in a stage whisper.

Leena shook her head.

"Did we," Nasrin said in a way that betrayed the cool tone she seemed to always exude.

Leena turned and saw them still locked together, prom picture–style. Eleanor couldn't see Nasrin, but Leena could. Like she was scheming on something. Leena turned away and busied herself with returning dishes from the drying rack to their cabinets.

"Sorry about that, Lee."

She hated the way Eleanor's nickname for her sounded coming out of Nasrin's mouth.

"That must have been awkward for you. I know you two are BFFs now, so hearing me and your ex-girlfriend fucking must have been uncomfortable."

The current of anger she had felt gave way to a dark blue numbness, as she struggled to defend herself. "You are way off base," Leena replied without turning around.

"Nas, what is your problem?" Eleanor asked, raising her voice almost at the same time that Leena spoke.

But then it was really quiet. Leena braced herself and turned around to find Dhaval standing there, bare chested and wearing her bright-yellow sweatpants that revealed his calves. "Hi? What?" He looked sleepy, almost doe-eyed. His confusion loomed.

An acute terror swept her body, a cold front that left her unsteady on her feet. She pushed past Eleanor and Nasrin, pushing Dhaval back into the bedroom and closing the door behind them.

"What was she talking about? What's going on?"

She stood with her back to the door and watched him sink to a seat at the bed's edge. She checked her pulse with a thumb at her wrist and confirmed that it was way over normal. She tried and failed to take a deep breath, panicked. This isn't what she had planned. This isn't what she wanted. She felt like she could die or throw up or both.

"Leena. Talk to me." His dark eyes were huge. Scared.

She couldn't look at him. Her gaze fell to the scuffed wood floor. "Eleanor and I used to date. In college." Once the words were out in the air, she felt solace. But the real killer, lurking behind the door in every horror movie, was not knowing the fallout of such an admission. "I—"

"No, I just, I need a second," he said, his voice climbing, rough and rocky.

She launched herself from the door and sank to the floor in front of him. He looked at her now, bewildered. Like he'd never seen her before, but knew he recognized her from somewhere. She sat back on her heels. Her heart was still racing.

"Why didn't you tell me." Dhaval's voice didn't raise at the end, but she still recognized it as a question.

"I was going to. I swear. This visit, actually. It was important to me that you knew."

He shook his head robotically. "You could have told me. I'm not some FOB. I went to college. I understand that people experiment."

She raised her eyebrows at his FOB comment. He looked at her like he was trying to understand. She shook her head.

"It's—" It was too late to turn back. "It wasn't experimenting. Eleanor and I dated, but she wasn't the only one."

"How many?"

She searched for a number, for a figure that would make him feel okay. "It doesn't matter. I'm with you. That part of my life is over." She rose up and unfurled her body, climbing into his lap, hoping their proximity would help her cause. He admitted her skeptically as she settled in, knees on either side of his legs, and wrapped her arms loosely around his neck.

He looked like he was waiting for more information. Honesty. That's what she owed him. "I've had four girlfriends." She watched his face go from shock to dismay.

"I thought, maybe," he said, "that you were the kind of girl who was traditional. Like, you hadn't dated before you were . . . serious."

"I'm serious about you," she said quickly, as if her cleverness could fix this. She stroked the back of his neck and tried not to be too hurt when he flinched. Then she searched for words that might soothe, might deliver her from this terrible dream. "You are the only man who has ever been in my life." The undeniable truth.

He shook his head incrementally, in tiny, jagged turns. "Were you ever going to tell me?" His question held an accusation. It said in blinking neon: *You are no longer trustworthy.*

She nodded quickly. "I was going to tell you this weekend, because I thought you should know, but I was going to tell you a hundred times before that too. I just didn't know . . . how." How she wished for a clean break from who she had been. But the ugly and plain truth was that the old Leena was also this Leena, living with her ex-girlfriend and keeping secrets from her boyfriend. This was who she was, her past and present, without a disguise. If she and Dhaval were to have any chance together, she had to own this burden of real honesty.

She lifted her arms and placed her hands on his cheeks, smudging at his cheekbones with her thumbs. She lightly kissed him, as if that could be a salve. His lips were tepid and inactive, present but not kissing back. He took hold of her shoulders and lightly squeezed, pressing away. He wanted her to move. She ached looking at him, to see hurt and anger slicking his face, knowing it was her fault. She moved wordlessly, backing up, crossing her arms.

"I would never do this to you. I would never . . . live with an ex and not tell you."

Leena shook her head. She wouldn't care, but that wasn't the point. "It's different. Women. Queer women. We—they . . . they can be best friends who seem like they're dating when they're not. They can be best friends who used to date, like me and Eleanor. You know it's not easy for me to make friends. When I do, when there's someone like Eleanor . . ." She thought of how lonely she had been in New York by herself, and how her life had bloomed with Eleanor in it. "It's different. You can't compare it to you living with a woman."

"So, it's different for straight people. Like me." He paused, taking a breath like he was gearing up for a sprint. "Are you bisexual?"

No, she longed say. *I am not anything notable. I am a simple girl with simple desires and pleasures. There's nothing to see here.* But it was a good question, one she had asked herself before in some form or another. In the lull before bed. As Dhaval slept at her side. Alone in a girl bar. But the answer to these questions never produced very much because she wasn't willing to listen. Couldn't listen. Didn't want to know. "I don't know what I am."

He started dressing in his shorts and T-shirt from the day before. "I can't be here."

Leena grabbed his arm, desperate. "No, wait. Stay." If he left and they didn't finish talking, didn't mend what had torn, she didn't know how it would end.

He shook her off. "I can't stay. I can't look at you. I have to go."

I can't look at you. The words struck her square in the chest, a jolt of hurt right from him into her. She watched as he pocketed his phone and wallet, and jammed his bare feet into low-top sneakers, his face like stone.

She watched him disappear—the back of his bare neck, a T-shirt she had given him for his birthday—then sank to the floor. Feeling powerless.

His leaving felt final. He'd have to come back for his stuff, but he could change his flight and head home, fleeing the disaster that she had exposed herself to be.

Her parents. Ba. Binita. They'd be so disappointed in her, that she hadn't managed to keep such a good man. And that's what he was. She now regretted not telling him sooner; earlier on might have bought her more of his acceptance. There had been so many times where she could have opened her mouth and just told the fucking truth. In retrospect, she felt reckless with her own life. Like she had been working off the wrong script.

A geyser of anxiety and fear and shame rose up next and stuck. The feeling that she had fucked up, that there was a wave of awful heading toward her. The feeling that she had been exposed: as a girl with a past, as dishonest, as someone with secrets that meant no one would want her.

Eleanor had this cutesy Japanese lunch container with one big section and two smaller compartments walled off from each other to ensure wet food didn't contaminate its dry cousins. The dressed salad, the rice, and the tofu. Leena stole it for herself as often as possible because she loved its order and simplicity. This was how her life had been organized: Everything and everyone in their places. Clarity on a need-to-know basis. This was how she could have it all. She could be Leena from Lowell, brainy Leena, Leena with girlfriends, Leena the good daughter, Leena with Dhaval. Depending on where she was and whom she was with, she could be exactly that.

Now she had been laid bare. Maybe he'd tell her parents, which brought another cold front over and through her skin. It would be terrible for them to find out that way. But—then she'd be free of her secret. That thought, however remote and horrifying, was satisfying for the briefest blip. She couldn't fathom how her parents would process that information, but the idea that she didn't have to be the one to do the telling was thrilling. No hashing words, no struggling through a tearful admission. Only the mess of the cleanup. They would have confirmation of something that they must have already known, deep inside of them, in a compartment they wouldn't admit existed. It was cowardice, but it was the only solid idea that didn't make her feel like she was drowning.

She stripped out of his clothes. As much as she felt flayed and stunned, she felt calm, somehow. She dressed in cutoffs and a sports bra and a black tank, and braided her hair loosely.

When she opened the door, Eleanor was square in front of it, cross-legged on the floor, like her guard dog. She looked up from her mug of coffee and copy of *Bitch* magazine. She smiled before her face fell. "Are you okay? He left so quickly."

Leena stole the mug and joined her, the floorboards cool against her warm skin. "Where's Nasrin?"

"Shower. Seriously, are you okay?" Eleanor pressed a hand into Leena's calf. Holding on. Buoying her.

Her touch felt like a brand. Leena got up to fetch

her own coffee, her feet on the floor, moving forward. "I'm fine." She knew that wouldn't satisfy Eleanor, but she had to try, because she couldn't bear the truth: She was caught, frozen in midair, between two flying trapezes. No net. With no idea what would happen next.

Eleanor followed her, not saying anything but speaking volumes with her hovering, her hip wedged against the counter and her body turned toward Leena as she prepared her cup of coffee. "I wish Nas hadn't said that. Not only because of Dhav, but because she was wrong. Right?"

In all the commotion Leena hadn't considered Nasrin's accusation. She leaned against the counter, drinking from her mug. The flashes of memory from last night—moans heard, arousal spiking, ensuring her own release—made her blush. She committed herself to telling the absolute, unvarnished truth this morning, but not to Eleanor. Not now. "I was uncomfortable. Just like I'm sure you would've been uncomfortable to hear me and Dhav."

Eleanor tilted her head to the side. "Yeah. But. I think she was saying—"

"She was wrong," Leena interrupted. Her confusion as it related to Eleanor wasn't going to be up for conversation. She needed her friend.

Nasrin slid out from the bathroom. Her short, curly hair was wet, and she was wearing a tank top with deep armholes, a sports bra, and almost-to-the-knee shorts. Her light brown skin glistened with lotion. She would be really hot if she wasn't deeply infuriating.

"Hey, Leena, sorry. About, uh, you know." Nasrin nodded that lesbian-nod, chin jutting up once, and locked eyes with her to cement it.

"Thank you," Leena said, as if she accepted the apology, which she didn't.

When Nasrin stole Eleanor's coffee and wrapped an arm around her shoulder, kissing her neck, that's when Leena decided to make her exit. "I'm gonna go. I need to—errands."

She escaped downstairs as quickly as possible, and took a breath of morning air drooping with humidity.

She had no errands, as she had prepared for the visit with methodical detail. Now she found herself burdened with the luxury of time and the desire to be nowhere with no one. She walked toward Prospect Park, past two toddlers losing their shit and a woman, presumably their mother, trying to placate them in Spanish. She passed a white woman with a fancy stroller, narrating to the kid about the day they were to have. Leena walked faster to get away from that, across the monstrosity of Atlantic Avenue and down a stretch of Vanderbilt, with its bodegas and laundromats mixed in with coffee shops and bars too cool to have names on the outside. She braved the tumult of Grand Army Plaza, looping toward the park, grateful when she was past the arch. The giant bloom of green beckoned her forth.

Inside, she felt cooled by the shade and density of trees. She walked along the drive into the park as the sounds of traffic melted away, blinking into the bright sky matted with clouds. Her thoughts wandered through branches of possibility. Staying in New York. Getting a job. Continuing to live with Eleanor, late nights and bars and brunch. Sharing a life. Maybe she would meet a nice person, though no one was as nice as Dhaval.

Dhaval. Good, patient, kind, sweet, loving Dhaval. He was going to call it quits on them. They would be done. Or maybe he could forgive her. Or maybe he couldn't. Her future was unclear for the first time.

Frozen in her terror, she spotted a man who looked like Dhaval walking along the path. Or—it was him, actually. Same beard. Same face. A lanky posture she would recognize anywhere. The probability of his being in the park was admittedly high, but for them to cross paths still meant something. Like seeing Eleanor on the street in San Francisco, hurtling back into her life. She had no patience for signs or fate, but this felt undeniable. Like a Bollywood movie, only with the absence of an overwrought soundtrack.

"Dhaval!" she called. She squinted against the sun's glare and ran over to where he'd paused, underneath a vaulted arch that looked like an overgrown mushroom. She heard kids laughing and the familiar sounds of a pop song blaring through a portable speaker. He stared back at her, still looking dismayed. For the first time, she didn't know what he was thinking.

During their brief separation, she had traveled everywhere: to the end, through the sadness, all the way to a new life. Looking at him now, she was just happy to see him. She wrapped him in a tight hug. "I love you," she whispered into his ear.

She felt his body sag into hers, and felt his relief.

"I love you too," he said, then sniffled.

She kept their hold, rubbing his back in slow circles. He was heavy in her arms.

"I want us to be a great team, Leena." He pulled away, taking her hand and lacing their fingers together, sweaty palm to sweaty palm. He kissed her hand like they were in a period romance, instead of sweltering in the park, half-broken. He looked into her eyes, like he was trying to see into her essence. Searching for safe harbor. A safe bet. "Will you marry me?"

"That's a really weird reaction to this morning," she blurted out, the first thing that came to mind.

His face was stone serious. "I thought about it a lot. I don't like that you lied to me, but . . . I believe you when you say there's nothing there." His eyes brightened, full of love. "You said I'm the only man who's ever been in your life. Maybe I'm the right one too. The right person. The one." On second thought, his eyes looked manic. He looked desperate.

In her reptilian cortex, a reply was ready: *There are billions of people on the planet and it's empirically impossible for there to only be one person for someone.* But those were not the words to be said aloud now.

Still, a response with heart and an outpouring of emotion was also not within her reach. She felt her own version of desperate, helplessly trapped between a wide-open, unknown path and comfortable convention. He was her future; despite her gut reaction, it almost seemed destined. To lose him would be a blow to who she was supposed to be. And. Yet. The wild, restless, tangled unknown beckoned.

She was distracted by a whoop, her head turned by a group of Latino men playing pickup soccer. They were celebrating a goal but quickly got back into formation.

"We need to start our life. We shouldn't wait anymore. We should get married and you should move to San Francisco." He tugged her hand and brought her attention back to him. He was trying to look relaxed, she could tell. "You haven't said yes," he said, teasing, but his insecurity leaked through.

She studied his face. Skin the color of her father's, but darker—dark eyes, thick eyebrows, impossibly white teeth because of his sister-in-law, the dentist. Anxiety in his eyes. She couldn't believe he didn't have more to say to her. *Do you still have feelings for her?* Or, *How can I believe anything you say when you hid such a huge thing from me?* Nothing.

But she wasn't Dhaval. He dropped to one knee and took her hand. She shook her head vigorously and tried to yank her hand away. This was mortifying. She could feel people watching.

"Leena, you can trust me."

She looked down into his plaintive face. It was ridiculous that he was the one asking for her trust when she had violated his by omission. But it was this gift that moved her. His generosity. His kindness. He was a good man. He was a good person.

Either way, Dhaval held the key to her future: one with her family's love and approval, or one without it.

She pictured her secrets like sand cupped in his hands. There was nothing more intimate than this, giving fears to another person to help hold.

This proposal was the one that did it.

She went back to her apartment, engaged.

PART THREE
ELEANOR, 2010

MAY

"Nice fucking work," Eleanor fumed to Nasrin, eyes locked on the closing bedroom door that swallowed up Leena and Dhaval. She stomped to her own room, feeling sick, her stomach churning, gastric juices furiously burning away. Leena had had a plan to talk to Dhaval in a way that was of her own choosing—and that had been thoughtlessly, perilously crushed. Nasrin's words thundered through her head: *BFFs. Ex-girlfriend. Fucking.* She was not envious of Dhaval.

Nasrin trailed behind her. "I didn't do anything." She put her hands on her hips.

Eleanor sat on the floor, back to her mattress, and crossed her arms, staring up at Nasrin. If only her eyes could shoot powerful, harmful, eviscerating lasers. "What you said was bad enough. Leena is with Dhaval. She doesn't want to be with me, we're just friends! Like, how many times do I have to say that? But you had to go and be a jealous asshole. Now Dhaval knows, and in, like, the shittiest way possible. She was going to tell him this weekend. I can't believe you."

Nasrin shrugged. "She should have told him a long time ago. Secrets are poison."

Eleanor shook her head, grabbing a fistful of hair at the root. "Were you born without the ability to show compassion? Like the way you can't process gluten?"

Nasrin got to her knees, kneeling in front of Eleanor, dark eyes wide and bright in front of her. "You're being dramatic. It'll be fine. Leena will be fine." Nasrin leaned in and kissed her, gentle and pleading.

Eleanor found herself trapped between blaring, unabridged anger and the aching pull of attraction. She had gone many long weeks without being kissed, so she accepted the gesture, reveling in Nasrin's plump, perfect lips, but barely gave anything back.

When it was clear that Leena and Dhaval would not be out soon, they settled into Eleanor's bedroom with coffee and reading: Nasrin with *The New Jim Crow* and Eleanor with her own thoughts, her magazine open but ignored. She was ragged with nerves, so hungry for something, anything, to happen. An explosion of an argument, a loud crying jag, something, because so far she was in the dark and had to paint her own scene about what was transpiring. She hoped they were breaking up, because despite Leena's protests of happiness, Eleanor knew better. Whatever her stated or actual orientation might be, Dhaval wasn't the one for her; that was obvious by how casual she was about him. There was clearly no chemistry between them. She needed something more exhilarating—to live in New York City and meet women and fuck up. She needed to live.

She crept to her doorway when she heard stirring, and spied as he left in haste, pulling on his shoes as he went. *Well, that was quick.* Maybe they had broken up, and maybe Leena would get the clean, fresh start that she deserved. She scurried out of her bedroom.

"Give her space," Nasrin advised, trailing behind her, her voice low and rough, rougher than usual.

"Yeah, sure, I will." Eleanor returned to her bedroom to grab her coffee and magazine, then settled in on the floor in front of Leena's door. Whenever her friend was ready to talk, she would be there for her.

Nasrin sighed loudly and unfairly. "*That's* space? That's helpful?"

She looked up at Nasrin. How could she be so cavalier about the drama that had unfolded? "No, I just—I need to be here. You did a lot of damage, so."

Nasrin pointed to herself, a question mark painted across her face. She shook her head, rolling her eyes, and beelined to the bathroom.

Eleanor rolled her eyes. "Unbelievable," she muttered to herself, sipping on coffee that was making her jumpier than she already was. Nasrin's inability to take responsibility was mind-blowing. The proof was right in front of them. Dhaval gone, Leena cloistered in her room, all because Nasrin had to shoot off her mouth, her sharp tongue at work, giving voice to her own fears. It wasn't the first time. Her girlfriend had spent months slyly—then directly—levying accusations at Eleanor, weaving the story of a love nest in New York. "There is no way there's nothing between you two. That's just not how this works," she had said on one of their Skype dates that had concluded in a mutual two-day silence.

What Nasrin couldn't understand was devotion. Leena had committed herself to Dhaval, and whether Eleanor thought that advisable was not the point. Her friend had hitched her wagon to this man. For now, at least.

She tried once again to read her magazine, barely focusing on a feature on Yoko Ono's artwork and instead listening for sounds, until the door finally opened and she was on.

Leena tipped out, dressed, hair in a braid, like she was about to play a sport. It suited her, made Eleanor smile, until she remembered what had just transpired. "Are you okay?" Eleanor asked. "He left so quickly."

Leena sat down on the floor, taking a slug from Eleanor's coffee cup. She watched Leena carefully, searching her eyes for tears, for signs of distress. Right now she seemed . . . neutral.

"Where's Nasrin?" Leena asked.

Like that mattered right now. "Shower. Seriously, are you okay?" Eleanor pressed a hand into Leena's calf. She needed to connect, to show how she was there for her friend, for whatever she might require.

"I'm fine."

Leena lumbered to her feet, eyes trained on the kitchen, and Eleanor followed. She stayed close, watching Leena prepare her cup of coffee. She really wanted to say something, literally anything, to make this right. She wanted Leena to be okay. She wanted them to be okay.

Nasrin had been unfair and uncool. She had said something petty out of jealousy, and Eleanor worried it was reverberating around Leena's skull as it was hers. She had to clear the air before it brought chaos into their relationship. "I wish Nas hadn't said that," Eleanor finally offered. "Not only because of Dhav, but because she was wrong. Right?"

Leena leaned against the counter, drinking her coffee, nodding slowly. "I was uncomfortable. Just like I'm sure you would've been uncomfortable to hear me and Dhav."

Eleanor tilted her head to the side. Leena was missing the point. "Yeah. But. I think she was saying—"

"She was wrong," Leena interrupted, her face resolute and stony.

And that was that.

Eleanor deflated to hear that, to think that there wasn't an inch of Leena that was jealous, and she sat with that discomfort, and her discomfort with the discomfort.

Nasrin popped back in, fresh from her shower, radiating body heat. Eleanor was still mixed on how she felt about her, whether she was enraged or frustrated or worse.

"Hey, Leena, sorry. About, uh, you know," Nasrin offered.

Her eyes lasered in on Leena, wanting that apology to mend what was destroyed. Eleanor searched her face again, scouring for evidence that everything wasn't ruined.

"Thank you," Leena replied, quickly and quietly.

Her hard and leathered girlfriend apologizing for wrongdoing, her best friend accepting—that was all it took for Eleanor to relax, even more so when Nasrin wrapped an arm around her shoulder, nuzzling into the crook of her neck.

"I'm gonna go," Leena said quickly. "I need to—errands." She was out in a flash, before Eleanor could properly process her disappearance, ask a question, confirm that she was okay.

She sighed, watching her disappear. "Today is fucking terrible."

Nasrin kept up her nuzzling, hot on Eleanor's neck, with wisps of mint toothpaste on her breath. "It doesn't have to be." She moved her arm around Eleanor's waist, tight and intentional, claiming her. "Eshgham," she whispered. "Nafas-eh man."

My love. My breath. Eleanor's grasp of Farsi only included words Nasrin wafted into her ears. "Are you trying to have sex with me? Is that what's happening now?" She felt Nasrin nod her head and she sighed again.

Nasrin kissed her soundly, with intention, with coffee-fueled forward momentum.

Unlike earlier, she felt her body respond, leaning farther into her. This while her brain swam, flooded, overwhelmed. "I don't know," she said in between kisses. "You fucked up. I should be mad at you."

Nasrin kissed her neck, a trail below her ear, then licked slowly along that same line. "Maybe . . . this will help."

Eleanor closed her eyes, shutting down one sensory channel to light up another, and led them to the bedroom. Nasrin was all over her, doing all the work, roaming her planes and slopes, kisses and tiny bites, hickeys blooming on her skin. She groaned amid her pleasure. "People are going to notice," Eleanor said.

"People? Who, Leena?" Nasrin asked, her fingers inside of Eleanor.

Her brain was slow, fuzzy, short-circuiting as she tried to focus on Nasrin's words while her fingers did so much. "Uh. No." Her pleasure pushed out through her limbs, straight into the air. "Like, people at work?" But Nasrin had been right. It had been about Leena— and thinking of her aroused memory in her body. She remembered the way her ex-girlfriend had nipped at her inner thighs, leaving her mark, how it tickled and escalated her desire for more. It wasn't ideal, to be thinking of her friend this way, and yet her mind wandered, and lingered.

When Nasrin's tongue joined her fingers, her mind went right back into her body, shuddering with what her girlfriend could do. After the upheaval of the morning, she surrendered to less emotional parts of herself and let go. This was what Nasrin could always do for her, and she held on as Nasrin rocked inside of her, so close, so close.

Eleanor was spread out on the bed, almost comatose, reeling from her orgasm, when she heard the front door open. They hadn't closed the door. Why hadn't they closed the door? She yanked the sheet up over their naked bodies and waited. She imagined what was about to happen. Leena would come in, crying. "It's over," she'd say. Then Eleanor would take care of her, a steady diet of stupid movies and takeout and wine.

But instead, she heard Leena's bedroom door close, then nothing but the hollow absence of sound. No tearful admissions or angry outbursts. She wished for X-ray vision and the gift of clairvoyance.

"Leave her alone," Nasrin said as if she could read her mind, and got out of bed to close the door. "If she needs something she'll—fuck, is this how you always are?" She slid back into bed, head resting on her bent arm. "You're not her mom. You're not her girlfriend. She can take care of herself."

"She's my best friend," Eleanor argued. She toyed with the tag on the sheet, fidgeted with the fabric. There was something else, a guilt that hung above her head like rotten mistletoe. "It's our fault that he found out."

Nasrin sat up, chest bare. "You mean my fault," Nasrin said. "Listen, it was fucked up that she didn't tell him sooner. It was a favor. Or, like—"

"Outing people is a favor? Are you hearing yourself?" Normally Nasrin's naked chest was a distraction, but not today. Eleanor glared at her breasts, undeterred.

Nasrin shook her head. "I didn't mean it like that." She got out of bed, rummaging for her clothes, bending and contorting her lean frame. "Let's eat something. Let's get out of here. Let's try to salvage this weekend."

Eleanor fumed as she pulled on a sundress. "Just because you had a turbulent coming out doesn't mean that everyone else has to." She winced once the jumble of words left her mouth. That had been low, to exploit the stories she had heard of Nasrin's Persian parents, who took years to accept the queerness in their daughter.

"That's not what this is about," Nasrin shot back, buttoning her shorts. "I'm not taking responsibility for a grown woman who wasn't honest with her partner. Should I lie to you like that? Is that okay?"

Eleanor didn't have anything more to say, not to her, and began texting Leena: **Hey! We're going out. If you want to come with, text back. Otherwise we'll give you a little time xo.** She opened the bedroom door and saw Leena and Dhaval on the couch with a laptop between them. Eleanor felt that she couldn't trust her eyes, so she blinked, and blinked again. But each time she saw the same scene spread in front of her: Leena and Dhaval, their heads bent toward each other. Not looking broken up, not looking destroyed. The message went unsent as she shoved her phone into her dress pocket.

When they turned toward her, she couldn't decipher

276

his expression. What was he seeing when he saw her now, that was different from yesterday? Was he judging or jealous or angry?

"Hey," Dhaval said with reticent cheer to her and Nasrin, who joined them in the living room. "Kind of a strange morning. But we have good news." He nudged Leena, who smiled shyly and didn't meet Eleanor's eyes. "We're engaged."

Eleanor's ears started ringing at the news. She almost asked Dhaval to repeat himself, but of course she heard him correctly. *Engaged.* She was shocked, though shocked was an understatement. If her mouth hung open, she could not be blamed.

"We're gonna buy a ring today," he added.

"Wow, you two handle news in really interesting ways, but whatever works. Congrats," Nasrin offered.

ARE YOU FOR FUCKING REAL? she wanted to scream. This was no way to start a marriage, and it was delusional to think that an engagement ring was a panacea.

But she looked at Leena's face. She didn't look conflicted or coerced or compromised. She was breathing easy. When her friend finally met her eyes, she saw pleading there, a smile on her lips.

"So amazing!" Eleanor pressed forward and hugged Leena, and then she hugged him.

JUNE

Eleanor woke to the strains of Alicia Keys's "Wreckless Love" playing out of her phone. Her alarm, which wasn't all that alarming, was a slow push off the cliff and into the morning. Its intention was gentle, because every workday morning made her feel only dread. She pulled the sheet over her head, hoping to hide from the day for a little while longer. She heard a thump against the closed door.

"Eleanor, oh my god, stop your alarm."

A smile spread across her face. Leena, her roommate and best friend. Leena, the only reason she didn't quit her gig and hightail it back to San Francisco, crawling back to her old job, with ginormous apologies to Nasrin and as much oral sex as her girlfriend's clit would take.

She stopped the alarm but stayed in bed, sheet thrown back. It was sultry in her room, with stale air hanging low even in the freshness of the day. She heard a garbage truck on her street, and early morning scuffles between children and parents wafting in from other apartments.

Another pound on the door. "Are you up yet? We need to leave soon."

As much as Eleanor appreciated Leena, appreciated her every day, Leena with a job was A Lot. Previously her day had been ordered by classes and schoolwork, and certainly her postgrad and job-hunting life had contained structure, but this was something else. A weekly schedule chiseled with precision. Intense nightly preparations for lunch the next day. And this, the prodding and nagging that rivaled every Jewish mother. "Jesus fucking Christ, oh my god," Eleanor muttered under her breath.

She grabbed a T-shirt and boxer briefs off the floor, and headed out into the living room that was drenched in sun. She drank the coffee that Leena had prepared for them as she watched her zip around, her black hair blown straight, wearing a pencil skirt and a teal blouse—a stark contrast from her usual boxy jeans and T-shirt look. This outfit accentuated her hips, her ass, the curves of her breasts. Her ring glinted on her left hand.

"I thought we were going to commute together?" Leena asked, passing from the kitchen to her bedroom.

Curled up on the couch and staring at her phone, Eleanor scanned the news, taking a final sip from her chipped Tokyo Disneyland mug. "Yeah, but I think I have a different timeline this morning."

Leena stopped short in the doorway of her room. Her face was clouded over. "Okay. I just thought—"

"No, it's cool, I'm ready to go." She wasn't about to disappoint Leena, and got to her feet.

"You are not ready to go." Leena's eyes swept over Eleanor's underdressed body.

Eleanor shrugged. "Okay, fine, I'm not ready, but give me, like, two seconds, and I'm all yours."

"What a gift," Leena deadpanned, turning toward her room. "I'll do the bagel. You get ready."

Eleanor cycled through her bathroom routine. In the shower, she sang from that Alicia Keys song, still stuck in her head. *"Let's go back in time when our kiss was brand-new, an adventure not perfected, a little hesitant—"*

"El," she heard, paired with an exasperated sigh. "The echo. It's so loud."

She soaped her back as far down as her arms would contort, and peeked out at Leena, who was applying facial moisturizer in the mirror. "I'd like to amend our open-door policy during showers."

Leena laughed, a stream that trailed behind her as she left the room.

All told, it took her more than five minutes to get ready, but not much more. Deodorant-lotion-underwear-dress. She threw her hair up into a wet knot, and tossed lipstick and a cardigan into her tote bag, along with her phone and their leftovers from the night before that she'd won in a Scrabble game, her sweet defeat over Leena clinched with the word *pacifist*.

"Okay, let's fucking do this," she called to her roommate, who emerged from the kitchen bearing buttered bagel halves, one for each of them.

They walked to the Atlantic Avenue stop, the air dry and still against Eleanor's skin. When they got underground to the subway, the atmosphere was sweltering, like heat was seeping up directly from the earth's core. Once they boarded the train, the air shifted again, frigid from the air-conditioning. Speeding toward the city, Leena held the pole in the center, Eleanor the bar over seats occupied by an older Asian woman and her squirmy grandchild.

"Sorry I was in such a rush. But it's only the end of

my second week. I have to keep making a good impression." Her face showed concern as she said this, but Eleanor could only concentrate on her hair, which had a tiny leaf in its wake. She reached out and gently pulled it from Leena's strands. Her friend smiled, grateful. "Thanks."

The rest of the ride, unfortunately, was business. Leena filled their conversation with when they'd do laundry, when they'd go grocery shopping, when they'd make a list for grocery shopping.

"We are so Felix and Oscar," Eleanor said with a laugh.

Leena's brow furrowed. "Are those friends of yours?"

"No. You know, Felix and Oscar, like from *The Odd Couple*."

Leena's face stayed blank, with no recognition of what Eleanor was saying.

"*The Odd Couple*. Like the old TV show. The old movie. No?"

Leena shrugged, meek. "I have no idea." She opened her mouth to say more, but was preempted by the conductor mumbling through the staticky speaker above, saying something like there was traffic on the bridge. When the voice ceased, she smiled. "There are holes in my pop-culture knowledge. Being the child of immigrants. I didn't grow up with parents who, for example, listened to the Beatles."

"*All you need is love,*" Eleanor crooned.

The train finally lifted up and out onto the bridge, sailing toward Manhattan.

Leena scrunched up her face. "Who are these men? Felix and Oscar? What did they accomplish?" She wore her scrutiny so seriously and without constraint.

"They were two dudes who lived together. One was sloppy, the other neat. An odd couple."

"And they're gay?"

Eleanor considered this question soberly, with the attention it deserved. "No, straight. But with homo-erotic subtext, like most things."

Leena nodded her head like she was thinking, pondering, doing mental math. "Which one of us is Felix? Oscar?"

Eleanor booped Leena's nose with the tip of her pointer finger. "Felix. With the cleaning, organizing, and lectures about socks on the floor."

Leena shook her head, looking away, a wisp of a smile fading from her face. "You say it like there's something wrong with that."

"Just like a Felix." Eleanor hopped off the train at Grand Street, waving at Leena from the platform as it left. Her shoulders sank. The best part of the morning would now morph into the worst. She trudged up the stairs and to the street.

At first she loved her job, so happy to be out of the fundraising game, to do the work instead of securing money, exhilarated to support girls' leadership. Psyched to work on the Lower East Side, which felt so real and unsanitized, unlike other parts of New York. She could smell puke and urine on the streets as she walked to work, a rough morning after for some, a city pulsing with people and their guts. But the reality was that she mostly updated databases, sent emails to the girls and their families, and helped out with the fund-raising mailings. It wasn't glamorous or challenging or fun. And the puke stench got old quickly.

She pushed open the street-level door and went up

the narrow stairs to the office, the open-plan brick-walled room of secondhand desks and aging computers. Her small band of coworkers were all much cooler than she was: born-and-braised New Yorkers with innate cynicism and sparks of excitement in spades. Even the way they dressed was infinitely more hip: Analiz, her boss, with tattoo sleeves and pinup-girl dresses; Mic, with their bow ties and shaved head; Jane, in her black T-shirts and black jeans, her gray hair in a stern pony-tail. Eleanor was unaccustomed to looking like the most conservative one in the room, with undyed hair and thrift-store duds, just this kid from a suburb in an H&M dress. She said good morning to everyone, recognizing the Le Tigre song pulsing from the stereo, and sat down to check email, hunkering down and bracing for her day.

At midmorning she sat in on a meeting by default, because there was no conference-room space. Mic and Jane were reviewing plans for the upcoming mentor-ship program cycle once school was back in session, and through her eavesdropping, she learned they were having a problem with recruitment. Women mentors wanted to help, but didn't have the time, or weren't bringing any diversity to the table.

Eleanor had a million thoughts to bridge such a gap. She turned in her chair. "Sorry, you two, I couldn't help but overhear. What about utilizing existing mentors' networks? Those women probably know other women like them. Or reaching out to colleges in the city? Tapping women of color organizations? There's probably a lot of ways to address this."

Mic and Jane exchanged glances. "Thanks," Jane said, her voice wilted, a patent-leather smile on her face. "We've tried some of that before. But, thanks." She turned back to Mic and lowered her voice.

Message received. Fuming, Eleanor put her headphones on, turning back to her computer screen. M.I.A. pulsed through her ears, bleats and drums and angular sounds. She hated feeling ignored, impotent, without anything to contribute. She had been on this earth for twenty-six goddamned years: she had ideas, she had experience. All she required was trust from these supposed feminists, people who were supposed to uplift young women, even her. Her shoulders pinched with tension, thinking of her paycheck that did not reflect how hard she worked or how much she cared for their mission. To do what she was doing and feel disrespected—well, *fuck this job.*

Her eyes glazed over later as she made sure the email copy in front of her was accurate and error free, when she saw a text message come through. She checked her phone, seeing a message from Nasrin confirming their Skype date, and one from Leena.

Drinskf tongjy?

Eleanor smiled, imagining her stealthily tapping out the message at work, then squirreling her phone away. Leena's work ethic was epic and all-encompassing, and she thought any diversion from it would be seen as incompetence. Such a mindset reminded her of her parents, also the children of immigrants, who cast employment in a different light than Eleanor did. From her father: "Your obachan and ojichan had it so hard. Taking whatever work they could find, before and after being in an internment camp in Arizona. That was real struggle. You should feel lucky to make copies." Or from her mother: "Your grandparents didn't flee Nazis and rebuild their lives so you could whine about not being promoted fast enough."

Her grandparents had taught her parents to be uncannily conscious of the thin membrane that existed between staying afloat and the deprivation that could have sunken them all. She got it. She really did. When faced with her parents' unsympathetic retorts, she had an answer ready: "I am so grateful to my elders, who wanted me to have a better life, and I do. And so do you, with your house and cars and vacations and wine clubs, so let me fucking complain about work."

A phone rang and she was brought back to the four brick walls, the windows that faced out onto Hester Street, the remaining hours before she was free.

At 5:59 p.m., she shut down her computer and barreled out with a quick blanket goodbye, then went down to the subway with a temperature of inferno Fahrenheit. She waited impatiently for the train, missing the much more civilized countdown clocks in San Francisco. The unknown was a beast. She read *Bitch*, sweating and silently cursing, until the train pulled in with a whoosh of near-fresh cool air. The silver cars thundered past her, a wave of power and blurred faces, until they stilled, gears halting, brakes applied.

And there was Leena in the window, her face cast down, reading from a sheaf of papers, appearing as if by magic right in front of Eleanor. What were the odds? She was here, right here, face slightly dewy from the humid weather, hair limp, in commuting sneakers like she was someone's mom.

Eleanor boarded the train, squeezing past a mother and toddler, then two teens sharing an iPod, one earbud per person. She stood in front of her friend, grinning, but Leena didn't notice her, staying focused on her printed document. She bopped her on the shoulder with two taps after the train lurched from the station.

Leena's whole body shook, startled, eyes raising toward her eyebrows. "Holy fuck!" she sputtered. "You scared the shit out of me."

Eleanor tried not to laugh too much at her.

Once Leena shook off her surprise, she beamed. "I can't believe it. Here you are. There's just so many trains. To catch the same one, at the same time, in the same car, in the same spot . . . Anyway. Hi."

"Hi."

They walked to their favorite happy-hour spot, pausing at the corner before crossing to the bar. Out of the corner of her eye, she noticed a group of Asian tourists huddled around a paper map, and as she listened in and detected the subtleties of attire—nice clothes and accessories, wearing one too many of both—she confirmed they were Japanese. Her heart swelled. Her people. If only her Japanese was better, she could swoop in and solve their travel issue. If only they saw her as one of them, instead of reading her right on glance as Not Exclusively Japanese, and therefore Not Really Japanese.

Eleanor shook it off as they drank beers at the bar, the air-conditioning making her shiver as late afternoon light poured through the windows. She tried Leena's beer and preferred it, ordering that once her own glass was drained.

"How was your day?"

Eleanor rolled her eyes. "Fine. Or, like, an approximation of fine. I can do so much more, you know? I'm ready to handle more. But there's just so much admin work to get done. I know someone has to do it, but still." She sighed, tapping her fingertips on the bar.

"That does sound frustrating," Leena said in solidarity.

"Yeah." She brushed it off; she was done talking about work. Wasn't she out with her best friend? Drinking delicious beers? With the summer over their heads like a lazy fan? "How was your day?"

Leena looked like she was revving herself up to something positive, bobbing her head, eyes wide. "It was good. I'm still learning how to do the job, but everyone is so nice."

Eleanor smiled encouragingly, hoping to egg her on.

"I'm glad, obviously, to work for Physicians for Reproductive Choice and Health. The work they do to support doctors and women, well, I can't think of anything more important," Leena continued. Eleanor admired Leena for working somewhere that really made a difference. She used to think that about her own organization and loved having the chance to impact the lives of young women, but often felt so detached. That work, mostly done by others, was remote to her daily professional life. Maybe she should go back to school, get her master's in public policy or social work, or some degree that would get her further, garner respect, change her life.

"And even though I'm just an assistant, like, I can really play a part. Maybe work my way up into a health role. Supporting med students. Maybe."

Eleanor nodded her head like she understood and agreed, even though neither one of those things was true. Her best friend's capacity for settling, for compromising herself, seemed to be limitless. She was willing to accept whatever came her way. Maybe there was safety in such hope, to believe that marching in place could actually yield results if one worked tirelessly toward a goal. Eleanor's mind wafted to Dhaval. He wasn't so different from this job.

She realized, blearily, that she hadn't yet replied. One thing was for sure: she believed in Leena. She nodded. "Yeah, for sure. I can totally see you climbing the ranks. Killin' it. Telling those med students what's up."

Leena ordered another beer and asked for the check at once, all efficiency. "I think we should go food shopping tonight."

Eleanor shook her head. "And I think we should eat empanadas and cake."

Sometimes Leena looked at her in this way she couldn't quite read. It might have silently said, *You are incorrigible. What'll I do with you?* But it also could have been, *You are annoying. I tolerate you.* Either way, it made her feel warm and known, and loved. It was a heady feeling.

"You know, we haven't talked about what we're doing for Pride." She was so excited for her first Pride in New York. San Francisco's festivities were old hat, and she was ready to experience something new and unfamiliar. She wanted to open her mouth and consume it all. "There's the Dyke March and a big dance for women and then parties the next day. It's gonna be great."

Leena fidgeted with her hair, pulling it out of its ponytail and wrapping it into a messy knot on the top of her head. "I . . . don't think that's my thing."

"Why not? Because your partner doesn't have a vagina?"

Leena winced. "He doesn't, but that's not it. It doesn't feel like a space for me anymore," she said, her voice compact and far away.

Eleanor hadn't considered that Leena felt this way. "It doesn't matter. It's for anyone. Like—straight people love going to Pride. Showing up, being such good model allies, wearing their 'Straight But Not Narrow' shirts."

"But that's not me either," Leena protested.

"So, who are you?" she asked, leaning forward with her hand cradling her chin, teasing and serious all at once.

The check arrived and Leena scooped up the carbon paper clipped to a postcard. "Let me treat," she replied hastily, pulling a credit card from her wallet. "New job, money coming in." She busied herself with flagging down the bartender.

"Thanks for treating. So. How do you—"

"I don't want to . . . Eleanor." Leena's eyes pleaded, drawing a line.

She could let it go, if that's what Leena was asking. And despite her own clawing need to understand Leena's inner workings, when Eleanor really scanned her own body, she realized that Leena wasn't the only one caught between worlds. She slid off her barstool. "I never feel Japanese enough."

The skin around her friend's eyes crinkled, her mouth in a bemused smile. "You've said this before. It's not a feelings-based thing. It's family heredity and DNA." She led them out of the bar.

Eleanor groaned. "No, I know, I just, like, I have

this face, but Asian people always make me feel so . . . white."

"Asian people? Me?" Leena asked over her shoulder.

Eleanor scoffed. "No, like real Asians." She smirked when Leena looked back with narrow dagger eyes. "No, seriously, like Japanese people. They don't know what to do with me."

"Then they don't matter," Leena said matter-of-factly.

They were words that Eleanor needed to hear, and she stopped them both in their tracks, in the middle of the sidewalk on Fulton Street, and embraced Leena tightly, like a balloon she was desperate to keep from floating away. There were no adequate words for her gratitude.

Eleanor and Leena wandered the aisles of Key Foods, collecting chocolate chip cookies and broccoli and tofu and ginger ale and ice cream. She looked at their haul in its basket. "There's a dinner in there somewhere. Oh!" She grabbed tampons from the shelf. "Still can't believe we're not on the same cycle yet." Eleanor steered them toward the checkout line. "Me and Nas sort of duked it out for a while, like, who had the alpha womb, you know?" She handed her debit card over to the cashier.

Leena laughed. "I don't."

"When women live together, there's often one leader, whoever is the strongest, who gets the other wombs to follow her. It happened on my study-abroad trip. I'm sure it happened in your house. Three women?"

Leena shrugged. "We didn't talk about that."

Of course. "Well, it'll take time. It'll happen for us. Who do you think is the alpha?"

Leena raised one eyebrow, turning her head, smirking, walking out with their canvas shopping bag.

Eleanor followed her out. "Wait, what does that mean?"

ELEANOR SHOWERED AFTER dinner, rinsing away the grime of the city, of work, of her day. With the hot water sluicing down her body, she rolled her shoulders and relaxed, letting her mind wander. She thought idly about planning a trip home to see her parents, hear about Fitz's first big-boy job, and visit Obachan's bookstore, which her uncle recently began running. It had been months since she'd been to the store, but there was no forgetting the smell of paper, the lingering scent of pulp past its prime. The business of the bookstore had never been a part of her life, only eating Pocky and flipping through manga, but she thought of it now and imagined running it herself. Being in charge, making decisions. Welcoming customers, stocking shelves, learning how to handle finances more complicated than her own. It seemed so fulfilling to continue her family's legacy, and so much simpler in the face of her current job. She yearned for escape. The dread of going back to the office, to a place that didn't excite her—that was a drag, and felt like all of her efforts toward good were pointless. It turned her relaxing shower into a hotbox of stress.

By the time she sat in front of her computer and booted up Skype, she was exhausted. She already processed her day, bedtime was coming, but she needed to be fresh and alert for Nasrin. It was their chance to connect. Once they began talking, she'd be all in. It would be so wonderful to have her person staring right at her, however remotely. And the Skype sex wasn't bad either.

Nasrin immediately initiated the call once she logged in. The connection was patchy for a second, pixelated, stilted, but then it cleared, giving way to Nasrin's face, her new Oakland bedroom in the background: empty white walls and vertical blinds.

Seeing the room always made Eleanor feel guilty. They had lived together in a well-located, beautiful studio, with abundant sunshine and good vibes. A place for two of them to tuck away in the middle of everything. Now Nasrin lived in a house share that was a ten-minute walk from the MacArthur BART station. "Hey, there's my beautiful girl," Eleanor said.

Nasrin was so many hard planes and angles, but her face was soft, with a round chin and huge, brown eyes. When she heard Eleanor speak, her posture went stiff and still, ramrod straight. "Hey, baby," Nasrin said, rubbing the back of her neck.

Eleanor could practically feel the texture of Nasrin's hairline, her fingers running across the short hair there. "How was your day?" Eleanor asked, stifling a yawn.

Nasrin pursed her lips, then put a hand to her chin, sliding it up to cover her mouth. She nodded. "Good. I think we should break up."

Eleanor blinked slowly, waiting for her brain to catch up. *I think we should break up.* "I'm sorry, what?"

Nasrin sighed and looked away. "This isn't gonna work."

Eleanor shook her head vehemently. "No, it will. It will. Of course it will. You'll get into grad school like we planned and move here, and we'll get a place, and—that's it. Or, that's the beginning, whatever—but of course this will work." Her heart was beating so fast, fear and adrenaline bubbling in her body. Her stomach in a knot, pulsing and aching.

Nasrin leaned in, eyes aimed right at the camera, directly into Eleanor's screen. "You and Leena. It's gonna happen. And I'd rather be on this end, doing this, than getting a call later when you say, 'Oops, I fucked up. We fucked.'"

Eleanor scoffed. "Leena and I . . . that's not going to happen. You're wrong." She could feel the heat of self-righteousness rising in her body. "You know what, you've been paranoid and jealous for months. You can't put this on me."

"I have eyes, El, please. Anyone could see what's happening here. Don't be so obtuse." She carded a hand through her hair, those dark curls that Eleanor loved, springy and loose, with sparse strands of gray starting to set in.

Eleanor folded her arms over her chest and shook her head. "You're wrong."

"Fuck," Nasrin said under her breath. She crossed her arms, shook her own head. "I thought you could at least admit it to me now, that you're not mine anymore."

Eleanor leaned back, bowled away by that. "That's how we talk now? Like we own each other? Yeah, maybe we should break up," she said with initial bravado, but her voice faded out at the end, and the *up* died in her throat, the *p* sound on her lips. Nasrin put her face in her hands. Eleanor wasn't sure if there was more to say, or what to do. It felt like her heart was bleeding out, beat by stuttering beat.

When she removed her hands, Nasrin wiped her face with a clumsy forearm. She was crying, her upper lip quivering. "I don't want to do this. But I don't want you to hurt me."

How much she wished she could reach through the screen. "I'm not gonna hurt you, baby, I promise."

Nasrin sniffled. "I've thought about this a lot. And I talked to Joan, and she thinks—"

"Joan Liu? Your ex? Are we talking about the same—"

"We're just frien—"

"I knew this wasn't about me." Eleanor shook her head. "You and Joan. You, spending time alone, Joan on the lookout for pussy. It's so obvious. I should have seen this coming."

"Oh my god. I am not fucking Joan. That's, like, the last thing on my mind," Nasrin said, strained.

Nasrin had the voice of a liar, but it was impossible to tell via video connection. They were too far apart when they needed to be in the same place, breathing the same air. "Look, tensions are high. I get it. Me too, maybe, but let's just cool off. Let's talk tomorrow, and I can book a flight to come see you soon, and we'll work this out." She would say anything to keep them afloat.

Nasrin hunched her shoulders. "I wish. But this is it. I love you, but, this is . . . We can't. I can't. Not anymore. I'm done." Her face crumpled, crying. A vulnerable creature where her indomitable girl usually sat.

Eleanor felt hollow. She couldn't think of anything else to say or do, since Nasrin had clearly made up her mind, so she closed her laptop and slid it under the bed. She turned the lights off and removed all of her clothes, letting the dark cocoon her. She heard music blare by outside, loud and big, and then slowly fade. Laughter on the street. She wished she was dead so she didn't have to experience anything so painful or thorny as the feeling of loss that had taken residence in her body, expanding and expanding, stretching her skin taut. Principled, hot, devious, charming, infuriating Nasrin.

She couldn't be alone. She half dressed in her T-shirt and underwear, and bolted for Leena's door, knocking insistently, knowing she was on Skype with Dhaval but caring little about that.

"Come in," she heard, muffled.

Eleanor opened the door and saw Leena sitting cross-legged on her bed, wearing headphones. She waved, then pointed down to the screen. "I'm talking to Dhaval. I'll be done in a sec."

Eleanor burst into awful, angry tears, her shoulders drawing forward with the force of it, her stomach clenching. "Nas just fucking broke up with me." Her gaze stayed on the hardwood floor.

"Oh, no. Dhav, I have to go. Did you hear that? Oh. Nasrin broke up with El . . . I know. Love you. Text you later."

Eleanor heard Leena putting her computer away.

"Do you know you're not wearing any pants?" Leena asked, her voice so serious that Eleanor couldn't help but laugh. She looked up, laughing, and Leena looked petrified. "I'm so sorry. I don't know what to do. What should we do? What will help?"

Eleanor sniffled. "Nothing. Everything is terrible." She slumped against the doorframe, feeling exhausted.

Leena shrugged, then nodded. "We have ice cream? And we definitely have wine."

Eleanor burrowed into the bed while Leena went and gathered supplies. She selected a television episode to stream that she'd seen a million times, the drumming striking up before "Previously, on *The West Wing*" played, a show Nasrin hated.

Leena arrived with a pint of ice cream and a bottle of wine. "Felix has decided that you can eat right out of the container and drink from the bottle," Leena said, handing Eleanor a spoon.

Eleanor beamed, her worn heart feeling one degree less jittery. She was the one to mostly partake in the sweets and wine that night, and to watch television, as Leena fell asleep soon after, but Eleanor stayed up, warm in her bed. Warm in her presence. Close to her. In her bed.

She queued up the next episode and admitted to herself in the dark: *Maybe Nasrin was right*. Ever since seeing her on the street in San Francisco, she'd felt a certain mélange of friendship and tenderness and desire. Eleanor let all of it simmer on the stove, but now it was—to push the metaphor a bit harder—boiling. She looked over at Leena, her hair spread across the pillow, looking angelic. Then she let out a snore, which was alluring all the same because it was Leena doing it. Everything about Leena was beautiful.

Except, perhaps, that she was engaged. Eleanor made herself look at the ring, that plain band inlaid with discreet diamonds, the symbol of the decision her best friend had made. She had set her own course, and as much as Eleanor disagreed with it, she would never violate what her friend wanted.

As the opening credits of the next episode played, Eleanor recommitted herself to Leena. To be her friend, confidant, roommate. To not cross any more lines, spoken or unspoken.

She picked up her phone and scrolled her contacts until she found Zoe's name. Zoe, who had reached out the month before to welcome her to the city. Zoe, who broke her heart six years ago. Zoe, who wasn't Nasrin or Leena. Eleanor texted her to see if she was free for a drink the next evening.

JULY

"Hey! I'm back!"

Eleanor opened one eye, shutting it immediately against the bright sunshine filling her room. She had neglected to close the shades the night before and was paying for it now—all that light pulsing in against her hungover eyelids. She groaned and checked the time on her phone. 11:03.

"Hey. Oh. Sorry."

Raising her head just enough to see Leena in her doorway, she then turned to where Leena's gaze had landed, on the woman next to Eleanor in bed.

Right.

"No, it's okay," Eleanor croaked and sat up, pulling the sheet up past her naked chest. She looked at Yara, slowly waking at her side, and took in the long, dark curls unfurled on her bed and her lush, round hips barely disguised by the sheet. A body so unlike her ex, and better for it. Yara stretched, her breasts rising with the effort, and blinked slowly, offering a peaceful smile.

By the time Eleanor looked back to the doorway, Leena had disappeared.

Yara didn't stay long. A shimmy into her underwear, a rousing kiss, and a promise to meet up again on Thursday night.

When Eleanor got out of bed, she realized that she ached from sex, and the pride of that raised a smile on her lips. She yanked on shorts and a tank top, threw her hair into a ponytail, and drifted into the kitchen, where Leena was.

"How was Binita's bachelorette party?" Eleanor asked brightly. "Was there penis paraphernalia after all?" She began making a full pot of coffee, trying not to look directly at Leena's inquiring stare.

"Yep. Penis straws." Leena went and grabbed something from her duffel bag. A white sash that, in a pink sparkly script, announced: *I'm the Bride's Bitch*. Leena plucked at it with disdain. "Binita's best friend bought these for us."

Eleanor grabbed the garment and placed it on her own body. "And what was the bride-to-be wearing?"

"One that said, *I'm the Bride, Bitch*. It was very classy."

Eleanor boosted herself up on the counter as Leena cracked an egg.

"Sorry I burst in on you. I thought you were alone." Leena's eyes were locked on the pan. "What was this one's name?"

Eleanor let that loaded question wash over her head and shoulders. The coffee pot gurgled, and she scooted off the counter, grabbing two mugs, getting half-and-half from the fridge. "Yara," she finally said. "And your disapproval has been noted." She poured coffee into both mugs, handing one to Leena.

She took it, eyes wide and caught. "No, El, I didn't mean it like that. It was an honest question. I'm sleep-deprived from all of the bachelorette party shit. I'm sorry."

She didn't know what to believe; she had heard what she'd heard. Because Leena's egg was starting to brown, she turned off the stove and moved the pan to another burner. Leena liked her eggs runny, but apparently she wasn't paying attention. Maybe she actually was sleep-deprived. Eleanor relented and took Leena at her word. "We met at that Rapture on the River thing the night before Pride, in a long line for the bathroom. I was there with Zoe and Ayana. And I went home with Ayana, but I got Yara's number." She'd thought about kissing Yara once they were free from the line, holding on to her hips as they danced wrapped around each other, getting her number before the near-impossible task of finding Ayana and Zoe in a massive crowd of dykes. "I like her. She's funny."

"And cute," Leena added.

"And cute," Eleanor agreed.

They sat at their small, round kitchen table from IKEA, wedged into the corner, drinking coffee, eating breakfast.

Leena cleared her throat. "How did you two . . . reconnect?"

"Well, I was without my buddy for the weekend," Eleanor admitted, with a scallop-edged gesture in Leena's direction. "So I invited Yara out, we had drinks, she came back here, and we talked."

Leena raised an eyebrow.

"No, really! Talked. But then we made out and then, uh, more than made out?" She hid her smile as she sipped her coffee. "It was fun. I had a good time." She nodded her head, putting a stamp of approval on it. She *was* having fun, not focusing on falling in love or building connections or giving herself to someone.

There was no point. There were only Nasrins and Lee-nas, and neither was interested. Instead: new life, new women, no looking back.

Leena quickly finished her egg and got up to put her plate in the sink.

"Will you defrost a bagel for me?" Eleanor asked, slumping on the table. Her hangover, which had momentarily receded, was back.

"Yeah. Split one?"

Eleanor's phone vibrated in her pocket. "Yep," she said, distracted, and read Zoe's text.

Ginger's tonight? I'm meeting up with Adelaide, that chick from the Dyke March

Eleanor barely considered the invitation. "We're going to Ginger's tonight," she announced, typing a **Yesss!** back to Zoe.

"Who is the *we* in that sentence?"

"You, me, Zoe." Eleanor heard the microwave slam behind her, and she turned around.

Leena was rummaging through the fridge. "I can't. I have to prep for the week," she said, her words muffled.

Eleanor made a buzzer noise. "Boring. Let's go out."

Leena plunked a plate, a knife, and cream cheese in a foil block on the table. "I can't."

Eleanor rolled her eyes and finished her coffee. "You're being really weird. Drinks. Women. It'll take my mind off Nas, and yours off work and shit. What's not to like?"

"I get jealous."

Eleanor looked up. She must have heard those words wrong. Leena, for her part, jumped when she heard the microwave's beep, and Eleanor turned to follow Leena with her eyes. Slicing the bagel, placing two halves in the toaster. *I get jealous.* Jealous of what? Of whom? Eleanor's heart fluttered with possibility. There was so much to ask after that admission, but Eleanor was afraid of spooking her, so she didn't say anything, and just poured them both more coffee.

"I mean. My engagement. It's hitting me that I'm going to be married. You're meeting new people, and it's something that I won't get again. And I'm . . . envious." Leena kept her body half turned away, but Eleanor could still see her face in profile: eyes down and dreary, lips stitched together, troubled. When she saw Eleanor taking her in, and their eyes met, she shook her head and a resolute smile appeared on her face. "Never mind. I'll go. Because it's really not a big deal. Sounds good."

The bagel halves were closer to burnt by the time they reached the table.

AUGUST

The air was thick and hot, and Leena rushed Eleanor through it, out of the apartment building and toward the subway. She was already exhausted at eight in the morning.

"We need to line up for the bus. We need to get there early," Leena instructed for what felt like the twentieth time.

Eleanor rolled her eyes. "We have tickets and so much time. We're fine. Can you slow down, please?" She was practically running to keep up, her rolling suitcase barreling behind her.

"This is the difference between us," Leena said over her shoulder. "I won't risk being late, and you tempt fate."

"I don't tempt fate," she replied, hurrying along. "I'm just not, like, asking for the universe to curse me."

It felt like they were cursed, though, when their C train into Manhattan slowed, and then didn't move. By minute thirty-one, Leena wouldn't even look in her direction.

"You can't blame mechanical issues on me." Eleanor smelled sweat and annoyance in the ether, in the absence of air-conditioning.

"I can and will, but it's not that. I'm just feeling . . . anxious, or something."

Eleanor swiveled her head, surveying Leena's visage. Her eyes were alarmed, her skin drawn taut, looking as if she could hollow in on herself. She put a hand to her friend's back, guiding her head to rest between her knees. "Breathe deep, in and out." She hoped this would be helpful. It seemed to be in movies and TV shows.

"The reminder to keep breathing is really helpful," Leena replied, her voice faint from its position. After a few more breaths, she resurfaced, flushed and looking grateful. "Thanks. Even though, again, I'm blaming this on you."

Eleanor couldn't tell if she was being serious or not.

"This is going to put us behind. We'll have to get new bus tickets, then wait for that bus. We'll throw off the entire schedule. And then everyone will be pissed for the rest of the weekend, probably longer. Indians have a long memory."

Eleanor turned to her histrionic friend, amused. So she was serious. "And then democracy will fall, and the sun will swallow the earth—the end."

Leena smiled, as Eleanor had hoped she would. "It's important! There's a schedule."

"What, with a spreadsheet?" Eleanor asked.

Leena looked at her incredulously and produced a one-inch-thick binder with timelines, contact information, and schematics.

"Have you been moonlighting as an event coordinator?" Eleanor asked, agape, flipping through the pages. "I had no idea a wedding was this complicated."

"It's not just a wedding. It's the mehndi party, followed by the sangeet, and then the ceremony and reception tomorrow. Every event has vendors and music and decorations."

Eleanor shook her head slowly. "Is this typical?"

Leena sighed and checked the time on her phone. "Some are even more ostentatious."

There had been a time when the idea of marriage was alluring and radical, illegal while not technically a crime. Two brides atop a wedding cake. But the fairy tale of happily ever after had soured in her mouth years back and embittered her on weddings, marriage, the whole of it. "I'm never getting married," she announced from the most hurt and fatigued place inside of her.

"Good that you can't legally get married, then," Leena said, prickly. "I can't believe we still haven't moved."

It was a rude thing to say, a burn tinged with the blush of homophobia, but she understood Leena's mental state: stressed to the roots of her hair, to the backs of her knees. "Maybe if we wish really, really hard," Eleanor teased in a delicate, pixie voice. She could live with Leena talking to her that way, at least for this weekend. She could be the bigger woman. The train lurched in one gasp, then stilled. She did indeed wish very, very hard—and the train took off at a slow crawl, the air-conditioning shuddering back to life. She squeezed Leena's hand in celebration, and Leena's hand lingered in her grip. After a half hour of iciness, it was everything.

"I'm sorry I said that thing about getting married," Leena said quietly. "That was rude."

Eleanor nodded. "It's okay. You didn't mean it." She knew that without hearing confirmation. "And I was kind of . . . dismissive. We're going to a wedding." She swallowed. "And you're getting married soon too. Even if I don't think it's necessary."

Leena sported her thinking face of befuddlement

and argument crafting. "It's about family. Joining histories. Those long lines of people before you who made families and homes together. Who stayed a strong unit when it got tough."

To Eleanor, all of that could be achieved without marriage. It didn't compute, but Leena looked so stalwart, and she wasn't about to argue, not when her argument was: love doesn't last. There was a time when she thought love and romance were what would save her from a normal, boring life, but she could no longer trust in being saved. Maybe her disillusionment made its way to her face, because Leena wrapped an arm around her, their sticky skin shifting and rubbing against each other.

"Did you ever want to marry Noa?" Eleanor asked. "You were together for a while."

Leena shook her head. "No." She laughed to herself. "No, I wanted to wear her. I wanted to be her. I wanted to surgically attach myself to her."

"Gross," Eleanor replied, but she was struck, shocked, by the intensity and poetry of those words. She knew Leena had never felt that way about her, and it seemed clear that she did not yearn to wear Dhaval. Maybe Noa alone had engendered that in Leena. Not for the first time, Eleanor was jealous.

Leena shrugged, slowly pulling her arm away, releasing Eleanor. "We were too much to last. I think a good marriage is about being friends, and I craved too much of her. Plus, it wasn't legal anywhere."

"Massachusetts," Eleanor corrected. "Where you lived while you two were dating. But I guess that's irrelevant. You'll be able to marry anywhere now."

Leena nodded, smiling, eyes falsely bright, like she was attempting cheer.

The train shoved into the High Street station. A trickle of grumpy people exited, replaced by a bottle blond with a dog peeking out of her bag and a worn, older Asian woman, who took a sleepy seat next to them as the train departed and another one screeched into place across the track.

A fragile parade of expressions flitted over Leena's face: disagreement and agreement and revulsion and joy. "If I'm getting married, I'm glad it's to Dhav." Said like a politician on the stump, diplomatically, with a theoretical relationship to the truth.

She longed for Leena to be honest about what she wanted, because Eleanor knew it wasn't convention. It wasn't a three bedroom in the South Bay with a nice guy. It wasn't a minivan and two ungrateful brats. But knowing Leena, all her facets and intricacies and blemishes, Eleanor wasn't sure what she wanted for her life without constraints or limits. If she could speak her future into existence, what would she have said?

They were sitting in front of a subway-system map, and a skeptical tourist with a French accent asked them to move their heads. Leena obliged, and so did Eleanor, begrudgingly.

"I'm glad you're happy." That was all Eleanor could manage. "When is he flying in?"

"Tomorrow. And his parents are driving up." Leena's words were limp, her face equal in exhaustion. But then her visage changed, a pinched smile appearing out of nowhere. Maybe that was all Leena could manage.

When they emerged aboveground, they ran like hell up Eighth Avenue and over to Thirty-Sixth Street, Eleanor's bag skipping, catching air. The bus was almost full, with two aisle seats near the bathroom still empty. Adrenaline pumped through her body as they took their spots, Eleanor in front of Leena. She turned around to see Leena with her eyes shut and head against the headrest, in recovery mode.

"Shit!" she said to her. "We forgot something!"

Leena's eyes shot open as Eleanor silently laughed. "I'm sorry, I couldn't help it."

Leena shook her head and closed her eyes, and didn't say a word to Eleanor until somewhere in Connecticut.

IT WAS BINITA who picked them up at South Station in Boston, pulled to the roadside while they jumped into the gracefully aging Toyota, Leena up front and Eleanor in the back. "I had to get out! Mom is driving me up a fucking wall. Hey, Eleanor. Are you two dressed alike?" Once buckled in, she launched them into the voracious, jumbled traffic.

Eleanor cast an exploratory glance at herself and Leena. She hadn't noticed it before, but they both had on black tank tops, jean shorts, sturdy sandals, with their hair up in messy knots. In another car, she would have remarked how gay this was. She nodded. "Your sister is always copying me."

The last time she had seen Binita, she was helping them move in, and she had been casual, with little makeup. This version of Binita was in a dress with her hair done, and bright-red lips and fake eyelashes and contoured cheeks. Her skin looked lighter, like she'd been inside for two years.

"How can you drive in heels?" Leena cackled in a menacing voice only heard when she talked to her sister.

That voice, that tone—it sounded like it was from the Little Sister Handbook. She knew its companion, because she had heard it from her little brother many times before. **Hey nerd**, she texted Fitz, in a swell of nostalgic love.

She watched Boston from the back seat. The last time she was here, she was graduating college, with Suzukis and Schwartzes descending on her and the city. She had been itching to get out and start her life, to bring about substantive change. With wiser eyes, she looked back fondly on twenty-one, before any cynicism had entered her bloodstream, and wondered what her younger self would think of where she'd ended up and who'd she become.

"Seriously, Mom is following me around, asking me a ton of questions, questioning everything I do. Leena, distract her, okay? That's your job today."

At the light, Leena turned around and made a face at Eleanor, eyes squeezed shut and tongue out. She wasn't sure what that meant, but she inferred it was a reaction to Binita and her dictates.

"So, what's new?" Binita threw over her shoulder, toward Eleanor.

"I hate my job and my girlfriend dumped me. So, I'm great."

Leena turned around again and shook her head in what looked like disappointment. Her eyes went comically wide and she wore a giant plastic smile on her face.

Eleanor took the hint. "But, Binita, this weekend is not about my woes! It's about your wedding!"

"It is, you're right," Binita said cheerfully, and Leena nodded. "I hope the sun stays shining." Binita turned the radio on and way up to a song about a DJ and love and commands to dance, a bumping synth beat underneath everything.

They drove on the highway, city giving way to suburbs, and meandered into new terrain, local roads that ran past groves of coniferous trees. She watched very carefully, observing this foundational place from which Leena had emerged, plunking down their upbringings side by side in her mind and imagining them the same: Girl Scouts, team sports, violin rehearsals, first bras and periods in the same year, experimental drinking, aimless driving, fervor to get away. California, Massachusetts. It was all the same.

In time, they pulled up to a perfectly average yellow-sided two-story house. She'd always thought houses in New England were charming, the model on which kids drew with crayons: a triangle sitting on top of a square, with a squiggle of smoke coming out of a tacked-on rectangular chimney. Her childhood home, long and ranch-style, was a snore to render.

They stepped inside, where it was somehow warmer than it was outside. Mrs. Shah appeared, yelled at Binita in Gujarati, then hugged Leena briefly before releasing her. "Hi, Eleanor. Have you been to an Indian wedding before? It's exciting, yeah?" And then she was gone, tugging Binita away.

Once Dr. Shah got off the phone, he beelined to Leena and Eleanor, wrapping an arm around his daughter's shoulders and releasing her quickly. "Hi, Eleanor. Thank you for coming. It's a special day. And by that I mean, Leena will actually dress up. That's the special occasion." He laughed at his own joke, and she couldn't help but join out of politeness and the intimacy they shared by both wanting to poke fun at Leena.

"I know, right? Something that's not jeans?"

Leena glared at Eleanor then at her father before getting rushed away by Binita.

Her father grinned. The spare times Eleanor had been with them, he always seemed so delighted by Leena. She knew the feeling.

"Eleanor, I don't think you have met Leena's grandmother, my mother. Ba, tamari dava lai ledhi?"

She saw the short old woman walking toward her in a plain, emerald-green cotton sari. Her mostly gray hair was swept back in a bun. Eleanor focused on her face, wrinkled and beautiful brown skin. She was reminded of her obachan, old and lovely too. As with her obachan, she had the expectation of a language barrier.

"No, I did not. But I will," she said solemnly to her son, in English, with a light and airy Indian accent. As he walked away, she winked. "Eleanor, it's very nice to meet you. Have you had anything to eat yet? We just made some dhokla. Are you vegetarian? It is vegetarian." She took Eleanor's arm and kept talking, pulling her into the kitchen. "Your name is Eleanor. That is a beautiful name."

"Um, yes, thank you. My mom named me Eleanor, from a character in a Jane Austen novel. Spelled differently, though."

Leena's grandmother yanked down hard on Eleanor's arm. Her eyes were ablaze. "*Sense and Sensibility*. One of my favorites! I read it when I was a girl and completely understood. The struggles of family, responsibility, and love. I went to a British school," she said with a note of pride. "We learned about the great works."

That surprised Eleanor. She didn't think Indian people would take pleasure in anything British.

"Not like my son and daughter-in-law. Education changed after Independence. Children of my son's generation do not know the graceful words of Austen."

Here she was with Leena's grandmother, who she would only be thoroughly polite to, and yet she seemed to be praising British colonialism. She looked around for Leena, or anyone else, any eavesdropper. *I need someone to explain what the fuck is happening.*

Her walking companion fixed her a plate of something that looked like cornbread. She sat her down at the small table in the kitchen. "You must drink this with milk. I will get it for you."

Eleanor wasn't even hungry, but she dutifully took a bite. She drank the milk too, as ordered. It was delicious, and she had another slice as Leena's grandmother argued about the relatability of Austen for an Indian audience.

"Ba!" she heard behind her, and whirled around.

Leena and Binita surged into the kitchen, Leena ducking to kiss her seated grandmother. "So, you've met Eleanor. What do you think? Can she stay? Does she pass your test?"

Leena's grandmother nodded, smiling. "She does. Are you hungry, Beta? What do you want? I will make it."

Leena shrugged. "No, I'm okay. I'll finish Eleanor's dhokla."

"You should eat. You've been traveling," Mrs. Shah said, joining them in the kitchen. She wiped down the counter and scanned like she was looking for something, anything, to do. To fix.

Binita popped open a Diet Coke, which made Leena scoff. "Binita should eat," Leena mumbled under her breath.

"I am eating, Leena," Binita replied, saying her sister's name with knives in the consonants. "I'm watching myself carefully so I don't look fat in wedding photos that will last my whole life, so excuse me."

"You're also using Fair & Lovely, I can totally tell. Your skin looks really weird."

"What is Fair & Lovely?" Eleanor whispered to Leena.

"It's skin-lightening cream for dumb Desi women," Leena replied, her voice audible to the whole room.

Eleanor's head ping-ponged between the two sisters, deadlocked in an intense glaring match. If she were younger, and if she had had a cocktail or three, she would have roared about feminism and the mutilation of women's bodies and the betrayal of one's ancestors. But this was Leena's family, and she could shut up and help keep things on track for Leena.

"So!" she said with forced cheer. "What needs to get done? I'm here to help."

"You're a guest. Please, be a guest," Mrs. Shah replied with a curt nod. "Leena has things to do, though, and she knows."

"I do. And I know," Leena replied sharply. "Let's get settled," she said to Eleanor, leaving the kitchen abruptly.

"Thank you again, really, it was so good." Eleanor retreated from the kitchen behind Leena and upstairs with their suitcases, the air even more stifling on this level. She rounded into a room, the first one on the right, and found herself in a museum frozen in time. A Mia Hamm poster tacked to the wall, sagging on aged paper. Another poster detailing constellations. A white particle-board desk and office chair. A pink bedspread on a twin bed. Eleanor explored every inch, fascinated, reading Leena's first-place certificate at a science fair, and gazing on a photo from a dance recital, Leena and Binita and their squad in heavy makeup and sequined bike shorts.

"I hated it. I hated the mirrors and the lights in the dance studio."

"But you love dancing," Eleanor said as she struck gold: a line of yearbooks on the bookshelf.

"That's different."

Eleanor pulled out one volume to study and stretched out on Leena's bed, leafing through *Lowell High School 1998–1999*. All yearbooks were the same: portraits and club group shots and ersatz school spirit. A younger, more serious Leena stared up at her from the soccer team photo. She turned to look at her now. "I forgot about your illustrious soccer career."

Leena settled gingerly on the edge of the bed, her hip tucked in next to Eleanor's. "Ha, yeah. Illustrious until I hurt my knee."

She could imagine a teenage Leena on the soccer field, running around, kicking, ponytail flying. A carefree girl with her eyes on the goal. The nostalgia shifted from the imagined to the real, as she was reminded of the Leena and Eleanor they had been. Younger, more awkward, sitting on beds together, as they were now. How they'd transitioned to more. Sleeping next to Leena, sex with Leena, kissing her, kissing her thighs, that first hit of her . . .

But she had told herself that she wouldn't do this, no matter how much her mind wandered. Leena needed support, stability, a friend. Eleanor opened her mouth and let her inane chatting skills shine. "Have you seen my room? My room at home. At my parents' house. Well, maybe you haven't. They actually redid it once I moved out, and now it's my dad's office. Now I sleep on a futon in the basement when I go home. You'll see it all eventually."

"How are your parents?" she asked, like she genuinely wanted to know, curiosity sprinkled across her face.

Eleanor was awash in gratitude. Bringing up her parents was cold water on the hearth of her desire. "My parents are fine. Good. Taking care of my obachan. She's ninety-one, and she *just* retired from the bookstore. My uncle is running it now. Did you know my family has a bookstore, a Japanese bookstore? Anyway, my grandmother is still really sharp and agile, though my dad says that's slowly, um . . . changing." Her chatter slid into real life: the concerning signals of her grandmother's decline. It struck her soundly, like it had her dad, frightened and refusing to admit it.

"Shikata ga nai," he'd said during a phone call the other day, his voice absent of the usual breeze and shrug it usually had when he extolled the wisdom of their people. His lack of assuredness made her scared in turn, for him and Obachan, and her, rounding it out. Her own mortality would come knocking on the door someday or another.

She was no longer grateful to Leena.

"Um, speaking of family," Leena said, pulling at a loose thread on her bedspread, "you know mine is so

. . . traditional. We can't talk about things. So it's better if they don't come up."

Eleanor trailed her eyes over the back pages of the yearbook, where Tina wrote, *I mean, how would I have gotten thru honors trig w/o u?* Roshni thanked her for being a good friend. Donna was psyched that they had gotten to know each other through soccer. Siobhan said she seriously loved her and wanted to *K.I.T.* "For sure I don't know what that means," Eleanor said to her friend, pointing to the page.

"Keep in touch!"

Eleanor grinned. "So, what were you talking about?"

Leena sighed. She stood, wrapping herself in a hug, eyes on the worn periwinkle wall-to-wall carpeting. "In front of my family. We can't talk about anything gay."

"What, like aggressively tight ponytails? Loving astrology?" she joked.

Leena's face pinched with a painful smile. She wouldn't be entertaining any humor. "No, that's not what I mean. We can't talk about your breakup, or Ginger's, or that Prop 8 decision."

Don't tell them about who we were. Leena left that off the list. She had asked her earlier in the year not to disclose their history, and at the time, in that moment, Eleanor said no. She wasn't a liar or an obfuscator. In January, Leena so freshly back in her life, she didn't want to meet Dhaval, didn't want to know anything about this left turn. Eventually she relented and met him, all for Leena. Everything was always for Leena.

A fragile silence hung in the room. She watched her best friend look devastated, worse than when she thought her boyfriend, now fiancé, would break up with her. She closed the tome and said nothing, just slid

316

it back onto the shelf nestled between *The Island of the Colorblind* and Leena's sophomore yearbook. She felt a deep sadness and disquiet for what Leena had to endure. The endless ducks and weaves, the exhaustion of hiding in plain view. She felt sorry for her and pulled Leena into a hug.

"Thank you." She felt Leena clutch her like a life raft.

"Of course," she replied without a beat.

After they showered, when it was time to get dressed, Leena opened her closet. Inside was an array of beautiful Indian clothes in pinks and reds and blues and greens that were absent from her Brooklyn wardrobe. Beading. Shimmery fabric. Eleanor cast a look to Leena, who was grimacing.

Leena shook her head. "Okay, so my mom probably got me something new to wear, and we'll fight about that for a while. For you, tonight, I am recommending a suit." She pulled out a long top with matching bottoms in iridescent blue. It was beautiful, as everything else was, but too small. Leena was then more selective, finally going with an outfit in gold fabric, a long, short-sleeved top that fell to Eleanor's knees, and pink pants that were tight to her calves but otherwise baggy.

Eleanor's eyes lit up. She would never buy something like this but thought it was wonderful, and even though it was tight, it was too lovely not to wear. She stayed dressed, following Leena downstairs.

"Mom? Did you buy something for me?" Leena yelled, prowling around for her mother.

In the time that they were upstairs, the house had swelled with people. Women milled around, dressed in saris and kurtas, while men wore short-sleeved shirts and pants. It was always women who caught her eye, and this moment was no exception, as the women colorfully stood out in olive greens and bright purples and peacock blues; with hair up in knots, or down and straight, shimmering; lips painted red or deep plum. She was startled by the sound of Leena's voice shouting in Gujarati, but followed that into what looked like Mrs. Shah's bedroom. Mrs. Shah was already dressed in a turquoise sari with a pink patterned blouse underneath. In their past run-ins, Leena's mother had worn generic Mom clothes, but today she was regal.

"Mrs. Shah, you look amazing," Eleanor couldn't help but say, breaking through the argument. She hadn't noticed before the ways in which the two women in front of her looked alike.

Looking flattered, Mrs. Shah gave a weary smile, like she was exhausted from receiving compliments. "Thank you." She turned back to Leena.

Eleanor hung back, sweeping her eyes across the various skirts, tops, pants, and saris laid out on the bed. Except for a bright-orange choice, everything seemed like a winner.

Mrs. Shah threw up her arms. "Fine! Wear whatever!" She left the room, gathering her sari in her hands so as to not trip on it as she walked.

"Can you shut the door, Eleanor?" Leena asked.

Eleanor did as requested as Leena shed her clothes and pulled on a black top with beading that hit her midstomach, then a long, full skirt with folds. She tied a matching piece of material over her shoulder and to the other side, like a sash. She had never seen Leena look so glamorous. It wasn't a look that fit her at all— she looked uncomfortable in these clothes—yet she was beautiful, that was an undeniable fact. Radiant, luminous, and all of those things Eleanor wasn't supposed to think.

"Okay, cool, let's go." Leena rushed out of the room before Eleanor could do or say anything else.

The party was already in full swing in the backyard, the small space taken up by a huge, white tent, where people wandered around, eating and talking. Binita now wore a pale-pink sari, her makeup amped up even more than before. She was surrounded by young and old women as two others bent over her, applying mehndi to her hands and feet.

Leena was immediately swept away, and Eleanor stood alone, unsure of what to do in this sea of Indian people she had never met. She hit the food first, a long stretch of snacks: samosas, pani puri, chaat, pakoras, desserts. She filled her plate and watched everyone filter by, aware of her non-Indianness, and though no one was paying her mind, she felt like she stood out. She wished there was booze.

Leena's grandmother maneuvered into place at her side. "Do you like Indian food?"

She caught Eleanor with her mouth full. She nodded, swallowing. "Yes. Very much so."

"Does Leena make Indian food in your apartment?"

Eleanor felt like this was a Grandmother Trap, designed to interrogate. "Sometimes? But she's so busy with work."

"And preparing for her own wedding," Leena's grandmother added.

Leena's wedding. Two words that inspired much in her mind, none of it good. Leena's wedding. She wondered if it would be like this. The same outfits, people, and food. Leena wouldn't want all of this fuss. It wasn't for her. She was wearing black, for god's sake, in a crowd of people bright and energetic with color.

"Do you have a boyfriend?" Leena's grandmother leaned in when Eleanor shook her head no. "You know, Indian men make very good husbands," she said quietly, then pressed a finger to her lips, and looked around. "There are many young men here today."

Eleanor scanned the room. The older woman was exaggerating. Most of the men were her father's age, or children. The few men that might be marriage material were fine looking. She wasn't closed to the idea of a man; it didn't repulse her; love was love was love. But if there was to be a spouse in her future, it wouldn't be a man, because only women inspired longing, desire, and heartbreak in her. She held her tongue as Leena requested, despite the fact that it felt like the worst kind of lying, to squash one of the things about herself that Eleanor felt was most true and great. "Thank you," she replied, looking away. "I'll keep that in mind."

With the mehndi drying on Binita, Leena, their mother, and other women, the sangeet commenced with speeches in a mix of English and Gujarati, platitudes about Binita's beauty, backbone, wonderful family, and her prized choice of fiancé. Eleanor took in the softening night: the twinkle lights hanging around the inside of the tent, the chilled breeze emulsifying with stilted heat.

Once the last speaker cleared the parquet wood floor, Leena and a cluster of other young women gathered, barefoot, getting into position. The bubbly and synth-based Indian pop music cranked up, and the women danced in tandem with movements of sheer athleticism and stamina, but paired with coy and feminine hand movements. She watched in wonder and surprise. When had she learned this intricate routine? When did she rehearse? Something about this revelation was even more impressive than the dance, which was itself impressive—the skirt twirling and hip undulating and constant grinning.

When they finished to great applause and enthusiastic whooping, another shift began. Tables and chairs were pushed back as new percussive music blared and everyone gathered into a circle. Eleanor was handed sticks wrapped with bright fabric and gold thread, but she hung back on the outside, watching as guests fell into a rhythm, swinging their own sticks to tap others at the appropriate time. A smaller circle formed inside the larger loop, containing Binita and Leena and their parents.

Eleanor loved dancing, even if rhythm was absent from her body, but at the moment she could only think ahead to Leena's wedding. It would come soon enough, before she was ready, and she would be here again, probably in this backyard and maybe even in this exact spot. She didn't want to keep going in circles. When Leena caught her eye, she flashed her the brightest smile she could muster.

"WHY ARE YOU going to steal Sagar's shoes?" Eleanor asked, interrupting Leena's to-do list rundown.

"It's not personal. It's just what you do."

"But why?" Eleanor shifted on the air mattress, the land raft squeaking against carpet.

Leena sighed. "He gives us money to give them back. It's a play; it's about joining families. Everyone has roles. And Nita's best friend Tejal created a whole plan. We practically have walkie-talkies and earpieces. It's very Secret Service."

"It's literally extortion."

"Yeah, but it's fun and cultural extortion. I'm sure there are Japanese traditions that are difficult to explain."

She racked her brain. "There's this holiday, Setsubun, where my dad would put on a demon mask and we'd throw dry beans at him." The last time they'd done it she had been in high school, Fitz in middle school, and they behaved like brats, so sarcastic and over it.

"Huh? Sorry, Dhav just texted that he landed. What did you say?"

Eleanor rolled away, wide awake. "Nah, never mind. I'm just gonna go to sleep. Good night." But she couldn't sleep. She tortured herself more with thoughts of Leena and Dhaval's wedding. Maybe she'd be sleeping on this exact same air mattress before her friend's wedding, before she became someone else entirely, out of reach.

The bedside light flicked on with a sigh. She heard Leena open a book.

It was inevitable. She was going to lose Leena again. She barely felt rested when the alarm went off at six a.m.

Leena groaned and stumbled out of bed, away somewhere, and returned a few minutes later with steaming mugs. "You can go back to sleep for a while, or you can hang out with us. Up to you."

Eleanor rubbed at her eyes, leaning up on her elbows. "I—coffee?"

Leena shook her head and held out a cup. "It's chai. But I can drive you to Dunkin' Donuts? It's Massachusetts. There's one on every corner. There's a DD inside a DD."

Eleanor squinted and accepted the cup, slurping down the hot chai mixed with milk, almost thick like a hot chocolate. She got up after a few sips.

The preparations commenced in Binita's room, with a makeup artist and hairstylist already on hand. Eleanor hung back and watched in fascination as the transformation began on Binita, Leena, and Mrs. Shah. With a base layer of beauty applied, the photographer joined them and began shooting the process.

Eleanor went to retrieve water bottles for everyone and practically knocked into Dr. Shah.

"I'm staying out of the way!" he said over his shoulder, retreating back to his room.

She balanced the bottles in her arms as she climbed the stairs, back to the room across from Leena's.

"Long, loose curls, Leena," Binita said huffily. "You're not being waterboarded."

"Leena, Beta, it will look so nice. Do this for your sister."

"I don't need anything. Just a blow-dryer. Straight hair, that's all I need," she said, turning to the hairstylist. "I don't need a lot of look. It's not my day."

"But you're my sister. There's going to be a lot of eyes on you. You should look nice."

Leena was eyeing Eleanor, with expectation in her expression, demanding advocacy.

"Leena will look nice no matter what?" she offered limply.

"Leena," Mrs. Shah said pointedly with a look that would have been clear from a hundred feet away—*You will obey me.*

Leena sat sullenly as her hair was sculpted with a curling iron.

A few hours later, makeup and hair done and documented, the women separated to get ready. Eleanor borrowed a stretchy choli, more comfortable than the tight top from the day before, and tied the petticoat's drawstring at her waist.

"No, tighter. And lift your arms up," Leena instructed, swooping in close.

Eleanor obliged, tying tighter and lifting her arms up, as Leena followed a learned pattern of looping the sari around her waist several times, then pinning the remaining fabric's end in place over Eleanor's right shoulder.

It reminded her of being dressed by her grandmother and her strong, sure hands. There was a slip, then the kimono, that one-size-fits-all garment pulled up high enough so as not to trip, then the sash to hold it in place, then the obi over top to secure everything at the waist. Obachan would always tie it too tight, and when Eleanor would complain, her grandmother would mutter in reply, "Ganbare, ganbare." *Hang in there. Be strong.*

Despite dressing Eleanor by rote, Leena looked harried and stressed, like she was unraveling. Eleanor could see it on her face, the tightness of her mouth, the knit of her eyebrows. It contrasted with her polished hair and makeup, a magazine version of beautiful. Eleanor liked her best with no makeup, hair in a ponytail. That's how she pictured Leena when she wasn't around.

"So many pins," Eleanor said. "What if one busts open and sticks me, and then I start bleeding everywhere?"

In the mirror, she could see Leena rolling her eyes.

"Just, like, a trail of blood," Eleanor continued, "spurting all over your family and on somebody's white boyfriend, who everyone wishes wasn't there anyway."

Leena's mouth relaxed. "If you're trying to gross me out, you know that won't work. I was premed."

"I'm trying to make you laugh. You seem like you're on your last nerve."

Leena smiled to herself, continuing her work of pinning and tugging. Her eyes flitted to Eleanor's, jumpy and nervous. Addressing it head-on didn't seem to be the solution. But then she nodded, slowly, with a minute movement of her head. "I guess. There's a lot to do today. I want everything to go well." She stepped away from Eleanor, appraising her, circling her, and nodded again. "You're good to go. You look good."

Eleanor looked in the mirror. She loved it—the multicolored fabric wrapped and draped around her, contouring to her figure, transforming her into someone else. It was like playing dress up. So, this was what cultural appropriation was like.

"Dhaval and his family are coming today," Leena said, in the voice she used before a deluge of truth. Unrehearsed and vulnerable, pitched and wavering. "It feels like a lot of pressure. It feels like . . . this is the start. First this formal meeting of the families, then our own timeline begins." Leena looked stricken by her own words, but then she waved her away. "I'm sorry. I didn't get enough sleep. I'm being dramatic. The answer is Dunkin' Donuts on the way to the venue. The answer is always Dunkin' Donuts." Leena applied a bright smile to her face before starting to dress herself, then called for her mother to help her the rest of the way into her lilac sari.

They arrived at the hotel early to put everything in place in the reception hall: card box, guest book, extra supplies in the restrooms, ticking items off on Leena's list as they went. The room where the ceremony would be held was dressed and quiet, chairs set up auditorium-style, facing a platform with what looked like a huge chuppah, and ornate pillows and chairs underneath.

"It's a mandap," Leena replied when Eleanor asked what it was.

Eleanor's eyes traced the draping in red and cream, and the floral garlands that followed the fabric. She turned to Leena, who had tears in her eyes.

"My sister is getting married. I didn't let it sink in until now." Stoic, edged, steeled Leena. The tears were streaming down her cheeks. She stepped up to the platform, holding out a hand to Eleanor, and she accepted. "She is making a lifelong promise to the future. It is breathtaking, and so overwhelming."

Once on the platform, Eleanor observed the two fancy chairs in the center, low to the ground and covered in white satin, along with the regular hotel chairs to the right and left.

"Those are seats for me and my parents, and Sagar's sister and parents," Leena said, sniffling. "And that little plate-box thing in the middle, that'll be for the fire. Their clothes will get tied together by Sagar's mom, then they'll circle the fire seven times. There will be so much Sanskrit that no one understands. And then, she'll move over and sit with her new family." Her face, forlorn, stayed locked on the mandap floor.

Eleanor gathered Leena in a hug. It was different, hugging her like this, in these clothes, on the stage of someone else's marriage. It felt like they were other people. "She's still your sister. That doesn't change."

"Yeah, but things change when you get . . ."

Leena didn't finish, but Eleanor filled in the blanks. That this wasn't all about Binita. Maybe she had been suffering in the same way that Eleanor had been, because the flame that once roared between them, which went out years ago, started flickering back to life. She pulled back just enough to see Leena's face. Tearstained, eye makeup jagged. She looked worn, like she was tired from fighting, but nothing could keep her from looking beautiful to Eleanor. "I really want to kiss you," Eleanor whispered. They were so close she was sure that her breath touched Leena's lips. "I know I shouldn't want that, or say that, but it's true."

Leena didn't look surprised or scared, like Eleanor had imagined. Her eyes were watching, waiting. "We shouldn't want that," Leena replied.

A jolt of electricity spiked through Eleanor's body. *We. We shouldn't want that.* That was all Eleanor needed to put a hand on the back of Leena's neck, stroking softly, and pull her into a kiss. Leena, who had unfurled such sadness and heartbreak within the walls of her body. She closed her eyes and thought of six years before. It had been a bad kiss: rushed, their teeth clashing, off by a centimeter. Leena pulled Eleanor back to her, and this kiss was the one to ruin empires and build cathedrals and change the universe, with flashes of yearning that went beyond kissing, with a passion first honed as college kids. Their lips pressed together, then Eleanor kissed back with her tongue.

"Rehearsing?"

Shocked by the sound of someone's voice in the enormous room, she jumped apart from Leena and turned her head, trying to locate who had shattered their moment.

"Sorry," said a sheepish young man in a uniform, pushing a cart of chairs. "I couldn't resist. We haven't had a lesbian Indian wedding yet. Congratulations, you guys."

"Thank you," Leena said, taking Eleanor's hand in hers.

Eleanor's pulse beat irregularly and quickly, her palm sweaty.

Once he was gone, Leena dropped her hand and climbed off the platform. "That could have been anyone walking in. We shouldn't have done that," she said over her shoulder, making quick work of getting out of the room, as if she was trying to outrun an ominous, crashing wave.

Eleanor sat on the edge of the platform, trying to catch her breath while her head spun. She was in suburban Massachusetts at eight a.m. She could get a ride to the house, then to a train station, then back to New York, where she could pick up her passport and leave the country forever, never to face Leena again. Seemed like a sensible, realistic plan. But instead, she hitched up the skirt of her sari and left the mandap, straightening the chairs and doing anything she could to be of help. That's why she was here with Leena, and no matter how much a fool she felt, and how scared she was for her future minutes and days, that was her job today. To help. She thought of her obachan saying "ganbare." She greeted Mrs. and Dr. Shah when they arrived, keeping Leena's grandmother company and offering her arm as she walked around. She gave directions to family and friends, to the bathroom or the nearest outlet to charge a phone. She helped corral people toward the entrance when Sagar arrived in the back seat of a convertible as his family danced around him, toward the hotel. There was so much effervescent joy and color and music, but she felt disconnected from it, with this looming storm cloud over her head and the fact that Leena would barely speak a word to her on a day when everyone else was celebrating.

During the ceremony itself, she took a seat in the last row, giving Leena as much space as possible. From here she could watch her unabashedly, on the small stage with the rest of the wedding party, as her friend fought to keep her emotions in check. Eleanor wished she could sit at her side, holding her hand, telling her everything would be wonderful, that nothing would change, and anything else she wanted to hear.

Of course, change was now inevitable, with the kiss still smoldering on her lips. She reached out and brushed a hand over her mouth, like she could conjure the moment back to life. Her heart buzzed, her blood sparkled in its stream. There were sure to be consequences, fallout, and destruction—but for a minute she let herself drown in feeling kissed.

The ceremony seemed intimate, just for family. Everyone else was a passing bystander, accustomed to this, had seen it all before, and seemed to have little interest in the rituals. But Eleanor loved it, the practices and the connection to lineage, even if she couldn't follow what was happening.

She felt a knock on her shoulder, shocked to see

the person at her side as she looked up, up, up his tall body. "Hey, Dhaval," she said with forced cheer. She moved aside in the aisle to admit him and his parents, panicking. In all the commotion of the morning, of the weekend, she had sort of forgotten that he existed, but here he was in the flesh, with parents even, because his fiancée's sister was getting married. His soon-to-be sister-in-law. They were a family, and Eleanor was somebody's straight friend without a man.

"You look so nice in Indian clothes," Dhaval said kindly, finally.

She felt bad for him. She wished she could shove him down a hill.

"Thanks," she said after clearing her throat twice. "And you clean up nice! In a suit." She brushed a stray piece of lint off the shoulder of his charcoal-gray jacket.

She watched him watch the stage with a soft, misty expression. Maybe he was imagining himself up there with Leena, at their wedding. Her heart tugged, desiring to be let loose from her body. She turned back to watching the action underneath the mandap.

At the reception she was seated far from Leena and her family, and Dhaval too. She had those ambient sensations of feeling awkward, like her first day of college all over again, but she managed to smile like she had never felt strange a day in her life. She was seated with other young women who were very nice, including Neha, whose eyes lit when Eleanor said where she was from.

"That's where I'm living now! No way! Shut up!"

She made friends with Neha and the other women, whose names blurred as booze eased into her bloodstream, and she ate all of the food that was passed her way, served family style at the table. Eleanor danced with her new friends, and by herself, and moved her line of sight when Leena and Dhaval were on the dance floor together. When the reception ended, Neha told her about the after-party in someone's room at the hotel, but she was ready to call it a night. Too much pretending. It was exhausting. With limited involvement, a ride with Mrs. Shah's best friend was coordinated, and they dropped her off at the house.

Eleanor took a shower, drank a gallon of water, and tucked into her pallet on the floor, exhausted. A day to raze all other days. An early morning, a late evening, with bruising events in between. Maybe Nasrin had been right, that what happened between her and Leena was inevitable, the only conclusion to a slow car crash. They could survive this, though, if they were honest and then pushed through. Leena had been sad, Eleanor tried to comfort her. It was a classic situation. It wasn't remarkable. They could get through far more, far worse, together. They could weather any quakes that came their way.

She was almost asleep when the door opened.

"Eleanor? Are you awake?" Leena knelt at her side, alcohol on her breath. "I'm so sorry."

Eleanor opened her eyes. Leena looked like a zombie. She wasn't drunk, or at least wasn't anymore.

"I pushed us. Or something. I'm so sorry. It had nothing to do with you."

She sat up. Leena was still dressed in her sari and weighed down by a huge necklace, earrings that pulled on her earlobes, and bracelets up her arms. She always seemed tethered to earth by gravity, but this was something else. Very carefully, with precision, Eleanor began to remove the jewelry and set it to the side, piece after piece. She hoped that this would relieve Leena, leaving her lighter and freer. Instead she looked naked, smaller.

With Leena in front of her, she no longer felt that they would survive this and get through it.

"I don't think that's true," Eleanor whispered. "And I don't think you're sorry."

Leena's face was unreadable—like every possible emotion was in battle with each other. She shrugged and directed her eyes away.

Eleanor kissed her without invitation, pressing their lips together, taking from her, tangling her hands in Leena's drooping curls. She waited to be stopped, to be told they were just friends, and pulled back ever so slightly while still keeping their lips locked. If she misjudged, she needed to be told.

Leena gathered Eleanor's hands in hers. "Be careful with the pins," she whispered against her mouth.

Eleanor took that direction eagerly, heartily, undoing all the pins and taking Leena apart. She felt twenty again, with a craving like there was nothing else in her life, and pressed Leena into the air mattress as it weaved and waved with the pressure of their bodies. With Leena naked underneath her, she licked and kissed paths all over her skin, relearning the geography that once kept her up at night, gently biting the birthmark on her inner thigh, moving right on past the engagement ring as if it wasn't even there. She pushed inside Leena and found her wet, and that drove Eleanor forward, her desire notching up slowly, unending.

After she made Leena come, her head back on the shared pillow in a daze, Leena turned to her. There was no strangeness between them now, the air clear and crystalline.

"I don't think I'm going to remember how to do this. I don't think I'll be any good," Leena whispered.

"Lee, there's no way. You used to be great. At all of it. It's like riding a bike."

Leena raised an eyebrow.

"Okay, it's not like riding a bike. It's like . . . Wait. Do you want me to go down on you? To jog your memory? Was this all a ruse?"

Leena beamed, relaxed, shaking her head.

Eleanor was sure she hadn't seen her like that in ages, but she didn't have time to focus on that for long. Leena kissed down her body in one long trail, from her mouth to her neck, down between her breasts, past her stomach, down to her inner thighs. To her clit. Eleanor shuddered at the whisper-softness that at first felt too ethereal to be believed. She started slow, but as Eleanor's hips started writhing off of the mattress, Leena upped her pace, and Eleanor stuffed a pillow over her mouth. It was too much, too good, her orgasm was going to come before she was ready, and she so yearned to savor this, just in case this error would be the only one of its kind. She didn't scream, but she felt as if she could have. A climax from this moment, that really began in January.

They didn't talk, after. They lay side by side for hours, with Leena stroking her hair.

SEPTEMBER

The sounds of "Wreckless Love" by Alicia Keys played, and Eleanor stretched her body awake, greeting the summery morning with a slow response. *"Let's go back in time, when seeing your ID on mine made me crazy,"* she sang along to the first verse.

"Eleanor, for fuck's sake, stop your alarm."

She did as requested, then rolled back to Leena. With morning breath fermenting in her mouth, she gave her a peck and curled into her side. She pressed her smile into Leena's bicep.

"I'm up," Leena mumbled. She ran her thumb over Eleanor's bottom lip, over and over again. "So, you're off today. What's your plan? Oh, that reminds me." She cleared her throat. "L'shanah tovah!"

Eleanor broke into a grin. Her pronunciation was a disaster—*el-shann-ah-toe-fa*—and it was adorable. She was adorable. Eleanor pushed a lock of hair off Leena's face. "L'shanah tovah to you too. It sounds like you were practicing." She nipped in for another kiss.

Leena shut her eyes, a small smile playing on her lips. "I need to get up. But somehow, for some reason, I can't get out of bed."

Eleanor leaned forward, applying her lips to Leena's neck. "Cannot imagine why." She couldn't quantify the taste of Leena's skin, but it was salty and sweaty from the stifling air.

Leena pushed her back, pinning her to the bed by her shoulders, towering over her. "You're going to make me late again this morning. I can already see it coming." She leaned in and kissed Eleanor again, and then hopped out of bed. "Shower?"

Eleanor followed her naked body with her eyes, the sway of her hips, the perfect round swell of her ass.

It had been almost five weeks. Kissing and sex and cuddling on the couch, and sex. Sex in the kitchen and on the living room floor and on the coffee table, and one time in Eleanor's closet, for reasons she had since forgotten. They sailed through overwrought admissions of adoration and guilt, simply and effortlessly together. Like college but better. Finally, a hulking weight had been lifted off of Eleanor. She could feel herself coming back in like the tide, gently. She could feel her blood brightening. Eleanor and Leena could move forward as a "they," like how it should have always been.

She followed Leena into the shower, bodies pressed together, the cool water flowing over their backs and in the small space between them where they weren't touching.

Leena put her arms around Eleanor's neck, kissing her. "Earlier this year I thought I wasn't a sexual person. Can you believe that?"

Eleanor arched her eyebrow. She truly could not believe that, and wrapped her arms around Leena's body, then slipped them lower, then slipped a hand between her legs.

Leena was indeed late, still wet from their shower at 8:30 a.m. From her perch on the bed in boxers and a sports bra, Eleanor watched with slow, insatiable eyes as Leena dressed.

"I'm thinking . . . I'm thinking I might call in sick." Leena looked at Eleanor with wide eyes, a mischievous smile tugging at her lips. Then she coughed the worst fake cough ever attempted in the history of humankind.

When Eleanor eventually recovered from that adorable act, she nodded slowly, incredibly thrilled at her influence. "You sound really, really sick." She opened Leena's laptop and handed it over.

Leena's grin turned wide and thrilled as she composed aloud: "Hi Diana, I'm so sorry for the short notice, but I'm not feeling well today. I'm throwing up every few hours. I hope to be in tomorrow. Regards, Leena." She looked up from her screen. "I've never called out sick before. How does that sound?"

Eleanor, a pro at calling out sick, took over and finished the draft, and hit send. "It's a classic. What should we do now?" She closed the laptop and set it on the floor.

Leena flopped to the bed, still only in underwear, and rolled to face Eleanor, looking up at her. "I don't know. What were you going to do? Go to temple?"

She scrunched her face and shook her head. No. "I thought about meditating in Prospect Park, or cleaning out my closet, or going shopping. Something New Years–y."

Leena leaned forward and trailed a soft line of kisses on Eleanor's knee. "Or we could do none of those things." She pulled Eleanor down so that they were on their sides, facing each other. She stroked her cheek, then brought her chin forward in a kiss, lips pushed together.

Eleanor felt delirium in her drowning, in her disbelief that this was really happening. It felt too right, and she felt too whole.

Leena's stomach complained loudly, and Eleanor laughed.

"Breakfast first, maybe, but then," Leena said, eyes hopeful, "back to bed?"

This woman was unrecognizable from the one she knew five weeks prior. Maybe she changed, with the change manifested by Eleanor, or maybe the passion had been there the whole time, but this new Leena was not passionate about work and meteor showers alone.

They walked up to Mike's and squeezed into one of their weird narrow booths for eggs, toast, coffee, and grapefruit juice. Their knees grazed under the table— light, sudden touches that aroused comfort and passion in her. With arms on the table, Eleanor leaned in, wanting to be closer to such a sweet, beautiful face, one she could see with her eyes closed. "Can't believe you called in sick."

"Me neither," Leena whispered, beaming.

Eleanor felt her phone vibrate in her pocket and quickly checked it.

Torts class canceled for the Jewish holiday. Thank G-d for Prof Adler :) You're off today, right? Heading to you. I should get there in like 30 minz.

She groaned. "Fuckin' Tomás, man."

Leena stole Eleanor's last piece of toast. "Huh?"

She sighed. "His class was canceled and he's already on the train heading to us."

Leena shrugged. "So? That's great! We haven't seen him that much since he moved here."

Eleanor stole the last bite of toast back, delighted to hear Leena's excitement in seeing Tomás—despite this visit being poorly timed. "Yeah, I've been kind of busy. But I had other ideas for the day."

Leena tightened her ponytail with two hands. "Such as?"

"Licking your clit until you're sore," Eleanor said with a shrug. "Stuff like that."

"I can tell you're just so proud of yourself." But Leena's teasing contrasted with a piqued interest in her eyes.

Eleanor nodded, holding her gaze. "I really am."

Summer still hung in the air as they walked home, hands in a loose grasp, folded then apart, together then not, so casual, like they'd never stopped holding hands. When she saw Tomás sitting on their stoop, she couldn't help but notice how quickly Leena dropped her hand, their bubble apparently popped. She surmised that they wouldn't be telling Tomás today.

He stood, so different from the boy she always expected to see, and he hugged them both in turn. "Hi, gals. Where to?"

They decided to visit the Brooklyn Botanic Garden, where they could use student discounts—at least, Tomás could, and Leena had her expired ID.

"How's your place?" Leena asked as they walked down Washington Ave.

His shoulders raised in a big shrug, then nodded, hands in his pockets. "Pretty good. I mean, it's a tiny square basically, but I like being in Washington Heights. It reminds me of the Mission, when I was younger."

She remembered that time, when she would tag

along for Tomás's family visits. Thinking of home, especially today, inflamed a pang inside of her for California and its open skies, a place that had become mythical only with her leaving it.

"How are classes going?" she asked.

"Oh god. I'm basically dead. It's killing me. Homework and reading and the actual, like, sitting up in class and getting called on and being present with your whole brain." He stopped them, grabbed her shoulders and shook her, eyes wild. "Tell me why I'm doing this."

She shook off his theatrics. "Because you're going to make a huge impact on the immigration system, and it starts with your JD." That's what he said, at least.

"That's true. How are you two doing?"

"Oh look, we're almost there!" Leena interjected awkwardly, blocking any answer to Tomás's question.

Eleanor threw a desperate look in Leena's direction. They had not discussed this—how they'd handle this transformation in their relationship, of describing who they were to other people.

Feeling thrown, Eleanor paid admission and found their first target: the Japanese hill-and-pond garden. She suddenly felt so precarious and unsure, such bizarre sensations to feel around the people she was closest to in the world. They stood on the covered observation platform that jutted out over the murky pond, and for a quiet moment she looked out at trees and shrubs and flowers, a bright-red torii gate, a bridge—all so disorienting, like she was suddenly transported to Japan. Feeling cognitively dizzy fit her current moment.

Leena stepped away to take a call, probably from her mother. Eleanor watched her walk away, one hand in the back pocket of her shorts.

She had been so happy, bursting with it, drowning in her deepening feelings for Leena. Nasrin and Zoe, and all of those other distractions, no one compared to the chemistry and compatibility between her and Leena. Real, all-encompassing, go-for-broke passion. The kind of love that could make someone break up with their fiancé.

But Leena hadn't done that yet. She hadn't told Dhaval. Any time Eleanor would bring it up, Leena would burst into tears. "I only want you," she'd say, wiping her nose. "Let's not talk about it. I promise I'll break things off—soon." And so they hid in a new closet. No details for anyone, apparently not even Tomás.

"This is really cool," he said.

It was really cool, but she lacked the wherewithal to enjoy it.

"Hey, my aunts got engaged."

The news put some levity back in her lungs. "No way!"

Tomás nodded. "With that district court ruling in place, they're feeling better about their chances of getting married, so they decided to put some wheels in motion. Nothing planned yet." He batted his eyelashes. "Except that I'll be the flower girl."

"You wish."

He smiled, but in that beat-up way she was used to seeing when he was down and the reason was a girl.

"What happened with this one?"

He looked taken aback. "This one?"

Eleanor racked her brain for a name. "Nicole?"

Tomás sighed. "No, that was the other one, who I met on OkCupid. This one, her name was Malika." He sighed again. He was so good at looking pathetic, like a puppy begging for the last bite of a sandwich.

She put an arm around him, offering comfort in the face of his woman troubles, for what she knew would not be the last time. "You'll eventually find someone wonderful, who thinks that you're charming and smart and kind. Because you are those things, when you're not being a huge dork." He made a face, then stuck his tongue out at her.

Her point, proven.

She had also found someone, or rather rediscovered the right one. If it was possible for her, someone so flawed and annoying and impetuous and generally unlovable, it was possible for anyone.

Their trio walked the grounds, observing an abundance of roses and lily pads and herbs, and she and Leena told Tomás about their jobs and the apartment, avoiding anything real. It was a relief to finally put Tomás on the subway, the charade of stasis dropped.

They walked home in silence, no hands held, with only the sounds of traffic and other people. Inside their apartment, Leena closed the door and pressed Eleanor up against it. She put a hand between her breasts, approximately over her heart, and stroked over her T-shirt with a thumb. Into her ear she whispered, "I missed you today."

Eleanor laid her cheek against Leena's, taking a deep breath. "I missed you too."

"But it was so nice to be with him. I'm glad he's nearby. I feel lucky that he's becoming my friend too." Leena paused. "We'll tell him soon, El."

She pulled back to see Leena's beautiful face stitched with trouble, and smoothed out her cheeks. Knowing what she'd find there, she took Leena's left hand in hers and kissed it, kissed where that ring stayed, standing between them and their future. "It was weird today, to not tell Tomás about us. I know you need time, and I get that, but it's just, like, I can't keep secrets about something . . . that's this important to me."

She watched Leena's head bob, acknowledging what she said. But the woman in front of her, from whom she wanted everything, committed to nothing.

She felt sadness well in her eyes. She couldn't hold back, even if the saying was painful. "I want to tell everyone, Lee. Everyone I love." She leaned her head against Leena's, forehead to forehead, breathing in the small space between them. She knew what she was asking of her, to completely shift the course of her life, to be out and unrepentantly public with personal affairs. She held her breath, waiting for a reply.

"You know this isn't easy for me," Leena whispered.

"I know." And furthermore, she understood who Leena was. Careful, thoughtful Leena. Eleanor hadn't been a part of her life plans, and so remapping them would take time. She had to be patient. She could try to be patient.

Leena cracked a smile, shaking her head. "You didn't go to temple today. I thought that was a thing you were supposed to do."

Eleanor took Leena's hand and led her toward the kitchen. "I'm Jew-*ish*," she said, hunting through the refrigerator for leftovers. Temple on the holidays was something she had given up years ago, uneasy with God and Israel and the prostration, the flagellation. It no longer held the mysticism for her that it once had. This year, though, some atoning would be appropriate. "Maybe I'll go for Yom Kippur. Maybe to the gay temple I read about. Hey!" It occurred to Eleanor that, while they weren't out as a couple, this might be one place where Leena wouldn't have to worry. "You should come with me."

"What is *gay temple?*" Leena asked, smelling a carton of leftover Chinese food.

Eleanor popped her eggplant parmesan in the microwave. "It's gay temple. The rabbi is gay. Gay people are in the congregation. I don't know, I haven't been yet. But we can go together."

"When?"

"Next Friday and Saturday."

A smile tugged at Leena's lips and she leaned in. "So it's a date, us going to temple."

Eleanor's heart swelled. She nodded.

After dinner, Leena's organizational nature won out and they readied for bed, each with their nighttime rituals. Leena's were much more exhaustive, with flossing and lotions, taking her contacts out, securing a glass of water. Eleanor stripped to her underwear and brushed her teeth, hopping into Leena's bed to wait. She set the alarm on her phone, then put it to the side. Friday, back to work. But then a whole weekend with her girl, winding walks and afternoon cocktails and lingering mornings in bed.

"Ugh," she heard Leena say as she entered. "I think I'm finally getting my period."

"Finally! Same cycle. I win."

Leena's eyes and smile were aflame for a second, then disappeared as she extinguished the lights. "You think you've won, but my uterus is covert. It lets you think you're winning, but then I'll change your cycle. Just watch."

Leena slipped into bed, grasping for Eleanor, rolling her so that she was cuddled. It inspired no shortage of giddiness in her, reaching all the way back to college when it had first happened. Although she was comfortable with Leena, more than with anyone else, ever, being in the shelter of her embrace was still exciting, a key to the door of a new world.

It was dark, the thick curtains blocking out traces of light from the moon and the street. Eleanor felt like they were truly alone in the world. She craned her neck to kiss Leena, who kissed back with the vigor of someone who wasn't yet ready for bed.

THOUGH IT WAS rainy in the morning, the clouds parted by the time they hauled it to the Javits Center a week later, avenues away from anywhere familiar. The glass facade sprawled far and wide, tall on one side, giant cubes stacked like an unwinnable game of Tetris. They entered the vast and foreboding building, and she felt her own smallness in the world as she looked up through the ceiling to the sky.

"Come on." Leena tugged her hand. "We're gonna be late."

They took escalator after escalator, up and up, until reaching their destination, a massive room wrapped in glass with an unrivaled view of the river, filled with seated people facing a makeshift bimah and ark. They found two seats toward the back, and she had to shield her eyes from the glare of the late afternoon sun, stunning as it pummeled through the glass panels that lit the room and ceiling.

The instruments, the voices, the arrangement, the melody—it was all unfamiliar, and yet the wistful sounds reverberated within her, the feelings unearthed like old friends from summer camp, pinging and lighting her up like a pinball machine. There had been so many Yom Kippurs in her life. Eleanor had been so many different people, dating Micah in high school or nursing a hangover, throughout the years when she dragged her carcass to temple. The music was habitual, a structure that belonged to history, the music of her mother, grandparents, beyond that, back to Germany, the music of people she never met. Eleanor felt a calm rinse through her to feel tethered to something that could last.

Her eyes basked in Leena at her side, who was lit with the glow of fading sun, hair haloed like a goddamn angel, with eyes suddenly so bright. She was always so unbelievably, untouchably gorgeous. But the light, and how it reflected off this woman she loved—and maybe also this intimate moment between them in front of thousands, and the stirring music of millennia—was overwhelming, striking her momentarily still and silent for once.

But she always had something to say. Eleanor looked to Leena again, studying her face. What was she thinking about? So out of her element, a sponge, taking in her surroundings. Eleanor wanted to know everything.

"Is this okay?" she whispered to Leena. "You don't understand Hebrew. I didn't think about that."

Leena shook her head with the slightest head tilt. "I don't understand Sanskrit either," she whispered back. "But really, this is all familiar to me. It's about

. . . the feeling. Legacy and community. Something bigger than you or me."

Eleanor looked at Leena again, trying to hold her with her gaze. Leena was here as Eleanor's date to temple, willingly spending time in contemplation and reflection, and she understood the feeling—of course she did. Eleanor was gone on Leena all over again.

The singing and music faded, and the rabbi welcomed everyone, generously, sumptuously, welcoming all parts of the LGBTQIA community by name, welcoming all Jews no matter their background, welcoming those who never felt like they belonged, ever. When she specifically welcomed people of all faiths, including Hindu people, Eleanor nudged at Leena with her elbow. She saw Leena roll her eyes in her periphery, but then she felt a slight grab at that same elbow, a touch that landed, stayed. She felt the heat that radiated from Leena's grasp, rooting her arm then her whole body in something real and tangible.

As the sun set, the fiery glow dimming with twilight, she listened to the rabbi explain Yom Kippur and its purpose: getting back to the essence of who we are, to clean ourselves of the gunk. She also reminded the growing crowd that they were not the sum of the worst things they had done, words that spoke themselves right into Eleanor, into her heart, into the crook of her elbow where someone else's fiancée's hand rested. The rabbi continued on with a battery of questions, an atonement primer: Where were you at this time last year? What happened this year in your life, in school, work, and love? Who was in your life last year until you lost them? She cautioned everyone to be aware of the fragility of life.

Eleanor took the thorny points, absorbing them into her bloodstream, and yet they could only get in so far, because of the woman on her arm. Of course, she felt doubt and guilt, but with Leena so present at her side, she also felt vibrant and alive, and as she surveyed her year, she only came up winning. Her ebullient joy was unmatched; her heart swelling red and sweet to have the person she wanted most.

At some point in the service, in the roll of readings and singing and temple-president speeches intermixed with moments of quiet contemplation and tranquility, the sky faded to black like squid ink, the glass panels dark with night. She looked up into a ceiling of obsidian and saw a reflection of herself, and them, surrounded by a swell of worshippers and observers.

Before the vidui began, the rabbi offered a preface: "As we atone, as we lift our words up to God, we tap on our chests. Lightly, not violently. We tap on our chests, because when we do that, the doors on our hearts fly open. And that's when forgiveness and healing can begin."

The rabbi read and the cantor sang a litany of wrongs, one after the other. She knocked on her chest as she was taught, even for the statements with which she didn't agree, because this wasn't a picking-and-choosing situation. She would knock even if she hadn't wronged her neighbor, because everyone had, collectively, like the way everyone was racist. But in fact, she had wronged her neighbor—even if using that definition loosely. Suddenly she recognized the guilt that she'd buried in her elation. She had done great disservice to others and needed to atone. Nasrin, whom she had stopped loving but held on to because she was scared of being single and alone with Leena. Dhaval, an obstacle in her way despite being one of the only straight men she could tolerate, with a good and giving heart. She gave them each two extra knocks on her chest, eyes squeezed closed.

She prayed for this moment to clean her conscience, to wring her guilt out to dry through honesty and apologies. She was a good person who had taken a wrong turn. She and Leena could move on, be more, have more—and she ached for what she couldn't yet have and felt like she didn't deserve.

Her mind a whirl, she barely noticed when Leena took her hand. But then she felt a pulse, a squeeze. Her eyes drew to where their hands were linked, fingers threaded together, and she let go of the squirrel's nest of her mind to focus on what mattered. Leena, and how deeply satisfying it was to hold her hand in a blessed space, humming with promise and the possibility of the year to come. Tears pricked Eleanor's eyes as she squeezed Leena's hand back and the rabbi concluded her speech: "May this be a year to forgive and be forgiven, full of love and kindness." From the rabbi's mouth to whoever existed in the universe to make that come true.

After the Mourner's Kaddish, the rabbi requested that everyone refrain from speaking until they left the room, to hold the spell a little while longer, and she shared a reminder for the next day's Yom Kippur services at nine a.m. that would last all day, until the blast of the shofar. She could almost hear the bleating horn tones from so many years past echoing through her mind.

In accordance with the rabbi's wishes, she and Leena

were silent as they left together, shoes on industrial carpet and down the escalators, down, down, down.

The wind was brisk at their backs as they walked toward the train, close but not touching, Eleanor's hands jammed in her pockets. She could feel a touch of cold in the air. It would be winter before she knew it.

"I'm gonna go see him. And tell him."

She craned her neck to the side, to Leena. "Really?"

Leena nodded with pressed lips, grave, but then smiled. "With what money I do not know, but I'll fly out there soon. Next week, maybe."

It made her heart squeeze faster, tighter, redder. Leena was planning steps to pull away from Dhaval so that she could fall further into Eleanor. But at the same time, the idea made her pause. Would she kiss him, would they have sex before she told him it was over? "Why? Why do you need to go see him?"

"Because I owe him that, at least. He'll be fine. He's a great catch. Some other girl will scoop him up."

She was surprised to hear Leena be so capricious about someone she almost married. Maybe that's how she was in the face of a relationship's end; maybe that's how she had been when they went bust in college.

Leena stopped them in their paces and grasped Eleanor's chin. "After it's all settled, we can move on. And really be together."

In Leena's eyes, Eleanor saw so much warmth and love, yet was scared to trust in this fragile thing. "What about your family?"

Leena's face, which had been half-enamored, went blank and solemn. She shook her head. "That's . . . harder. You know that."

Eleanor nodded. She knew the entire depressing landscape.

"I'll get there, El. It's just going to take time."

They walked in the dark, in the quiet between them, and she was about to ask Leena what she thought of the service, and joke about conversion, when Leena's phone rang.

"Hi, Mom. I'll call you back, Eleanor and I—" Leena's face went slack, shocked, and she put her hand over her mouth.

Eleanor's stomach tightened.

"What? But she can't. She's so hea—okay. I can come right now . . . No, I want to. I'll call when I'm on a bus or train or whatever." Leena hung up, her face frozen. "My grandmother had a heart attack."

She saw Leena's grandmother in her mind, pasted over with television images of what a heart attack looked like. Hospitals and tubes and a frail old body. Her heart fell, and she took Leena into her arms, her body heavy with a sprawling, boneless heft. "I'm so sorry, Lee. Let's go back, pack up, I'll come with you." She unwrapped Leena, but kept an arm snug around her, moving them forward.

"I don't know what to do. I can't even think," Leena said flatly.

She needed Eleanor to take charge and make it all happen. Unfortunately for both of them, that wasn't her specialty—but she could fake it, for Leena. "Amtrak? We're right near Penn Station. Maybe there's a train?" Eleanor opened her phone and found the schedule right away. No luck. The buses seemed hard to figure out. Planes, then. "There's a late flight to Boston out of JFK. I'll book it for us."

Leena nodded numbly.

Eleanor hailed them a taxi as soon as she spotted one, and steered Leena in first. She held Leena's hand tight as she booked a flight on her phone one-handed. But as Eleanor began the process, she realized their reality. To Leena's family, she was her best friend—and best friends didn't take this kind of trip. Though tectonic shifts had taken place, as far as Leena's family was concerned, she was still ready to marry Dhaval and go forth with the life they had planned. A younger Eleanor would have spared no time in puncturing their delusions, but that could wait. She and Leena had time. With a peach pit of discontent stuck in the side of her gut, she booked one ticket. "You'll be okay without me. You have Nita and your parents. Plus, I bet it's not that serious. You'll be back for work on Monday." She put all of her optimism into her voice and words, all the forced belief she could muster.

Leena sighed, dropping her head to Eleanor's shoulder. "I think you're right. Thank you."

Eleanor thought of Obachan, Grandpop, and Grandmom. Her ojichan, whom she had never known. All time on earth was fleeting, but time with grandparents felt borrowed. She thought again of her living grandparents. Their complications, their endurance, their love. *Please don't die on me yet. There's still so much we haven't discussed.* She squeezed Leena's hand, imagining her own thoughts to be the same as those going through Leena's mind.

"I did this to her," Leena said quietly.

Except that—they weren't.

They were nearing the airport and seeing signs for car rentals and terminals. Eleanor turned to look at

Leena, who was still the same amount of dazed. "No, Lee—"

"I did. What I've been doing to Dhaval, it's wrong. I brought this on my family. On her. I've been too happy." Her eyes beaded with tears, her lips pinched together. She started shaking her head. "If she . . . it'll be all my fault. I don't know how I'll live with it."

"Leena, you're a scientist," Eleanor pleaded. "You know this isn't how it works."

Leena shrugged, her face crumpling as she cried, as she wiped her nose with the back of her hand. "And it doesn't matter how much I love you, or how wonderful this is. It's still all my fault."

They were in a car, rushing to the airport so that Leena could be with her grandmother, but it didn't matter. Eleanor was in a Notting Hill bookstore, a New Year's Eve party seconds before midnight, Riverside Park in a field of wildflowers, a downpour of rain after a failed wedding, every romantic movie that shaped her—only this was her life, her own love. *Leena*. It had always been Leena. "I love you too. And it's not your fault," she said fiercely, hoping she could be heard over all of Leena's fears and doubts.

I love you. Their words crystallized and cemented their path forward, who they could be. She could see a fusion wedding that might please Leena's parents. Marriage was serious, and it would make them understand. Eleanor saw her and Leena under that mandap. They would kiss again, and seal their fate.

Leena reached out and touched Eleanor's cheek, caressing it. Then she pinched it, and smiled.

The car pulled up to the departures gate at terminal 5.

Leena laughed to herself. "I don't have anything—clothes, underwear. Do I even have my license?" She rifled through her bag and pulled out her ID. Then she turned to Eleanor and took her hands. "When I get back, we'll talk a lot more, and figure out next steps. I'll tell Dhaval. I'll tell my family." She took a deep breath. "I'm praying she's okay." Then she kissed Eleanor gently, putting such tenderness on top of turbulence. "My brain is all over the place. I have to go. I'll call when I land. I love you." She bounded out of the car and Eleanor watched her go.

"Can you take me to Clinton Hill?" she asked the driver.

He looked in the rearview mirror. "Yeah. Is everything okay?"

She sighed, settling back against the seat.

NOVEMBER

She rushed out of the subway stop at Forty-Second Street, sprinting against wide slabs of concrete. *Fuck fuck fuck. She's never going to let me hear the end of this.* She almost knocked over a tourist in pursuit of her destination, turning the corner to Fifty-Third Street, the early winter gusts catching her loose hair.

Her grandmother's disapproval was evident from twenty feet away, arms crossed, tapping a foot in her sturdy navy-blue flats, making a show of checking her wristwatch. "Eleanor, the show is about to begin. We had no way of reaching you."

She rolled her eyes. "Grandmom, you really need to get a cell phone." She stooped to kiss the older woman on both soft, wrinkled cheeks.

"I got one!" her grandfather crowed, pulling it out of the inner pocket of his blazer. "I saw it advertised on television for old folks. Look at these big buttons," he said, flipping it open.

"Those *are* big buttons," she agreed as her grandmother shooed them into the theater and up one level, to the front, where they squeezed past other theatergoers in their row, offering hushed apologies.

The dark theater, the stirring of the orchestra—it was all a relief. Here she could focus on some inane musical romance that lacked the complexity of her life in this moment. Except that *Promises, Promises* wasn't inane or romantic so much as it was a sad tale of patriarchy at work, culminating in the female lead attempting suicide because her married lover prioritized his wife. When the curtain fell on the first act, she looked to her grandparents on either side of her, back and forth like a tennis match. "What the hell kind of musical is this?"

Her grandfather shrugged. "It's based on *The Apartment*. Jack Lemmon!"

"It's Burt Bacharach music," her grandmother added in defense. Whatever that meant. "And that gay fellow from *Will & Grace* is in it. That's a reason for you to like it, yeah?"

"I wish we were seeing *In the Heights*," she grumbled.

Her grandmother sighed, opening her Playbill and scanning it. "You know I don't speak Spanish."

Eleanor rolled her eyes, checking her phone, and saw a missed call from Leena. "Damn. I . . . I'll be right back." She rose, nudging out of their row and into the lobby, putting in her call only to hear Leena's voicemail greeting.

"Hi, it's me. I'm so sorry we keep missing each other." They kept missing each other on the phone, but there was an entire other type of missing at play, a type that cut into her heart and left it bleeding. She saw Leena in her mind's eye as she'd seen her last—back in New York for a few days before returning to Lowell. She had been so distracted, doing laundry and packing and making constant calls, that her presence in their home was otherworldly, only a ghost of herself. But at least Eleanor was able to hold her, to look into her soft, dark eyes. "I hope your grandmother is doing better. I hope her doctor's visit went well. Was she able to walk with you a little up and down the street? I know you wanted to do that." Leena's remote life, unavailable to her, gleaned through bits of voicemails. "You must be such a help to your mom, and such a comfort to your dad. You really are some kind of superhero." The lights in the lobby dimmed, blinking. "I gotta go. I'll call you later, or you call me." Then, a whispered indulgence with eyes tight: "I love you." She pocketed her phone and headed back to her seat.

She loved her, and she wasn't scared to say it. She loved her and it was the truest thing she knew. And it was painful to love someone so far away. This perhaps was what it would have been like if they'd stayed together through Leena's study-abroad trip, waiting on an email or phone call via calling card. Thank god for the passage of years and leaps in technology.

The curtain rose and she settled in, but she couldn't ignore the weariness in her bones. She supported Leena, but the time apart was gnawing on her. She wanted her home, and for Leena to tell Dhaval and her family. Then they could start their life together. Eleanor didn't want to wait any longer.

Maybe I could come up and visit with you? she texted stealthily.

"Eleanor, put your phone away," her grandmother hissed.

Not stealth enough.

AFTER THE MATINEE and before her grandparents' trip back to Philadelphia, they took a brief stroll to an early dinner at a white-linen steak house. Knowing they were treating, Eleanor placed her order for an old-fashioned and shrimp cocktail and a roasted half chicken.

"Eighty years on this planet and I still haven't tried shellfish," her grandfather said with a remorseful shake of his head, his German-British-American hybrid accent as familiar and comfortable as a worn sweatshirt.

"You don't keep kosher," she reminded him. "I can split my shrimp with you." This was the conversation they had every time mussels or cheeseburgers were consumed.

He shrugged, his still-thick gray hair gleaming under the lights. "Maybe next time."

Her grandmother took a sip of ice water, then blotted her mouth with the linen napkin in three neat pats. "Tell us everything about work and your roommate. Is she a slob like you?"

Her grandparents on both sides had parallel upbringings and trajectories, and yet her maternal grandmother's voice was sturdier, almost Victorian, and no-nonsense, even when she was teasing.

Thankfully their server delivered her cocktail. She took thirsty pulls from it. "Work is . . . I don't know. And my roommate is great. She's neat, actually, very much so. A total Felix."

Her grandfather turned in his seat. "Helga, didn't we see *The Odd Couple* on Broadway? With Jack Matthau? I think it was in that theater we just went to."

"*Walter* Matthau. Who remembers? I think we saw the movie in the movie theater."

She finished her drink and checked her phone. Nothing new, from no one in particular.

Her grandmother patted her hand. "So glad we finally made it up here. We've been meaning to come see you in the big city." She smiled, pushing Eleanor's hair back and off her face. "We've just been so busy. We went on one of those Alaskan cruises and saw whales and glaciers. I meant to bring our photo album." She snapped her fingers with a shake of her head. "Darn. Next time."

Her grandfather picked up the thread. "And I'm volunteering at the temple a fair amount. We're helping to keep the local food pantry stocked. I've met some nice people from churches and a mosque too. Did you know that women choose to wear that head scarf?" He shook his head with wonder. "I'm learning so much."

Eleanor had grown up with Afghan and Afghan American girls in Fremont, and was a women's studies major, so this was not new information. But she welcomed his remedial learning, was even heartened by his ability, despite his age, to meet people beyond his insular community.

"Speaking of good works," her grandmother said as their food arrived, "Goldie is becoming a rabbi."

Eleanor raised an eyebrow, cutting into her chicken and wolfing down the first few bites. She hadn't seen her cousin in years, but could only recall her muted bragging about Penn's business school and her internship at Comcast—as if Eleanor actually understood or cared what all those words meant in combination. Straight-and-narrow Goldie becoming a rabbi. She scoffed. "I bet she ran out of better options."

Her grandmother clucked. "She found herself on the wrong track is all. She thought about when she was most happy, and it was actually her bat mitzvah project when she learned Spanish, all in service of teaching recent immigrants English. And that made her really think about giving back. She volunteered at temple and eventually felt called to the rabbinate." Her face transformed with restrained pride. "You two should get together sometime."

Eleanor could not process this information. Goldie was locked so firmly in Eleanor's mind as blond and vapid, with all her concerns in the wrong place. People capable of change, of growth, of forging a new way. What a new concept.

"Eleanor, did you go to services?" her grandfather asked.

"Uh, yeah. Kol Nidre and Yom Kippur. There's this gay temple, but they do services at a big convention center." Kol Nidre, the night when Leena fled New York and never really returned.

"Gay temple?" Her grandfather's eyes went wide. "Really? Maybe we could go sometime." He leaned in, setting aside silverware. "Have you met any nice young ladies?"

She immediately shook her head, but he wasn't to be deterred.

"I hear there are all kinds of technology. I don't know what, but they say it can help gay women have a baby. Make me a great-grandfather before I die." His eyes pleaded, half-serious, with two clutched hands over his heart.

"I—haven't met any nice young ladies at temple." A political answer. He would be upset to hear she was with an engaged woman who wasn't Jewish—and never mind that Eleanor was almost sure she herself didn't want children. "And besides, you're going to live forever." She made a fist on which to rest her chin, smiling at both of them. She was lucky to have them, and her obachan, even if she was in rough shape. The dementia was picking up at the speed of an unyielding hurricane, with worsening symptoms and her parents putting more time into her care, ferrying her to appointments and coaxing her to take her meds.

Unlike Leena, who ran without a thought to be with her ailing grandmother, Eleanor received updates remotely. No doubt lingered in her mind that they loved their grandmothers the same, and as much, but there was something different about Leena that made her selfless and unafraid.

About this, of course. Breaking up with fiancés was another matter.

"I hope I won't live forever!" her grandfather said. "How terrible. I'd look like a weathered old beech tree."

"Otto, don't start talking about trees," her grandmother dismissed. She pierced into Eleanor with her brown eyes and steely determination. "You don't have to become a rabbi, but you need a path. You're just floating."

She shook her head. "I'm not. I'm not. I'm fine. Really, I'm good." She tried to smile defiantly but her lips wavered, and then the worst thing possible happened. Tears began flowing from her eyes in a giant, ugly cry.

It wasn't about work. Or—it was about work, and Leena, and New York, and her life, and the people she loved. It was all too much to bear, too much weighted matter.

Her grandmother stroked the back of her hand and watched her cry, offering no words of comfort. But she watched, witness to all the things Eleanor was feeling and could not name.

The server approached the table and quickly backed away.

After dinner she rode with them in a taxi to Penn Station, and kept them company in the lounge before their train home. Her chatty grandparents filled in the blanks—impossibly more information about their cruises, how much they loved the faster Amtrak trains—and she asked questions at appropriate intervals, but still felt drained from crying.

They both hugged her too hard with their bony, stooping bodies. As she pulled out of her grandfather's embrace, he stopped her, hands on her shoulders. "Goldie told me something interesting about Yom Kippur. The shofar blasts have meaning. It's one long note, then three broken notes, then nine staccato bleats, then one long note. It means: I was whole, then the world and life happened to me, sadness and defeat. That last long note means: but I can be whole again."

"Otto, we need to go," her grandmother said irritably.

She watched them go, descending out of view on the escalator, her grandfather waving over his shoulder, his words with her all the way home.

TWO WEEKS LATER she closed the front door, her mouth fresh from Leena's kiss. They were two weeks into Leena's new schedule: working remotely from Lowell on Mondays and Fridays, to lengthen her weekends with her family. But they were months into this separation, this untogetherness that felt worse than when Eleanor had been yearning for an engaged Leena from the next

361

room. At least her friend was around then, available to her.

There was good news on the horizon, though. Dhaval had planned a trip east to see his family and Leena over Thanksgiving, and that's when she would tell him—though in fleeting moments, Eleanor fretted that she wouldn't do it, that when the big moment came, Leena would clam up, unable to make that clean break. But she said she would, and all Eleanor had were Leena's words.

But their last few days together had not gone well. At night when they both returned home from work, there was a morass between them that they couldn't cross. There were catch-ups, there were shared glasses of red wine, there was sex: but it all felt perfunctory, like gears in habitual motion.

Eleanor's whole life was about pulverizing obstructions, going deep, getting dirty, scaling the highest peaks of a challenge. But a malaise had set itself into her cells, one that made her want to pull back for the first time, and protect her fragile, pink heart.

She dragged herself to work, late, on a commute with nobody to talk to, laugh with, or make the swell-crush-crash of the subway feel less alone and suffocating. She held herself tight in her jacket, missing a needed layer in the brisk air, and faced the rest of her day: Preparing for their fundraiser next week. Sending reminder emails, confirming comp tickets for sponsors, checking in with the venue, hand-holding board members. Enough tedium to melt her brain, especially since it was already taxed by being elsewhere.

She hated feeling like this, so lonely and apart, distraught and broken. It was also Leena who had last plagued her in this way, so young and lovesick, beset with stomachaches that had no cure. Eleanor hadn't let anyone in in the same way after college, and now she remembered why. It felt like barren death.

"Hey, Eleanor," Analiz said, suddenly appearing at her desk. "Do you have a minute?" she asked, a stern frown on her cherry-red mouth.

Eleanor pulled the earbuds from her ears, Joni Mitchell still softly leaking through them.

Without waiting for Eleanor's reply, Analiz helped herself to a slice of the desk, taking a seat and crossing her arms. Her face stayed severe, in contrast with the cutesy ice-cream cones printed across her dress. "I got a very irate call from a board member. Talia Barger said that the invitations to her friends arrived in duplicate. I need you to check your work, and if it's your error, I need you to call and apologize. Okay? Thank you." And off she went, no room for questions or conversation, or hearing her take.

I did fuck up, but only because Talia didn't send me her lists on time.

Who fucking cares about duplicate invitations? Rich old women got their invites. Case. Closed.

Flames licked her stomach, all the way up to her face, swirling in a toxic brew of embarrassment, annoyance, frustration, and Over It. Young women of color and their promise, their potential, all mattered so much to her, but she was done with the bureaucracy and her lack of agency.

She did not call Talia, but she did look for new jobs online. First in New York, looking for higher salaries. In another tab, she typed in *Bay Area jobs*, just to look, just to know. At the end of the day, she took off early without a word to anyone, a bat out of hell. She walked up Chrystie Street and kept going as it turned into Second Avenue, hands clenched in her pockets.

She descended down into Nowhere, eyes adjusting to the blaring darkness and red lights over the bar, the ceilings low even for someone short like herself. Zoe was already waiting in a blue suit and white button-up and brown wing-tip shoes like somebody's dad, with a squat glass of whiskey on the rocks loitering on the bar.

Eleanor climbed onto the rickety wooden chair and drank. "Should have gone to Cubbyhole."

"It's always so crowded in there. And I always trip over someone I know."

"Someone you fucked," Eleanor corrected, eyes scanning, not looking for anyone or anything. It was too early in the day for this scene, chairs sparsely populated with older gays and two worn lesbians in zip-up sweatshirts. She was tired but didn't want to go home to an empty apartment with Leena's lingering scent in the air. "Thanks for the drink, by the way."

Zoe waved it away. Working in finance, she always treated, was always the most lavish. "You're someone I fucked," she said without heat or defensiveness, just casually, stating facts.

"Oh god, don't remind me," Eleanor replied with mock horror. Ever since bumping into Zoe at Ginger's, she did her best to categorically recategorize her ex, draining her memory of who they'd been to each other. Time marched on, and they had become different people.

"How was your day?" Eleanor asked.

Zoe traced the rim of her glass. "It was satisfactory."

She peeked up at her under heavy eyelids. "The sex wasn't bad, was it?"

Eleanor contemplated that, an ice cube melting in her mouth, poking her tongue through the hole in the center of it. The ownership Leena had over Eleanor's body and brain left no room for memories of other women. "It was satisfactory."

Zoe laughed, high-pitched and girlish, a sound that seemed like it belonged to someone else. "I remember you. You were good."

She shook her head. "How many whiskeys did you have before I got here?" She finished her own, wanting to catch up to Zoe.

Her drinking companion tilted her head, turning fully in her seat until she faced Eleanor. "Two, but that's not the point. I don't know, we're compatible, right?" Her face was serious, more than usual, her dark eyebrows knitted together. "I've been thinking. I like you, and you like me, and maybe we could . . . be around for each other." Her eyes searched Eleanor's face, confidently hopeful. "Since we're both single."

Once her shock dwindled, she parsed her feelings. There was a world where this proposed friends-with-benefits offer would be one to accept. Idling in a parked car with Zoe until the right one came along. And there was some part of her, deep and tucked out of the way, that bloomed whenever someone desired her.

"I'm with Leena," she said. "She's cutting things off with her fiancé, but, yeah. I'm sorry. I guess I'm not so single." It was freeing to voice, after keeping quiet for so long. She took a deep breath, and it felt like the first in forever.

Zoe barely blinked. "Wow, Suzuki. You two are a Joan Armatrading song."

Eleanor let out a bleak laugh into her glass before asking the bartender for a refill. Her shoulders relaxed, falling out of their tight hunch.

"I gotta say, I'm surprised you told me. We must really be friends."

Eleanor shook her head, equally surprised. "I guess we are. Huh."

"It must be killing you that she's away like this."

Any distraction she'd felt from Zoe's proposition vanished, and she felt herself near tears again, like she always seemed to be these days, the feeling of gagging before vomiting in her throat.

Eleanor was so worn, so weary from feeling overwrought and dramatic. Maybe sex without emotion would be simple. She contemplated this on her trek home, first on the train and then as she walked to her apartment, the first flakes of snow falling on her shoulders.

DECEMBER

"So, you're not coming home," Eleanor said slowly, her back to the brick wall outside her office. She shivered in her down coat. Her body had forgotten how to survive an East Coast winter. The wind whistled down the street, creating feedback in the phone, and she couldn't be sure she was audible on this side of the conversation, but she was prepared to scream.

"I—no. But I'll come visit. This weekend, even. And you'll find a great roommate, I'm sure of it."

She was prepared to scream and throw her phone into a slushy street puddle. It was caustically cold outside, but an inner heat burned inside her, keeping her focused on the conversation. "Leena," she said patiently, "that's not why I'm upset."

There was a deep, pregnant, sad silence.

"My grandmother is sick, El. And my family needs my help. What else am I supposed to do?"

Not violently pump the brakes on your life.

Be here with me.

Invite me to be with you.

"It's not your fault she had a fucking heart attack." There. She said it. Truth in black and white. What Leena needed to hear.

Or not, actually, because the line went dead. For a split second she imagined the connection was lost, but she knew what had happened. She shook her head at her petulant friend. Girlfriend. Passing ship. Whatever she was.

On her way up the stairs back to work she texted Leena. **I'm sorry. I don't want you to be upset. But it's not your fault she's sick. I love you.**

There was no answer, and there was no answer later in the afternoon either. She was as good as gone. Eleanor was alone.

The end of her day was a blur, reading Joni Mitchell's song lyrics instead of working, planning for a shared cab to the airport with Tomás later in the week. She was ready to shed her everyday skin, needing a break from all of the things in her life she could not change.

Analiz knocked on the side of her computer, no-nonsense in a light-up Christmas sweater and plum-tinted lipstick. "Eleanor, the list for the auction items isn't done. I need that before you go."

Eleanor took a shallow breath, her teeth rattling in her mouth, and she took a bite of her tongue to keep from shrieking. She looked down at the keyboard, mucked with crumbs, and looked back up at Analiz, at the visible wrinkles at her mouth. She was an angel of doom.

Fuck you, Analiz, she thought. There were too few precious hours on earth to waste being disrespected and devalued. Cast aside, ignored, alone.

In one clean motion, Eleanor flung her keyboard off the desk, thrilled with the clattering sound it made against the linoleum floor. That was one way to get rid of the crumbs.

"Fuck you, Analiz," she said, giving clear voice to the bracing wildfire inside.

In their small office, speakers pulsing with Grace Jones, with a background of winter awfulness visible through the windows that needed a good cleaning, everyone was struck silent. Everyone but Eleanor.

"I'm so goddamn sick of being told what to do and on *your* timeline. It's not fair and you don't trust me, and I'm so done. I'm so fucking done."

Her heart raced, her hair felt like it was pulsing against her skull, and in that moment, she had never felt so clean and purged, her nerves singing but standing perfectly in place, eye to eye with her boss.

Analiz stared back at her, boring holes into her skull, but then her visage transformed into what almost looked like a smirk, like there was something savory on her tongue.

"It's too bad you feel that way, Eleanor. But I'll take that as your resignation. Jane will take care of the loose ends. You need to leave right now."

Her calm was a douse of cold water over Eleanor's head, and a gut-punch moan left her mouth involuntarily. *Oh god wait I fucked up I fucked up so bad I take it all back.* Her eyes widened, and she nodded quickly. She needed to leave. In the snow-globe silence of the office, she shrugged on her coat, slipping her phone into her pocket. There wasn't much else that was hers. Head down, she left, descending the narrow stairway out to the street. She hailed the cab she could no longer afford but needed very badly.

Replaying her poor decisions made her eyes squeeze shut in pain and embarrassment. She lost both her roommate and job in one afternoon, and possibly Leena altogether. The sky turned from gray to black—an apt metaphor for her mood.

Back at her apartment, she turned to a bottle of red wine and Joni Mitchell, bumping around in underwear and thick wool socks, trying desperately to forget that she had wrapped sticks of dynamite around her life like a daisy chain.

But she had. She had done that. She had been reckless with her life as if it were yesterday's garbage, when it wasn't that at all. It was her life, and she valued who she was and what she offered to the universe. She was better than an adult-size tantrum.

At least, she hoped she was.

In two days, she would fly home to California for the holidays. She wished, as Joni wished, for a river she could skate away on. Home would be an ailing grandmother, two frantic parents, Fitz playing video games in a childlike trance, and no relief from her own lovelorn, doomed self.

She checked her phone. Still no reply from Leena, but she hoped she could coax and beg, and Leena would return, at least for a little. Eleanor had no shame when it came to her.

In her chaotic romping, she literally collided with her bookshelf, wiping traces of wine from her mouth. Her eyes tried to focus on titles, names, authors, the odd mix of their books. Leena's science-y reads. Eleanor's college books, for the most part. Had she stopped reading after graduation? Was her mind atrophying?

She slid her thumb down the spine of a red-and-white book. *Communion* by bell hooks, subtitled *The Female Search for Love*. Over the years she had flipped it open, read a page, and placed it back on the bookshelf, but now she sat with it, wine bottle wedged between her moldable thighs. She remembered vaguely that Professor Post, her favorite, had offered it to her one afternoon.

Women talk about love, pronounced the first sentence of the preface. bell hooks elaborated on love and its relationship to feminism, how fathers who withheld love set the stage for those desperate to find and know it, how people learned early on to search for love, as hooks put it, *beyond our own hearts.*

Eleanor was infatuated. She inhaled hooks's words and exhaled disappointment, loneliness, disconnection. The words spoke to this exact moment, leaping off the page and into her eyes and cheeks and into the nod of her head.

hooks's words echoed through her brain: *Self-love was the key to finding and knowing love.*

As a girl, she had thought of her religion as love, but then her heart had been fractured, unsure of the world and what she could expect from women. She put steel beams around her most precious organ, keeping it safe, avoiding the romantic sweep that she knew so well from movies. But then she'd gone all in on Leena, and she was still all in if Leena wanted her. *If.*

She had never in a million years thought of loving herself; no amount of feminist education had sparked that thought. Self-love could be liberation, could even be the path back to love, but it started with her. A commitment to herself. An ownership of herself.

As the words blurred with intoxication and exhaustion, she kept reading, reading until she lost grip on the night.

It was December, in the middle of the night, but as she fell asleep, she swore she could hear that one last long note of a shofar.

PART FOUR
LEENA, 2017

OCTOBER

Leena packed her bag like she would for any other wedding, strategizing practically and tactically through the various scenarios that would necessitate her belongings. Of course, this bag was different, as was this wedding and this day. She finished her task, eyes sweeping the room for anything she'd neglected to include, but she was in good shape. Jacket on. Ready to go.

But she didn't want to go.

She sat at the bed's edge, keys edging into her palm, bag at her feet. Her nerves wrenched. She forced a deep and cleansing breath into her lungs, then blew it out. A small moment of calm sat between her lips.

Then she heard the jangling of keys and her mother's heavy sigh. "Leena? Jaldi kar! I'm meeting Urvashi massi for lunch."

Leena looked up and saw her mother: shorter than she used to be, the tiniest bit of white roots showing, with eyes that looked exhausted beyond their years. She'd dressed in a tan velour sweat-suit set, with her one designer bag hanging from her arm. And she looked, as she had for years now, thoroughly disappointed. She turned and left without waiting for a reply.

Leena shouldered her bag and descended the stairs,

with no one to say goodbye to in the empty house. Her dad was on a shift at the hospital. No one else. She locked the door behind her.

It was a balmy day in Lowell. She shed her light jacket as she climbed into the passenger side of the Toyota. Leena flipped down the visor, checking her hair in the mirror. She was not yet used to its short length, cropped close, finely tuned by a barber. She inspected it, fingers brushing at the sides and at the base of her hairline.

Her mother eased out of the driveway, still so cautious after decades with her license. "How long will you be gone?" her mother asked, pausing at the stop sign and placing big-framed sunglasses on her face.

"Back tomorrow afternoon. Don't know what time."

"Who is getting married?" her mother asked stiffly.

Leena got the sense sometimes that her mother was bursting to ask questions, and not just some but all of her questions, like she used to before this cold war befell them. She studied her mother's face as she guided them out of their neighborhood and into town. "My friend Tomás from college." She brightened a little to think of how they'd kept up over the years, despite it all, and how selfishly thrilled she was that he and his wife would be moving to Boston.

Her thoughts strayed to other college friends who would be at the wedding. She considered this fact with prickly unease before she forced it away.

Her mother nodded and said nothing in reply, only switched on her Celine Dion CD.

Leena pulled on sunglasses and sat with the uncomfortable silence. She felt her phone vibrate in her hand and looked down. It was a photo from and of Siobhan, her old friend from high school, draped in a sari, Ba looking on in the background, proud of her handiwork. Leena's heart clenched to see her grandmother on this device she used every three minutes or less.

She remembered being so embarrassed that day, at the way Ba had unearthed their otherness in front of her friend. Ba spent that afternoon teasing her granddaughter. "At least *someone* likes to dress like this."

Going thru old photos and found this. Isn't it the best? I loved her. I miss her. How are you holding up?

Someone loving Ba, claiming her like that, was irritating. *Love* was a big word. **I'm okay**, she replied. She was now used to this question, lobbed gently and patiently by friends. What they really meant was: Is the trauma of your grandmother's death palatable yet?

The answer was no, because every day she went into Ba's old room and saw only memories of what was once there: The hospital bed with railings for elderly hands and bodies. The walker, the ventilator, the wheelchair. All gone. Tears welled and fell from her eyes, a common occurrence in these past few months. She directed her face, and her sorrow and grief, toward the passenger's side window, curling her body away from her mother, who couldn't stomach emotions of this magnitude.

They arrived at the train station. *Call me when you get there, call me when you're coming back.* That's what her mother used to say. Now she unlocked the doors. "I have to go." She turned her head away.

Leena used to wish for more silence from her mother. The incessant questions, calls, demands. They seemed to be endless. Yet when their rift began, their relationship torn apart, all she wanted back was her mom's vigilance. Without it, she was left off-balance in the eerily silent home they now shared.

She climbed out of the car and walked away quickly. She headed upstairs to the track, her bag heavy on her shoulder, weighing her down. The onset of her thirties had brought many things, and now three years in, her right shoulder often performed with complaints. She waited, and waited, because she was early and the train slightly late.

Once she boarded, she settled into a seat on the familiar commuter train, which brought her into the city each weekday. She slumped against the car wall, gazing out as the train lurched. Normally she checked work email and listened to podcasts, but today she observed the towns dotted along her train line. The thicket of trees and aboveground pools. Ponds with lily pads. Five jet skis lined up in a neat row. Charming Winchester with its grassy square and church. God, she was so sick of New England quaintness.

Eventually the city crowded into her ride, as back-yards receded and train tracks bifurcated neighbor-hoods, and new high-rise apartments loomed. Leena pulled into North Station and merged with hockey fans, jerseys on and faces painted, walking past home-less people in old coats with piles of bags. She walked past too, thinking in public health statistics, but dou-bled back, offering one desperate woman a protein bar from her bag—and then she was off again, on the T to the hotel.

As she went through the motions of check-in and leaving a card on file for incidentals, she was reminded that she didn't want to be here. Beige hallways connecting similarly neutral-colored rooms, featuring black-and-white photography of iconic Boston scenes. The Citgo sign, Fenway Park, an aboveground train. Generic, without personality. And despite her fondness for Tomás, she did not want to be here at his wedding. It was another wedding, another commitment, watching everyone else move on.

She flopped backward on the bed, holding her phone up with outstretched arms, and logged into her dating app, greeted by a smiling cartoon robot with heart eyes. **Hi Leena!** said the text bubble. **Here are your potential matches.** Logging on in Boston was always more fruitful than Lowell; there were so many more women. Danica, 27, frosted blond with a steely gaze. Laili, 38, with dark eyes and great eyebrows. Ashley, 35, wild brown hair and a beautiful smile.

Eleanor, 33. Her long hair now short like it was back in 2004. Her smile the same as it was the last time Leena had seen her, years before. She tapped to see more. **Formerly: Suzuki Booksellers. Now: MSW candidate. I'm interested in safe communities for QTPOC folks, yoga, bookstores, mindfulness, and whatever else you think makes a good profile.** She scanned through the photos Eleanor uploaded: a beach shot with cliffs in the background, a photo with an older Japanese woman who must be her grandmother, Eleanor in a furiously verdant place with Japanese architecture behind her, Eleanor stuffing a giant slice of pizza into her mouth and laughing at the same time.

If she was some woman Leena had never met, she'd be enchanted by this pretty girl with a sense of humor. Her pulse would race with possibility. But she knew better than the app. Eleanor lured women in, transfixed them, only to pull away when the going got tough. Investing in her would leave anyone without.

Leena unpacked her navy-blue shift dress to iron out the creases, smoothing away undesirableness the way she couldn't in her own life, then hung it in the closet, finding herself at three p.m. with two hours before the wedding began. Neil deGrasse Tyson's new book was burning a hole in her bag, but a drink in the lobby bar was a more appealing way to spend down the day.

Leena settled onto a stool, gazing at the flow of people in the lobby. Black and Brown people, probably fellow wedding guests. She'd be sitting next to someone, all of them, tonight and tomorrow. She sipped at her tea, which she chose over scotch at the last minute. She wished she could still day drink without getting sleepy.

"Hey, Leena?"

A man's voice, one she didn't recognize, came from behind her. She spun around and saw a Filipino man with a familiar face.

"It's Sam," he said, and was joined at his elbow by a woman.

Cath, if memory served, though more voluptuous than Leena recalled. Sam was a lesbian last time she saw him. He still had warm, brown eyes and the same broad smile, but where he once had soft curves, he now had planes, slim and lean, balding with a five-o'clock shadow.

"It's so great to see you two! It's been such a long time!" Leena hopped off her perch to hug them.

Cath backed out after they embraced, wincing.

"Sorry. My breasts are so sore. The baby is at home this weekend, and I need to pump."

"Baby?" She could feel her eyes soften. "Congrats, you two. Seriously."

"Thanks," Cath replied. "It's nice to have a break, though. And wine." She saddled up to the bar, her back to everyone else.

Sam scrolled through his phone. "I can't help it. I'm such a proud papa," he said, handing over his device to Leena. On the screen was an image of a baby looking up, dazed. Curly, dark hair with fair skin. Biracial like their parents' coupling. Probably created in a lab, with determination and love.

She handed back the phone. "Gorgeous. You should be proud." Leena wasn't sure how to ask her next question. "And you—you and Cath—how are you? Apart from the baby?"

Sam pierced her with his eyes. "I've never been happier in my life," he said with such conviction that Leena felt winded. He held her gaze for a second, smiling, then turned to put a hand on the small of Cath's back.

She watched the tableau in front of her: two people standing together, every day, no matter if the days held life-changing events or just plain-old routine. As she often did when observing a couple, she wondered how they kept something as fragile as love afloat. Was it possible to spend decades sweet on the same person? She had no idea how people did it.

Leena left them at the bar on round two as she headed upstairs to shower and get ready, looping toward the elevator, waiting, then boarding. As the doors closed she heard someone yell, "WAIT!"

A woman with short, dark hair slid in. Bags in her arms, sweating, dragging one behind her, a tote bag spilling onto the floor.

"Hi, Eleanor."

The woman from so long ago looked up as the doors closed behind her. "Oh. Shit."

Leena knew it had to happen eventually, and yet it wasn't any easier. Her nerves had run her ragged at the prospect of seeing Eleanor, confronting the things she had left behind, but actually seeing her didn't make Leena nervous. She noted the bags under Eleanor's eyes and the wrinkles at her mouth. Time had passed for both of them. In another world, she would have never noticed Eleanor aging, because she would have seen her every day, making the slight shifts imperceptible.

Being reminded of what they didn't have made any traces of anxiety burn away. She had nothing to be nervous about. It was just Eleanor, as familiar to her as the skin behind her knee. Leena hadn't done anything wrong. Eleanor was the one forever at fault.

"I knew I'd see you eventually. I knew you'd be here. I was excited to see you, Leena."

Her blood boiled in the face of Eleanor's amnesiac reaction, as if it hadn't been seven years since they'd last seen each other. As if they'd parted amicably. "Yeah, same," Leena replied sarcastically. She watched the floor number slide from three to four, then felt the elevator bounce, shake, and still. "Oh, for fuck's sake," she muttered. She advanced on the control panel, pressing the call button. "Hello! I'm stuck! I need to get the hell out of here." She heard Eleanor laughing behind her, which was utterly infuriating. "Anyone? Hello? I cannot be here."

"Ma'am," a bored and relaxed voice replied, "we apologize for the inconvenience. We'll take care of this issue immediately." The voice crackled at the other end, then silence.

Leena leaned against the back wall, as far from Eleanor as she could get, crossing her arms over her chest. She checked her phone. No service.

Eleanor wasn't saying anything either, but she planted herself on the floor, organizing her things. Everything back in her tote, making space for that in her roller board bag, repacking.

Being stuck in a confined space was not on today's to-do list. Without anything else to do, Leena observed. Eleanor was in jeans, Doc Martens, and a leather jacket, like a bad girl from a nineties movie. She smelled different. Less fragrant, less like jasmine. More like earth.

"This is ridiculous. Don't you think this is ridiculous?" Eleanor asked, looking up at Leena. "We're trapped here together. Is that not that poetic? Or tragic? As I get older, I've started coming across moments where I'm like, holy shit, this is like a movie. This is so ironic. Or poignant. I've been alive to have been through it all once."

"I think that sounds like things are repetitive." Leena sunk down against the wall, trying to take a deep breath. She checked her phone again: still no service. Then she checked her watch: 4:02 p.m. The wedding was set to begin at five and they needed to get out of here, especially because Eleanor was Tomás's *best (wo)man*, as gleaned from Tomás and Kemmi's wedding website.

"You cut your hair," Eleanor observed.

"So did you." She tented her legs, resting her forehead on her knees so she didn't have to look at her.

"It's a good look. I'm just surprised that you'd do something so drastic. So dykey."

When Ba died in July, the mourning hit her immediately and all at once. No stages. It felt so foreign to experience such deep despair, like an archaic sequence of DNA had been suddenly activated. In the few days after, she went through the motions of being alive, eating and sleeping and breathing, but it all felt plastic and phony.

Her father shaved his head, as was custom. She watched him do it, leaning against the bathroom wall. They didn't talk anymore, not really, but he didn't tell her to leave, even as silent tears ran down his cheeks, a scene unknown to her until that day. She knew they were bound by the same grief, though they couldn't share those words. But she still wanted to tell him—tell everyone. Quickly, quietly, she picked up her father's electric razor and took it to her own head, letting years of hair fall to the tile. She had never used this device before, and her hand shook.

He pried it from her hand and finished the job, his doctor's grasp even and still. He set his hands on her shoulders, the first time they had touched in years, and they both looked at each other in the mirror. His eyes were red and inflamed. Hers, tearing up. She cleaned up after them, her long and his short black hair mingling together on the bathroom floor. Now they were the same.

Leena touched her hair now, growing in new. "Yep. Dykey."

"I . . . We matched on the app. Did you see that?"

Leena groaned. "I match with a lot of women. I don't know what you're talking about."

"Leena." Eleanor's voice was stern, authoritative like a teacher's, and Leena popped her head back up out of habit. "I get it. You're fucking pissed at me. I get it. But weren't we friends once? Wasn't I someone to you?" Her face was pleading and distraught, along with her voice, her body straining forward.

Leena leaned in, spreading her knees and folding her legs into a pretzel. When she was younger, she would have stayed silent, letting manners and good conscience rule. Years of pressing down, and down, on things she had to say, had worn her patience. "When it got hard, you gave up," she countered in a strong, clear voice.

Eleanor looked away, her head hanging heavy. "I know that." Her chin raised, pointing forward. "But you abandoned me first."

Like it mattered who struck the first blow. "My grandmother was sick. My family needed my help. And I needed you, but you were nowhere to be found." She remembered the lonely bus trips to Massachusetts on Thursday nights, back to New York on Mondays. Sleeping facing away from each other. Eleanor fading away.

"You moved out," Eleanor shot back. "Was I supposed to follow you? Like, live nearby, come over when everyone went to bed? I'm a whole fucking adult."

"I fucking came out for you!" Leena shouted, the words that had lain dormant inside her body for years, until now. "I came out, and I didn't go back. I tore down my relationship with Dhaval. When he told my parents before I could, and they took it terribly, you were nowhere." Leena stood up now, towering over Eleanor, and it felt incredible. Powerful. "I lost myself in you." She shook her head. "I was under your spell. And it made me give away so much." She thought back to those floundering moments and how she had ceded control. Moving in together when it was an ill-advised idea at best. Letting hormones drive the ship when they kissed and fell into bed. Pressured to tell Dhaval, to blow up her life. "So. Yeah. I'm *pissed* at you," she said in light, clipped words. Her chest heaved, adrenaline pumping at having emptied herself of what had weighed so heavy in her heart, and she sagged into a corner of the elevator.

"You lost yourself?" Eleanor asked faintly, so quietly Leena wasn't sure that she even heard it. "I made you do that?"

Leena rubbed at the back of her neck. "Yeah. You did. All women do. I lose control, I stop worrying about myself, and put all of my energy into that relationship." Her mind surveyed the graveyard of her past involvements, and to what would await her. Women were who she wanted; women were pain.

Eleanor shook her head. "That sounds awful." She bit her lip. "But it also sort of sounds like . . . falling in love. And complete abandon. You do lose something. But you would've gotten *you* back."

That was ridiculous. She knew what falling in love felt like. Or maybe she didn't. Either way, Eleanor was wrong. Leena advanced through the small space, hitting the call button again. "You guys are killing me. What's taking so long?"

"It's a Saturday," said the bored voice eventually. "We apologize for this inconvenience. We're working fast to reboot the system. Please be patient. Thank you."

She leaned her forehead against the cool metal of the panel and took a deep, expansive breath in and out. When she failed to relax, she began feeling claustrophobic. The walls were closing in. The air tight. Danger around the corner. She took another breath, pulling it in through her nose, down her throat, and out again. She sank low to the floor, back against the wall.

Eleanor cleared her throat. "It seems like things are good with you. I saw you have a great gig. And you seem happy. At least, in your profile photos you do."

She glanced at her without looking up. She didn't need her cheerleading. "Pictures lie. I'm trying to sell myself to women. On how smart and funny and cute I am. It has to be lies to look that good."

"'I'm a scientist working for the government. Ladies, form a queue to the right,'" Eleanor quoted from Leena's profile. "That's pretty cute and funny, and smart. I'd date you."

Leena rested her cheek on her kneecap. She watched Eleanor smile at her. "You already did. How did that go?"

Eleanor rolled her eyes. "Lee, all I'm saying is that you're further along than you think. A few years ago you were going to lock it down with a dude—"

"Who I loved—"

"Whatever! This is what you want, isn't it? This path? Isn't this who you are? Aren't you on your way?"

It was true: She did have a good job. She went on an occasional date. She had Binita, her nieces, Siobhan. She had researched that gay soccer league in Boston and was thinking about joining. But she wanted more. She wanted to live abroad and bring her medical skills to where they were really needed. She wanted kids— soon, before her eggs went rotten. She wanted a partner who would let her be herself. In that order. "I don't really know where I am. But, yeah, I guess. On my way."

Eleanor reached out slowly, one timid hand landing on Leena's knee, resting from its journey. "That's all I want for you. To be happy. And to have your own ostentatious wedding at a library." She rolled her eyes again.

"I know!" Leena crowed. "I can't believe it. It's so not Tomás. I figured maybe a backyard-barbecue wedding." She realized now that they were gossiping together, sharing an intimacy in roasting Tomás. She hadn't meant to let her guard down.

"I hadn't been there until yesterday for the rehearsal. It's really nice, obviously, but that's all Kemmi. A spectacle, a splash," her voice tinged with judgment.

"God, El, tell me how you really feel," she replied.

Eleanor lifted her hands. "She's fine. She's not who I would marry, she'll totally knock him over at every turn, but hey, it's his life."

It was almost sweet to see Eleanor be protective of Tomás, someone as close to her as a sibling. Leena remembered how difficult it was when Binita married. She liked Sagar, but it was tough to see that change speeding toward her when she wasn't ready for it. She thought of that wedding and now this one, neither of which she would have chosen. "I can't imagine getting married in that way. I wouldn't want to be the center of attention like that."

"I remember. No eyes on you, no attention, no PDA. It, like, offends your sensibilities."

She looked at Eleanor with critical eyes. Her ex was leaning on judgment like a crutch. Simplifying someone as if she could diagnose them. Eleanor was almost always wrong, like she was now. "It just isn't something I crave. I don't need everyone's attention all the time."

Eleanor scoffed. "And I do? Is that what you're saying?"

Leena was caught by her intimation. "I—yeah. That's what I'm saying."

Eleanor let out a shaky laugh. "I guess I can see how you'd think that. But people change, Lee."

She looked at the woman who once represented so much. It was onto her that Leena had projected promise, the future, love, everything. She couldn't imagine that Eleanor had really changed from what she remembered. In her mind, Eleanor was trapped in her self-centeredness and chaos. *But people change.*

Leena tried to shift her view like a kaleidoscope, to see through new eyes. Then the elevator jerked back to life, sliding smoothly up two floors, and the doors opened, wiping away the formidable long pause that settled in the car. Maybe it was Leena's imagination, but she felt like she could see the bad energy creeping out and away, fresh air pouring in.

"Is this your floor?"

Leena looked up, focusing. "Yeah. Yes." She got to her feet, dazed, a baby deer finding its legs.

"I'll see you soon?"

Leena nodded, almost not wanting to go, but not wanting to stay either. She stood in front of the doors as they closed. Then she rushed to her room to get ready, her hand faltering with the keycard, not inserting it the right way at all until she finally did. She stripped off her clothes and got into the shower, and once the spray hit her naked body, she began to cry— for all of the things she didn't get but wanted, for all of the Leenas she could have been but wasn't, and for the relief of finally confronting the scars on her heart.

Emerging from the shower in a cloud of humidity and catharsis, she zipped into her dress and examined herself in the mirror. She thought about how much more comfortable she'd be in a suit. She styled her hair. She still didn't have the hang of it, not yet, but she was getting there. In quick minutes, she was done, ready to go, opting for the stairs over the elevator this time. Just in case. Outside, as she crossed Huntington Avenue, rounding the corner to Boylston Street and to the front of the main branch of the Boston Public Library, she started to see streams of people going the same way. Those same Black and Brown people, now robed in their finery: suits, some tuxedos even, strapless dresses with shawls thrown over top to beat the evening chill. Then, some Black women with their heads wrapped, wearing bright blouses and skirts, all in complementary fabrics. The array of colors was familiar, like her family weddings, and it put her at ease.

The library's courtyard was beautiful. It didn't look like Boston at all but like pictures of Italy: open to the elements, with a garden and a fountain in the middle. Moving from that busy street, through a solemn institution, and into this otherworldly place made the transition feel sacred. The courtyard's beauty was sullied somewhat by the continuing rain as guests gathered under the portico, cramming underneath the length of the overhang. The wind picked up the water, blowing a mist onto everyone's formal wear.

Tomás arrived in place with Eleanor, both of them holding giant golf umbrellas. She'd never seen him in a suit or with his hair slicked to the side, or looking this nervous, but he couldn't hold her attention. Her eyes fixed on Eleanor, consuming what she saw: her blush-pink suit jacket that matched Tomás's bow tie; her white blouse buttoned up to her neck; her tight black pants; her short hair, styled with a pouf at the front. Eleanor looked gay and glamorous and beautiful. Had she always been this annoyingly stunning?

Leena's thoughts were interrupted as Kemmi entered, the bride poured into a strapless white-cream gown cinched around her hourglass figure. A mermaid dress, which she could only name because of mindless bridal reality shows that Binita liked to watch, with ruffles like waves covering her legs. Her hair was in braids, woven together in a side bun, and kept in place with a diamond clip. She hung on to her mother and father, the mother in a lace top and skirt with her head wrapped, and the father in a long top and robe, both in matching patterned fabrics. Kemmi's face was tense, anguished, and if Leena had to hazard a guess as to why, it would be because of her six-inch high heels on the wet pavement.

Their officiant was Kemmi's uncle, who spoke with a booming voice and lyrical Nigerian accent. He invoked God more than once and Leena saw Tomás twitch every time. Kemmi's sister read something from the Bible about the different qualities of love, then Eleanor stepped forward and took hold of the microphone.

She cleared her throat and began to read. "No union is more profound than marriage, for it embodies the highest ideals of love, fidelity, devotion, sacrifice, and family. In forming a marital union, two people become something greater than once they were. As some of the petitioners in these cases demonstrate, marriage embodies a love that may endure even past death. It would misunderstand these men and women to say they disrespect the idea of marriage. Their plea is that they do respect it, respect it so deeply that they seek to find its fulfillment for themselves. Their hope is not to be condemned to live in loneliness, excluded from one of civilization's oldest institutions." It was here that Eleanor choked up, paused, and sniffled. She roughly wiped at her eyes. "They ask for equal dignity in the eyes of the law. The Constitution grants them that right." She smiled stoically, then stepped back into place beside Tomás.

Leena couldn't help but tear up a little too. Those words from the Supreme Court moved her when she had heard them years ago, in the thick of caring for Ba. Now and in this day and age, with insanity run amok in the news and government and White House, progress felt far away. She wondered if Eleanor had asked to read it, to stick it to all of the traditional older folks in the room. Or maybe the lawyer in Tomás valued those words on the onset of his own marriage.

The rest of the service streamed by. Tomás and Kemmi were pronounced man and wife, kissed for too long, and then departed down the aisle along with the rest of the bridal party, Eleanor included. Leena's eyes went with them.

She followed everyone else inside and up the stairs,

ushered into a large reading room with long tables accented by green glass-shaded reading lights. Moody and regal. Books along the walls on shelves. A sweeping arched ceiling with architectural details that she could appreciate but not name. Leena could only imagine the expense of renting such a space, then decorating it, stuffing it with food and drink and guests. She sipped her champagne, gazing around and guessing at the price. Twenty thousand? Fifty? More?

Cath bumped into her, splashing bubbly of her own into the air and a little onto Leena's shoes. "Whoops. Collision. Sorry. I've had one glass and it's gone right to my head." She shook her head, almost sadly. "This is what having a kid does to you."

Leena looked Cath over, in a gauzy olive-green dress that cascaded against her pale skin, covering her postpregnancy figure of larger breasts and weight on her belly. Her eyes caught on two rings glinting from a chain around her neck, landing at the edge of her low neckline. She looked so lovely and ethereal in a way Leena didn't remember from when they were in school—and then she felt bad for casing Cath like that, a jewel thief before a heist. These dating apps had warped her brain into making split-second appraisals, even offline. Leena looked straight ahead, as if she were reading titles and not restraining her eyes. "What did you think of the wedding?"

"Wet, but nice. He's such a good guy. So nice and funny and sweet. I bet he'll be such a good husband."

Leena thought of other nice, funny, and sweet men, being good husbands to other women. Dhaval called a few years back to tell her he was getting married, though they didn't speak; she had been afraid to pick up. He left a voicemail about meeting Anjali and falling in love. "I hope you'll wish us well. And I hope you find what you're looking for," he'd said.

"You're lucky to have a good husband of your own," she said now to Cath. "Seems like things are going well."

Cath slung her long, red hair over her shoulder and chuckled. "Do they? Good. At least someone thinks that. Are you married?"

No, I dodged a bullet. No, it feels like defeat. She shook her head.

"Why not?" Cath asked belligerently, swaying a bit in place. "You're so smart and hot. Why hasn't someone scooped you up?"

Hot. Leena's cheeks reddened, flattered and flustered. "I—I like being single," she replied. She wasn't sure it was true as it left her mouth, but out in the air it felt right. Close enough to right.

"Being single," Cath said wistfully, her gaze elsewhere. "I've been in a relationship since 2002, since I was a baby. I bet you have time to date around or fuck whoever you want. God, that sounds great. To meet someone, to connect, have sex, and walk away. No conversations." She rolled her eyes and shook her head. "I'm so far away from that. My body and my time are not my own. I'm nursing, pumping, a human feed bag. And Sam and I haven't had sex in . . ." Cath attempted to count, then gave up with a sigh and a plaintive look. "When he started on testosterone, his sex drive was out of control in the best possible way. But when the baby came, we both changed. It's just become that kind of thing."

Leena knew this was a possibility if, and when, she entered another long-term partnership. She'd seen movies that documented the phenomenon. She was well aware of the comfort that could settle in like ambient dust over people's sex lives. But it was quite another thing to hear about it from someone she knew, live in front of her, and she felt her jaw hanging open, slack. She'd never been with someone long enough for it to become *that kind of thing.*

"Marriage is all of the good things that are promised and all of the bad shit that makes you shudder," Cath continued.

Leena could not follow that thread, but nodded, allowing the intoxicated soliloquy to continue.

"Then again, it's different for us. We're gay—well, I'm still gay—which means our marriage is different. Not traditional, or conventional. More open. Less boundaries. You know." Cath's eyes refocused on Leena, even as they remained cloudy. Now Leena was the one being cased. A lazy smile spread across the other woman's face. Then her fingers grazed Leena's shoulder, her thumb stroking at the area around her deltoid muscle. "God, I love this dress. The material. It's so gorgeous."

Leena looked down to the hand at her shoulder, not so far away from her breasts. She blushed, enjoying the lavishing of attention. It was not within her understanding of the world, of marriage, to see it take this form: envious, open to whatever the wind might bring, and fully aware of what was needed. It did not compute, and neither did the feeling of interest stirring in her belly, and lower. Maybe she didn't understand anything. Her eyes slid up, taking in soft lips and white teeth and smooth, pale skin. Cath's burning brown eyes.

"Hi?"

Leena turned around and saw Sam holding two champagne flutes. She tried to be elsewhere, blending into the bookshelves, taking a small step backward and looking around.

"Hi, honey," Cath said cheerfully. "Thanks for getting us drinks."

Sam shook his head. "What is happening right now?" His critical gaze darted from Cath to Leena then back to Cath.

Leena's eyes swept the room as if for the first time, fascinated by details she had already seen. She chugged her champagne. "Refill! I'll be back." She wouldn't be back. She strode to the bar, where a familiar pink suit jacket was unavoidably and unfortunately waiting, and she steeled herself. One awkward situation to another.

"Hi!" Eleanor said exuberantly. "Have you tried their signature cocktail? It's bourbon and maple syrup, or something. It tastes like fall."

Leena pushed her lips together to avoid smiling. "I haven't, but I will."

"I'm glad we talked before." Eleanor closed the gap between them, her voice dropping. "I feel like we cleared the air as much as we can, and now we can be civil this weekend. For Tomás."

Leena didn't mean to, but she locked onto what she said about being civil. As if without their exchange, Leena would have flipped a table or something. The hidden accusation didn't strike her well, and made her want to be the opposite of civil.

The DJ requested—but more demanded—that everyone find their seats, and Leena took her gold-embossed table card to where Cath and Sam were already seated, having a hushed and animated conversation that Leena pretended not to see. Another couple she'd never met before was also seated at the table. She took a seat between Eleanor and the white guy with curly, dark brown hair.

"Micah," he said, introducing himself.

Seated with Kemmi at the sweetheart table, Tomás tapped his glass with a spoon, the tumbler filled with something amber and glowing where the light hit it. As he stood up, Leena saw that he was dressed in a different suit now—a black one with silver floral embroidery all over the jacket and twin silver buttons down the sides of his pants.

"Hi, everyone! Hola, bienvenido! For those of you who don't know, my wife and I—my wife!—met a few years ago. We met online and had a date, and I thought it went pretty well. I was in law school at Columbia, she'd just started at McKinsey. It felt like we could be a power couple. But I guess she didn't feel that way? Because my post-date texts were met with silence."

Kemmi looked pained by the start of the speech, which contrasted with how lovely she looked in her draped cream lace blouse with her head artfully wrapped in a crisp taupe fabric. They both looked so sharp now, out of their gown and tuxedo pairing, and into traditional clothes that held traces of their families across borders and oceans. Blended together now.

Leena had once envisioned such an occasion of her very own. An Indian-Hindu–Japanese-Jewish wedding. It had been inchoate and fleeting in her mind, but it had taken root, until it was clear that nothing would need to grow. Anyway. Maybe there would be someone else. An Indian-Danish wedding. Indian–Sri Lankan. Indian-Kenyan.

"I gave up," Tomás continued. "On her, not on love. See, I know this isn't particularly masculine or good for my street cred, but I actually wanted to get married. My parents have been through a lot, but they are such a good, strong team. I look up to them. They are here today in spirit."

She heard his voice falter. Her heart clenched.

"I also had the privilege to live with my aunt and her wife during high school and after college. I spent years observing what love can look like. I wanted that in my life."

Her gaze shifted to the women he indicated. Women with beige-brown skin, big dark eyes and wavy hair, their looks drifting into each other. One in a modest black suit, the other in a teal dress. His aunts, whom she'd heard so much about over the years. Their faces shone with adoration for the remarkable man he had become. Tomás had been molded by his aunts and his friends, and by himself. He had learned not to need his parents. Maybe a self-crafted family could be as good, or better, than one formed by blood.

"So, I moved back to California, and was killing time in the northern part of San Francisco, a place where I never am, and I went into a bar to watch a game. And I saw Kemmi—that smart and beautiful woman I'd gone on one date with. In town for work, she was at the counter alone trying to bribe the bartender to put on the Patriots game." He looked down to his seated bride. "You were up to a hundred, weren't you?"

She nodded, a big stage gesture.

"Yeah, so she's delusional—because no one is turning off a 49ers game in San Francisco—but she's scrappy. If I wasn't already bummed that we weren't dating, I was then. I tapped her on the shoulder and offered her more cash to help make the bribe. I can safely say I became an option for the first time."

She nodded again, but something only for him, her face tender.

"Becoming Kemmi's husband is literally a dream come true, a desire that withstood distance, time, and change. We're moving to Boston, starting over together, ready to face what's next." His gaze fixed on his new wife. "We're a team now too."

Kemmi, who had been so stoic at the start of his speech, jolted out of her seat to wrap her arms around Tomás's neck and kiss him. It was an ostentatious move, but that was what weddings were about, and Leena found herself so stirred by the authentic display in front of her. Never mind weddings. This was what love looked like.

Everyone clapped, Eleanor wolf-whistled, and the kale and butternut squash salads were swept out onto the tables.

Micah leaned in, chewing and swallowing his bite before speaking. "You're here with El?"

Leena shook her head forcefully. "Nope. I'm a friend of Tomás's, from college." That wasn't inaccurate.

"Oh, gotcha, gotcha. That's cool. I went to high school with them."

Her eyes scanned his face. He was pretty. And his name was suddenly familiar, her brain unlocking the details. "Micah, like the one who dated Eleanor?"

He chuckled. "Yeah! That's me. Her last stop before Gayville." He cleared his throat, looking sheepish. "Not that . . . that was a bad thing. We all have our own path. It's all good."

She watched his face contort as he tried to gobble up his words, to pull them back into his mouth. He regretted what he said because he was reading her as gay. Because of the hair or her demeanor or both. She had always been pleased with her ability to hide in plain sight, shape-shifting circumstantially when she wanted to be seen by another queer woman. But now the hair gave her away. It was a style she shared with plenty of straight women—she saw it in Boston all the time—and yet there was something undeniably queer about her. It was obvious to everyone. There was no need to hide. A freedom she never knew she'd wanted.

Leena finished her salad in a daze of this discovery. She looked around at her tablemates. Micah and his wife. Cath and Sam. Eleanor. Without realizing it, she had a date to this wedding. She was, as Micah had put it, here with El. She turned to Eleanor, leaning in as a herd of waitstaff descended at once, taking their plates. "Micah is sitting next to me. Your ex-boyfriend Micah."

Eleanor sat back, smiling at the server who zoomed in and out. "I don't really think of him as my ex. It was a million years ago."

"I'm your ex too. You're at a table with two exes. Is that weird?"

Eleanor squirmed in her seat. "Only when you say it like that. Jesus."

Leena laughed into her lap and took a sip of her drink, the one large ice cube beginning to melt and dilute the potency and sweetness. She found herself watching Micah out of the corner of her eye: his smile as he listened to his wife, the bob of his Adam's apple as he drank. In another world, Eleanor could have been the woman at his side, and Leena wouldn't be here at all, because they would never have met. Never have become friends. Never have shared an apartment. Never have fallen in love. And without Eleanor, Leena would most assuredly be Mrs. Dhaval Patel.

Dinner was predictably a vegetarian lasagna for those not partaking in the rainbow trout or duck. She watched as Eleanor picked at the top layer of noodle and wrinkled her nose.

"So, Leena, what do you do?" Micah asked.

"I work for the city. I do data analysis in the epidemiology and data-services department."

"So, like, counting herpes outbreaks?"

Eleanor swiveled to look at Leena directly, right in the eye. "That's exactly what you wanted to do. Not that stupid shit Micah said, but the work, the department." The smile on her face was radiant. "Good for you, Lee."

It was exactly what she wanted to do, serving the public and government with health information. But in practice it didn't give her what she thought it would. She didn't feel a sense of purpose sitting behind a computer, eyes glazed over, looking at spreadsheets. "Thanks. What do you do, Micah?"

"I'm a software engineer. I work in the Bay Area. That's how I met Min Jin." He indicated to his wife, who was deep in conversation with Sam. "She's a product manager."

Leena thought of the one software engineer she

knew in the Bay Area. "You don't know Dhaval Patel, do you?" She didn't know why she asked. It was a silly game—*Oh, you live in Tennessee? Do you know . . . ?*—that people couldn't help but play.

His eyes lit. "Tall? Kinda beardy? His wife's name is Anjali?"

She could see Dhaval in some boring ranch house in Silicon Valley, his arm around a basic but pretty woman, watching television. "Yep. That's him."

"We worked on the same team, but he's on a year-long paternity leave now. How do you know him?"

"They're old friends," Eleanor rushed to say.

"We used to be engaged," Leena corrected. She didn't need protection or coddling. She shook her head. Dhaval was on yearlong paternity leave with his tiny, probably adorable baby. Taking them for walks in the stroller, to playgroups, feeding them solid foods. Watching them grow. Shaping a family that could have been hers but was now someone else's. As much as she'd let go of who she was supposed to be, the news left her numb.

"I can't believe that. The odds are, well, they must be astronomical." Micah turned to Min Jin. "Leena was engaged to Dhaval Patel, that front-end engineer with the great beard. What are the odds?"

Min Jin made a face. "It's probably not that high. It seems like it would be, but you have to consider social factors of knowing young people in urban areas, and the interconnectedness of those networks."

They continued to debate probability. She excused herself to the bar as the lights lowered, making the green table lamps that much more ethereal. The synth boomed and beats of a Whitney Houston song kicked in.

As she watched Tomás and Kemmi dance, she weighed what to order next—back to wine, maybe, or keeping on with cocktails—aware that she would be hungover either way. It was a pleasure to see her old friend beaming with so much joy, to finally have attained the thing he wanted: A woman to love. A new family.

Cath and Sam got up to dance, as did Micah and Min Jin and Eleanor. She watched her ex sway, her arms and hips out of sync as they moved. Leena had spent so much time watching her dance poorly, a non-skill she made up for with zeal and fervor and joy. For a split second they locked eyes across the dark room. She didn't want to see Eleanor as beautiful, lacking in the twitchiness and self-consciousness that marked her twenties. She seemed calm and at ease now, and it was lovely on her, but Leena disconnected their gaze.

The next song was a jumpy pop tune, a guitar twanging lightly from underneath, someone telling someone else to shut up and dance with them. It was one of those songs that was on the radio constantly a few years back, when she'd take long drives to escape her parents. Hearing it now, she wanted to reclaim the way it once made her feel, and she joined the fray without a drink, where her various acquaintances and friends of friends and ex-girlfriend were dance-jumping around. Her body moved with the rhythm and she felt total relief, like she could let go of all the detritus that had been leveled at her. Things with Eleanor were complicated, and Dhaval had a fucking baby, and her life wasn't where she wanted it to be—but she could dance and close her eyes. "SHE SAID SHUT UP AND DANCE WITH ME," she yelled along with everyone else.

The song finished and another in Spanish began,

coaxing Tomás's family back to the dance floor after taking a break during the white pop song. Leena kept dancing through that tune too, and the next, until it slowed down.

During the slow song, Tomás and Kemmi clung to each other in the middle of the dance floor, eyes closed and whispering, while others looked on reverently. Leena watched too, but with strains of envy and cynicism, competing emotions that nipped at each other but didn't win. Other couples joined the bride and groom on the dance floor. Kemmi's parents, Tomás's aunts. Her tablemates. Leena looked around for her date-by-default, but didn't see her. She moved out of the ring of guests who surrounded the dance floor, slinking back and surveying the crowd, suddenly so frantic that she couldn't find Eleanor. And then she saw her, hanging back and by herself. She was watching, smiling, but Leena could see something else on her face. Like loss.

She sidled up to her. "Hey."

Eleanor glanced over and her smile grew. "Hey." Then her face went suddenly overcast. "Hey, are you okay? That thing about Dhaval having a kid? That can't have been easy to hear."

A lie bubbled in Leena's throat: *No, it's fine, I'm happy for him.* But this was Eleanor leveling with her, saying it plainly. Caring for her. "It wasn't. And it's not that I want him to be my guy, but . . . I don't know. This isn't where I imagined being in life." She felt better to say words that she meant. It was Eleanor that taught her that, so many years ago. Eleanor the teacher, the worst, the best. Leena held out her right hand. "Would you like to dance?"

Eleanor stared at Leena's hand like a foreign, unknowable object. "Are you trying to prove a point? You don't have to. I get it. You've changed. You're not afraid of PDA."

She took hold of Eleanor's hand herself, pulling her onto the dance floor. Not to the center, but not in a dark corner either. They had spent good hours dancing together over the years, but never like this, swaying in time to the music, in sync with each other. She wrapped her arm around Eleanor's waist, tight, feeling her firm and solid in their embrace. They were so close together, she could smell the fruity alcohol on Eleanor's breath. Leena took Eleanor's right hand with her left, tucking it between their bodies, and she felt Eleanor put her arm around Leena's shoulders. It was nice. More than nice. She was tipsy, but was pushed over to intoxicated by the feeling of Eleanor all around her. Only this moment mattered between them, Eleanor's thumb slowly kneading against Leena's hairline, the nape of her neck. The arousal in her body went from five to a trillion.

The song ended too soon. They dropped their arms and moved apart as Shakira kicked up, Leena transported to the past. Cath's birthday, or maybe Sam's? Dancing with Eleanor, their bodies close, their hips tight together. They had sex for the first time that night in a cloudy haze of desire that simmered in Leena for weeks. The past wasn't all bad. There were still some things that could work between them. "I know you probably have some duties as best woman," she yelled into Eleanor's ear over the music, "but after you're done we should have sex." Her heart thudded in her chest.

"What?" Eleanor shouted back. "I think I misheard you."

Leena shook her head no, taking Eleanor's hand and squeezing it. "No. You didn't."

Eleanor's eyes were wide as she processed, nodding slowly. "I have to make sure their suite is all set up. Do you want to come with?"

"Yes," Leena said without thinking. They walked out of the hall, music and the sounds of laughter and jubilant shouting streaming behind them. Passing marble columns and frescoes and lions carved from stone, their footsteps echoed in the grand staircase. The details stood out now as they hadn't earlier; something to observe instead of cringing about what she said. *After you're done we should have sex.* The bravado and swagger of such a thing. Outside the rain had subsided, replaced with a cold heaviness that hung in the air. She ducked closer to Eleanor. "I'm remembering lots of walks in college. Walking everywhere together."

"I remember you held my hand in Brookline and I thought I'd die," Eleanor said, tugging them into traffic as the light changed in their favor.

Leena thought back to those heady days of being young and in college, when the expectations of being a woman, an Indian American woman, a professional, a doctor, a daughter, and a wife and mother were known and yet felt so far away. At the time, she could set those pressures on a shelf. Eleanor had been a part of that escape. She didn't remember holding hands and feeling like she would die, but she could recall when time was hers. Hers to spend or lose. When the future felt like an open field and not a narrow bridge.

Tomás and Kemmi's suite was on the top floor.

Eleanor admitted them with the press of a keycard and Leena followed, taking in the views of the harbor and the lights from buildings and traffic, glimmering in the dark. "What's supposed to happen?" she asked.

Eleanor grabbed for a plastic bag stashed in the corner. "The champagne is already in the ice bucket, with glasses. Great. There are candles, but I'm going to leave the matches nearby instead of leaving them lit for hours. And I just need to hang up this banner. Can you help?" It read JUST MARRIED, each letter on its own folksy paper tile.

Leena tied one end to the bedpost while Eleanor handled the other. "You've gotten skilled at wedding planning," Leena teased. "You used to think it was advanced physics."

"It is," Eleanor grumbled. "I planned his fucking bachelor party, and I'd rather vote for that asshole in the White House than do that again. Oh god, I can't even joke about that."

When they finished hanging the sign, Leena sat at the bed's edge, topped with a fluffy white down comforter. Her words from earlier came flying back. *After you're done we should have sex.*

Eleanor straightened the letters, kneeling on the bed. Her black pants clung to her thighs. Her arms strong underneath her pink suit jacket. "How does it look?" she asked.

"Great." But Leena wasn't looking at the sign. She stood and walked to Eleanor, and kissed her. To do it, to meet in the middle, she was up on her tiptoes and Eleanor was leaning down, like Juliet on her balcony. Eleanor's lips were slightly chapped, the way they were when summer faded into fall. The feeling, the sensation of a connection made and a spark ignited, it was like all of their kisses. It was all she wanted, to bury herself in this night, in this place. Everything else could wait, on pause. She could be here, now.

"We can't fuck in here, he'll be so mad," Eleanor said, gasping.

"I don't think he'd be mad." Leena kissed where her neck was exposed, right above the collar of her shirt. "He's on our side. Or whatever."

"Couch?"

Leena tumbled them over to a couch, velvet to the touch. She laid Eleanor down, her head on a bolster pillow, and rested on top of her, getting back to kissing and ridding her of clothing, jacket first.

"Lee, my neck is going to break on this pillow." Eleanor craned her head, wincing.

Leena scanned the room, looking for another surface, pressing against her. She had her, right here. Leena ran a hand up and down Eleanor's bare arm, toned in a way it didn't used to be. "Yoga?"

Eleanor nodded. "For my lower back pain. It helps. So, yes, my body is depreciating in value, if that's what you were asking."

Leena snickered. "I like it. I mean, I like that you're doing that for yourself, but I like how strong your arms are. It's new."

"And I like this," Eleanor said quietly. "You're so . . . bold. Throwing me around. That's new too."

Leena began unbuttoning Eleanor's top, surging forward to claim her mouth once again. She freed the top buttons and looked down at her work, to Eleanor's tan bra, lacy at the top of the cup. She applied her mouth to the lace there, kissing a combination of fabric and skin. While there, her hands wandered to unfasten Eleanor's pants. She didn't pull them down or off, but followed her impulse to snake her hand inside, past the waistband of her underwear. Sinking inside of her. Pure bliss.

"I don't want to have to stop," Eleanor rasped.

Leena couldn't comprehend what that meant, due to the blood rushing to her vagina. She stilled her hand and stood up straight, her eyes level with Eleanor's, curious.

"If this happens now, we'll be here for a while, right? I don't want to be found. So." She removed Leena's hand, woe on her face as she did, moaning. "I've missed that. I'm missing it now. You always know what to do."

There was already warmth pulsing in Leena's body, heavy and staggering, but this made it grow, spreading like wildfire. Leena inserted the fingers that had been inside Eleanor into her mouth, sucking on the taste, and watching her heavy-lidded eyes as she did.

Eleanor advanced, pressing their bodies back together against the wall.

Eventually they made it to Eleanor's room. Once there, Eleanor peeled Leena out of her dress, unzipping it, letting it fall. The bra was next to go as they kissed on the bed, Eleanor unhooking the garment like a lockpicking expert, then she rolled Leena's underwear down her legs and licked at her thighs and clit, on a mission. Leena held Eleanor's head as she strived with soft licks, then more pressure, then a finger inside her. A tight, fierce hand at her hip, holding her down. Eleanor's muscle memory must have kicked in, remembering the playbook of what Leena liked.

Maybe it had been a while, because Leena's orgasm

was slow going. Maybe her vagina was out of practice. No. That was not a medical possibility. But if her vagina had intelligence, as she was sure that it did on some metaphysical level, it was probably withholding: *Why are you letting Eleanor back in? Why are you falling into bed with her again? Is this motivated mostly by your loneliness?*

One of Eleanor's hands snaked up to Leena's breast, rolling her nipple between her fingers, and all of the ongoing work in combination suddenly shifted her brain offline. Pure pleasure. Sensation.

"This feels so good," she gasped out. "Did I say that? Did you hear me say that?"

Eleanor nodded, speaking some words that vibrated against her clit.

"Fuck, that feels so good," she moaned. "You're going to make me come."

And there was enough magic in that statement to make Eleanor's tongue work faster, to catapult Leena over the edge, to orgasm with a reverberating cry. Then she sank back into bed, back into her body. Solid. Done. Drained. Her body completely relaxed against the mattress.

Eleanor scrambled up her body. "So, how was that?" she asked, voice husky, wiping her mouth with the back of her hand.

Leena blew out a breath. "Yeah. That was okay."

It made Eleanor laugh, full smile, teeth too. "'Okay' is what I was aiming for, so, good." She rolled her eyes.

Leena tossed her down to the mattress. "That was really fucking great," she said, leaning down to kiss her. "Have you gotten better? I remember you being good, but that was . . . skill."

"Craftsmanship? Craftswomanship?" Eleanor said, arching an eyebrow. "How many stars would you rate me?"

There weren't enough stars in the sky. "Cassiopeia." Leena looked down at Eleanor's body, still in her hastily buttoned top and pants. She yanked the former off and dueled with the latter, and pulled her underwear down. She found her clit and touched it with the pad of one finger, a soft hello.

"Oh," Eleanor said, her mouth trapped in an O.

Leena kept it up, with her mouth at Eleanor's neck, kissing and licking and sucking. She increased the speed of her finger with the escalation of Eleanor's breaths, like an equation. If two trains were headed to Boston at one hundred miles per hour, how fast would Eleanor come?

"Oh, Lee." Eleanor sighed. "I'm coming."

Evidently, quite quickly. It was such a quiet, simple experience, and not what she remembered. Wasn't Eleanor loud and screaming? Was she remembering wrong, or had Eleanor changed? She kissed Eleanor's lips, her cheeks, chin, everywhere.

With an arm above her head, Leena cast a glance to the glowing green digital numbers: 9:03. "The wedding is still going on."

Eleanor rolled to face her, looking serene and soft yet elusive, like if Leena tried to pin her down, she'd fail. She yawned. "Want to go back?"

Leena saw the steps in front of her: getting dressed, explaining to anyone who asked why they both looked so postsex delirious. Out into the cold and wet, when it was so cozy in the cocoon of their own making. "If you do?" she replied diplomatically.

Eleanor propped her head up. "Should we swap clothes and see if anyone notices?"

Leena snorted. "Should we make out on the dance floor?"

"Or find a deserted library stack? I bet that's a kink you've always wanted to try." She popped her eyebrows twice, trying to be suggestive.

Fifth-floor stacks on campus. Sophomore year. Noa's idea. But she shrugged now and played along. "I'm open to a lot of things these days."

Eleanor grinned and leaned in to kiss her, soft and quick. "I feel bad. It's Tomás's wedding, and I just . . . left." She bit her lip.

Leena nodded, because she, too, understood guilt, but wasn't feeling particularly moved in this moment. "There are a ton of people there. He'll barely notice we're gone." She closed the gap between them to kiss her some more. Boneless. Languid. Happy.

A placid silence filled the room, in the spaces between them. There was so much to say, and nothing.

"We haven't even done the 'how are yous,'" Leena said. "I know nothing new about you."

Eleanor made a pillow of her left arm. "What do you want to know?"

"I saw in your profile that you managed your family's bookstore. When did that happen?"

Eleanor shook her head sadly. "My obachan passed away. When she died, I was working at a consulting firm in DC for nonprofits. I hated it," she said with a grim sigh. "The firm, my boss, everything. And when we lost her, I couldn't bear to tread water any longer. So, I quit and left to run the store with my uncle."

Leena was aghast at the audacity to leave on a whim. It was a move her mind could barely compute.

"It was a disaster," Eleanor continued. "I didn't know anything about running a business. I just . . . it was my obachan's store."

This Leena could understand. Loving a grandmother so much that it moved you toward illogical action.

"Closing the store was like losing her all over again." Eleanor's face clouded over, before revving up. Rallying. "Once I whined and got over it, I decided to get my MSW. I missed so much of her final years, hiding in myself. Older people deserve better than that. I want to make sure they're supported."

Leena nodded, trying to process such magnanimity. "I did not expect that. Not even a little. You were always fighting for something huge."

"These days, for me, it's not necessarily about movements. We need to take care of people who might get missed in all of the chaos." Eleanor cleared her throat. "Like you. Running to take care of your grandmother. That wasn't my favorite thing you've ever done? But I get it now. I so, so get it now."

Leena didn't need absolution, but what she took to keep was Eleanor's understanding. She reached out to stroke Eleanor's cheek with her knuckle, a gesture that was welcomed with a press back into Leena's hand.

"So, you're still in California, or are you—"

"Yeah, I am. I go to UCSF. I'm living at home." She hid under a hand. "I'm some cliché. A woman in her thirties who moved home to save money. We're a CBS sitcom, but with fewer white people. Feel free to judge accordingly."

Leena thought of Eleanor's parents fondly, of parents she could actually talk to. "How are things with your parents? What's it like living with them?" She imagined white wine and invasive, hysterical conversations. "They turned your room into an office, right? Do you still sleep in the basement?"

"They converted it back. How did you . . . how did you remember that? Who are you?" Eleanor asked with wonderment, twinkling stars in her eyes.

There wasn't an appropriate response, so Leena just smiled.

"Things with my folks are good. I can't believe it, but it's good. I go to therapy, which helps with the minor scrapes, but as an adult I find them much more enjoyable than I did when I was younger. And I really missed California. It's good to be back."

Leena hadn't spent enough time there to feel any of that. There was only that one visit to see Dhaval. For her, California was a future she'd escaped by the skin of her teeth.

"I didn't mean to imply there was something wrong with living at home," Eleanor said quickly. "I just heard myself. I'm sorry. Did I offend you?"

Leena shook her head. "Not at all. I want to move, now that . . ." She kept shaking her head as her eyes welled with tears. *Don't talk about it don't talk about it don't get into it.* "Ba died a few months ago. I'm sorry. I don't want to cry after sex, but here we are."

Eleanor cradled her body around Leena in an approximation of a hug and stroked her hair. "Oh my god, Lee, I'm so sorry. I didn't know. That's just awful. I was such a fan of your grandmother."

She sniffled. "It's still really hard. I miss her so

414

much." She wiped her nose with the back of her hand.

"I'm sorry that we're both in the Dead Grandmothers Club," Eleanor said with absolute sobriety.

Leena burst into laughter. "I know you were trying to be helpful, but that was so . . ." She laughed until she was crying again.

"So, you stayed at home to help take care of her, like some kind of saint." Eleanor kept stroking Leena's hair. "But now what? You can do whatever you want." She propped her head up. "What's next for Leena Shah?"

"I don't know. I haven't gotten there yet." These questions that Eleanor liked to ask felt like the slight prick of a hundred needles. "We reek of sex." Leena leaned in to kiss Eleanor. She needed to shake off her sadness, and ideally this line of questioning. "I'm sweaty and sticky. I'm gonna shower. Do you want to join me?"

Eleanor nodded, then kissed her, and they kept up their kissing on the way to the shower, in a long journey that involved backing up into walls and against the sink in the bathroom.

Leena turned the water on, finding the right balance. Hot but not scalding. She climbed in with Eleanor behind her, the spray falling across her shoulders and sluicing over her breasts.

"But there must be something you want to do next. In your ideal world, what happens?" Eleanor asked.

Leena squeezed the small bottle of hotel shampoo that smelled of rosemary and mint. "In my ideal world, I play soccer in the Olympics, and I'm amazing." She didn't want to put words to her real desires, but Eleanor was looking at her so seriously and earnestly that she felt compelled to share her seedling of a thought. "I've thought about going abroad. Using my MPH in service of epidemiology elsewhere in the world, where it's really needed." She lathered her hair.

"I don't know, it seems needed here too. All these parents not vaccinating their fucking kids."

Leena shook her head vehemently. "Don't even start on that. It's all based on one flawed study, and that guy's not even a doctor anymore! There's barely correlation let alone causation with autism."

Eleanor's eyes flashed, eyebrows raising. A small smile on her lips. "Don't even start, huh?"

She was being teased, by Eleanor, by her old friend. Like it was years ago, miles away, sharing an apartment in the heat of summer. So much unspoken between them.

Eleanor rubbed an insistent hand on Leena's hip. "So, abroad, somewhere. Anywhere specific in mind?"

She unwrapped a bar of soap, challenging her already wet hands. It smelled of lemons and herbs. "South Africa, maybe?"

Eleanor smiled, almost looking beyond Leena. "South Africa. Your canceled trip, right? Thwarted by the powerful Noa?"

Leena soaped her arms, then torso. She turned away to clean her crotch, a ridiculous nod to modesty. "Yeah."

"Do you think your life would be different?"

It was hard to imagine her life being anything else than what it was. "I'd have gone to med school. I'd be a doctor. So, yeah, my life would have been different."

"You know, it's not too late for that either. Med school?"

She turned to face Eleanor. "Would you do my back?" She handed over the bar and turned back around. "It *is* too late for med school. Turning thirty, I learned, is about saying goodbye to the person you thought you'd become."

Eleanor gently bopped her back with the soap. "Do you really believe that? You're not dead yet. You can still make changes. You're employable with an advanced degree, with enough privilege to fuel you to the moon."

She smiled, flattered by Eleanor's hyping. "Are you suggesting I become an astronaut?"

"I think you'd be a great one," Eleanor said, sweet and adoring.

Leena rinsed entirely, her body under the spray. She turned back around and kissed Eleanor, because she didn't know what else to say. Eleanor had no grasp on the real world, on how things worked. Not everyone had that much ability to shape their life.

"Besides," Eleanor continued, "we're all gonna be dead one day. You don't want to have regret in your veins when you take your last breath."

Leena sucked in air. "That got dark."

Eleanor shrugged, sheepish. "It's true. If this god-awful year has taught me anything, it's that there are no guarantees. A maniac is running our country. We have to take our time where we can."

"You only live once." Leena's words drifted into the air, along with a yawn.

"Exactly."

It had been a long evening. Exhaustion hit her in waves, as she climbed out of the shower and dried off, looking around for her clothes.

Eleanor cleared her throat, the towel still tucked around her. "Do you . . . want to stay? Do you want pajamas?" She rifled through her messy suitcase, open on the floor. "I probably have . . . Oh." She stood, pink cheeked. "Think fast," she said, tossing a blur of cotton at Leena.

She unfurled the ball and marveled at the T-shirt. Her beloved Lowell Soccer T-shirt, which had disappeared years back. She looked at it now. The holes along its hem. The fading of the print. The garment would not have been out of place as a rag, but someone had seen its value and cared for it. It had been well loved. Leena looked up at Eleanor. Though they had had sex, this was the instant where she felt true intimacy between them again, growing like ivy, like unwanted but stunning weeds.

Leena tossed it back. "You've had it this long. You gonna wear it to bed?"

Eleanor dropped her towel and the shirt, and climbed into bed, slinking up Leena's body and kissing her. "I'll just be like you. Naked. If that's okay."

"That is okay," Leena replied against her mouth.

After a second go, and after Eleanor was sacked out at her side, Leena tried to make sense of the day. An elevator, a dance, then more, then the shirt. She'd spent so much time arguing against odds, probability, and chance, but she couldn't anymore. Here they were, in the same place, finally on the same page, ready for each other. Finally. Eleanor was the one. She knew it like she knew the quadratic equation, the Pledge of Allegiance, and the Gayatri Mantra. They were meant to be.

IN THE BLEARY light of the following day, hungover and dehydrated, she felt less sure. She rolled over and headed to the bathroom. Alone, framed by glaring mirror lights and textured taupe wallpaper, she considered the danger. Of letting Eleanor, or anyone, in again. Of being swayed by unruly tendrils of desire, for work and love and excitement. If she knew anything for sure, it was that she couldn't have everything that she wanted. Leena and Eleanor had been a disaster every time they'd tried being together. Perhaps she, and they, were utterly doomed to repeat this pattern over and over and over. She turned on the tap for water and gulped it from a glass. When she left the bathroom, she pulled on a towel for modesty's sake. Ready to confront Eleanor, to discuss where they were and what last night meant.

The bed was empty, save for a folded note on the pillow. *I'm so sorry. I had to get to the brunch. Come downstairs and join me. xo*

She ran her fingers across the hotel stationery and ink, where Eleanor had left her mark. She stood for the longest time, slowly processing the empty room with no one there to receive her remarks. Finally she set the note aside and got dressed in her clothes from the previous night, stepping back into her ankle boots and darting into the hallway.

Tomás was already in the elevator, his eyes lighting up when he saw her. "Hey! You disappeared last night." He dipped in to kiss her cheek. "I'm pretty sure it's because of the discarded pink blazer I found in my room."

"You're married!" she chirped as her cheeks burned. "How does it feel?"

He held up the gold cardigan in his hands. "Already fetching," he replied, rolling his eyes. "No, seriously, it's great. It's great! Will we see you downstairs once you, uh, change?"

We. The couple *we.* She nodded, giving off a closed-lip smile. She was relieved when the elevator opened on her floor and he was swarmed by new Nigerian relatives greeting him with exultation. At a wedding, the people getting married belonged to the world.

She slipped out, back to her room, where she shed her dress, underwear, and bra. Feeling so different from how she did a day earlier. Sore. Achy. Satisfied. In the shower she soaped her breasts, her thighs, her mound. Where Eleanor had been. She felt the tide of her hangover recede a bit as the hot spray washed away traces of her evening.

She yearned to talk to Ba—to the woman she was before she got sick. The woman who didn't drive, and so walked to pick Leena up from school as a little girl. Who endorsed Leena's love of school and science, and disinterest in the conventionally feminine. Who had wisdom and mischief and grace flowing through her veins. Who left the only country she had ever known to help her son, to care for her grandchildren, only to be alone in a house most days and clash with her daughter-in-law.

"If you tell her, it'll kill her," her mother had said early on, after she'd moved back home. Her father had said nothing, but he'd looked through her in a way that had signaled his dismissal. The mandate had been clear. She closeted herself, because she feared they were right. She already felt responsible for Ba's heart attack, and she wouldn't cause further damage.

On the sporadic night that she'd steal away from the house to go on a date, she would lie to everyone about where she was headed, cursed with a teenager's lot and guilt.

In the end, it was her grandmother's heart that did her in. Too old, too weak, too compromised. Maybe if Leena had told her that she preferred women, it would have lengthened her life. As it stood, in Ba's eyes, Leena was a spinster who lost Dhaval and hadn't found anyone else. Maybe it broke her heart to think of her granddaughter alone.

She put on jeans and a long-sleeved shirt, sneakers, and sat at the edge of the bed. Ready to go.

She didn't want to go.

Leena flung herself back on the bed and stared at the ceiling. She felt aimless, vulnerable, in need of guidance. From someone who knew. One person fit that description. The giver of excellent advice and some of the worst moments of her life. She scrolled in her phone book to Don't Fucking Call Her, Ever, and considered it for a second, then another. It was a great idea. It was a terrible idea. She ripped off the Band-Aid before she could think better of the decision, selecting the contact from the list. The phone rang and rang, and she readied herself to hang up.

"Hello?" said the voice like a time warp.

She took a deep breath. "Hi, Noa. It's Leena."

There was a long pause on the other end. "Oh. Hey. Did you . . . mean to call me?"

It had been so long since they last spoke that she had forgotten the nuances of Noa's voice. Strong, deep. Full of conviction and vim. Someone who once made her feel safe. "I'm surprised you picked up."

421

"I'm a doctor. I always pick up. I'm surprised you're calling though. It's been . . . years."

It was surreal to be on the phone with Noa. Her original agony. They left things so badly, she had been sure she'd go a lifetime avoiding her. But she had kept her number, and Noa had picked up. It felt destined. "Were we in love?"

"Whoa."

"I know that's . . . sort of . . . a big question. I'm at this wedding, and old thoughts are stirring up, and I just needed . . . I don't know what I need."

She heard Noa sigh. "You've done some crazy shit, but this really takes it. I mean, yeah, we were in love."

"How are you so sure?"

"Because I was there. I loved you, I fell for you. You fell for me. It's the simplest thing in the world. You used to make everything so complicated."

Leena disagreed that it was the simplest thing in the world. Love, to her, felt like the most difficult. The highest Everest. The meshing and colliding of two people and lives. "I was also, like, a teenager when we met," she argued in defense, at that last part. "But, thanks," she said in a softer voice. "I was worried that I—I don't know, that I couldn't recognize the symptoms of falling in love."

"I think you do, or did, but I can see how you'd worry. You needed everything to be so orderly and organized and contained. Love is fucking guts, it's messy and gross. It's nice things too, but it's mainly human, so it's disgusting."

Leena smiled at this assessment, at Noa. "So, where are you, as you take this strange call from me?"

"Driving my twins to soccer practice."

That combination of words—*twins, soccer practice*—threw her for a loop. Like a punch to the boob, delivered by Binita while fighting over the remote. "That's great! Congrats." Then she was struck with an unpleasant thought. "Is your wife in the car? Have I ruined your weekend?"

"I'm divorced," Noa replied matter-of-factly.

Knowing her ex as she did, Leena was not surprised to hear this. She felt grateful to have escaped what she was sure would have been the same fate. But they had been friends. No matter what had transpired, she imagined divorce wasn't easy, not with children involved. "I'm really sorry to hear that."

"No happy couples get divorced."

"So, my questions about love were really tactful."

Noa chuckled. "Yeah. You always had a way with timing. No, really, it's fine. Here's what I'll say: trust the universe."

Leena wrinkled her nose. That hippie advice was strange coming from Noa, believer in the facts, the empirical truth. "With everything going on in the world, you're telling me to trust the universe? I don't think we can. The universe is on vacation."

"No, I'm saying, when something comes along, grab it. Because you don't know how long you'll have it for."

There was a wistfulness in Noa's voice that wormed into Leena's heart. Leena had always loved the broken parts of her best. "Thank you. That's good advice."

"It's really good to hear your voice," Noa said, her tone less gruff and didactic. Softer, kinder, engaged. "I've missed it."

Leena could feel the quicksand materialize around her. They'd been here before. It started with giving

423

away a slice of themselves to the other, then ended with howling dissolution. If she'd learned anything, it was that they were done, for good. That was a door she was happy to keep closed. "Noa, thank you so much for taking my call. This was so helpful. I hope you have a great day with your kids. I have to go." She hung up for self-preservation's sake, which was rude, but she felt better for it. Accomplished.

One decision begat another. She headed down to brunch, to a dining room with splatter-patterned carpets and white-cushioned chairs, and helped herself to the breakfast buffet in chafing dishes. Eggs, fruit, lightly toasted toast. She saw Eleanor immediately, at a long table with Tomás's aunts and Micah and Sam and Cath and Min Jin. There wasn't room near Eleanor, so she slid in next to Cath, the only empty chair at the table. Flashes from the early evening filled her brain, but she kept her mouth shut and recalled none of it aloud. She gave her an awkward smile. "How are you?"

Cath, who was wearing sunglasses inside and wolfing down eggs and pancakes, kept her eyes on her plate. "I had a night. I'm glad I'm still in one piece. I can't drink like that anymore," she muttered.

Sam sipped his coffee, then grinned at Leena. "You had a night too. We didn't see you and Eleanor for long."

She shoveled toast into her mouth. "We were busy. We had to decorate Tomás and Kemmi's room."

Cath and Sam exchanged a glance, then returned to their breakfasts.

Leena felt a warm hand between her shoulder blades.

"Hey. How are you?" She turned and saw Eleanor

smiling down at her. Her hair tamed with product, in a green plaid shirt. Her expression buttery and saccharine.

"I'm good. How are you?"

"Tired. Hungover." She dropped into a squat, holding on to the back of Leena's chair with one hand. "Are you okay?" she asked in a low voice, her smile knowing.

Leena felt her own expression falter. "Yeah. I'm okay." There was a tackiness to Eleanor's expression. She wouldn't be surprised if she had bust out with a *Last night was amazing, babe.*

"Good." She stood, her smooth smile never wavering. "I'm glad we're getting the chance to say goodbye. I need to leave in a few minutes, actually. I have class tomorrow."

She had class tomorrow, in California, where Eleanor had a life. The cold-shower shock of this reminder kicked Leena out of her spell. Of course. Real life: Commuting and work. Silences at the family dinner table. Everyone else waltzing by, on their way to somewhere else. She was foolish to think she could gallivant back into Eleanor's life. She had pinned her hopes on the wrong wall.

"It's gonna take a while to do my rounds. I'll start with you." Eleanor gestured for a hug, arms outstretched and rounded, one hand urging her in.

Leena hugged her, hating the way she melted into her arms. She had been in battle with herself all morning, fighting her way through obstacles and emotions. She felt defeated as she drew back and away, out of the embrace.

"Bye, Lee," Eleanor said, before starting her goodbyes with Sam and Cath.

And that was that. The end of the affair.

Leena finished her breakfast in solemn bites, as fast as she could. Eleanor had made herself entirely clear: It was one night. It was over. It was, it seemed, a rote experience for her to dismiss last night's hookup. Leena did a smaller route of farewells once she had swallowed breakfast, congratulating Cath and Sam again, and putting a tentative dinner on the books for when Tomás and Kemmi were back from their honeymoon and visit to Mexico. As she waited for the elevator, she recategorized Eleanor. Eleanor could no longer belong to the Maybe Again One Day designation. After this weekend, the only safe place for their archived relationship was Done for Good. Leena could close the door. Move on. Consider her options.

In her room she packed recklessly, sweeping clothes and toiletries back into her bag. Now that she knew the score, she was ready to go, itching to get back to, of all places, Lowell. Maybe Binita would fetch her at the train station, and she could hide out at her house for the night. Watch a princess movie with the girls. Drink wine. Anything to stop her brain from meandering down old, dark paths.

After turning in her keycard at the front desk, she slung her bag over her arm, ambling out to the covered entrance. It wasn't fate at play, or if it was, it was fate without much of an imagination—because Eleanor was here, again. This woman who couldn't seem to stop crossing her path, now waiting at the taxi stand with her bags, looking at her phone.

The door was closed. She had closed it, like she did with Noa. Restraint and steely determination could be her guides. It simply took concentration not to act with the heart. She walked the other way, toward North Station.

It was possible.

It was easy.

But instead, she turned around and sprinted back toward the taxi stand. "Hi! Eleanor! Hey!"

Eleanor's head raised. Her face softened. "Hey."

There were words she could have put in order, to be made into a sentence, but she had none. A taxi pulled up and her throat went dry, a desert forming in her mouth. "Uh." Cold, crazy nerves danced on her skin as she endeavored to find the right words. "I don't think we're done."

The driver collected Eleanor's suitcase and stowed it in the trunk.

"That almost sounds like a threat."

Leena opened her mouth. "I want to be in love with you again. Given our track record, I guess that is kind of a threat." She buttoned her lips together, unwilling to let anything else out, any other words that wanted to declare sentiments that she barely understood. But it was true. It was all true.

Eleanor shook her head this small, almost imperceptible amount. "You can't just decide that. That's not how it works. And I have to go to the airport."

Leena was a thirty-three-year-old woman who had been in love before, had lost herself in others. She could decide whatever she wanted to and proved it by climbing into the cab.

Eleanor huffed out a breath and climbed in after her. "Leena, I don't know how to have sex with you then act like it didn't happen. You're not other people.

You're not just some woman. Logan, please? Terminal C?" she requested of the driver.

He nodded, with his eyebrow arched, then turned the radio up.

"Why did you have to act like nothing happened?"

"Because I thought you might. Later," Eleanor said with half a shrug. "Last night, you told me about so many wonderful things you want to do. Be. Explore. I would be so upset if I got in your way."

The cab wound them out of Back Bay and onto Storrow Drive, rounding the tip of the oldest parts of the city, with sun shining on narrow roads and quaint brownstones.

"I'm asking you to get in my way," Leena said, her eyes locked on the sights while not seeing anything at all. "You're being so unemotional. Measured. I hardly recognize you."

"I've spent a lot of time jumping into things without looking. It's worked okay, but I don't want to do that anymore. Therapy is helping me be more intentional."

Leena tossed her head back against the padded seat. "I don't know what I'm doing. But I know how I feel." She turned her neck ever so slightly, so she could look over to Eleanor, and groped for her hand, which she gave limply. "I think there are forces at work, invisible bands that keep pulling us back into each other's orbit. And I'm sort of mixing metaphors here, but the point remains. Don't you feel it?"

Eleanor rested her head on the seatback, eyes trained on Leena. She nodded. "You sound like me. The romantic me. The young me."

"I love her," Leena said with as much conviction as she had ever held about anything.

Eleanor leaned in, the littlest bit, to close their gap and kiss her. It was sweet. Then she shook her head slowly, sadly. "I don't think she exists anymore."

That, Leena didn't have an answer for, and they spent the remaining minutes of the ride staring at each other, faces so close they could have kissed again, but they didn't. She wished they had never met. She wished they had married years ago. She wished they were children and could redo their lives, every decision and scrape and triumph, all over again. She wished she had not climbed into this cab.

"Uh. Ladies? We're here?"

"Thank you," Eleanor said faintly. She didn't lift her head as she addressed Leena. "This was magical." Eleanor kissed Leena's cheek and opened the car door, and Leena followed behind.

They hugged again, this one just for them. She tightened her arms around Eleanor's shoulders, wanting to sustain this feeling of comfort edged with fear—a feeling she had once accepted as her norm. She knew now it was the fear of losing something so good.

Eleanor dropped her arms and reached for her tote bag to pay for the cab. As she gave over her credit card to be swiped and processed, she developed a wry smile. "Let's do this in another six years or so."

"If not annihilated by nuclear war by then," Leena muttered.

"Something to look forward to, then." Eleanor took her receipt. "I know this seems odd, sir, but this other woman is actually headed back into Boston. Maybe you can take her?"

Leena envisioned an impetuous flash: buying a ticket, flying with Eleanor, starting a new life in

California. Maybe she could come around to it. Maybe it would help her mend. She saw the water crashing against the coast. Deserts, palm trees. Fiercely, almost unbearably open skies. Droughts, earthquakes. Everything on fire. Maybe not, then. There were limits to how nimble she could be.

If not California, then South Africa, or somewhere that she could be of use. There was work to be done. She climbed back into the car. "You keep finding new ways to be good to me," she said, peering up at Eleanor, hair aflutter in the wind. "I—" She wanted to make a promise, to seal them together even as she couldn't be sure of what was next. *This is it for me. You are it for me. You fit. No matter where I go or what I do, that'll still be true*, she wanted to say.

"I'll see you soon," she said instead.

As the taxi slowly pulled away, Leena watched Eleanor underneath the winged overhang. It was impossible to see all of her at once, but she tried to catalog with a sweep of her eyes: short, dark hair that looked like it did thirteen years ago, but better; broad, strong shoulders; hips and legs that grounded her to earth like a trunk. There was so much history, so many paths trod, lives lived together and apart. Leena tried to drink in more and more, until the car merged toward the airport exit and Eleanor disappeared. Then, she looked ahead.

ACKNOWLEDGMENTS

I'd like to express my deepest thanks and gratitude to the following people, entities, and experiences:

- Sarah Schulman, who both named this book and taught me how to write it, and continues to champion me at every turn;
- Robert Guinsler and Sterling Lord, for believing in (1) this funny little feminist romance and (2) me;
- The Feminist Press team, especially Lauren Rosemary Hook and Nick Whitney, with extra claps for Jisu Kim (for all of the hand-holding);
- My one year as a college student in Boston, wandering lovelorn around old streets;
- My women's and gender studies education at Rutgers University, with special appreciation for Professor Nancy Hewitt;
- My parents, for cultivating in me a creatively curious and restless spirit, and asking technical questions about contracts and advances;
- My in-laws, now a Table for Nine, especially my father- and mother-in-law;
- My days as a coordinator at nonprofits, which taught me humility and how much I didn't actually know;
- The Wayback Machine, for answering questions like, "What kind of scents did Yankee Candle sell in 2004?";

- Sydney Spector, for providing legal counsel, early reading cheerleading, and an abundance of support;
- Everyone in my VONA LGBTQ Narratives workshop, for helping me to feel like a writer for the first time;
- Queer | Art, for providing community and access;
- The F train, for being so slow and terrible as to facilitate copious writing time during my commute;
- Congregation Beth Simchat Torah's excellent video archive of Kol Nidre services;
- Early reader-writers Celeste Hamilton Dennis, April Greene, Minal Hajratwala, CQ Quintana, and Laura Robitzek, for their support and critique;
- All of the Indian Americans in my life, who informed my writing about the life of an American-born Desi. I was eating samosas at six and in the India Day parade at twelve and have attended more Indian weddings than any (non-Indian) person I know, but none of this makes me a full member of this community. I feel blessed to be a witness to what movement and change look like firsthand. An extra-special thank you to Sweta Shukla for her editorial support;
- My wife, who is both not in this book and everywhere.